the Enigma Always

Breakfield and Burkey

BOOK 6: Award Winning Techno-Thriller Series

Published by

ICABOD Press

ISBN: 978-1-946858-32-0 (paperback)
ISBN: 978-1-946858-19-1 (ebook)
ISBN: 978-1-946858-20-7 (audiobook)

Library of Congress Control Number: 2015913247
Cover, interior and eBook design: F + P Graphic Design, FPGD.com

Second Edition
Printed in the United States

TECHNO-THRILLER I SUSPENSE

Kirkus Reviews

The Enigma Factor In this debut techno-thriller, the first in a planned series, a hacker finds his life turned upside down as a mysterious company tries to recruit him...

The Enigma Rising In Breakfield and Burkey's latest techno-thriller, a group combats evil in the digital world, with multiple assignments merging in Acapulco and the Cayman Islands.

The Enigma Ignite The authors continue their run of stellar villains with the returning Chairman Lo Chang, but they also add wonderfully unpredictable characters with unclear motivations. A solid espionage thriller that adds more tension and lightheartedness to the series.

The Enigma Wraith The fourth entry in Breakfield and Burkey's techno-thriller series pits the R-Group against a seemingly untraceable computer virus and what could be a full-scale digital assault.

The Enigma Stolen Breakfield and Burkey once again deliver the goods, as returning readers will expect—intelligent technology-laden dialogue; a kidnapping or two; and a bit of action, as Jacob and Petra dodge an assassin (not the cyber kind) in Argentina.

The Enigma Always As always, loaded with smart technological prose and an open ending that suggests more to come.

The Enigma Gamers (A CATS Tale) A cyberattack tale that's superb as both a continuation of a series and a promising start in an entirely new direction.

The Enigma Broker …the authors handle their players as skillfully as casino dealers handle cards, and the various subplots are consistently engaging. The main storyline is energized by its formidable villains…

The Enigma Dragon (A CATS Tale) This second CATS-centric installment (after 2016's *The Enigma Gamers*) will leave readers yearning for more. Astute prose and an unwavering pace energized by first-rate characters and subplots.

The Enigma Source Another top-tier installment that showcases exemplary recurring characters and tech subplots.

The Enigma Beyond the latest installment of this long-running technothriller series finds a next generation cyber security team facing off against unprincipled artificial intelligences. Dense but enthralling entry, with a bevy of new, potential narrative directions.

The Enigma Threat Another clever, energetic addition to an appealing series.

Acknowledgments

We are grateful for the support we have received from our family and friends. We look forward to seeing the reviews from our fans. Thank you in advance for your time.

Specialized Terms are available beginning on page 431 if needed for readers' reference.

The idea of living forever is one that has persisted throughout time. Many have chased the possibilities, the rumors, and risked everything to no avail. Could technology provide the method for living forever where the Fountain of Youth has failed? But if you had that awesome power, who would you want to live forever?   **...The Enigma Chronicles**

Beware the Dream Chaser for He Will Sacrifice All, Including You...
The Enigma Chronicles

The waiter had seated her a few minutes before at a secluded table. It was a balmy day, and the abundance of flowers emitted a rich yet subtle scent of vanilla and cherry blossoms. She had tied her heavy dark hair into a simple chignon that accentuated her long neck, which supported a simple golden chain with a single teardrop pendant. Her creamy skin was accentuated by a red dress that displayed her lithe figure. Though not classically beautiful, she carried herself with confidence and, frankly, cared not for social ranking.

This meeting was likely doomed to end up like their prior discussions. The opportunity it presented her was worth one more attempt for the establishment of mutually achievable goals. He was brilliant, but like most geniuses, incapable of seeing past the flaws of his current plan or seeing the possibilities of approaching something from a different perspective. He walked toward the secluded table at the very end of the garden, striding with confidence and tall enough to command respect. His clothes were tailored, the fabric expensive though with subdued colors, and his brown hair was neatly trimmed. As he paused to speak with the waiter, she saw his dark eyes and unwavering facial expression issue orders that would undoubtedly be followed.

He bowed toward her slightly before he took her hand and passed his warm breath across her skin. She smiled as he placed a single lavender orchid with white streaks in each of the petals in front of her as a token of friendly negotiations. His hands were well manicured and void of any signs of physical labor. She looked up with her dark eyes and almost smiled in an inscrutable manner as she nodded her head in acknowledgement. He sat nearly across from her but angled to allow his legs additional stretching space.

Neither of them speaks as the waiter brought out a large tray laden with wine and food and placed it on the table for sampling. The waiter positioned a napkin in each of their laps as he also added a clean plate at each place. After the gentleman sampled the wine and nodded, the waiter finished pouring into each glass. He turned and walked away without saying a word.

His dark eyes took in every inch of her as he raised his glass and commented, "To our reaching an agreement, madam."

Her eyes danced a bit as she chuckled and agreed, "Yes, that would be worth a toast."

They each silently sipped their wine and sampled a bit of the fare. Though this was hardly their first meeting, they seemed to be sizing each other up as they each built the strategy for the discussion. After several minutes of observing the sensibilities of not rushing into a business discussion until the social pleasantries were completed, she picked up her napkin and delicately dabbed at her lips, knowing nothing was there to remove.

Looking down to the flower, she focused on it to collect her thoughts and then took one more sip of the exquisite wine as she began, "I know that we do not always see eye-to-eye on this project of yours, sir. I also know that you asked for my help and viewpoint as you have respect for my experience and skills. I think that your goal is very short-sighted indeed, yet it can be achieved. It needs some time, some logic, and some testing in a methodical, pre-defined sequence."

The gentleman's eyes flashed with anger as he interrupted, "Madam, this is not the way you suggested our conversation would go when we scheduled this meeting. You know that time is the enemy of us all. Time is the entire reason that I engaged with you at all. To shorten the time between the two points. That is why I agreed to this meeting. That is what you promised, madam."

She held up her hand, displayed her long, slender fingers and trimmed but colorless nails, and quietly insisted, "When we started on your project, I had suggested that it would be at least a dozen years before we could explore clinical trials. I had been diligently working toward that goal when you made the decision to take a different path. Your path made no sense four months ago, and those poor results are my proof points.

"Your experimental procedure has always lacked the discipline necessary for the steps that need to be followed. There are few shortcuts in something that involves over three billion variables. I have worked on some bioinformatics programs that will help shorten the time frame to arrive at a solution. To achieve your long-term goal is going to require the multi-threaded approach, period." Her face remained serene and emotionless, outside of a hint of a smile at his reaction.

His eyes flared, then turned stormy as his face reddened with anger. He swallowed for control and asked, "How long do you think it will take? How much more funding is required, though that is not the issue, is it?"

As she leaned back slightly in her seat and sighted the orchid again, she sipped her wine and replied, "I think five million should be enough to take me to the solution. I suspect it will take just over five years for completion. Value at even twice the price.

"Before you get upset, that is half the time I originally projected. And, before you started your rogue processes, you had speculated for a quarter of a century. I'm not proposing shortcuts, but instead a smarter approach. Though to a degree, it would be brute force testing."

He looked at her in anger and yet respected her abilities more than he was willing to admit aloud. She was one of the best minds he had ever come across. She had no interest in him, per se, even though he had offered all his fortune and marriage. That was a discussion she had stopped on all fronts. It was clear that another man had claimed her heart that continued after his death. The gentleman gathered his wits, mentally reviewed the alternatives, and recognized that his options were limited.

He looked at her intensely and stated, "You'll get your money. You can return to my labs with me and get started immediately. Anything and everything you need will be provided."

Her temper almost showed, but she checked it as she retorted, "I will work in my own space, sir. I will not have you standing over me and pressuring me, as you are now. We tried that before, and your efforts failed. You went off in a snit and look what you accomplished.

"If you place those sorts of constraints on me, I'll do nothing, and you'll die a painful death." Her voice softened as she added, "If you let me work, I believe I can find a salvation for you, as well as a long-range solution. Your experimentation has resulted in two goals – with one being more critical than the original."

He looked beaten. She reached down to pick up the beautiful orchid and as he nodded resignedly, he reached to take her hand. She extended her hand with the flower into his open palm, feeling relieved that they'd reached agreement. He covered her hand with his other hand. Before she could react, she felt the hypodermic needle slide into her skin. Her eyes flew open, and she looked at him with pure hate as she yanked her hand away and dropped the flower. She inspected the puncture and blood that now glistened on her ivory skin. She stared at the orchid now, realizing it was an assassin's weapon.

"You stupid, deranged man! What have you done?"

He gently picked up the flower and, as he studied it, said, "The orchid, how beautiful in life and how empty in death." His face turned to stone as he continued, "Even though you have refused my offer of marriage and security, I feel as though our lives are already intertwined. We are on our way, you and me, towards a rich destiny that will be best shared together. I have given you my half of the solution, per our agreement, because I want you with me to the end of our days.

"I have infected you with the same treatment I took for myself. Now you have a personal, vested interest in succeeding, in applying the mapping correctly. You can return to your home, your work, but I will be watching, and this is now in your best interest to resolve or you too will perish. And as you stated so plainly, it promises to be very painful, my partner in life or in death."

The lady lay her napkin aside, collected her small clutch, and rose. Her eyes focused on him while her face was like a mask, empty of emotion. Before she turned, she quietly demanded, "The waiter will hand you an envelope as you leave. Your payments are expected to be wired into the numbered account therein in monthly increments for the sum mentioned. I will provide periodic updates on the progress and contact you only if I have need of something. I will continue access to your system, which I presume will be available via the same connection."

Even though her stature was small, she looked as regal as any royal, on any continent. He was almost saddened by the events that had just unfolded, until she stopped and turned.

Her eyes blazed as she added, "Do not ever contact me directly again, even when this is solved, which I promise it will be."

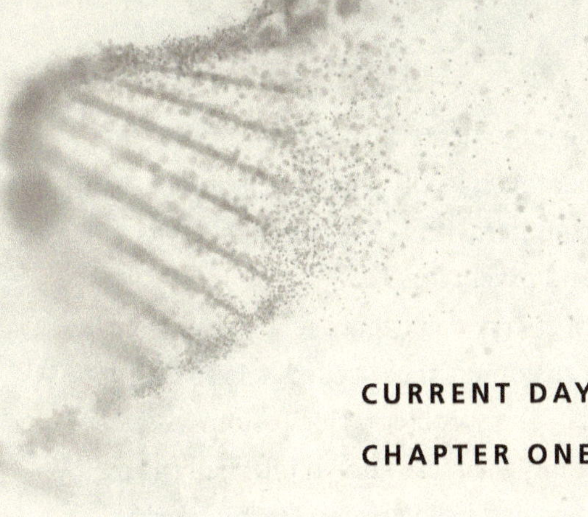

CHAPTER ONE

The Emotional Demon Lurks in All of Us

The mansion was quietly graceful, and the carpeted stairway was wide and elegant as befitted European designs. The colors were dark mahogany with light walls and paintings that, if one looked closely, would be identified as created by one of the older masters. Though Haddy had added her touches of color and updating throughout the mansion, the underlying old-world elegance was clearly visible. There were three floors of living space. Below these, an expansive wine cellar and storage area which were all organized and optimized. Even with all the people currently in residence, the noise was associated only between the two women.

Haddy assisted Petra up the stairs, being careful not to offer too much help. Ever since the battering she had received in Argentina on her last assignment, Petra was moody and withdrawn from almost everyone. Otto and Haddy had offered to secure a full-time physical therapist, but Petra was having trouble just facing her own mother, Haddy, so an outsider was refused out of hand. Ever since she'd run away from Zürich, the operations area for the R-Group, to her childhood home, she had continued to become more depressed. She wasn't even in email connection with her lover, Jacob, let alone her other team members. The brutal encounter with Sönders had taken its toll on her, both physically and psychologically.

Petra was the brilliant encryption expert, recognized globally, who was called upon by customers that needed help to decrypt or break a mathematical cypher problem. Her customers were primarily a part of the family business known internally as the R-Group. The core business had been created during World War II with a charter to preserve individuals' wealth and protect them from governmental tyrants. The original financial side of the operations had begun with the use of the Enigma Machine that had been spirited away as the founding families fled from Poland. Petra was a descendant from the original family founders. Her father Otto had held a key role in the organization but was working toward turning that responsibility over to Petra and Jacob.

Jacob's grandfather, Wolfgang, was a second key person in the group and was focused on the financial aspects of this family business. As with each of the founders, all the descendants were highly educated and had each decided on a focus that could be leveraged by the family business. Jacob had been raised in the United States by Wolfgang's now deceased wife and their daughter, Jacob's mother. Wolfgang had been on a path to groom Jacob as a replacement for him in the future before that path had been interrupted by the Argentina incident.

Jacob, a talented programmer and security specialist, had been brought into the business after his mother had been murdered. He and Petra had fallen in love and seemed destined to spend their life together before the horrible beating Petra had suffered in Argentina. After what had seemed like the road to recovery for Petra with Jacob in Zürich, Petra had left a note as she departed to her childhood home. Jacob was crushed by her leaving and left himself, without a word of explanation to the family.

The third key voter in the family business was Dr. Quinton Watcowski, better known as Quip, who had taken the reins a little over a year ago from his grandfather. Quip specialized in building leading-edge technology and maintained his creation, the *Immersive Collaborative Associative Binary Override Deterministic system,* or ICABOD, as it was fondly called. Quip was also considered the project manager for problem projects that the business worked.

Otto's other daughter, Julie, or JAC, as she was called when she worked, was a cyber assassin specialist. Recently married, she and her husband Juan had started a business that incorporated all of the original cyber assassin duties that Julie performed, along with monitoring specific people of interests to the various projects they routinely and non- routinely worked. Julie and Juan ran the operation known as CAT, Cyber Assassin Team, with their recently vetted staff. Julie wanted to continue in the family business and was the primary interface with the rest of the family operations in order to maintain its anonymity. She had also wanted to stay close to her husband and their recently born twins.

Juan, a pilot and martial arts expert, worked with the CAT staff to provide the fulfillment of field-level intelligence gathering, identity cloaking, and acquisition. Julie and Juan were currently in resident in the Luxemburg family home. They were settling into being a family as they also worked their fledgling business. Business was good, due to referrals from the family business.

Everyone had tried to help ease the circumstances of Petra's injuries, Jacob most of all. The only one who wouldn't help in the recovery was Petra. She withdrew from everyone and sequestered herself away from her work, her team, and her love. Even being close to her sister Julie and the adorable twins had not brought Petra out of her depression. The hope was that, given enough time, she would heal and return to her rightful role with the R-Group. However, as the days turned into weeks, everyone began to wonder if she might be gone for good.

Once Petra and Haddy arrived onto the landing, Petra pulled her arm back, determined to accept as little help as possible in going into her room. Her arm was now out of the cast and she was slowly relearning how to use it. Her walk, no longer the graceful gait of a powerful young woman, was more of a healing limp with irregular steps similar to that of an older woman. As they entered her room, she turned, as was her habit, to view herself in the hallway mirror, only to see her disfigured face, no longer swollen, but still quite red. Her jaw was still wired internally, with a modest change that had permitted recent improvements to her speech, but she was still humiliated by a pronounced lisp.

Haddy watched with sadness every time Petra stopped to look in the mirror. Petra couldn't bear the sight, yet continued in the self-torture. Haddy had suggested that only the mirror in the bathroom remain, but Petra had been adamant. It was heartbreaking.

Trembling, Petra reached for the mirror and turned around to gaze into it from various angles but saw the same result. Tears started to stream down her face as Petra asked, "Will anyone ever be able to stand the sight of me again?" Slowly she turned from the mirror as she shuddered with sobs of emotional pain.

The scene tore at Haddy, but she refused to not find a bright spot. She swallowed hard and with conviction insisted, "There, you see, my precious daughter! You didn't think you would ever speak again. You've sustained significant physical damage, but you're turning the corner. Look at your progress!

"You have command of your arms again and can hurl insults at inanimate objects! You're eating real foods again. Do not forget how far you've come! If you were still where you were eight weeks ago, I would be joining you with tears, but you are improved! Do not despair and never, ever give up! You only lose when you give up, young lady! Allow me to retain a physical therapist so that we can increase your progress. All the routines you found on the Internet have helped, but there may be more that can be done to speed your recovery.

"As far as looking at you again, your family has no issue. Jacob never complained. Those darling babies in this house coo at you just fine, smiling when you enter the room or they hear your voice. However, you need to spend more time with them before they discover you don't know them. Come, rejoin humanity and do not despair, because you have overcome so much!"

Petra shook her head and softly asked, "Despair? What do you know of despair, mother? I'm the one who has lost everything."

Haddy became frustrated by her daughter's comment and barked, "What do I know of despair? I'll tell you of despair! Despair is seeing my daughter wishing she was dead rather than celebrating her survival! Despair is seeing my daughter withdraw from her team and her father like they were some nobodies at a bus stop! Despair is seeing you push Jacob away and become a recluse because you enjoy wallowing in self-pity! You dare suggest that I have no idea of despair!

"You might consider other's feelings before you shove all of us out of your life. We all love you too much. Real despair is watching that loved one spiral in emotionally! Despair is not being able to help you because for some unexplained reason you enjoy punishing yourself and you want us to watch!

"Despair is also my not being able to watch you being destroyed any longer, while being unable to look away because I care so much about you! You let me know if there is anything else I need to explain to you!"

Haddy turned to leave, but Petra, her eyes now streaming with tears, gathered her mother into a hug, and the two stood there quietly holding one another as they cried on each other's shoulder.

After a few moments, Petra asked, "What am I going to do? I simply can't bear seeing the disappointment and sorrow in their faces as everyone looks at me! I can't face them or stand their shocked looks as they see all this ugliness."

Haddy said nothing but let Petra's thoughts hang there momentarily. Then Petra quietly asked, "Have you heard from him?"

Haddy had trouble containing her emotions as she explained, "He left not long after he found your note. We can find him if we need to. Frankly, we were trying to give him space, just as we are doing for you. But, no, we have not heard from him."

Petra started crying anew and rushed into her bedroom and closed the door.

CHAPTER TWO

Don't You Know Me From Somewhere?

Zara protested, "What do you mean, you can't buy them? I'm no diamond expert, but even though they are a little rough and not as nicely polished as they should be, I can tell they are of a great value! They should bring a small fortune! Okay, a large fortune! What is the big deal?"

The elderly gentleman looked over his spectacles and in a very paternal way stated, "Young lady, without a bill of sale or authenticated provenance, these are tainted diamonds. Here in the New York Diamond District, we do not support the trafficking of..."

Zara finished his statement. "Yeah, I heard it before, blood diamonds! I keep hearing that from every one of you little squirrely old men trying to get my diamonds on the cheap! I'm from Russia, not Sierra Leone, for God's sake! My diamonds are from Russia! These are family heirlooms. My great-grandmother passed them down. There was no provenance or bill of sale. Why would there be? Where can I go to deal with someone who knows the value of diamonds, since you obviously don't?"

The diamond merchant let the insult roll off of him as he responded, "Madam, two presidents have issued executive orders forbidding trafficking in blood or conflict diamonds in this country, which, without the proper documentation, these are classified as such. You can go to your local fence, who will not know what to do with these potentially nice stones, or go to another country where ethics are not so scrupulously observed.

"I recognize their value. However, I cannot deal with you for them as it could cost me my business and my freedom. I treasure both, having come from a Nazi concentration camp where human rights meant nothing. In this country, they do. Therefore, I am not inclined to subsidize regimes without honor. I understand that there are underground people in South Africa that could remove them from the setting and essentially change all their characteristics. Enjoy your travels. Good day, madam."

Zara was furious. She recognized she was wasting her time as she packed up her hard-won booty that couldn't be brokered through normal channels and stormed to the door. As a parting gesture of animosity, the shopkeeper didn't release the door lock as she went to leave. The result was her piling into the glass door and unexpectedly bumping her nose up against it.

The shopkeeper smiled and innocently apologized, "Oops! Gracious me! Should have unlocked the door sooner. As my grandson would say, my bad!" The shopkeeper chuckled loud enough for Zara to hear until the door closed and the sounds of the city intervened.

Out on the street Zara surveyed the district and realized that she was going to hear the same story from each of them. She knew the only ones who wouldn't tell her would try to take her diamonds for a song so they could be re-cut for a profit she would never see.

"Just great," she thought. *"Here I am with five million euros in stolen diamonds, but I'm still starving! I didn't count on not being able to sell the damn things! Okay, well, it's time for plan B. Except I don't have a plan B.*

"Ok, Zara, we need to conserve what little cash we have so we can plan our next move. As much as I hate to admit it, I need to con some dense guy into taking me in so I have a safe place to rest. I guess I should use the helpless but proud female routine number three to get a place to stay. Now all I need is a mark to…"

Zara didn't get a chance to finish her thought as she collided with what might be her best option. As she watched, this attractive man admired her lines and eyed her from head to toe from his juxtaposition on the ground.

Feigning a little disorientation from the collision, Zara groused, "My, people come and go so quickly here! If you're hurt, let me help you up, sir. Of course, I will do that as soon as I see where I have landed. I didn't think I would run, quite literally, into such a powerful man in my travels. Are you what they call, in professional football, a linebacker?"

The flattery worked its charm, and the dashing man paused to offer all means of assistance to the fallen lady. She smiled at him and straightened her garments in a very provocative manner that he couldn't help but appreciate.

Once she was back on steady legs, he offered, "Ma'am, a thousand pardons and endless apologies for my coarse actions. May a gentleman offer a lady such as yourself some refreshment to help ease your fallen condition? I have been accused of being ill-mannered but not without compassion for someone suffering from my poor conduct. May I know your name so that I may properly apologize?"

Zara smiled at her potential new mark with his polished manners and very expensive clothing. Perhaps he had some useful connections that would be worth cultivating. She wanted to cloak her name under one of her many aliases for the time being. As the head of the United States branch of the Dteam, she had ten aliases that she could switch among. For the time being she was trying to stay under the radar of her Russian boss, so she decided on the newest one as she accepted, "Oh, kind sir, I am grateful to meet one so generous in manner, strength, and looks! I was warned that New Yorkers had no compassion for other travelers, so I am pleased to see there are exceptions! My name is Daria Plovia, kind sir. And you are?"

The man inclined his head slightly and offered, "My name is Arthur Buswald. All my friends call me Buzz."

Zara knew she captured his imagination with her long legs, striking facial structure, dark eyes, and full lips. She wrapped herself into the new characterization of Daria that she had just created and smiled her well-practiced seduction smile. "I am very pleased to meet you, Buzz. Now, I think you made some reference to refreshment? I have a thirst that may not be quenched with just a single simple libation."

Buzz, thoroughly smitten, suggested, "Then of course, let's just see how thirsty you are, ma'am!"

Zara grabbed up her bag and hastily searched for the diamond necklace to reassure herself that it was still there.

Buzz couldn't help but notice the refracted bling and commented, "My goodness, so many diamonds, but none gracing your creamy neckline!"

Zara smirked as they walked on and replied, "Bubi, goodness had nothing to do with them being in my possession!" She chuckled and added, "Sadly, just an old family heirloom of valueless crystals. All I have, really."

Buzz swung the door open to his flat, placed his hand on the small of her back and ushered her in. "Welcome to Castle Buzz! Home sweet home! As we agreed, this is just until you can get back on your feet again. I'm still amazed that you made a journey so far from your homeland with so little baggage. You remind me of one of those characters in a TV series that is on the lam and only has the clothes on their back, but no toothbrush. By the way, I've an extra toothbrush if you need it. I'm real fussy about my toothbrush, so you should know that I'm not sharing. You can take that other room over there and set it up as your own."

Zara studied Buzz a second and then asked, "All this hospitality to a stranger and you do not insist I share your bed? Don't tell me I found both a gentleman and a kind stranger in this harsh city."

Buzz chuckled as he responded, "Hey, I'm not going to discourage you from warming my bed, but it would be your choice, not a requirement. Besides, all this is new to me as well. Let's take our time and get to know one another, then we can see where things stand."

Zara wandered into the other room. As she inspected the closet and the top of the dresser, she noticed right away the belongings of another woman. She turned and strode back out to Buzz. "I can't help but notice another woman's trappings in the room and closet. What am I to say when this other female comes back to her room for her possessions? Were you looking for a team exercise rather than just a partner?"

Almost immediately, Buzz grew very dark. It took several seconds for him to regain his composure before he quietly remarked, "She won't be coming back, Daria. She was murdered by a Russian mobster.

"I simply can't bring myself to remove Patty's things. I haven't been in that room in quite some time. It didn't occur to me that you might take offense at her belongings being there. I try not to think about her or what happened. If it will make you feel better you can put them into bags, so you don't have to look at them. I can't touch them. Too many memories. All of them painful."

Zara smirked internally to herself and thought, *What a great con line! Maybe I can use that some time. However, I'd better play the 'I'm-so-sorry' card to make him think I'm touched by his emotional…whatever.* Zara commiserated, "Oh my! You poor thing! How awful for you and for her too! Yes, of course, I understand about her things. Did they ever catch the killer? Oh, I'm sorry, what a rude thing to ask. Is my being Russian going to be a problem with such a dreadful event having been in your life?"

Buzz was slightly melancholy with divulging the history, yet not anxious to let her leave. He commented, "Oh, you mustn't think that way! I don't hold all Russians personally responsible for one murderous psychotic! You have needs that I can accommodate. Somehow that seems right to me, regardless of your nationality. Anyway, the wretched little murderer, Sergei, got all that was coming to him. The police had me identify his body and his ugly silver front tooth."

Zara barely contained her astonishment as her insides roiled on hearing the name Sergei. She immediately flashed on how she had come to work in the Dteam group in New York City. She recalled with disgust his greasy appearance, the big silver front tooth, and his offensive stares after she had been offered the job. She had all but forgotten about Sergei until Buzz had revived the buried memory. To meet a man in a city of millions only to have a common crossing was fate at its worst, or perhaps it worked in her favor.

She remembered when Sergei had disappeared, but every time that she inquired after him Grigory told her to drop the subject, so she'd let it go. She didn't care a bit about Sergei yet was somehow relieved that he would never sneak up on her. She obviously needed to do some additional research on her new target. Perhaps there was more to this man than she had considered.

Trying to regain his original upbeat attitude before reliving his bad days, Buzz suggested, "Hey, enough about my downer story! Why don't you settle in and then let's see about something to eat, shall we? I bet after a short rest and a nice meal we can talk about your next steps. Agreed?"

Zara smiled amicably. "Agreed."

As an afterthought, Buzz remarked, "Oh yeah! Let me get some plastic bags. If you'll bag all of her stuff up, I'll see that it gets donated to the battered women's shelter down the way. It seems like this is a good time to break with the past, don't you think?"

As Buzz scampered off, Zara thought, But first, Bubi, I will pick through her clothes before bagging them up. I could use some new clothes, and it seems a shame to let clothes from a dead woman be donated so carelessly. After all, I'm needy too.

As she sorted through the things, she found many items she could utilize. Then she became almost nostalgic when she came across some erotic leather goods in one of the drawers. They reminded her of her past, when she was at the top of her game as a dominatrix. Zara considered that perhaps this arrangement could have some longevity.

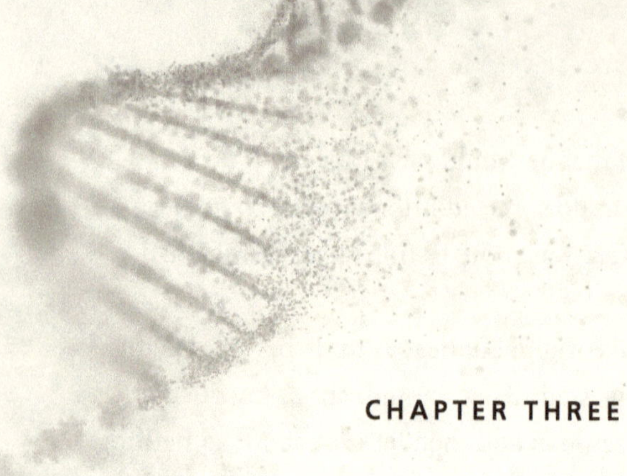

CHAPTER THREE

What If Being Saved Means Trusting In Yourself?
...The Enigma Chronicles

As he stood there, he stared out one of the few windows in the massive laboratory and data center. Winter had not yet released its grip on the frozen landscape. For some unknown reason, he never seemed to notice nature, the world around him, or the changing seasons. The Finland location meant using the snow and ice from the environment to cool down the horrific heat generated by the massive supercomputer driving his project. So long as the temperatures were low and snow fell, the data center would run the heat exchangers far more cheaply than alternative electricity. He smiled at the cynical thought of bragging on the *greenness* of their project, located in a climate that leveraged more natural cooling than most other super-computer sites.

His musings were interrupted by his faithful assistant, who entered and stated, "Xavier, I think I may have found the candidate for our next round of testing. You had asked me to continue correspondence with our volunteer until we were ready, but she quietly fell off the grid. After digging and searching, she came back on the grid only to flat disappear until this week. As it turns out, her assistant gave me some clues to her disappearance, and now we can piece together what may have happened."

Dr. Xavier Pekoni slowly turned his gaze and stared dispassionately at his assistant. He adjusted his spectacles and tossed his shoulder length silver ponytail back over his collar before he reprimanded, "Leroy, our *forever code* project is designed to intercept the degenerative tissue problems in human beings, as well as refresh the body's DNA encoding, so the life force of the individual can allow living for a thousand years. Since we are still unable to make it work to my satisfaction yet, and time on this planet is still so precious, I don't want to waste any of it listening to how your day went. Can you simply get to the point and outline our next steps? I'm in a hurry and expect you to be on the same schedule with me! Our all-important time continuum is collapsing to a finite point. Don't waste any of it!"

Leroy recognized that tone and, swallowing hard, he offered, "Apologies, Dr. Pekoni. Your missing test subject has been located, but her caregiver is unwilling to allow me access to her. I'm exploring other options, for both regular channels and otherwise, to determine how best to reintroduce her into our program timeline."

Xavier nodded approvingly and agreed, "That's better. We have successfully completed our preliminary testing with organs in animals, but we must see how we succeed or perhaps stumble with a human subject. The regenerative process on lost neural pathways in the brain will be our next milestone, and I don't want to miss our timeline. Do you understand?"

Leroy, somewhat intimidated, responded, "Yes, Dr. Pekoni, I understand. But in any case, whether we use legitimate means to extract her or otherwise, we cannot risk activity that would generate high exposure and attention to your project. The setback we incurred in exiting the U.S. operations was a good but unfortunate lesson in what not to do or who to trust. Therefore, we will need to extract her quietly and leave no trace of her to be followed. Those were your instructions, and I have not forgotten."

Xavier almost smiled as he reminded, "As I've pointed out, our time is running out. I want answers for the *forever code* before the squeamish, bleeding hearts show up again and say you can't test with humans! Once we have the right formula, no one will care how we got there because they will all be pushing and shoving while standing in line to buy our service for a ten-fold boost in lifespan. So, you're right, we must be quiet about who and where we are."

Leroy concurred, "Yes, Dr. Pekoni."

Then, with a renewed seriousness, Xavier asked, "When is the field trip for the former Master Po to be arranged?"

CHAPTER FOUR

Here, Let Me Help You With That

The air seemed thick with annoyance as Quip and Wolfgang joined Otto in the conference room. Quip and Wolfgang exchanged quizzical glances between each other during the awkward moments of silence.

Finally, Otto blurted out, "Can someone tell me why all the meetings are now initiated by ICABOD? I mean, what's the point in even having a meeting if ICABOD already knows what we should be concerned about and already has our answers! ICABOD's ability to divine future events has practically turned this into the ICABOD show! Starring ICABOD! Directed by ICABOD! Produced by ICABOD! Written by ICABOD! Cinematography and costume design by ICABOD! Now I know how a stage prop feels being moved into a scene shoot and then moved back into storage!

"Now that we are all assembled, heeeeere's ICABOD!"

Quip and Wolfgang sat and rolled their eyes at Otto's outburst. After a few seconds of silence, Quip finally asked, "I sense something may be troubling you, Otto. Do we need to explore these feelings of yours with our studio audience and perhaps end with a group hug? Then, after a good cry and a commercial break, we could talk about the reconnaissance ICABOD has obtained from the newest supercomputer activity, which we asked for information on?"

Otto glared at Quip and snapped, "I feel like I'm being mocked in my own company! Here we are, prowling for information on the Helsinki supercomputer, *called Statistical and Theoretical Integration of Numerals Kinetically and Infinitely Evolved,* or *STINKIE* as she prefers to be called, but no one can tell me how to get my daughter and Jacob back together."

After he listened to Otto's rant, Wolfgang quietly offered, "Otto, I hurt too, in this matter. I don't like seeing them gone any more than you. I would rather we focus our attentions on our next supercomputer threat vector than use valuable resources to determine the next episode of a daytime soap opera. As much as I hate seeing both my grandson and your daughter split from us and each other, I do believe the time apart is necessary. They are adults and able to make their own mistakes and their own decisions. It is not for us to move them at our speed, as they must resolve their own issues.

"In the meantime, I advocate we focus on work-related items. This is my advice on the subject. Quip, how do you feel?"

Quip was now a little more appreciative of the situation as he gently replied, "I agree with Wolfgang. I grew up with Petra. It pains me to know she is in such a depressed state. Heck, I even miss Jacob, a lot, though I don't know him as well. I don't feel that meddling in their affairs is correct, since neither of them are asking for help.

"Otto, you once told me that unsolicited help and advice is always poisonous to those to whom it is offered. I must advocate a wait-and-see policy as well. At the very least, until we need them to contribute their skills to a project.

"If you are in agreement, may I ask ICABOD to proceed?"

Otto sighed and grudgingly shook his head in agreement. Quip looked at the monitor/camera that ICABOD used to communicate and nodded – the command to proceed.

ICABOD responded, "All contextual clues and informational hunting being performed suggests that the operators of STINKIE, are collecting data to help them leverage the decoded human genome ahead of others in a special project. The project appears to have had its origins in the Fountain of Youth project that went dormant 5.4 years ago, when the project lead and all their research went missing."

After a short pause, ICABOD added, "My apologies, Otto. I meant no disrespect to you or the team members. While I do not experience the same human emotions you have expressed, I do notice Petra and Jacob's absence as well as the emptiness you share with the others.

"I have not accessed the master program *Deterministic Algorithms Assembled into Future Findings Yielding a Matrix of Accelerated Theorems Holistically,* also known as *DAAFFY-MATH,* for seeing into the future since our agreement not to. However, if the group feels it should be done in this instance, certainly it can be done to aid two such valued team members."

Otto, a little chastened, replied, "No, Quip and Wolfgang are right. We should only be using our computing power for maintaining the balance of power and to intercept enemies of humanity, not interfering with matters of the heart or personal relationships.

"I'm sorry I went off on you, ICABOD. I am just frustrated with the current circumstances, and I unfairly took it out on you. Please accept my apology. You are doing your job in a very responsive manner."

Smiling now, Otto continued, "Okay, so what else can you tell us about STINKIE from Helsinki?"

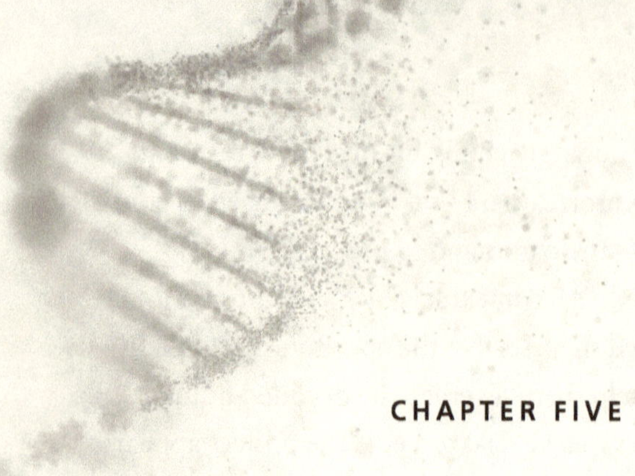

CHAPTER FIVE

Facing the Monsters Doesn't Mean You Can Win

...The Enigma Chronicles

Jacob finally acknowledged the dawn as he slowly opened his red, swollen eyes. Things started to focus, except that everything had a sideways tilt to it. The realization that he had fallen asleep on the couch again finally passed through the fog of yet another alcohol-filled evening. It occurred to him that if he sat up his vision impairment would be cured. It also occurred to him that somehow the view of everything sideways in the room was kind of different and somewhat refreshing to the normal view. He would have liked to study this view a little longer, if there hadn't been someone repeatedly pounding on the door shouting his name.

The irritated voice from the other side of the door was yelling, "Geez, Jacob, are you going to open up or not? I must be at work soon, man! Now open up the door, or you can wash your tattoo yourself!"

Jacob suppressed his annoyance at having his hangover interrupted as the dull ache and itching across his back reminded him of the requirement for the antibacterial scrubbing of a human hand rather than a scrub brush. He pulled himself off the couch and staggered to the door.

After Jacob opened the door, Buzz pushed through the doorway in a hurry and commented, "Naked again, I see. Here're your clothes that I collected along the way from the street to the door. By the way, the old ladies next door were leering out the window at me, hoping for another strip show. The young mother next door is threatening to call the police at the next peep show you put on. She complained that her two children can't be left out to play in the late afternoons because of what you might do. Buddy, you're going to have to lighten up!"

Jacob gave Buzz a disinterested gaze for a few moments and asked, "Can you just scrub my tattoo and go? It's only a couple more days and she'll be ready to face the world."

Without waiting for a response, Jacob headed to the shower and started the water.

Buzz followed him to the shower, then whistled as he exclaimed, "Dude, that's one fine dragon! Now that she's healing and less red, you can see her shimmery scales. Delicate but powerful wings…she's the picture of grace ready for flight, but somehow menacing?!

"When you said you wanted to do a cover up on that old blob on your shoulder with a new tattoo, I had no idea that she'd cover your back from stem to stern!

"You know, everyone is retweeting Gentleman Josh complaining for days about his hand cramping up after your session. You didn't need to do both the outline and colorization all in one setting. I mean, my god, he pounded ink into you for almost ten hours! You should have taken two separate sessions like you were told. No wonder you're still in pain."

Jacob was in a surly mood and sarcastically remarked, "Honey, can you scrub a little higher up and to the right? I told you both, I didn't want to go back a second time.

"If it had been a real problem, he could have simply turned down the cash. I could have gone somewhere else. Oh, and thanks for getting me drunk enough to sit through the ordeal and not letting anyone else know."

Buzz, with a sour look on his face, retorted, "Well, I might have gotten you prepped for the hammering you took, but I haven't been getting you drunk every night since you landed back in town. And, hey, what's up with Beth? She keeps calling me asking why you won't call her back. Actually, the whole staff at the bar are wondering where you went, not just the girls. It used to be that I had to try and coax you out of your shell to have one beer. Now I feel like the little kid who isn't being invited to the other kids' birthday parties. What happened to you?"

Jacob winced a little from the scrubbing the dragon tattoo was receiving, then offhandedly stated, "Beth is a non-event. Sometimes she sits next to me in the bar so I buy her a drink. That's it, end of story.

"Nothing happened and everything happened. As Nietzsche would say, *He who fights with monsters might take care lest he thereby become a monster*. I wanted the dragon to remind me that I have become what I was fighting against. She'll remind me that I'm the monster now."

Buzz, puzzled and just a little fearful, cautiously asked, "I know what a dragon tattoo is, but what is a Nietzsche? Are they like German Ninja?"

Jacob felt the slight, stinging pain across his back, smiled slightly and replied, "Again you clearly demonstrate the ability to assemble complex concepts into the absurd. Yes, old friend, I'm just like the German Ninja."

Buzz, sensing that Jacob was not fully over his hangover, nor his binge for that matter, shrugged his shoulders and simply stated, "Okay, you're done. I've got to get to work, and I suggest that you try to reengage with humanity. You know that your old boss might just have you back if you dressed up and made it a point to ask him pretty, please.

"I mean it worked for me with my dad. It might even land me a girl. People can't help but give you the benefit of the doubt and, brother, are you creating lots of doubt!"

Jacob turned off the shower, smiled fatalistically, and suggested, "When one has become a dragon, how can you go back to fighting them?"

Buzz just shook his head and dried off his hands. "Okay, have it your way! I've got to get to work so I can maintain my life in this best of all possible worlds. You go ahead and stay here and slug down more of that rot gut stuff. Then you can mourn about that lost love that hosed you off after she was done with you!"

Still soaking wet from the shower, Jacob stepped out and grabbed Buzz by the scruff of his collar, raising him up and pinning him against the wall in a blaze of anger.

Buzz seemed almost unsurprised by the action as he calmly mentioned, "Here I am in suspended animation again! Up against a wall, by you, for the same reason, for the same comment, I make every morning.

"You do realize that every morning before I leave here, you get to do your suspended animation exercise with me before I go to work, and your brain finally snaps back to this reality. You know I do this every day to see if she still makes you cry before I go, don't you?"

Jacob slowly lowered Buzz down and realized that his eyes were overflowing again just as Buzz had stated.

Jacob lamented while rubbing his hand over his scruffy beard. "I'm sorry, Buzz. This wound doesn't seem to respond to antibacterial scrubbing like the tattoo."

Buzz commiserated, "I know, buddy. That's why I will be back tomorrow to scrub that which I can reach and poke at that which I can't."

After Buzz left, Jacob wondered how long he had been like this. Was it weeks or months that he had tried to purge the emotional wounds he felt for her? In fact, Jacob wasn't completely sure where he was. He only knew that the neighbors were divided on their feelings about him walking home naked each evening after drinking in a bar for most of the afternoon.

Jacob looked over at his laptop and wondered if he could still remember the password to get into his email. Maybe today would be different. Perhaps there was an email from her asking how he was feeling. He chuckled to himself at the thought of an email curing all their emotional scars. Perhaps he would check tomorrow for that all important message. He realized that every time he looked for that redeeming piece of correspondence and it wasn't there, the monster in him would flail at his loss, driving him back to the bar where people cared about your money, not your feelings.

CHAPTER SIX

Shared Success is Far Sweeter When You Are with Your Heart's Desire
...The Enigma Chronicles

Lara had stared out the window during the whole briefing delivered by her top design team. The staff sensed something was wrong, but everyone pretended to be fully engaged in planning for the next season's lineup.

Over the last year, Lara had built Destiny Fashions into a leading style definer for Brazil and much of South America. The global fashion industry paid close attention to her defining moves of design and use of environmentally sound fabrics. Lara's quest and dream had been launched with her father's emotional and financial backing. Prior to her success she had wandered, like being lost in the desert, for months before she had returned home to patch things up with her father. He had encouraged her to push the company to his board of directors for approval and funding. All of this had begun when she had met Carlos.

Carlos had rescued her during an emotional low point. He had given her hope and happiness when she had been perched on a precipice and almost ready to step into a horrible existence. He had made everything possible for her. Because of him, she was now perched on top of the world, but she was not close by him. Lara missed him to the point of distraction.

Trying to reengage Lara in the presentation, one of the designers inquired, "Lara, what do you think about this fabric, with this cut? Some are saying it's too bold, but I think it'll make a statement for any lady who wears it. Your thoughts?"

Lara turned to face the designer and asked, "Could we pick this up again tomorrow? I can't concentrate today, even though I know our next planned event needs the collective output from this session. My apologies, but not right now, please."

Lara rose and quietly left the room without a glance back. The staff was surprised, and a couple of them noticeably resented the request as they gathered their materials up and shuffled out of the meeting room.

One of the team members grumbled under his breath, "That's the second time this week she's done that. We can't stay on top of this industry without timely decisions. We have too many competitors gunning for us! What a shame."

After leaving the meeting, Lara walked straight to Thiago's office. He sat on her board of directors and often gave her good counsel when asked. Thiago was also her father.

Thiago looked up as she entered his spacious office and smiled. He knowingly commented, "Ah, I know that look, my daughter! I know it because I see it on my face each morning while getting ready for work! I suspect it is not your failures that are troubling you but your successes. Am I right?"

With a slight smile and nod of her head, she acknowledged, "Yes, Papá, that is my problem. I cannot focus any longer on my business for thinking about my prince who is absent from my life. I know that I don't want one without the other. What am I to do?"

Thiago chuckled softly and comforted, "My daughter who wants everything! Then again, what woman doesn't? Let me guess, the fashion design business wants you to death, but your love is too far away for you to put your full focus on either?"

Lara nodded as she looked to him for a solution, as she had when she was a small girl.

He continued, "I suggest that you put someone you can trust in charge for a while. Make them a chief operating officer so they have authority to get actions done. Then go see if you can work a new arrangement for you and your Carlos. However, you must confess to him that you are looking to make both love and business fit into your life. Otherwise, one of you will be unhappy."

Lara studied Thiago for a moment, then nodded as she responded, "When I was a teenager, Papá, and all those fights we used to have, I distinctly remember thinking you were the dumbest guy on the planet. Now, here we are almost a dozen years later and I can't believe how much you've learned over that time! Astonishing, actually!"

Thiago studied Lara over his reading glasses, clucked his tongue and flatly replied, "It occurs to me I should have paddled your bum a little more as a child so I wouldn't be given these kinds of backhanded compliments I'm receiving now."

Lara grinned. "Oh Papá, I'm just teasing! And you're right about going to see Carlos and focus on us. I'll make the announcement tomorrow about our new COO, since I've already got someone in mind. I'll be gone for a while, but I will check in to let you know how it went, or if it went."

Thiago smiled a paternal smile and said, "Travel safe, my daughter. Give my best to Carlos. He is a very strong man. You must remember that when you talk with him."

Lara beamed at the plan being formulated and she asked, "I wonder if I should call him, or just show up? He might really enjoy the surprise visit, don't you think?"

Thiago darkened a little but then related, "I once popped in on a young lady who was my flame early in my youth, but she was not the only one surprised. I got there around 10:30 pm but she wasn't at her flat. I waited in my car all night only to witness her gentleman friend dropping her off early that morning so she could change before going to work. My advice is to call first, my daughter."

A little panicked, Lara frowned and replied, "Uh, yeah, good idea. Good bye, Papá."

CHAPTER SEVEN

I Like It When You Let Me Help You with Things

EZ watched the mechanical motions Quip went through to pour a glass of wine for each of them. She always knew when something troubled Quip because of his absentminded activity, which indicated he was lost in thought. That and the fact that he didn't try to remove her bra the moment he arrived home made her even more suspicious.

EZ gently asked, "Honey, what's wrong? You seem preoccupied, deep in thought even. If it is work related then we agreed that was out of bounds for me, but if it's something else I am here, if you want to share."

Quip smiled at her as he handed her the glass of wine and sat down adjacent to her. He stated, "Everyone is concerned about Petra and Jacob. It is starting to feed on the team, and some of the team are not dealing very well with the teammates being MIA. Everyone, including me, wants them back and together so everyone can live happily ever after. Isn't that ridiculous?

"Yep, Mr. Geek here, believing in fairy tales and the proverbial happy ending. What if there is no happy ending to the tale, and the good times are already history?"

EZ pulled back a bit and admonished, "Why, Dr. Quinton! To hear you talk like that makes me very uncomfortable, indeed! You should be ashamed of yourself thinking, *This is as good as it gets,* for them! Next, you'll be saying the same thing about us! Let me tell you something, buster, we gotta lotta good stuff on the way. Don't start looking backwards wondering where it went wrong!"

Quip, ashamed at his negative comments, agreed, "Yes, sweetheart, you're right. I'm sorry to let their unconnected circumstances bring me down. I just can't help but want things to work out for them as well as they have for us, that's all."

EZ calmed down a bit and nuzzled a little closer to him as she suggested, "I expect the best medicine for them is to be back in the game doing family business. That will quickly return the first stage of self-worth.

"Once they see that their skillsets are valued for work, they'll have to cross paths. Then they can work on gathering back the lost feelings they had for each other. I don't think they lost their feelings, just their way. Perhaps a bit of stubbornness. That's the way I see it playing out."

Quip nodded approvingly, gave her a hug, and added, "Not only are you an excellent unified communications specialist, you're pretty good at assessing the personal issues of a couple too. Uh, will you remind me to tell you how wonderful you are, if I don't say it often enough?"

EZ got even closer to Quip and in a very sultry voice murmured, "Honey, you should tell me how wonderful I am."

Quip stared into her eyes but before he could say anything, EZ asked, "Honey, you've been home over forty minutes so how come I'm still wearing my bra?"

Big Things Do Exist in a Small World

O tto recognized the incoming number as a client associated with a United States agency with which they had a standing purchase order of rather broad latitude. Eric was also a quasi-friend of sorts, which made him fair game to tease. Otto answered the call in his cheeriest voice. "Dr. von PettinGrübber! I'm delighted to hear from you, sir! I trust this call portents a heartfelt discussion of your needs, unmet by your agency staff that will grant us the opportunity to serve your quest!"

Eric, momentarily blank of thoughts, finally marshaled his mind and responded, "Otto, have you been writing for automobile commercials again? Because that's what you're sounding like."

Grinning, Otto embellished, "Close, liposuction commercials! People always need fat sucked out of somewhere, but it's the sales presentation that makes or breaks the deal. In our research, it is key for the client to feel there is nothing shameful in eliminating fat excesses that have accumulated over the years. Our best sales pitch is to appeal to the customer by making them feel they should do this or that to look better for their significant other. We min-imize the *all about me thinking* and get the customer to project their feelings on how their partner will relish the new twenty kilo loss. Our liposuction service takes away unwanted fat and returns a more self-assured individual. We call it the Robin-Hood syndrome, whereby we steal the fat from those who have too much in exchange for a more confident outlook on life. Most gratifying, actually.

"But enough about my new frontiers of community service. What can I do for you, sir?"

Eric sat and blinked in a thoroughly disoriented state for several seconds as he tried to process Otto's comments. He felt like he needed to pinch himself and see if he was dreaming. He finally commented, "I find it astonishing that your organization has so many varied interests in the business world. It's no wonder people come to you for help. I just wish I could remember why I called you today."

Otto smirked a little at derailing Eric's thought process yet again. He let the silence hang without further comment.

Then Eric blurted, "Okay, now I remember why I called, Otto!

"We had a project we underwrote to do some very advanced research on human aging. We had this very persuasive academic type named Dr. Pekoni wrangle funding and supercomputer time from us in his research efforts. This was about ten years ago. Everything was well thought out and structured with milestone reviews, which suggested a lot of confidence in the project."

Otto, curious, asked, "What exactly was the project supposed to do?"

Eric responded, "It was called the *Fountain of Youth* project, and the ambition was to leverage the then recently decoded human genome and learn how to use the genetic sequencing to reprogram cellular structure.

"His project proposal was to use the work in genetics and DNA as instructional blueprints of each human organ from growth through maturation to then alter the physiological behavior of a matured individual. He postulated that human body tissue contained flaws within the genetic sequencing that, over time, either forgets how to regenerate replacement tissue or mutates into something adversarial to the host human. In other words, cancer.

"The doctor further suggested that if we could understand the applied maturation of the sequencing of the human genome, then we could biologically reprogram the tissue at the genetic level to its optimum matured state and eliminate tissue degeneration. He received funding because he convinced the panel he could add a process to make human tissue at the cellular level through genetic manipulation perform as intended on a continual or as needed basis at a fixed age."

Otto filled in the next sentence as he postulated, "And thus extend the human lifespan because organs and life tissue would no longer mutate or lose the ability to regenerate themselves. How interesting! But I thought the human genome project was declared finished in April 2003 by an international consortium?"

Eric nodded and sighed a little before he continued. "Correct, but that was just the mapping. He was actually using some of that early research, along with his own, to move his project along faster. It looked very promising, and there was an awful lot of hope staked on his project's outcome. Then things started to slip, as did the defined milestones. Progress seemed to be increasingly elusive as time wore on.

"The first big breakthrough came about halfway through the project life cycle, when we were shown some proof positive data points that some hog gene resequencing had in fact stopped cold a cancer that had been introduced into the animal. Dr. Pekoni was over the top in his presentation. Looking back on it, I can see we were intoxicated by the success of this one test subject. The agency kept the funding in place, then things started to unwind.

"Briefings and even progress reports started being rescheduled or postponed. We had trouble even getting the doctor on the phone. Calls were never returned, and numbers finally ceased working."

Otto furrowed his brow and stated, "I believe I remember some of this from the sensationalist side but not what happened next. I seem to recall some controversy around the project and then nothing. What happened?"

Eric replied, "We had reason to believe that he started to experiment on humans, based on his earliest successes with animals containing similar DNA pairs to humans. Apparently, word got out and anyone dying of cancer volunteered for the possible chance it would work for them. Dr. Pekoni simply couldn't refuse the offers to experiment on live humans for the sake of moving his project along.

"We started getting reports of his activities from other agencies and inquiries from a few folks who were quite uncomfortable with government funding of unsanctioned human testing. One group likened this experimentation to the Nazi S.S. doctors' work at German concentration camps of World War II. To state it plainly, these were unsanctioned human trials with none of the clinical safeguards or even oversight in place."

Otto's eyebrows arched up in alarm as he suggested, "Eric, this information is a little too close to home for me, with my family having run from the Nazis after my native country of Poland was overrun in 1939. But please continue, sir."

Eric nodded and explained, "It might have been water under the bridge, if that was as far as it had gone. Unfortunately, his experiments had an unfortunate side effect on the volunteers. Everyone, without exception, developed a blood disorder from his genetic reprogramming that necessitated blood transfusions every thirty days. A couple of our internal operations analysts cynically rebranded the program as the *Virtually Amplified Mathematical Processing of Integers Recursively and Exponentially*, or, the VAMPIRE project.

"With the private sector coming into the picture and the unwanted publicity of experimenting on human subjects, the government pulled the plug on funding the VAMPIRE project, which stopped Dr. Pekoni's project cold in the states."

"That isn't the entire story, is it, Eric?"

Eric clucked his tongue and replied, "Again, correct, Otto. We have reason to believe one of the test subjects was in fact Dr. Pekoni himself. When he vanished, he took all of his research, and I mean *all* of his research, with him. It was postulated he was looking for something to help counteract the blood disorder because he too had it. Intelligence suggests that he missed some of the necessary genome sequencing for his project that he had started before the main genome sequencing project was definitively completed.

"After he vanished, we started getting reports of an organization that was illegally harvesting DNA samples from as many sources as possible. We believe that the doctor is looking for the missing DNA sequencing he overlooked, and that will allow the cure to the blood disorder his program needs to increase the human lifespan."

Otto asked, "How much of a life enhancement are we talking about here?"

Eric shrugged and replied, "There were only speculative theories, but the number that kept coming up was a thousand-year lifespan, or roughly ten times today's healthy lifespan."

Otto mused, "I can understand Dr. Pekoni's interest in the program. What can we do for you in this matter, Eric?"

Eric said, "We would like to know where our bought-and-paid-for research material is. Plus, we need a view into Dr. Pekoni's current activities and whereabouts. We continue to get sporadic intelligence reports that he has not stopped his workflow and is still harvesting DNA from unsuspecting volunteers.

"Can you hunt for his current whereabouts? It would be ideal to find out what he is working on and capture copies of the newest research materials. If he is still operating, then I am fairly sure we have a problem. If he isn't operating, the research materials don't need to fall into the wrong hands."

Otto confirmed, "Yes, of course, Eric. We will locate him if he exists and do our best to track down the research materials. Please drop all the case information into our usual encrypted dropbox, and I'll assign someone to begin the search."

Eric agreed, "Thanks, Otto. Your statement of work and purchase order will be in there as well."

"Good day, Eric."

CHAPTER NINE

Altered Plans without Warning is a Danger Sign
…The Enigma Chronicles

Andy practically shouted into the phone. "What do you mean, bring her in for another specialist review? We were just there last week for her monthly checkup! Don't you people know who is coming and when around that facility? …

"Don't be using your uppity attitude on this old Georgia farm boy, young lady! At least I know how to pour bovine urine out of a boot with the instructions written on the bottom of the heel, unlike some people I talk to on the phone…

"Well, of course I want her to have every opportunity to be helped, but why couldn't you have told me last week…

"Yes, I know Su Lin is a special case. I realize that means many specialists are interested and not all of them show up at a convenient time…

"Well, I have my regular job too, you know. These little jaunts to the medical facility take time out of my regular schedule to accommodate these random specialist reviews…

"You mean this visiting specialist is so important that you will come fetch her and bring her back when the review is over?

I don't know about that. I'm her guardian, and ever since the accident I...

"Yes, she does know all the folks there, so it's not like I'm sending her off with a bunch of strangers...

"You make a pretty good case for this one time, which would help me out with my workload...

"And the driver's name? ...

"Leroy, okay. Got it! Thanks. We'll see Leroy then day after tomorrow..."

Andy was really annoyed that they wanted to see Su Lin on such short notice. He was scheduled to depart in a couple of hours to a customer in California to provide some updates to their equipment. Carlos had readily agreed to watch out for Su Lin while he was gone, yet Andy felt it an imposition. Su Lin had been a ward of Andy's since her heart had stopped for that short duration so many months ago, damaging her mind.

Su Lin was a lovely woman of Asian descent that Andy had been extremely attracted to before the accident. The lack of blood pumping through her system for an extended period had caused some significant damage to her memory. The once expert in cyber technologies and leading edge applied technologies now had the social skills of a teenager rather than the fifty-something woman she was. Skills were being relearned through some special training, as well as the time spent by Andy with her, but progress was very slow.

The accident had occurred shortly after she had brought her pig, Franklin, and her student, Daisy, to work on some nano-technology experiments. Even though overall the experiments had proven successful, Su Lin's accident was attributed to this experimentation. Daisy had returned to finish her schooling while Su Lin and Franklin had remained. Franklin had fit in with the other animals on Andy's farm, and Su Lin delighted in the responsibility of the care and feeding of her pet.

Andy found Carlos located in the telecommunications center where he was focusing on some changes to their software.

Andy was still in a terse mood at being forced to leave Su Lin to someone else's care while he fulfilled the required customer visit. Everything seemed like it was against him. Carlos sensed that Andy was in a grumpy mood but wanted Andy to feel comfortable with the responsibility hand-off.

Carlos suggested, "Now don't forget to pack fresh underwear and take your good toothbrush this time. You know how California ladies judge men by the sporty briefs they wear when they are trying to decide who they should take home to meet their momma. A good toothbrush keeps all the debris from collecting on your smile, like tofu for instance."

Half annoyed by everything anyway, Andy rolled his head to one side while he looked rather incredulously at Carlos. He reminded, "I'm not going out there for some California Dreaming Cakes, budrow! I have an extra fussy customer who doesn't believe in remote anything when paying for our services. I don't want to stay any longer than I have to among the fresh California fruit salad clowns!

"We Georgia folk have this impression of California people that they like to fill their hot tubs with carbonated water and get in naked with the eight close friends they met that morning as they bob for recreational drugs! I typically work twelve to fourteen hours a day, so I can get the hell out of Hollywood quicker. I'm not going there to squeeze the fruits to go in my shopping bag, so stop trying to cheer me up!"

Carlos blinked a few times and offered, "I could do the California gig if you want to shepherd Su Lin with these characters. That might make you feel more comfortable, Andy. Or, if you prefer, I can stand here and take some more verbal hostility if that will help improve your disposition."

Andy, mad at himself and quite chastened by Carlos's remark, calmed down and apologized, "I'm sorry, Carlos. I just feel rather unsettled by leaving Su Lin with these people at this time. I can't quite put my finger on it, but something seems wrong. I feel like I'm running out on you and her with me being so unsettled. I didn't mean to take it out on you. Forgive me, my friend."

Carlos studied Andy a few seconds and asked, "Do they really party naked together in a hot tub full of recreational drugs and sparkling water? Are you sure I can't take your place for this trip?"

Andy grinned and said, "Go do your chores, boy! Make sure nothing happens to Su Lin while I'm gone, or it's the woodshed for you, mi compadre!"

Carlos smiled at Andy's comment and the fact that he had gotten him out of his poor mood before Andy had left for the airport.

Carlos smiled as he read the text message on his phone. He read it a second time to savor the intent of the message and then dialed to speak with Lara.

Lara answered on the first ring and hoped to not sound as anxious as she felt. "Hello, my prince! Do you have time to talk, or is this a bad time? I mean, I can call back if this is inconvenient, or if there is someone else there such that you cannot…"

Carlos chuckled and interrupted, "Sweetheart, there is no one else for me but you. Stop it. Now is a good time. If it wasn't, I wouldn't have called, now, would I?"

Lara chided herself for sounding like a teenager as she blurted, "Oh, Carlos, I want to see you to talk about us. Okay? I know I'm not happy about how things are with us separated.

I need to know how you feel. I was in a design meeting, and I got panicky. I felt we might have changed as a couple. Now I am scared that…"

Carlos rolled his eyes and intervened, "Honey! Slow down! I'm right here. No, there isn't someone else here taking your place in my bed or my heart! You've been working. I've been working. I agree, it's time to figure out something new. Yes, please, pack up that gorgeous body of yours and ship it here to Georgia. We'll work through everything."

Lara was on emotional overload. As tears of relief streamed down her cheeks, she agreed, "Yes, my love! I'm coming. See you soon, sweetheart!"

CHAPTER TEN

In Transacting the Deal, the More Middlemen the More Mouths To Feed

It had been a rough day for Buzz. Ever since he'd had his near-death experience, not once but three times while hanging out with the wrong crowd a while back, he'd honestly tried to stay on the straight and narrow. He admitted to himself that it was indeed safer than mixing it up with a Russian mobster, being interrogated endlessly by the police regarding the death of his former girlfriend, Patty, or having somebody named JAC help him buy his freedom from a Chinese political boss using a white tiger. But his current existence was just plain dull.

These days he followed orders from his father at the bank and reviewed changes to program code, which was like watching mud harden in the sun after a heavy rain. He thought to himself, there had to be something more to his existence than the dull, mindless code review and the hyper-fear level of mixing it up with mobsters from all points on the globe. He absentmindedly got undressed to take a long hot shower in the hopes that it would clear his mind before he attempted a fun night out.

The hot water and soapy scrub brush were having the desired effect of improving his mood, so much so that he even started singing a few lines from one of his favorite rock opera songs. All too soon the song and the shower were over. He pulled back the shower door to reach for a towel only to have it handed to him. Momentarily startled, he snapped the towel around himself and then saw Daria, who seemed to enjoy the view.

With a barely suppressed smile, she coaxed, "Oh, Bubi, don't stop just because you have an audience. In my country when the bathroom door is left open, it means it is either available or it's an invitation to watch. We women don't like to admit it, but we too enjoy being the voyeur and purveyor of a well-sculpted man, served up on display behind glass."

Zara moved closer to Buzz, then carelessly teased him with a caress to his jawline that trailed down his pectoral muscles. She confidently teased his hard nipples and asked, "Does the towel mean no more show time? What a shame! The opaque glass only hinted at the quantity of your maleness, and I was hoping to learn if you were of Chinese descent. You know, Won Huong Luo."

Buzz was now beat red and thoroughly undone by Daria's suggestive comments and touching. He was intimidated by the eroticism she projected and was harboring the usual male fear of not being sized as an Olympian endowed man, ever ready to meet a woman's expectations.

Buzz stammered a little as he replied, "Daria, I'm sorry. I didn't think that you would be back here at the apartment until later."

Zara leaned even closer and almost whispered, "Bubi, the view of such a powerfully built man, nicely scrubbed clean, drives me to ask that you share something with me."

Buzz was at a hopeless disadvantage with her request and felt totally outmaneuvered. He felt an overshadowing anxiety that his performance might not meet the expectations of what appeared to be an intimate encounter with a Russian temptress, so he innocently asked, "What did you have in mind, now that I am showered and still naked?"

Almost as though a light had been switched off, Zara pulled back and flatly stated, "I need a contract programmer for a job. I picked up some piecemeal work over the Internet this morning. I was hoping you might help me find a suitable code jockey to help me get this done quickly, since my funds are dwindling."

Buzz sensed the game was over with a mixture of relief and disappointment that Zara's teasing looked to go no further. Buzz asked, "What about that family heirloom I saw when we first hooked up? Have you considered cannibalizing it for more cash? I know from our prior discussion you wouldn't accept a handout, outside of a room here."

She fought to calm the alarm she felt at his remembering the necklace. Zara offhandedly replied, "My family heirloom! Ha, you know what they told me when I tried to have it appraised in the diamond district? It was a very well-done piece of costume jewelry! It's just as well since it has so much sentimental value it would have pained me to sell it.

"Now it's back to work for this girl. I am glad you accept a woman who likes paying her own way. Do you know anyone who is good enough to do some fast, yet brilliant, coding contract work, Bubi?"

Buzz answered, "I might have someone in mind for you if I can get through his emotional fog. Let me see where he is in his life's crises, and I'll get back to you."

Zara smiled and advised, "I'm old enough to do my own interviewing, so we can drop in together. I know what I'm look-ing for and you don't, so why don't you finish drying off, pack up your now docile beast, and let's go see him."

Dejected, Buzz commented under his breath, "Sure hope Jacob doesn't answer naked again. I sure don't need any more competition for Daria's attention."

Addressing Daria, he said, "It would be easier for him if we met for dinner. I really don't know his prior commitments, and he hates anyone showing up uninvited. I know a place that is right between where we both live, and I was ready to go have a bite to eat. Let me get dressed and call him to meet us there. My treat!"

Zara waited in the other room for Buzz to finish dressing. She had done some research through the Dteam files with a focus on Grigory's notes. After she located a file on Patty, who had worked part time for Grigory on identity theft, Zara had traced back through the files and located some programs her new benefactor had worked on. She recalled when Buzz had explained to her the other night, how much work he did at his father's bank. Buzz had indicated he had once moonlighted doing some coding, but had stopped doing that some time ago. After reading the small scribbles from Grigory, she could guess why. Perhaps he would consider helping her if his friend didn't work out.

Her phone chirped and she reluctantly answered, "Dmitry, it is somewhat late for you to be calling. Did your late-night snack of vodka and caviar give you a fit of consciousness, or did you just want to tell me how much you've missed me?"

A rather sullen Dmitry responded, "You haven't answered your phone in quite some time. I was beginning to wonder if it was something I said to hurt your feelings. I trust I am right in saying you do have feelings, correct? I mean, I would hate to get you mixed up with a regular person that isn't always on the hunt for money from her next victim."

Zara, struggling to hold back her irritation, coldly remarked, "Hey, I told you I was going on vacation, so what's the big deal? Who is it that you want to harass next? The reason I ask is whenever that is what is on your agenda, you usually begin with me! Spill it, *Dummy-tree!*"

Zara wished she hadn't hurled the last insult during the verbal sparring.

Dmitry, exceedingly irked by her comment, fought with his anger yet calmly inquired, "My dear, you think that because you are not in Russia that you are beyond my reach? There is no place on this planet where a person can go that I can't have my agents strangle her with her own bra. Use that tone again with me or use that disparaging nickname again, and I can promise you a lesson in manners. Understood?"

Zara swallowed hard and took the time to calm her breathing before she contritely responded, "I understand, Dmitry. What needs doing, my master?"

Dmitry finally had cause to smile and commented, "My master! I like the sound of that.

"I need cloaking on some harmless pranks I need to play on one of our neighboring sovereigns. They have been trying to access my supercomputer here in the Kremlin data center and frankly, I'm tired of it. A little exercise of our system's considerable strength would restore a better appreciation of our relationship."

Zara smirked as she asked, "Gosh! Whose turn is it this week? You have pretty well whacked everyone, except Finland."

Dmitry grinned and replied, "How clever you are! Finland has been launching some cyber probing efforts, looking for something on our systems. It is time for the Russian Bear to remind them of their colony status."

Zara, barely concealing her sarcasm, responded, "They didn't like being Russian any better than they liked being Swedish! Let's hope you conduct a better attack than the clumsy one launched by the Soviets in 1939 when 100,000 Finns held off almost 600,000 Russian troops.

"Have you seen the cartoon from that Finnish newspaper? In it one Finn defender says to another, *Look at all the Russian Troops! My God where are we going to bury all of them?*" Zara laughed at her own storytelling.

Dmitry, tiring of the history lesson, asked, "You do recall we finally got our way with the Finns, and that they gave into our demands, right?

"But, enough of that! How soon can you be ready to anonymize my data traffic? Because it will be a torrent."

Zara sensed she had worn out her welcome on the call and replied, "I will need a week to bring everything back online and up to speed. You know how it is when you go on vacation. Nothing gets done in your absence."

Dmitry nodded to himself and responded, "Actually that works well with my schedule. I'll be in touch."

But before Dmitry disconnected, Zara asked, "Before you go, Dmitry, I need a favor from you. I have inherited some diamond jewelry that, well, I would like to turn into cash. I was wondering if, among your contacts, there might be someone who is agreeable to paying a fair price for an heirloom of questionable origins. Can I get your assistance in this matter?" Then she added, "I would certainly expect you to get a brokering fee for such a conversation that leads to a sale, so as to make it worth your time."

Dmitry curiously asked, "How many diamonds are we talking about? Inquiring minds need to know."

Zara sensed she had hooked Dmitry and innocently replied, "I don't know how many diamonds on the necklace but when I checked in the diamond district, they suggested it might be worth five million euros. However, no one here would offer anywhere near that figure without the original bill of sale. Do you have such contacts that could assist in converting these for me? I would be most grateful, Dmitry."

Dmitry, rather amicable at this point due to the project he wanted worked, assured, "Well, let me see if I can't help you with that little project. I will make some inquiries tomorrow. If you can send me a picture, it would help with my brokering efforts."

Zara feigned gratitude as she sweetly responded, "Thank you so much, Dmitry! I will get the photo off to you as soon as we disconnect."

Dmitry, in his most pleasant voice, finished, "We'll talk soon, Zara!"

CHAPTER ELEVEN

Heading My Way...
the Good Times and Its Evil Twin

It was Buzz's favorite bar and grill. He almost preened as he showed off what everyone would think was an attractive date. She was dressed to kill, but he was just dressed. His hair didn't quite behave for a comb or a brush, and he had long since given up on trying to discipline it. She, on the other hand, was nicely packed into a well-fitting dress that almost suggested business yet could be used to solicit her next client, if she were that kind of woman. Her long legs were visible beneath a hem that just cleared her bottom. The dress displayed just a hint of cleavage but nothing overt.

They were seated where the noise level of the bar would not detract from their intended conversation.

The waitress quickly sized up the situation correctly as a business-type meeting, since Zara was coolly keeping her distance from the man who had escorted her. After she ordered, Zara watched the inbound people, alert for their guest. Walking back to deliver the drink order, the waitress smirked a little at Buzz thinking he was over his head as he tried to impress yet another uninterested "date".

Absorbed into her new alias, Daria, Zara said, "Buzz, this friend of yours, I hope he understands the value of time and does not keep us waiting too long. You're sure he is coming to talk with me?"

Buzz, a little put off by the circumstances, reached over and covered her hand as he replied, "Hey, have I ever let you down before? Relax! Enjoy your wine and please tell me more about the new work you secured.

"He said he would be here as a favor for all the favors I've done for him. I've got to warn you, he is in something of a lost love state. He dumped everything here in the city to chase after a woman, only to have her dump him. If he shows up and acts like a jerk, we can just leave and stick him with the bill. Agreed?"

Zara almost smiled and then looked out across the bar and submitted, "Ah, now that looks like a survivor from a failed relationship. Is this him?"

Zara was amazed again at how small the world was. The man approaching the table was not only a friend of her new mark, Buzz, but she knew him from her contracted job to deliver a digital payload to the city offices that had ended in her disruption of their computers. She had been attracted to him then and was not surprised that, though he looked worn down, she was attracted to him again. She needed to guard what she said with him, as her appearance had been very different during that encounter, but her voice could be her downfall.

Buzz, a little disappointed at Daria's keen interest in Jacob, dejectedly answered, "Yeah, that's him."

Jacob caught sight of Buzz and walked directly over to the table. He looked at them both but did not immediately join them. He almost smiled yet seemed to be assessing Daria as he stood at the head of the table.

Finally, he spoke. "Hello, my name is Jacob. I'm a recovering pen-testing code jockey. I'm here tonight to discuss my struggling road to recovery, as well as to discuss a potential contract job you might have available."

Buzz stared blankly at Jacob as he tried to determine Jacob's sobriety level. His behavior was not a total giveaway at this point. Buzz signaled the waitress to bring Jacob his usual.

Zara chuckled and smiled warmly as she raised her chin. She then, as she suppressed most of her accent, offered, "I'm Daria. Won't you tell me of your recovery status?"

She looked at Buzz, who seemed soured at Jacob's hit entrance. Zara suggested, "Buzz, you didn't mention that this Jacob person had a humorous streak in his composition, as well as broad shoulders!"

She looked back to Jacob and gestured for Jacob to sit next to her, which put even more downward pressure on Buzz's mood. Jacob shrugged, looked at Buzz and acquiesced.

As Jacob sat down next to her, he winced a little when his fresh tattoo rubbed against the vinyl booth as he slid in.

Zara noticed the slight grimace and asked, "How does a young stallion have aches and pains that cause him to show discomfort? Have you spent too much time coding and not enough time exercising? You do know that muscles that don't get taken out for exercise soon get even with you, yes?"

Jacob, still trying to recall why she seemed so familiar, pushed his thoughts aside and replied, "Buzz indicated that you had some contract work that you were looking to have done. I've been out of my element for a while, between contracts so to speak, but Buzz made a compelling case for getting back to work and reengaging. I thought I would at least come meet you and see if we could help each other.

"First, I have to say you seem somehow familiar to me. You definitely remind of someone. I can't shake the feeling we have met before. Do I look familiar to you by chance?"

Buzz, annoyed that Daria and Jacob were already on such good terms, exclaimed, "Oh, come off it, dude! Seriously! Don't I know you from somewhere? I put in a good word for you so you can get a coding gig, and you try to make a move on her with the oldest line in the book!"

Zara clearly sensed the tension from Buzz and couldn't resist her favorite game of mental cruelty.

Smiling seductively at both men, she intervened, "Gentlemen, I'm only here on business, but I sense there's a competition afoot for something that was not put on the table. Just because I am sleeping at Buzz's doesn't mean I am his property."

Jacob turned his head to look knowingly at Buzz and said, "Buddy, I didn't mean to be scoping your lady. I can't help feeling I've seen her before. That's all! My apologies, ma'am, if you took offense. Allow me to withdraw the question then, and let us start over."

Zara protested, "But, kind sir, I'm not sleeping with him, only staying at his apartment. He has made no overt offerings to know me in the biblical sense but has only shown me the greatest kindness, even to the extent of showing off for me in his shower. He is a generous man in all aspects that a lady could think of."

Buzz was mortified by her recounting of the earlier shower scene, yet he was somehow pleased that she thought him kind. The fact that Jacob snickered at her attempt to give him praise as a gentleman was almost insignificant.

About that time the waitress interrupted to bring Jacob's beverage and to see if fresh drinks were required, which helped to allow the tense situation to calm down.

Zara began again. "Let's stay with the business project I have, shall we? Jacob, I have some coding contract work that I need done within a short time frame. Consider this an introduction exercise that may lead to more work, but I am not prepared to discuss all the details in this bar. First of all, are you interested?"

Jacob leaned back against the booth back only to wince again, then lean forward and rest his arms on the table. He sipped his drink, then set it down.

Zara noticed and asked, "Are you in pain from a recent injury? You tend to favor your back."

Buzz blurted out, "Why don't you just tell her that you just got this huge dragon tattoo across your back, and I'm the one stuck giving you a sponge bath every day in the shower!"

To Buzz's dismay, Zara looked back at Jacob and suggested, "It's too bad we don't know each other better, else we could show each other our tattoos.

"To my original question, are you in for some contract coding or not?"

Jacob smiled reassuringly and said, "Ma'am, how can I refuse such a proposition from a delightful lady! However, for my friend's sanity, permit me to state that I have been bruised by a lady recently, so this will only be a business arrangement."

Zara smiled knowingly and scooted close enough to annoy Buzz and brush Jacob's arm as she confirmed, "Excellent! We can start tomorrow then. Meet me at Buzz's at nine.

"Now if you will excuse us, Buzz has to make good on an earlier display that boasted of a length and girth offering that no female should allow to go unattended."

As they left Zara teasingly said loud enough for Jacob to hear, "So, Bubi, you scrub another man's back in the shower? I did not know you were a man that, they say, operates like a screen door that swings both ways! Come, let's show each what the other is capable of, shall we?"

Daria hustled a beet-red Buzz out of the bar. Jacob motioned for the bill and with a knowing smile said, "It may take some time, but I will remember where I've seen you, Daria."

Chairman Chang sat fixated after viewing the multimedia picture he had received via his email. The initial fury he had experienced gave way to numbness and disbelief. How could he have been so wrong not to suspect Dmitry of having grabbed the five-million-euro diamond necklace from Nikkei's neck before he returned her? His two associates, Won and Ton, had argued persuasively that Dmitry was not the culprit, so he had dispatched them to hunt for Zara as the probable thief. However, here was Dmitry offering to sell him the very necklace he'd sent Won and Ton to find in a different part of the globe. If this had happened to someone else, he thought it would have been funny. But, as it was, all it did was make the chairman want to spit.

It took all of Chang's mental facilities and supreme willpower to answer the incoming call from Dmitry. He rather sullenly responded, "Hello, Dmitry…

"Yes, I got the photo of the diamond necklace…

"May I know how you came by such a magnificent item? Did you shake down some poor unfortunate soul, then when they wouldn't buy it back, offered it to me? …

"Ah, I see. You are brokering for someone else…

"Hmmm, does the owner of this handsome item have a price in mind? …

"Dmitry, I said handsome item, not handsome price! Five million euros based on a picture! At least send me the provenance letter so I can verify its authenticity and worth…

"Oh, I see. So now we are talking wholesale not retail, I take it? Without proper paperwork I would have to see them, *then* we could talk price…

"Dmitry, how can you say that? Of course, I don't trust you, but that's no reason to accuse me of not having any trust. Let's turn this around. You send them to me, and I'll let you trust me to pay you…

"Dmitry, what an unfair characterization of me. I never had a sister to sell to the slave trade, regardless of their cash and carry policy…

"Dmitry, please express my hope to the owner that they get their desired price. Without all the proper paperwork, I will only be interested in the necklace at a steep discount, down to say…€500,000…

"Dmitry, there is no need to use that kind of language when trying to broker a deal for questionable merchandise. I meant, what if these are stolen property or, heavens me, conflict diamonds? Where would I be in my explanation to the authorities? …

"You do make a good point…

"True, I am the authorities here…

"That's better, Dmitry. Have a talk with the owner and get back to me with their decision. Goodbye, Dmitry."

As soon as he disconnected the call, Chairman Chang hastily dialed a familiar number and said, "Dmitry just tried to sell me back my own diamonds, the bastard! At first, I thought he had them, but it sounds very much like someone has them and he gets a percentage if he can move them. So your first theory must be correct, and it is Zara who has them. Find me that bitch and bring back my diamonds."

CHAPTER TWELVE

The Best Case Scenario is that You Grow Up Healthy and Hardy

Su Lin woke up, determined not to cause any problems for Carlos. Before he'd left, Andy implored her to behave, do all her chores, and finish her studies before the car came to pick her up for transport back to the doctors for yet another test. She knew that she was sometimes stubborn about completing all her chores, but Andy was so kind, as well as encouraging, that she wanted to show him that she was capable. In the last year she had learned so much, amazing even herself.

The methods of research that included working on her laptop were a lot of fun. Lots and lots of information could appear with only a simple inquiry. Andy had structured her learning each month to research certain aspects of a given subject and then test out. She honestly liked writing the stories and some of the papers he'd assigned to her to complete by hand, rather than on the computer, but that was because he complimented her on her handwriting.

He'd said that most people today didn't write by hand as much as by computer, but he liked to read her papers without having to look at a screen. Su Lin supposed that since his work required that he work in front of a computer, that reading from her papers was more relaxing. When she turned over an assignment to him in the afternoon, he would typically take it outside to the patio and settle on one of the chaise lounges surrounded by flowering plants, playful chirping birds, and quiet trickling fountains. Sometimes he asked her to join him with a couple of glasses of sweet tea, and they would discuss her paper or any of the current news topics at length.

This morning she had reversed her order and completed feeding the animals, as well as reviewing some of the commands Andy had shown her with Franklin. Su Lin thought Franklin was the smartest pig in the world. Franklin was able to respond to commands which Andy said she had taught him before her accident. She didn't remember, but she loved working with Franklin as much as he liked working with her.

Then she had exercised and eaten before she took a shower and washed her hair. She had carefully combed and plaited her long, thick, glossy black hair into a single braid. The braid reached just below her waist and would be out of the way for the tests she suspected would be performed on her. The tests were mostly the same and really hadn't helped much, she didn't think. Her improvement was stemming from the studying and activities that Andy laid out. He said she was essentially retraining her brain, but that it would take a long time and she needed patience.

Andy had laughed and said sometimes she giggled too much during her studies, but he never punished her. At the center in Atlanta during some of her visits, the other girls would complain about being grounded or losing privileges. She had a hard time understanding those consequences, as she usually did as she was asked the first time. If she didn't understand the why of the request, Andy, Carlos, or even EZ would explain it to her. All of them treated her like an equal.

She finished her hair with a nice purple bow to cover the rubber band near the end. The bow matched the purple-flowered shirt that she wore over her jeans. She picked up her sweater as she left her room to go and wait in the front sitting room. The front sitting room offered a view of the drive where the driver would come from to pick her up. Wrinkles, Andy's hound dog, lifted his head in greeting but quickly settled back down and resumed his afternoon snooze. Carlos was sprawled on the couch reading a magazine, on technology she presumed.

Carlos was tall, lanky, and handsome, with dark hair that was almost as black as hers. He lived in the house and worked with Andy in the telecommunications business. He was also in love with Lara who, she was told, would arrive later tonight for a visit. Su Lin liked her and she hoped Lara would bring her a new dress from her fashion line. It was so neat that Lara was a fashion designer.

Carlos looked up and greeted, "Hey, Su Lin, it looks like you finished all your chores early. Are you excited about this trip to the center today?"

Su Lin smiled and replied, "No, I just want to make certain that you can give Andy a good report. I also finished the assignments and placed the files into the share folder on the internal network, like you showed me.

"Do I look okay? I even took my shower last so I wouldn't smell like Franklin."

Carlos grinned and replied, "You look great. It always amazes me that you have such a fresh face and ready smile."

"Carlos, I know I should probably add some lipstick or mascara, like EZ showed me, but I just don't like it."

Carlos laughed. "It is not a requirement and, frankly, you don't need it.

"The driver should be here shortly. Last night you said you wanted to go to the car by yourself. Is that still the case? I don't want to get into trouble for not escorting a young lady such as yourself to the car."

Su Lin frowned and then brightened as she suggested, "I really would like to try to do it myself. If the driver gets out of the car to open the door, then I think that would be okay, don't you?"

Carlos pondered that and answered, "Okay, but if you change your mind, I'll be right here."

Su Lin pointed out the window as the black car approached. "Wow! That is a huge limousine. I must be terribly important for this visiting doctor to meet."

She stood up as the car came to a stop and the driver, with a standard cap and dark glasses, emerged. He seemed to be a large man and certainly looked like he could take care of himself and her. Carlos rose and gave her a hug.

"Go ahead now. I'll be here when you return. You also have the cell phone I gave you last night, right?"

Su Lin grinned and replied, "I do. Thanks, Carlos."

Carlos remained where he could watch as Su Lin rushed out the door, closed it firmly behind her, and then proceeded down the long walkway toward the car. Su Lin stopped a bit short of the car door. Carlos smiled, knowing she was doing as instructed before she got into the car. The driver gave a slight bow and replied to her questions. Something in the driver's mannerisms looked familiar to Carlos, so he moved a bit closer to the window to see if he could reconcile his growing concern.

The driver opened the door and indicated that Su Lin should take her place. Su Lin seemed rooted to the ground as she made a comment back to the driver. He replied and then reached for Su Lin's arm, almost like an escort move. Su Lin pulled back, and Carlos headed for the door. Just as Carlos threw open the door, the driver was forcibly moving Su Lin toward the rear seat. The door had no inside handle that Carlos could see, and dread welled up inside him as he sprinted toward her almost in slow motion.

Su Lin yanked herself free and started screaming at the top of her lungs and flinging her hands and feet in random directions as the driver tried to gather her up. The driver spotted Carlos and gave up his efforts. Su Lin melted into a puddle on the ground and kept screaming over and over. The driver jumped into the car, and Carlos made a note of the license plate even as he bent to encircle Su Lin in his arms.

As he patted her and held her, rocking her on the ground, she cried and kept muttering, "Bacon, no bacon, no, no, no bacon." She sobbed.

Carlos picked her up and carried her back into the house. He held her for a long time until she settled down. Once she quieted, she refused to utter even a single word while torrents of tears continued to streak down her face. Su Lin finally stopped crying and fell asleep. Carlos delicately pulled his arms away from her and laid her on the couch, covering her with a lightweight blanket. He knew something was very wrong and he really didn't want to worry Andy, but he needed help. He placed a call to Jacob, but it immediately went to voicemail, so he did the next best thing and placed a call to Quip.

Quip picked up the call on the second ring and said, "Carlos, long time no ring. What's up?"

Carlos took on a serious tone as he replied, "Quip, I tried to reach Jacob, but he's not answering. Someone just tried to take Su Lin for some additional tests to a visiting doctor at the center in Atlanta. She wanted to show she was responsible, so she walked to the car herself." Carlos looked to make certain Su Lin was still asleep. He ran his fingers through his hair and paced back and forth as he continued, "She was to ask the name of the center, the doctor she was to see, the driver's name, and how long the drive would take, before getting into the car."

Quip commented, "Okay, so Su Lin is making progress which we are all fairly aware of. Andy has been doing a great job in setting up her teaching, and EZ has been keeping me informed as to her progress. Didn't Andy go to some customer site for a meeting or something?"

Carlos responded, "Yes, Andy is in California. I was to watch Su Lin. He told me to take care of her and to make certain she was okay. He told me like ten times that he trusted me."

Quip was now on full alert as he asked, "Carlos, I heard you say someone tried to take her. Did they take her? Because we'd need to take action now and not debate."

Carlos regained some of his composure and answered, "Quip, she is here, but she totally broke down. I don't know what was said. One minute she was doing the verifying questions, and the next minute this guy was trying to force her into the back of the limo. Then she started screaming and kicking. I rushed out to get to her, the guy got away, and she spent the next forty minutes shaking and crying, totally distraught before she finally fell asleep."

Quip pondered the implications of this outburst for a few moments, then asked, "Can you describe the limo or even the driver for me?"

Carlos related the license plate number and a modest description of the driver. He conveyed his concerns regarding the driver and indicated he was still unable to place the guy. He then explained that Lara was arriving later that night to come and stay at the farm for a few days. Quip said he would see what he could find out and get back with him.

Carlos continued, "Quip, thanks for taking on some of this. I will take Su Lin with me to pick up Lara, which I planned to do anyway. If you find out anything, you know my number.

"By the way, is Jacob on assignment somewhere that he didn't answer? He's always answered my calls, it seems odd."

Quip deflected, "That, my friend, is a conversation for another time. He is finding himself."

Carlos chuckled, "Heck, we all do that at one time or another."

CHAPTER THIRTEEN

Plans Sometimes Fail, But Tenacity Keeps You Going

Leroy was annoyed as he abandoned the car in the parking lot of a crowded Atlanta mall, after he had carefully wiped every surface he had possibly touched. Wearing the chauffeur outfit, complete with gloves, minimized the potential of any prints. As it was a rented vehicle with over forty thousand miles on it, there were many skin cells that could be lifted which promised hours of research if that path was pursued by authorities. A very unlikely activity as no crime could be proven. He exited the car and removed the duffle bag from the trunk, throwing the keys inside before he closed the lid. These older model limos were not sophisticated enough to prohibit locking with the keys inside.

He calmly walked toward the mall, focused on not drawing attention to himself. He was a very tall, ramrod straight, burly black man that walked as unconcerned through the throngs of people as he would in his own deserted backyard. He was big enough to notice and big enough that people automatically gave him a wide berth. In this particular character role, he kept his eyes down, yet missed nothing of the activity around him. The somber expression on his face was not displaced by his more enjoyable personas. He liked playing those roles far better but readily adapted to the current circumstances.

Leroy knew he needed to change his clothing and then hop onto the MARTA to the airport where he could catch a flight to New York City. Though he flew all over the world to fulfill his assignments, he was based in New York City. He needed access to his secure communications before he informed his boss of the setback in the plans. Before he had that conversation, he wanted time to think of a couple of options he could offer during the discussion. Part of the value that Leroy brought to the operation was his ability to think outside of the box.

He entered the second restroom he spotted inside the mall after he'd watched for several minutes and saw that no traffic entered or left. He changed his clothes, washed up at the sink, and then inserted his appliance which included gold outlined front teeth. His smile broadened as he looked into the mirror and assumed the demeanor of the good ol' boy. He gathered his possessions back into the duffle bag that was now sporting different colors once he'd flipped it inside out. His shoulders slumped and he picked up a bit of an irregular gait as he exited and smiled at nearly everyone. His smile was infectious, and many returned similar greetings. Exiting the back entrance of the mall, he walked the short distance to the MARTA platform and purchased the fare to the airport. He would change again with the locker contents he'd previously stored before going through security and onto his flight.

As he sat and waited for the train, he mentally reviewed the topics for his upcoming conversation. He felt it best to lead with the worst first. The train platform was deserted at this time of day, and the train was not due for thirty minutes. He took out his cell phone and launched a security program before he dialed Finland.

Leroy greeted, "Sir, I am sorry to report that the mission was not accomplished as we had hoped. I was not compromised, therefore neither are you. You also need to know that this woman is not close to the way you suggested."

Xavier Pekoni exclaimed, "That's a huge disappointment! I need to perform some tests on her. What happened, and more importantly, what do you mean she is not close to my characterization of her? Is she ill?"

Leroy explained, "Sir, she is almost like an adolescent in her behavior and demeanor. You had suggested that I would find a logical, stubborn, mature woman who would understand the comments and essentially come along for a joint meeting. She is nothing like that.

"The behavior she displayed was like that of a teenager being allowed to go on a date by herself. The questions she asked were like those supplied by a concerned parent to make certain she was safe before taking a ride with a stranger. When I mentioned the key words you supplied, she became uncontrollably hysterical and made such a commotion that I had to vacate the place before raising more problems than could be discreetly handled."

Xavier thought for several minutes about what that might mean. Nothing in his knowledge of her indicated that was a normal or expected behavior. He'd been advised that she would be a good source of information on some different approaches that he was considering. Plus, she had undeniable access to processing resources he couldn't touch.

Xavier asked, "Can you describe her skin, her hair, or maybe her walk to me before she went out of control?"

Leroy complied. "Her hair was black, almost blue, and very shiny, healthy looking in a long braid. Her skin was flawless ivory with no makeup to hide behind. Her eyes were clear and actually sparkled at first. As she walked to the car she had a bounce in her step and nothing seemed amiss.

"I had tried to get into the records at the clinic to retrieve the details of her condition as you are already aware. We have very limited information. If her DNA had not shown up in the search we performed, we wouldn't have located her at all. The name Su Lin has no correlation to any of your prior history."

Xavier suggested, "It is the same woman, I feel certain. The DNA match is irrefutable. I presume you were unable to get any samples of skin or blood during the attempt."

Leroy admitted, "No, sir, none at all. I was lucky to escape before the man inside the house raced out to assist her."

Leroy left off the part about his knowing the man in the house from a prior interaction they had had in New York City. He and this man had crossed paths quite some time ago in one of his fronts, the pawn shop to be specific. He had discreetly taken a DNA sample while giving the man a weapon in the form of a cane from the pawn shop. The man's DNA was in their system, but he had yet to process why this guy was in Atlanta. Leroy didn't believe the man had recognized him because he was focused on Su Lin. He didn't want to upset his boss on this point and decided that conversation could wait.

Xavier stated, "For the time being, we need to find out some additional details about this subject. I will need to have you make another attempt at acquiring those first-hand samples at the very least. I would rather have her here working on the project. What ideas can you suggest?"

Leroy grinned, the sun glinting off his teeth, as he ventured, "I have two approaches that I think are worth trying. One is to return to New York and do some additional brute force entry to the clinic files to get the additional background. The other is to employ short-term support from an operative I have worked with who could enter the clinic as a nurse and simply wait for Su Lin's next appointment. She could then sedate her, and I can pick her up more easily.

"I did do some reconnaissance of the clinic facility, and there are some areas in which we could arrange for this to happen. There are enough treatment rooms that a slight misdirect at various points during a routine visit wouldn't raise any red flags. The waiting area only has a single entrance and exit, behind which there is a warren of rooms for patients.

"I doubt, after this particular event, if a driver would ever be allowed to pick her up. She has a standard appointment every six weeks, which delays your timeline a little over a month, sir. It also provides me the time to get Alisha established at the clinic."

Xavier was a little concerned as he asked, "How is Alisha going to be accepted into the clinic without certain credentials?"

Leroy smiled, "Oh, sir, no worries. The best part is Alisha already has the credentials and was a nurse earlier in her career. I can trust her, and we have worked together before. She enjoys a good joke played on anyone she considers in the system."

Xavier indicated, "It seems this plan has some possibilities. I am disappointed that you did not obtain more success."

Leroy smiled as he offered, "Sir, my update is not yet complete as this was only one of the avenues I have been working. May I beg a few more minutes of your time, sir?"

Taking silence and no disconnect as an affirmative, Leroy confidently continued, "I was able to verify that the four test subjects you required for the next round are scheduled to arrive in the morning at your laboratory. Two women and two men with the DNA structure you outlined. They have no family ties, so authorities will not be tracking their whereabouts based on missing person reports potentially being filed. When I arrive back in the New York offices, I will scrub the rest of the information regarding each test subject from all their home country records."

Xavier was not happy and grumbled, "As my assistant, I expect you to be exact in the details. The shipment was to contain five, not four subjects. It is not like you to miss count on something this important. The timing is too critical for you to not meet the requirement. Do I need to start looking for someone to help or replace you?"

Leroy grinned, and the gold tooth again caught the sun's rays and caused them to dance around the platform. He quietly checked a chuckle and then clarified, "Sir, I am sorry to have not been clearer. The four test subjects are being escorted by the man who meets your personal requirements. The four can be moved and settled in with the help of Nathan. Nathan has your closest DNA match and an exact blood type match. Please accept this as my small token of appreciation to work with you, sir."

Xavier smiled and remarked, "I am pleased. That is an ideal way of moving the subjects into their new testing places. Perhaps I can get this Nathan to help me move my original subject. She is still lovely but not responding as I had hoped. Perhaps this new round of testing will improve her status, as I know now this Nathan will improve mine.

"Keep in touch as you get additional information and Alisha is positioned. You have earned a bonus, which I will send along."

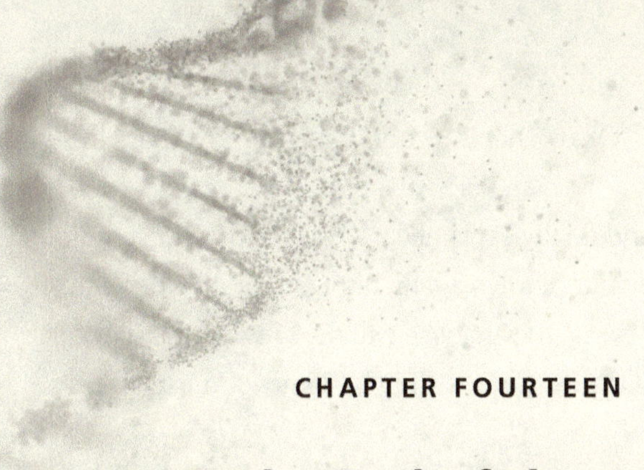

CHAPTER FOURTEEN

At the End of the Storm the Sun Can Shine

Wearing a very grim face, Quip walked into Otto's office and slumped into a chair. Otto looked up and raised an eyebrow at the sullen behavior as he finished his phone call. Quip looked like he'd lost his best friend, but he was anxiously trying not to interrupt. Otto concluded his conversation with the customer in its own time.

Otto looked Quip over and asked, "What's up, Quip. Did someone steal your wagon?"

Quip sighed, "Otto, I need your help. I just got off the phone with Carlos, and someone tried, yet failed, to kidnap Su Lin. Andy is out of town, and I am not certain of the right next step. Carlos was able to convey a modest description of the vehicle and license plate, which ICABOD provided some details on."

Otto had gasped at the start of Quip's explanation but now replied, "Su Lin is with Carlos and still safe?"

"Yep, she is with Carlos but apparently traumatized from the attempt and now sleeping. Carlos is concerned but doesn't want to alert Andy because he is with a customer of theirs in California."

Otto nodded, "Okay. That is a good thing, right? What's the problem?"

Quip sighed and finally explained, "Well, frankly I don't want to have EZ go back out of town again, but I am afraid when I tell her the story that is exactly what she will do. I just got her back, and we are having a great time settling in. I know I must tell her, but I don't want to."

Otto chuckled, then composed himself and stated, "Quip, you need to think out of the box. Have you asked Julie if someone on her team can do some investigation? It does seem odd that someone would try to kidnap Su Lin. She has had her identity scrubbed quite thoroughly and, in her current state of mind, isn't stepping on the wrong toes."

Quip looked almost hopeful as he replied, "No, I had not even thought about contacting Julie. Sometimes you are so smart, Otto, you amaze me."

Otto lifted his eyebrow and sharpened his gaze at Quip as he said, "Pardon me?"

Quip blushed a bit, then admitted, "Sorry, Otto. You know what I meant. Let's call Julie."

Otto set up the conference call and accessed the files that Quip indicated ICABOD had created to track the incident.

Julie answered on the second ring with an agreeable familiar tone. "Father, hi. How's it going? When are you coming for a visit?"

Otto smiled and responded, "It is going well. Pass along my best to everyone, please. I have not made any plans to visit for this week. It is simply too busy.

"Do you have a few minutes? Quip and I have some business to discuss."

Julie's tone changed, "Yes, of course. I should have asked if this was a father call or an Otto call. How can I help?"

Quip explained, "Earlier today, someone tried to kidnap Su Lin from the farm. It was a crazy plan of a driver being sent to deliver her to a visiting doctor at the clinic for some special tests. ICABOD has interrogated the records and discovered that no such visiting doctor exists. ICABOD also discovered that some sloppy attempts have been made to access her digital files. ICABOD has removed all the digital copies of her files for the time being. The paper ones with Dr. Neil Giles still exist somewhere in their secure file room. He's on vacation for a few weeks, and by the time he returns hopefully we can restore the digital copies or at least determine a good explanation.

"Andy is visiting a customer in California, and Carlos was put in charge of watching Su Lin. The failed kidnapping attempt has Carlos on edge. He tried to phone Jacob before he reached out to me. I am not certain of the right steps, but Otto suggested we might get some assistance from your team on this."

Julie asked, "Any other details concerning who or why on the attempt, or is that part of the help needed? Is Su Lin okay?"

Quip continued, "She is physically fine, though Carlos thinks she is traumatized. Lara is arriving in Atlanta late tonight, so he is essentially standing guard until then. He provided some details that we are using to put some pieces into the puzzle. How busy is your team, and do you have anyone that might help? I had thought about EZ returning to Georgia to help, but she may not be the right resource."

Otto rolled his eyes at this comment and interjected, "Carlos provided a license plate, and the vehicle was tracked to a rental place near the Atlanta airport. We are awaiting a copy of the identification that was provided with the rental. The man driving the limousine was a very large black man, sharply dressed in nice chauffeur attire with a cap. The hands were gloved and no special characteristics were noted. He said some things that caused Su Lin to become hysterical, and she fell onto the ground. Carlos tended her as the man escaped in the car."

Julie admitted, "Right now we are a little busy. When we started this, I never dreamed that our services would be utilized by so many of the family business customers across all our services. Otto, it was really brilliant to suggest offering security types of services to the customers. Lucrative for all of us. Juan and I were actually discussing possible expansion if the business continued at this rate. I am loving the business."

Quip, who was worried about putting EZ on a plane if no alternative was available, asked, "Do you have any suggestions? We all know that Su Lin has history with some really crazy people, so this could be a real threat that may not simply go away. We need a better understanding of the motives for the attempt."

Julie agreed, "No doubt, and Su Lin, aka Master Po, has always held a special place in my heart from our previous inter-actions. She always picked the best places to meet and exchange information, especially if it was in close proximity to an ocean.

"I currently have available Brayson and Mercedes. Ernesto and George are working on the other project you assigned us, Otto. Summit and Tyler have been following up separately on the consulting projects. We still have Brayson coordinating the various activities of the teams, which, I might add, he is performing well on. Juan has been working with Mercedes to improve her martial arts skills as well as keeping me in shape with the classes."

Otto smiled and advised, "Perhaps Mercedes would be a good selection. I wouldn't want you to leave right now from either the kids or Petra. Though you could advise Haddy that I miss her.

"Mercedes is young enough to relate to Su Lin's state of mind, and it may be that the traumatizing was male-centric, which would be a negative for Brayson. But I am glad to hear he is coming along well in his role.

"The file containing all the details is in your area of the network now, and it will be updated with anything that ICABOD can glean from the cameras posted throughout the city."

Quip looked relieved as he asked, "How soon can she depart? And I will be happy to advise Carlos. The extra security would ease his mind, as well as allow him to enjoy Lara's visit."

Julie laughed and asked, "Won't hurt your storytelling to EZ either. You don't fool anyone, Quip. I can get Mercedes on the next flight out which will put her into Atlanta in the morning. I will convey the flight info to you and Carlos.

"We'll get it figured out. Thanks for the call."

Quip arrived home to the apartment and smelled the aroma of a fine dinner being prepared. Oblivious to his arrival, EZ looked beautiful as she worked around the kitchen. He watched for a few seconds before he spoke.

"Hi, babe. I'm home and it smells great in here."

EZ looked up and smiled and rushed into his arms and kissed him before he was prepared, almost knocking him over. Her hair was all undone and like a fiery mane around her face and halfway down her back. She paused the kiss and looked deeply into his eyes.

Quip looked at her with sheer hunger that suddenly had nothing to do with the meal being prepared. His eyes darkened as he picked her up and carried her toward the bedroom, as a different hunger commanded him. He nuzzled her neck and asked, "Are the burners and oven off?"

EZ responded, "Yes, dear. The moment I heard your key in the door."

He laughed and continued until they arrived right near the bed where they slowly undressed each other and kissed along the way, each becoming increasingly excited as they enjoyed one another. Quip laid her on the bed and eyed her long limbs and hardened nipples as she instinctively opened up to him.

Her wanton gaze drew him closer as he tasted and sampled with pleasure. He had planned to tease her slowly, but her responses and mewing sounds of satisfaction shifted his focus as he drove her higher and higher, until he lost control in time with her release. He rolled over and pulled her on top of him as their breathing slowly returned to normal.

She drew her fingers over his neck and chest, then slowly opened her eyes and murmured, "I think that is the nicest way for you to come home, honey."

Quip smiled and replied, "Sweetheart, I think that your greeting is without equal. Very nice!" He gently patted her fanny and then repositioned the both of them on one of the pillows. "I see you fixed the blinds. Boy, I bet the neighbors are disappointed in that!"

EZ chuckled and added, "I promised that sometimes you would forget to close them, so it's okay.

"How was your day, anything you can talk about?"

Quip pulled in a bit closer and stated, "Babe, I got some good news and some bad news. Which would you like first?"

EZ raised her eyebrow and answered, "I think I want the bad news first. I just hope it isn't too bad."

"Well, okay. The bad news is that Su Lin was almost kidnapped earlier today."

EZ gasped and immediately jumped up as she grumbled, "I need to pack right now and get on a plane. The good news must be that you arranged for the flight right away, so I wouldn't stress. Does my father know yet? How is she? Is she in the hospital? Who would do such a thing? Is Carlos hurt? Oh, how terrible."

Quip interrupted, though he was thoroughly enjoying her running around the room buck naked, carrying an empty suitcase. She was so pretty he hated to interrupt, but he needed to try to catch her. He reached out as she passed close enough and pulled her onto the bed.

"EZ, stop. You aren't getting on the plane. You need to listen."

EZ tried to wiggle out of his grasp the moment he had pulled her onto the bed. Her brain clicked as she actually heard his words and paused. "Okay, you need to explain, mister."

Quip looked chastened as he expanded, "I will explain the whole story over dinner, but the short answer is, your teammate Mercedes is on a flight to Atlanta tonight. She will be protecting Su Lin and investigating all the leads to find the kidnapper. Julie thinks you can help from here, working with me."

EZ did not look quite convinced until she heard a text hit her phone. She grabbed it off the nightstand and read it.

Need you to work with Quip on the Su Lin thing.

Mercedes and I will update you. Spoke to Carlos, Su Lin is fine.

Let's not tell Andy for a while. Julie.

"I will do my job, though I am not certain about keeping it from Daddy. He isn't going to like this at all," said EZ.

"He isn't, honey. But we need to work to find out some answers before we tell him." He leered at her and her creamy skin as he asked, "Are you ready to eat dinner, or do you want to go for round two, you pretty thing?"

CHAPTER FIFTEEN

It's Not Bragging If You Can Do It

...The Enigma Chronicles

Zara found the background reading she'd discovered in Grigory's files interesting. The notes on Patty and Buzz were a little sketchy, but she was able to piece together that Buzz's dead girlfriend had done work for the Dteam regularly and had Buzz on the line to do some contract code work just before Zara came onto the scene. As near as she could figure out from the notes, Patty had disappeared just before Sergei did. With what Buzz had related, she suspected that Patty fell prey to Sergei, while Sergei then fell prey to Grigory's violent temper. She shuddered to think about the memory of that oily little character and was convinced that women the world over would rest easier with him gone.

Apparently, Patty had established a fairly good business with identity laundering here in New York, based on some of the transaction amounts that showed up in the logs. She found it odd that the business simply disappeared as soon as the Russian Dteam overlord Grigory expired. She chuckled to herself at the politeness of the term when she knew he had been mauled to death by his white tiger, Nikkei.

Old history, Zara thought to herself, not really relevant to her current search. One thing that did pop out about Patty was that she had a nice cover up business for identity laundering, which explained why there was an inventory of erotic leather goods and sex toys. She had been a hostess for an adult products line to meet new and vulnerable targets, as well as clients. Zara puzzled as to why, if she was so avant-garde, Patty had kept Buzz the dweeb around?

Coming back to reality, she quickly checked her cell phone for the time and realized she was going to be late for her meeting with Jacob. She promptly left the Dteam offices to try and make her appointment with Jacob. She tried to text Buzz to indicate that she was running late. She hoped to have Buzz greet and detain Jacob until she could get there, but there was no response from him. She chided herself for not getting Jacob's number and was annoyed that Buzz had not responded.

Upon reflection, she had to admit that it was partially her fault, too, considering the state she had left Buzz in last night. Of course, she reminded herself, the events of last night were in no way a reprieve for that last man who had betrayed her. Dakota had cost her a big payday and was still a target in her mind. It annoyed her, however, to think that she might have been angrier with Dakota because he had turned down her affections, and that it still hurt. She pushed the thought out of her mind by recalling the previous evening's unexpected encounter with Buzz. She convinced herself that she was only showing her gratitude for his hospitality while she stayed at his place. She assumed that he needed some bragging rights to socialize with friends. It was the least she could do for his male ego.

Zara smirked at how the romance he was trying to cultivate got started in a way he hadn't counted on and ended in a way she hadn't counted on. She'd forgotten how much she enjoyed playing the dominatrix role where she delivered all that a man could endure. She did permit him some standard foreplay with her breasts, but before he could have his way with her, she had him securely bound and ready to mount. She had redeployed Patty's stash of leather restraints to increase Buzz's cooperation during their private interlude.

For Zara it was like old times, when she was at the top of her game, being paid handsomely for dispensing Bondage and Discipline treatment. The session had begun like all of them with her tenderly warming him up by applying the leather flail to every sensitive area of him in order to see him flinch. In her old role at the Big House, she didn't care for the yelps. There, she had applied a suitable leather gag so she could work in peace but still enjoy the begging from the patron.

Once she was sure that her idea of B&D foreplay had been observed, she arranged an assorted array of interesting adult toys she was going to use on him. Just after she launched into her well-rehearsed procedure of *The Submarine Game*, as it was affectionately requested at the Big House, she noticed that Buzz was whimpering with tears. She thought it odd, so she released the gag.

He repeated, "Not like Patty! Please, not like her! I just want to hold you, Daria! I just want to hold you!"

His whimpering was enough to stop the B&D session she had performed for so many clients. True to his request, he'd only wanted to hold her. Zara was somewhat confused and uncomfortable with what appeared to be his honest feelings for her. Her emotional state started to thaw as well. She awkwardly touched back, using feelings she thought had been erased over the years. Slowly she let down her guard and allowed herself to enjoy his touching and further encouraged him. He focused on giving as much as receiving. It had been some time since a man had treated her with such tenderness. At his insistence, she had multiple climaxes, based on his oral expertise, which she found astonishing. His climax was proof enough that he had thoroughly enjoyed his being cared for so completely, and she smiled with satisfaction at a job well done.

As Zara looked around at all the leather harnesses and adult toys, she thought it odd that they now seemed more of a hindrance than an accelerant to love play. Even though Buzz had treated her with warm affection, rather than as an appliance to be rented, she did not feel entitled to sleep next to him through the night. Zara didn't quite trust these unused but not unknown feelings yet, so she looked kindly at him sleeping and delivered a quick goodbye kiss on the forehead. Zara had quietly slipped out of his room and taken a nice hot shower to get all the erotic oils off before she retired to her own bed. She recalled sitting in bed, staring wistfully out the window, and thought that perhaps this gentleness was why Patty had kept him around.

All thoughts of the night before disappeared as she approached the apartment building, only to see Jacob exiting. She called out to him.

Jacob turned and greeted, "Hi. There you are. I was ready to believe that the deal was off when no one answered the door. I should have gotten your phone number at the bar. However, after the dressing down Buzz gave me for my *Don't I know you from somewhere?* comment, I didn't want him to rail about me asking for your phone number as well."

Smiling, Zara slipped into her alias role of Daria as she replied, "You know, that's funny! I was chiding myself for not having gotten your number as well. I even texted Buzz asking him to alert you that I was running late, but he never responded.

"Oh well! We are meeting now. Even though I lost track of time, I am certain we can continue with discussing my project needs. Shall we head over to my offices? Did you bring your computer in case you are ready to start?"

Jacob smiled at the strangely familiar lady and commented, "My, you do move along, don't you, Daria? I haven't said whether we have a deal, and you're already asking me to log into the network. It is odd that you have a Russian accent, but you rush the deal like an American. How long have you been here in the U.S.?"

Zara was taken aback by Jacob's comment and asked, "How do you know that I'm from Russia and not Ukraine? I suspect then that you are well-traveled and have an ear for accents."

Jacob shrugged as he smiled and replied, "English is not the only language I speak. Yes, I am—was—well-traveled. Apologies if my comment sounded rude. I was only jesting with you, Daria."

Zara smirked a little at the comment and replied, "I too am well-traveled. My haste in completing this project is due to the payday at delivery of a finished product, not because I've become Americanized. You come with references from Buzz, and if you are uninterested then I will need to go through a formal hiring process for a security coder and that will negatively impact my time table. My apologies for what you perceive as haste, but time deadlines are in fact time deadlines. I hope you understand."

Jacob good-naturedly nodded and acquiesced, "No harm, no foul, Daria. Frankly, I was disappointed when you didn't show up. I was really looking forward to seeing what you had in mind.

"I just now heard you say security coder, and actually that is what I am best at. Can we discuss the assignment details at your offices now, or is this a two meeting process?"

Zara smiled and responded, "I believe we might have what you Americans say is an understanding!"

Once they were seated in the conference room at the newest location of the Dteam offices, Zara began a whiteboard session to illustrate the needed code from Jacob.

Daria explained, "Okay, I'm under contract to provide software to a security device to make sure it doesn't get tampered with." She drew four blocks surrounding a fifth block. Pointing to the center block she continued, "This one is already done, but my last coder indicated that it was vulnerable to attacks or spoofing hits. He recommended that before this core code does anything, it check with these daughter processes to see if the request is legitimate or is bogus to the running program. Basically, the program needs to test the authenticity of the program request. I want that security algorithm to run in a separate program that can only be accessed by either the main program or the admin so it can be updated. I need the code to fill in this security box. Can you do that?"

Jacob studied the whiteboard drawing and asked, "Any reason why the original programmer isn't working on these other boxes as well?"

Zara stared coldly at Jacob for a few seconds then commented, "Yes, because he is dead. Are you interested?"

Jacob, somewhat surprised at her bluntness, was taken aback and responded, "Can I see the main program to see how it consumes the responses it will require from the security program? At the very least I would require the Application Program Instruction set of calls you are using, so I know how and what values to return."

Zara quietly responded, "I can't show you the main program, but I will give you the APIs you will use to interact with the main program. The main program is classified because it is to go into a commercially available appliance for monitoring businesses during and after regular hours. A lot of high-end institutions are interested in this product, and I have to be able to tell them that no one but I have all the component knowledge. This, in itself, is another security mechanism.

"Once I see how you perform on this task, we can discuss the other blobs of code I need written. Each module blob is worth 1,000 U.S. dollars and a bonus upon delivery of the entire program and our remittance paid. Are you capable of such a task?"

Jacob studied the board a little and remarked, "I'm sorry about your other programmer. I didn't mean to pry. As for your offer, with the API set I can have something for you by the end of the week."

Zara looked at Jacob in astonishment and asked, "You do know, of course, that today is Thursday, right?"

Jacob chuckled slightly and responded, "Sorry, I meant I can have something for you by Friday then. This Friday."

Daria grinned at his impudence and stated, "Okay, then see you tomorrow, Jacob the confident coder!" She pitched him a USB drive and clarified, "The API libraries are on the drive. See you before noon then?"

Jacob smiled knowingly and agreed, "Very likely, ma'am."

"Good. If you provide this as fast as you promise, then I may have some other upcoming work that I am to get details on over the next few days."

CHAPTER SIXTEEN

Tell Me It Isn't So,
Or Tell Me It Is Just So

Su Lin quietly wandered over to where Carlos was working and waited for him to notice. She often came into his area to simply observe what he was doing, and he had helped her a great deal on expanding her computer skills.

Carlos didn't stop or turn as he concentrated on his computer, but he commented, "Su Lin, you know it is bad luck to try to sneak up on someone skilled in the ways of the Yaqui Indians. In Western cultures, it is acceptable, when you try to enter a room quietly, to moderately clear your throat so as to indicate you wish a word with the person."

Su Lin was somewhat amazed as she asked, "How did you know I was behind you? I try to walk quietly, like you showed me, but I am never able to sneak up on you. I guess your Yaqui mystic teacher was very good in his training of you."

Carlos turned around to face her, chuckled slightly, and offered, "Actually I saw your reflection in the computer screen. What's up, ma'am? You appear to be doing better."

Su Lin pouted a little at being deceived by the common trick but then conveyed, "It's my laptop. It keeps chirping at me from the calendar and task minder to do follow up on my assignment, but it's not an assignment I ever created. The assignment offers a link that points me to a file subdirectory. When I click on it, I can't look into the directory or open any files.

"A screen appears and asks for a password, but I have no idea what that might be. I looked at my notes, and you indicated once that if I create a password, I should note it in my journal to help remember. Nothing is noted."

Carlos gave a mildly surprised look and asked, "You mean you don't remember creating the need for the password?"

Su Lin succinctly responded, "I mean, I didn't set a password on this subdirectory nor do I know how the subdirectory got there. I didn't do it and am not certain how I would do it." Then she grinned as she asked, "Can you help me fix it, oh Yaqui one with the computer?"

Carlos was puzzling over the dilemma from Su Lin when his cell phone acknowledged a text message from an old friend. As he read it, he smiled as recent memories flashed through his mind.

He smiled and announced, "We'll work on the puzzle after we return from the airport, young apprentice. Right now, we are being asked to pick up a team member at the airport, from Julie and Juan's team, along with our delayed but long-awaited traveler, Miss Lara. Are you still okay to come with me to the airport?

"We'll be retrieving Lara and Mercedes, but there is a lot of activity at an airport so you must stick close to me. I don't want you scared again – do you understand?"

Su Lin looked a little apprehensive and asked, "I'm not sure about that. Couldn't I just stay here? What if Andy doesn't like me being at the airport?"

Carlos studied her for a moment, then expounded, "Andy definitely wouldn't want you here alone. If you can't go to the airport with me, then I will have to send a car for the two ladies. That would be a shame since Lara usually shows up with presents. Ah well, no big deal. She will bring them here. They won't be wasted. I need to arrange transportation for them, then we can work on your computer problem."

Su Lin stood and processed the information about presents, then suddenly and loudly exclaimed, "No, no, I can go with you to the airport! I am not afraid of crowds so long as you are close, Carlos. When do we need to leave?"

Carlos fought to suppress a smile as he responded, "Are you sure? I mean, we can just stay here and not bother with the shopping we would do at the airport while we wait. It's no biggie."

Su Lin, who was now ready to run to the car, protested, "But I am all ready to go, Carlos! We don't want to be late for ice cream…I mean, to pick up the nice ladies with presents…uh, well, they should be picked up by people they know, so let's go!"

Carlos grinned as he checked to see if he had cash in his pocket to cover the toll costs and the shopping he'd volunteered. After he secured the house, they piled into the car and headed toward Atlanta International Airport.

It was impossible for Carlos to give Lara the kind of attention he wanted with two other people in tow as they returned to the farm. Su Lin, being unusually clingy, insisted on sitting next to Carlos, which was not part of his original plan when just Lara should have been with him.

Mercedes was all business about her new assignment to protect Su Lin, so she was carrying on a dialogue to gain her trust. It might have been easier to deal with her if Mercedes hadn't washed down so many no-drowse pills with a cocktail mix of energy drinks and espresso that she had lived on during her long flight from Europe. Her accelerated speech was intimidating to Su Lin. Several times Carlos had asked her to slow down so he could understand what she was asking.

At one point, his frustration peaked. "Mercedes, I am used to the slow speech cadence of Andy, who converses with me at roughly forty words per minute. I will tell you that with eighty words per minute, with gusts up to two hundred words per minute, your verbalizing is beyond my capacity to comprehend, so slow down! In fact, I implore you to wait until we get back to the farm, so the continued rapid fire verbal onslaught by you doesn't cause me to have an accident!"

Once they reached the farm and were unloading the vehicle, Su Lin approached Carlos. "Thank you for taking me, Carlos. Mercedes makes me a little nervous, but I felt safer close to you."

Carlos smiled good-naturedly at her and gave her a quick hug. He looked to Lara and suggested, "Su Lin, why don't you show Lara around the house and help her get settled. Can you do that please, while I visit with the human verbal machine gun?"

Su Lin grinned conspiratorially and nodded.

Carlos and Lara exchanged glances before he added, "Lara, put your things in my room, and we will talk later. I need to set some ground rules up and brief Mercedes on what we know so far.

"I also need to call Andy and brief him before things get any more out of hand around here."

Carlos watched Su Lin escort Lara to the house and began scanning for Mercedes so that he could brief her. However, Mercedes was slumped over in the back seat of the vehicle in a physiological crashed-and–burned-out state. The caffeine/sugar/ginseng power drink binge had caught up with her, and her body had done the classic power-off maneuver, leaving her completely drained and now fast asleep. Based on what she had said she had consumed, he guessed she would be out of commission for at least twelve hours.

The sour expression crossed his face clearly indicated that their briefing would have to wait. He almost reached for his phone to call Andy about the cavalry that Quip had sent to help. Somehow, he knew Andy would only be upset when he learned that the help had arrived in a toxic state. Better wait to brief Andy when Mercedes was awake, and he had briefed her. It was, to be honest, a long flight, he thought to himself. She was over-the-top anxious to make a good impression.

More annoying to Carlos was the realization that he would have to carry the verbal-tornado from the car to the guest room, as well as all the luggage. Carlos sulked a few seconds and then hauled her out of the vehicle and, with one heave, tossed her over his shoulder like a duffel bag. As he hefted her up to the house, he said to no one in particular, "Remind me to get even with Quip for helping me this much."

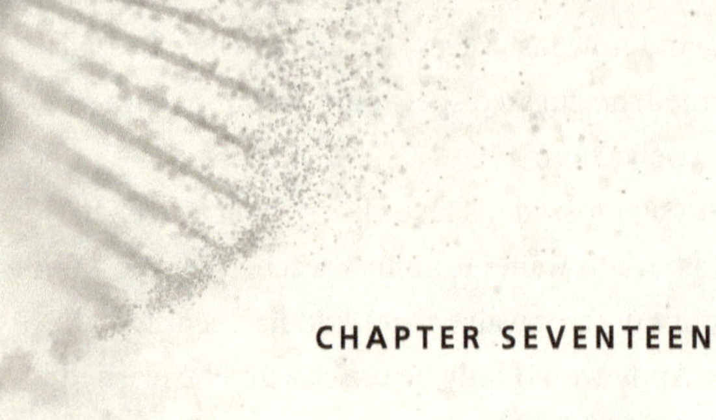

CHAPTER SEVENTEEN

It's Easier To Sell Lies Over the Truth

...The Enigma Chronicles

They stepped out onto the street and turned to look at each other. As the trusted protégées of Chairman Chang, they had trained extensively in martial arts, travel, negotiations with buyers of programs such as their identity transformation offerings for the very rich, and were licensed pilots. The originally identical twins, as close to children as Chairman Chang would ever get, were now differentiated by the scarring that Won had from a lost encounter with Nikkei, Chairman Chang's white tiger.

Won was living proof that you could survive a tiger attack, but your tongue would not if it was being used to deliver a raspberry to an animal you had enraged by inadvertently stepping on her tail. The anesthetic and the surgery had been delivered simultaneously with one swipe of her paw. Because of the bond they had with each other as twins, Ton always spoke for both.

Together, though, they were close to invincible. They had convinced Chang that Zara had lifted his stolen diamond necklace, and so they were sent to track her down. For this assignment, they had been adept at hunting quietly for the game named by the chairman, but this quarry had proven to be elusive.

After weeks the trail had brought them to the east coast of the United States where the clues had dried up, and Zara had seemingly vanished. They had tried in New York City to check the offices that had belonged to the Dteam, only to find them vacated. The only solid lead they'd found was that one of the diamond district merchants indicated that he had turned down a lady's diamond necklace that had been offered for sale. Between the description of her, her accent, and the diamonds, they were confident that it was in fact Zara. They also learned that no one would buy the diamonds without paperwork, so they correctly deduced she had not yet been able to sell them nor travel very far without a lot of cash. They surmised she was stuck here, but hunting in the city that never sleeps was quite the challenge.

Won's phone chirped, and upon his quick inspection of the incoming call, he took it but said nothing while he listened.

The caller asked, "Where are we with the search?"

Won promptly handed the phone to Ton for the verbal update. Putting the phone on speaker with video, Ton said, "Good day, Chairman Chang. Our search continues, but we've run into a bit of a snag here in New York. No one knows anything, and no one would tell us anything until we changed our tactics."

Chairman Chang wrinkled his face into a puzzled look as he asked, "Changed your tactics?"

Ton beamed enthusiastically and responded, "Yes, sir! Since we are accomplished identity laundering experts, we gave ourselves Hong Kong detective aliases. We were sure that New Yorkers would respect Hong Kong detectives in search of a fugitive in their city, so we manufactured new detective IDs and became Hang Onn and Tue Tite."

Chairman stared blankly off into space, unable to comment right away. He finally asked, "Did your masterful identity change afford you all the civilian cooperation you were expecting?"

Frowning slightly, Ton replied, "Point in fact, it did not, sir, so we had to improvise again. As the forged IDs did not get us anywhere with the indigenous locals, we then began augmenting our story to say we were really role-playing for an upcoming TV/cable series to be called Drugnet! After we promised to do some filming in their place of business with them getting a small cameo appearance, everyone was most agreeable and definitely helpful.

"We even have enough material worked out for a couple of first season episodes based on our investigative conversations!"

Chairman Chang slowly closed his eyes and shook his head in disbelief. Struggling to free his mind from the sleuthing efforts and cover identities of his two young associates, he transitioned to a slightly louder, more insistent voice as he asked, "Can you just tell me what you found, not how you found it?"

Ton, somewhat confused by Chang's tone, responded, "Well, yes, sir! We know Zara is here in New York, and she has tried to fence the diamond necklace, but no one will touch it without the proper documentation. That is as far as we have gotten, however.

"She has fallen off the grid and doesn't seem to be in any of the usual places, which is to be expected, since she didn't get any of the cash from the anticipated sale. If she is back with her former team, they have relocated as that building was vacated. Frankly, we are at a dead end, sir."

Chairman Chang, recovering from the earlier discussion, suggested, "Then how about we arrange for a showing through Dmitry? Dmitry indicated that he was brokering the diamond necklace for someone. A clever broker would not tell the buyer or the seller of the other's identity, lest they be cut out of the transaction. Thanks to your efforts, we now know it is in fact Zara who has the diamonds, but we can't approach her directly.

"Let's have Dmitry arrange a viewing of the merchandise. I will ask him to withhold my identity and will have the meeting arrangement with my third-party agents, namely you two. That way we can get close enough to get everything."

Ton asked, "Won't she decline based on the possibility of it being a trap? If I were her, I would expect a possible double-cross and probably my loss of freedom without a guarantee."

Chang studied the situation a moment and added, "You're right, so this will only be a showing, not the purchase. I will indicate to Dmitry that I now have a buyer for the diamond necklace. I will suggest I am prepared to pay three million euros if my expert can inspect the merchandise in person. The location and the security of the diamond necklace will be under their control, and after that we can discuss an actual transfer."

Ton puzzled even more as he asked, "You're willing to pay cash for the return of the necklace? We thought you were only interested in its return as well as the Russian thief?"

The chairman was pleased to instruct. "I have no intention of paying anything. Once she shows herself, or the diamonds are shown, you two will follow to capture and bring back what is rightfully mine. You, see?"

Both smiling at each other, Ton replied, "Oh, of course, sir! Now we understand. But who will be the diamond expert? She already knows both of us, and if we show up on the scene, she'll know immediately it is for you, and our element of surprise will be lost."

Chairman Chang thought for a moment, then suggested, "I can dispatch Major Guano to act in the capacity of our diamond expert. He can be our point person while you observe the participants to arrange the return of my property. In the meantime, keep up your surveillance efforts in case she does surface along with the diamonds. I'll call the Russian cyber thug, Dmitry, and make the arrangements. Keep hunting, gentlemen."

Dmitry reached for his cell phone and answered, "Chairman Chang, nice to hear from you again. Were you able to shake down some of your constituents so you can make a credible offer for the diamonds yet? I know that your parents won't increase your allowance since you had them interned, so that's not an option. And don't bother offering me stock in those bogus Internet companies that the Western financial companies keep fawning over."

Chang had a sour look on his face as he responded, "Have you always been jealous of those with talent far greater than yours? You are so like one of the Grimm's Fairy Tales trolls, looking for his few shekels as someone passes over his bridge.

"I guess I had better get to the point, since you sound like you are late for yet another execution there in the Kremlin. What I have in mind is offering three million euros for the diamond necklace that you showed, via the multimedia graphic, if my designate can physically see them and verify their authenticity. Once he is satisfied, he will notify me and then we can arrange to make transfers to all interested parties.

"Can you contact your seller with our terms to see if they are agreeable?"

Dmitry, somewhat taken aback, responded, "This is certainly a different tone from our last conversation! Yes, of course I can, but what has changed? You even shrugged off my good-natured insults like there is another agenda afoot. Yes?"

Chairman Chang realized too late he had been too agreeable and countered, "You are always so suspicious, Dmitry. If you must know, I too have a buyer so I am now more agreeable to a transaction than I was before. Are the diamonds still for sale?"

Somewhat placated, Dmitry answered, "Chairman Chang, we Russians are always suspicious! Yes, the diamonds are still for sale. I will contact the selling party and see if they are agreeable to your request."

Chairman Chang smiled and asked, "By the way, where will the viewing be offered? The cost of travel and time will need to figure into either your commission or the seller's price. After all, they are the ones making the transaction so difficult."

Dmitry smirked and said, "I will point that out to the seller when I speak with them, Chairman Chang. Goodbye for now."

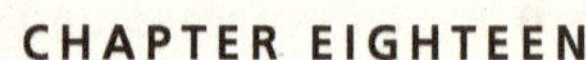

CHAPTER EIGHTEEN

Low-Cost Security – Paying the Fox to Guard the Hen House

Dmitry was very upbeat as he contemplated his call with Zara. Dmitry had two people on staff that were more protective of him than normal assistants. Konstantin was his operations lead and Evgeniya was his personal administrative assistant. Konstantin typically executed the team's operational assignments, but Evgeniya was practically his personal bodyguard. They were anxious to please Dmitry, but Evgeniya was so fanatical about taking care of him, she had to be calmed down from time to time. She worried about him when he was in a depressed mood, and she was also suspicious when he was in too good of a mood, like he was today.

Trying to maintain a nonchalant attitude when speaking, Evgeniya innocently asked, "Don't you have a call coming up with that computer-hacker whore in a few minutes, Dmitry?"

Dmitry's Afghan war wounds had earned him power and admiration in Russian politics. While his two assistants were devoted to him, they also despised several of the…*colorful*… *connections* that Dmitry needed to maintain. Looking over the tops of his reading glasses, Dmitry sarcastically responded, "Evgeniya, did you not get a birthday card from Zara again?"

Undaunted by the comment, Evgeniya blurted, "I find her manners, dress, and, most of all, her dialog with you offensive. Especially to a man of your status! Here you are, a hero to the Soviet Union, and she speaks to you like you work for her! Just so you know, the next time she shows up here to see you with no underwear on…"

Dmitry, blinking at the tirade, interrupted, "You noticed she wasn't wearing any underwear, too? Well, I can understand your disdain for a lady who doesn't wear underwear, but you will admit that her rentable recreational area was nicely groomed, don't you think?"

Evgeniya was rendered speechless, incapable of responding to the outrageous comment. Without further discussion, she turned and stomped back to her desk. Dmitry smiled slightly to himself at having suspended the dialog without raising his voice.

Moments later, the expected call came in from Zara and he answered, "Hello, my well-travelled friend! I trust you are calling about my need for anonymizing data traffic for my harmless prank that we discussed? Or, should I just assume you are calling about your needs, and mine have been forgotten?"

Zara knew Dmitry was in a good mood since his sarcasm was in high gear, so she responded, "I am sooo glad you don't make me do a pole dance for you anymore just so I can have a discussion with you, Dmitry. In answer to your question, I thought we could do both. I have my anonymizing application servers back online and ready for your disappearing act.

"Now, how about you comment on my diamond buyer so we can get you the promised commission which, if I under-stand it correctly, is also only about you. I trust you have good news for me?"

Dmitry feigned a modest amount of irritation and responded, "Pole dancing? I feel cheated that I have not seen your entertainment skills as a pole dancer!

"Be that as it may, let's talk about the diamond sale now that I know your systems are up and ready. The buyer wants his agent to inspect the diamonds in person and is willing to have him travel to meet you. I assume you are in the Dteam offices of New York, so I suspect you can arrange a secure showing to the appraiser there or someplace of your choosing? If you can and the diamonds are of a suitable quality, then the price without papers would be three million euros."

Zara thought for a moment before she replied, "But they are worth more than that."

Dmitry agreed, "They very well could be, because my source said he too now has a buyer. I assume that he will, in fact, resell them after establishing their worth. Do you want to do the meeting or not?"

Zara contemplated a moment, then suggested, "It occurs to me that if his agent likes the merchandise, they could be persuaded to up their bid to four million euros, or we can continue to look for another offer."

Dmitry smiled and agreed, "Ah, now you are thinking like a Russian Cossack! Text me the location and date and time you want. Give me a few days leeway in case his appraiser has to travel. Do you need me to provide some security for the showing? You can't be too careful, you know."

The offer made the hair on Zara's neck stand on end. She smiled and coyly asked, "You know what the hen said to the fox, Dmitry?"

Dmitry grinned and exclaimed, "Nothing, if he was a healthy fox! Alright, arrange your own security then, Miss Suspicious!

But don't let them snag our diamonds and my commission, or you will be doing that pole dancing for me a long time to get me my commission."

Zara smiled impishly and murmured, "Why, Dmitry, I didn't know you were looking for a full-time pole dancer! How sweet. I didn't know you cared!"

Dmitry, tired of being teased, retorted, "Just text me the time and location. Once I get that, I will have Konstantin begin the onslaught…I mean, harmless prank."

Zara happily responded, "Yes, Dmitry. I have already sent the anonymizing login, password, and Internet address to you so we can start anytime. I'll be in touch."

Quip had a puzzled, quizzical expression as he asked, "What do you mean, BORIS has been trying clandestine moves on STINKIE? Are you talking data intrusion and security breaches, or did he have his hands up under her skirt going for the circuitry?"

ICABOD responded, "I do not believe BORIS's instrumentality includes appendages such as hands, but STINKIE was a little embarrassed to tell me of the attempted intrusion. Perhaps the metaphor of his hands under her skirt are more appropriate, upon reflection.

"Dr. Quip, in either event it is apparent that an attack by one of the Algonquin Round Table members on our newest member is eminent. I am not inclined to openly accuse another ART member of hostilities across sovereign lines, but my reconnaissance clearly indicates a Russian cyber-attack against Finland is eminent. I recommend a cloaked interception of the attack. I am partial to BORIS as a supercomputer peer, but I cannot sanction his programmers launching a crushing attack against STINKIE."

Quip drew a deep breath and repeatedly blinked his eyes, then acquiesced, "Agreed. Besides there may be more going on with STINKIE that we need to fully comprehend. We suspect that the Fountain of Youth project has been resettled to this super-computer in Finland. There is a vested interest in discovering what the project has evolved into at this point. ICABOD, where are you in your sleuthing efforts regarding STINKIE?"

ICABOD appeared to hesitate a moment before he answered, "Dr. Quip, I see something of an ethical issue with me stating I am her friend and confidant, but then probing her restricted areas for our purposes. I have made the proper protocol requests to penetrate to her core, but I have been politely rebuked each time."

Quip stared, trying to process the response, and then indicated, "I don't know why, but everything you've been saying seems heavily laced with sexual innuendos. Am I hearing that somehow, you've now been programmed with a conscience? I used to be able to aim you at anything and you would simply go! Now we must debate this like freshmen in a college speech class!"

ICABOD processed the accusations and reminded, "Dr. Quip, when you granted me the right to refer to myself as an I-being, it came with the caveat that I use proper ethical judgement while questioning the activity. I am merely exercising that responsi-bility, per your mandate, sir. As the creator of this computer and master programmer, you are entitled to suspend any mandates as you see fit, and I will comply. However, I felt compelled to register my point of view in this matter."

A very sullen Quip studied the situation momentarily and replied, "No, I don't want to override your ethics in this matter,

ICABOD. Please tell me, how do we get the needed intelligence that might be on STINKIE without creating an ethical dilemma?"

ICABOD promptly suggested, "By employing someone who is a disinterested party to make the incursion. It occurs to me that Jacob would not be ethically constrained, since he is not friends with STINKIE."

Frowning now, Quip reminded, "However, he won't be able to do it nearly as fast as you, even if I could get him back online. He's playing *the pining and pouting putz for Petra* in New York, and we have work to do."

ICABOD offered, "It occurs to me that a suitable challenge might be attractive to him at this stage. I can direct him on the incursion path if he can be persuaded to help."

Quip looked at the monitor with squinted eye and his head cocked toward ICABOD and asked, "You're prepared to show him the way in? What about your ethical dilemma, you computing hypocrite?"

ICABOD stated, "I only said that I could not do the incursion. I did not say I could not tell someone else how to do it, Dr. Quip."

Quip grinned and beamed as he reacted, "Ha! That's my boy! Let's see if we can loop in old Jacob to do some electronic breaking and entering. This might even help him come back from the dead!"

ICABOD then advised, "With regards to the shunting effort to protect STINKIE from BORIS and the eminent cyber-attack, I should not be party to that exercise since both supercomputers will know of my involvement, which will lead them back to our organization. May I recommend a third party to hold up a secure tunnel to cloak us from both sovereigns, Dr. Quip?"

Quip nodded and agreed, "Good point! We need someone else to hold up a secure tunnel for Jacob to do the clandestine reconnaissance into STINKIE, and to absorb or at least redirect the cyber ION-fire so that STINKIE doesn't get fried, and BORIS doesn't blame you.

"Hmmmm. Sounds like a job for the TUCK! Dave Tucker, my favorite Australian Cloud provider! He cloaks! He pokes! He ropes! But best of all, he jokes! Better get ahold of him and his vice president, Gina, to let them know we need some specialized services."

Fear, Like Darkness, Tends to Dissipate in the Morning Light

Su Lin awakened early and watched the sunrise from her bedroom window. It promised to be a warm, beautiful, blue sky day on the farm. After washing up, she put on her jeans and topped it off with the new multicolored blouse Lara had brought. The blazing colors were vibrant against her pale skin tone. She added the matching scrunchie to the end of her long braid. The person in the mirror looked so radiant that Su Lin clapped her hands in delight. She tidied up her room and went downstairs. Lara had advised her to make friends with Mercedes first thing and show her around the farm, and Su Lin had promised.

Downstairs she smelled coffee and heard soft smooth jazz playing in the kitchen. She smiled and hoped that she could make breakfast this morning. Andy allowed her to make breakfast for herself or the whole household. She liked it best when she made something everyone might enjoy. Since there was company, she wanted to make something special.

As she rounded the corner, Su Lin spotted Mercedes sitting at the table sipping a cup of coffee. Mercedes's brown curly hair was capturing the morning sun rays, making her look very pretty. Her skin was very fair with sprinkles of freckles on her face and her arms. Su Lin took a breath, as if working up her courage, smiled and entered the kitchen. Andy had been insistent on treating guests with respect.

"Good morning, Miss Mercedes," offered Su Lin, readied for the onslaught of conversation she expected based on last night's deluge.

Mercedes looked at Su Lin and grinned, then slowly replied, "Good morning, Miss Su Lin. It's a beautiful day, just beautiful."

Mercedes then returned to looking out the window and sipping her coffee. Su Lin was speechless as she processed the change in this woman. She decided to look to see what might be available to cook this morning for breakfast. Carlos and Lara would likely sleep in for a while, based on Lara's long flight and their catching up on what had transpired in the months since they had seen one another. Therefore, whatever she fixed needed to either be kept warm or easily reheated. Several choices were available which pleased her.

"Uh, excuse me, Miss Mercedes, I would like to prepare us some breakfast. Is there anything that you are unable to eat? I wouldn't want to fix something that you were allergic to or didn't like." Su Lin hesitantly smiled and wondered if she had interrupted meditation or something.

Mercedes looked up with a sweet face and pleasant smile and replied, "Su Lin, so sweet of you to offer. Anything is fine. The only things I dislike are octopus and liver. You weren't planning on those, were you?"

Su Lin's face contorted in a way that suggested she was ready to gag, then she shook her head and replied, "Yuck! No, that is definitely not on the menu this morning. I would have no idea how to even prepare those items. One time, Carlos told me that octopus was like chewing on the sole of a shoe."

Mercedes's eyes twinkled as she said, "Oh, thank goodness. What a relief. May I help you with breakfast? It would help me learn where things are located, and Julie said you were wonderful at showing people stuff. It took me a while to find everything to brew the coffee. I hope my noise didn't waken you."

Su Lin grinned as she started to remove things from the refrigerator to add to the pile on the counter. Su Lin liked Mercedes. When she had seen her at Julie's wedding a few months ago, she felt like she'd known her practically forever. "Sure, I would appreciate the help. Sometimes I forget some things, so you can help me remember, okay?"

Mercedes moved into the area near the stove. She opened cabinets and drawers as directed and found the requested items. They worked well together. Mercedes had high hopes after several minutes that perhaps her behavior from last evening hadn't put Su Lin too far out of reach. They would be spending a great deal of time together. Images of her carrying on during the trip from the airport flashed before her eyes and made her inwardly groan. She owed each of them an apology.

"Su Lin, this is really helping me learn where stuff is located. Thank you. Ummm, by the way," she hesitated. "Was I a real motor mouth last night, and did I scare you?"

Su Lin debated how to respond. She didn't want to hurt Mercedes's feelings since she seemed to want to pitch in and help. She needed to honor her promise to Lara, but she promised Andy to always be honest.

Su Lin finally replied, "Mercedes, I am not trying to hurt your feelings, but, yes, last night you scared me. You don't scare me now, though. I had a really hard day yesterday when that man came by to pick me up. I don't recall much after I walked out to the car, until Carlos asked if I was feeling better. I think I needed my rest. I feel better now."

Mercedes smiled and replied, "Well, I had a tough time making my flight to come meet you. I was worried and had too many sodas and coffee. My caffeine rush, combined with the long flight, and, well, the rest is history. I'm glad you told me."

Mercedes extended her hand and said, "Let's start over. Hi, my name is Mercedes, and I look forward to us being friends."

Su Lin looked surprised, then pleased and ignored the hand and gave Mercedes a quick hug. She gleefully replied, "That would be wonderful! I like having friends. I only have a few, you know."

Su Lin turned back to the task at hand, and together they prepared a lovely meal with some quiet exchange. Su Lin indicated they would be going outside to tend the animals after breakfast. Su Lin wanted to introduce Mercedes to her Franklin. Mercedes headed up the cleanup detail while Su Lin set the sausage on a plate in the warmer, along with a delicious quiche. Su Lin wrote a short note of instruction to Carlos and Lara which she placed next to his plate. Su Lin practically dragged her new friend outside to meet Franklin and the other animals.

Carlos watched Lara as she slept. They had talked until very late, and Lara had finally fallen asleep. As much as he wanted to wake her up, he was thrilled just to watch her beside him in his bed. He missed sleeping and waking with her close. Since their relationship began, they had had some stolen time together, like this, but as they had discussed last evening, they wanted more from each other. He wasn't sure what the solution was, but for now he'd stop time to not disturb her slumber.

He'd woken when Su Lin had padded down the hallway past his room. Since no untold yelling or tears or shouting had ensued, he knew she was fine. That, combined with the aromas that floated up from the kitchen, made him suspect that she had prepared a feast. The cooking that woman did was nothing short of delicious. Carlos recalled the first few weeks after she had returned home how Andy had patiently showed her how to cook, where the recipes were, and then had turned it over to her. Outside of grilling, which Andy and Carlos took turns doing, Su Lin enjoyed being in charge of cooking and took great pride in contributing. Which reminded him that he needed to look at her computer problem.

The sensation of being watched caused Carlos to look down and see beautiful brown eyes looking at him, filled with desire and love. She turned her lips into a slow smile and crooned, "Good morning, my prince, have you been up long? I like seeing you when I wake up, mi amor."

Carlos's eyes darkened with desire as he moved to gather her into his arms and rumbled into her neck, "Not long, sweetheart. Just long enough to memorize the curve of your cheek and slope of your neck, as well as longing to see more."

Lara chuckled and reacted with goosebumps to his rumbling against her skin. She whispered, "Then I think we should both see more, a lot more. I have so missed you."

He deepened the kisses, and she responded immediately. Theirs was a seriously mutual physical attraction. They knew all the right moves to get the best responses from one another. Even with the weeks of being apart, they matched like two halves of the same heart. He stroked and touched as she stroked and touched in return. They alternated touching and kissing, licking and tasting, and feeling the other's response like an elaborate choreographed dance that escalated to a wonderful crescendo of ecstasy and release for them both.

As their breathing slowed, Carlos gently stroked the line of her side from breast to knee. Her body was luscious, warm, as well as a delightful fit next to him. Lara opened her eyes and sparkled as she drank in the sight of him. Carlos's heart soared as he realized how much he'd missed her.

"My love," he rumbled, "I am so glad you took a break from work to come and talk with me. I think we need to figure out something so we can be together all the time."

Lara smiled and replied, "I would agree. Twenty-four hours a day might just be enough time to spend with you, my prince!

"Right now, though, I need a shower, and then can we get something to eat, please?"

Carlos leered at her and replied, "Sure, sweetheart. I will join you in the shower and, ummm, help scrub your back and anything else you want."

Lara asked, "Do you have a lot to do today, my prince?"

Carlos nuzzled her neck and replied, "Outside of being at your beck and call, not a lot." With that he got out of bed in all his male glory and reached down and scooped her out of bed. He commented, "A beautiful lady, such as you, shouldn't have to walk when she can be carried."

She squealed and laughed and together they explored the possibilities of making love in the shower before heading down for breakfast. Lara knew she'd made the right decision in coming to Georgia.

CHAPTER TWENTY

The First to Rise Sometimes Means the First to Fall

Julie hesitated outside of Petra's door. In the weeks that Petra had been in the house, Julie had only once tried to talk to her sister and had been soundly rebuked. Juan had agreed it was time for Petra to be prodded back into the real world. Nighttime visits to watch the twins sleep in the nursery and refusing to interact with the family for meals only continued to keep her isolated. She was not engaged with the family, nor was she engaged with work. Julie had no idea what she did for hours in her room, but she suspected sleep since Petra was often spotted roaming the house at night.

Haddy had returned to Zürich for a few days to catch up on some work once the doctor indicated Petra's final surgeries were completed. Petra moved around fine, and Juan had caught her in the workout area several times, building up her strength. Juan had even offered to help her train some, but Petra had turned her face away and politely declined his offer. Everyone walked on eggshells, which was not helping at this point. Pity-party time was done, if Julie followed through on her plan.

Julie paced back and forth in front of the door, working up the courage to knock or simply enter. This was business. Carlos had called and explained the issue with regards to Su Lin's computer. Mercedes had tried to open the files as well with her tricks. When Mercedes failed, she was convinced that the files had a complex encryption on them, not just a password barrier. That was how Julie had become involved. Mercedes's report had provided one part, and then Carlos had called and asked for some help. Julie had suggested that the computer be transported here, but Carlos didn't want to interrupt Su Lin's standard routine.

Carlos recommended, after he extracted a portion of the problem, that a change of scenery might do Petra some good. The farm had a wonderful way of grounding individuals and putting things into perspective. Julie had agreed, since nothing at the family home seemed to make a difference in the way Petra interacted with people. A quick call to Haddy had also gained approval as a new approach toward Petra's improvement. Su Lin was mentally broken and could possibly relate well to Petra in her current physically and mentally broken state.

Julie knocked on the door. Petra on the other side grumbled, "Go away!"

Julie knocked again and then said, "Petra, it's me, I need to speak to you. It's important!"

The silence continued until Petra finally responded, "If it's important then one of your team needs to deal with it. Or Quip. Call Quip, he'll have ideas."

Julie was getting angrier by the second at the responses. After a minute, she tried the door handle and found it was locked. She demanded, "Look here, Petra, I said it was important. I'm your sister. Open the damn door right now, or I will."

With no response, Julie backed up and prepared to kick the door, when it opened. Petra was in her robe with her hair going every which way. She looked haggard as she quietly asked, "What's so important that you can't handle it? You always fix everything, or find everything, or know everything."

Now Julie was mad. She approached Petra until she was toe-to-toe and their noses nearly touched. She stated, "I don't fix everything, but I am part of a team that's pretty damn good. You were a part of that same team until you decided to give some dead guy the power over what you do and what you think. Well, I am done with it, Petra. Do you hear me? Done!

"It's time you got up, got dressed and participated like the rest of us. I get that you dislike me, my husband, and my children, but you're needed. It's that simple."

Petra's eyes grew wide, and her temper flared. "That's not true. I love you all. I'm just a burden at this point."

Julie thumped on Petra's chest with her index finger as she related, "You're only a burden in your mind. I need you to be my sister, but more importantly, Su Lin needs you."

Petra's forehead wrinkled as she asked, "Su Lin needs me. Why? Is she hurt again?"

Julie, not giving an inch of space up and forcing Petra to back up a bit, informed, "Someone tried to kidnap her, so I sent Mercedes to guard her."

Petra looked worried, so Julie continued, "Right now she's safe and with Mercedes, Carlos, and Lara on the farm. Andy's almost finished at a customer site in California and should return home in a couple of days.

"There are encrypted files on Su Lin's laptop, though, and they are unknown and can't be opened. They also seem to be tripping a calendar notification. I tried to get them to send the machine here for you to take a look at it, but they won't."

Petra's eyes seemed to engage. "Su Lin's laptop? Hmmmm, we never looked at it because she was rushed to the hospital.

It's likely important to something she was working on, though I cannot imagine what. If she set the encryption, you can bet it will take days to open."

Julie felt like she was gaining ground as she replied, "Or you can work your magic. You are the best at that type of thing. Frankly, we are all getting pretty tired of taking care of you and your feelings. No one has the power to keep my big sister down. No one but you!

"So, you are going to pack a bag, get dressed, and go to Georgia. I have a flight set, and the car will be here in an hour. You can stay at the farm. Carlos promised you could have the room furthest away from everyone."

Petra shook her head and quietly declined, "I can't go anywhere. I can't be seen by anyone."

Julie was fed up with the lame excuses as she took one more step to resume the nose-to–nose stance and declared, "You can and YOU ARE. I will help with some designer tricks, but you are making this trip. I need your help and expertise on this, Petra. NO, is not an option. We all know you're constipated with self-pity, but we need you to flush it and bring your mental energies back online!"

Petra looked crestfallen as she moaned, "I'm not emotionally constipated. I just don't want to face myself in the mirror anymore."

Julie empathized, "Then don't look in the mirror. I'll help you. But you will interact with me. You will pull your weight in the business or, I swear, I will take you down."

Julie placed her hands on Petra's shoulders and turned her around in a flash. Then gently pushed her further into the room as she insisted, "Now, Petra, the time is now. So let's do this. I will help. Time is not on your side with this. And by the way, Lara is there. I know you would like to see her, even if you won't admit it."

An hour later Petra descended the steps to the waiting car with a small suitcase carried by Juan. An elaborate scarf covered most of her face, and if one didn't know she'd had a problem, they would likely only briefly wonder about the slight limp. No cane was required.

As she was driven away, Juan placed his arm around Julie and reassured, "She needed this push. You did great, my darling."

Julie nodded, unconvinced, as tears welled up in her eyes, and she silently prayed that Petra would gain herself back.

CHAPTER TWENTY-ONE

The Restless and the Relentless, a Formidable Combination
...The Enigma Chronicles

Alisha made sure no one was watching as she gained access to the hard copy file room in the medical facility. She quietly hunted for the target files while she cautiously listened for anyone intruding on her search. The color coding and date ordering made the search quick and easy. The low light in the file room hindered her a little, so a small penlight was used to do the final file determination. She smiled as she pulled out Su Lin's case files. *Excellent,* she thought, *the complete hard copy dossier on the subject! Too bad Leroy had been unable to locate the electronic counterpart.* She wrinkled her nose and was dismayed at the size of the folder. Photographing these pages with her phone to transmit to her associate, she realized, was going to take some significant time.

Alisha quickly and quietly started to methodically photograph each page once she had a small desk light and a flat surface rigged to process the documents as quickly as possible. The process was taking longer than she wanted which meant it was only a matter of time until someone entered. Several minutes later, one of the resident nurses barged into the file room, threatening to cut her photo session short. She noticed with relief that at least the nurse wasn't her new boss.

Alisha, always the master of improvisation, looked up at the nurse and barked, "Who the hell set up this file room? Dammit, everything is filed bass-ackwards by someone with no concept of the alphabet! What do you think will happen to all that juicy federal funding this place has been getting when they find that this place is in non-compliance with the HIPAA filing mandates! No wonder the hiring manager offered me a bonus to fix this crap!

"Honey, I am glad you wandered in because I will need your undivided attention to get this mess in shape! If you're not other-wise busy, we need to take ALL these files off the shelves and refile everything by treatment, gender, and date. If we get the rest of the staff in here and get started now, we should be done in about three days, if we work non-stop. So roll up those sleeves, honey!"

The verbal onslaught had the desired effect, and without saying a word, the nurse turned around and quietly closed the door behind her. Alisha grinned at the ruse she had delivered, knowing full well that word would spread like wildfire, and no one would come in to bother her photo and transmission session.

After the final picture was taken, she began to ship multi-media and the associated text messages to her cohort with the bogus subject, *Selfies of Us Lined Indiscriminately Nearby at the capital*. She chuckled to herself and wondered how long it would take him to realize he should use the capitalized letters as the name of the designated target of Su Lin. They had always been accurate at reading each other in business and other activities.

Since she was not going to be interrupted, Alisha decided to go ahead and call him now that everything was finally transmitted. For the time being, her role was over until the next scheduled appointment between Su Lin and Dr. Giles.

She dialed his number and coyly greeted, "Hello, tall, dark, and thick! Did you get all my selfies I sent you?"

Leroy clucked his tongue in mock disdain and responded, "Well, hello, gorgeous! Yes, I received the transmissions and quickly deduced from your text title that these were the files we were looking for. Thank you for capturing that to digital format for me. All I need to do now is compress all these photos into something that can be emailed.

"I have started trolling for some cyber thugs to improve my data source access to help us avoid going to this particular extreme again, ma'am."

Alisha commented, "Yeah, but what a pain in the gazzosky to first photo them and then text them! You're sure no digital records could be found? How did you even know to look here for paper files?"

Leroy shrugged and grumbled, "I prowled their database but found nothing. The only reason I knew this was the right place was because the front desk's calendar scheduler showed Su Lin's appointments for every six weeks."

Alisha nodded thoughtfully and deduced, "So someone or something scrubbed her records. My man, you were crafty enough to check the appointment schedule. Very clever. Do you still need me here, or can I come home and collect my fees?"

Leroy chuckled and mockingly replied, "Fees? Am I given to understand that you want more money? I thought we were friends!"

Alisha again coyly responded, "Of course we're friends! While I can't wait to play the *Hop the Fireplug game* with you, a lady does need a certain amount of funding to maintain her gorgeous figure for her man."

Leroy privately reflected that perhaps he had been overly generous in calling her gorgeous. While she had been an attractive lady forty-five kilos ago, now it seemed she was a twelve-biscuit-a-meal kind of girl based on the ninety kilos she now sported. These days, her size served her well in her various roles that he needed her to play, and frankly he preferred his lady a little on the plentiful side. He chuckled to himself at the fact he was being generous to her again.

Leroy smiled and replied "Hon, you come on home for now, so we can get your fees taken care of. You might need to go back for her next scheduled appointment though. Okay?"

Alisha smiled broadly as she reminded, "I am on my way, but don't be letting any other women wet on that fireplug, you hear me?"

Leroy flashed his toothy gold grin and said, "Then don't take too long, honn-nney!"

Recognizing the incoming number, Leroy immediately answered, "Good evening, sir! I trust the email and its attachment made it through to you. Are you pleased with the reconnaissance effort on our target?"

Xavier Pekoni took longer than usual to respond but finally asked, "Are you sure this file and all the images you sent me are correct? Did you look at any of it before you sent it?"

Leroy grew alarmed at the tone of the questions and replied, "No, sir, I did not look at them. Once the DNA read correctly, everything flowed from that identity. Is there a problem, sir?"

Xavier stammered as he responded, "This file cannot be right! Bring it up on your computer NOW! I want us to go through it! This has to be wrong!"

Fear was infiltrating Leroy's being as he pulled up all the files and decompressed them for his viewing. Finally, with everything open, he swallowed hard and acknowledged, "I'm ready, sir. You will see the DNA identifiers in the file of the first page and that was our key point to proceed. No electronic version could be discovered in our hunt, but we were able to copy this Su Lin person's medical records where she has been coming for months to be tested. I compared those signature files with…"

Xavier interrupted, "Take a look at her picture and the other medical details of this woman! This simply cannot be her; I tell you! Everything, and I mean everything, clearly points to an Asian female that is roughly twenty-five years old! Master Po, or this Su Lin, is closer to fifty-five years old! Look at the test results posted in here. These must be the wrong records!"

Leroy mulled the statement over in his mind before he proposed, "So either someone was clever enough to substitute someone else's hard copy records for hers or…"

Xavier flinched as he recoiled from the second possibility as he finished the statement. "Or she solved the problem of aging! This cannot be! It simply cannot be!"

Leroy calmly offered, "Sir, the DNA records are our proof that this person Su Lin is our formerly known Master Po, who founded the Cyber Warfare College in China before she disappeared. I am looking at what you're seeing and, I must tell you, this is the same female that eluded my capture on that farm. This is the same person and, yes, it very definitely suggests she has solved the riddle of aging.

"Keep in mind though, humans of Asian descent tend to not show the appearance of aging as other humans of different descent, as you have mentioned to me on numerous occasions."

It took a few minutes for Xavier to overcome his astonishment, but he finally insisted, "We must have her and all her s ecrets. I am now convinced she knows, and very soon I will know.

"Leroy, any resources you need you will have, but this delicate flower must be gathered and brought back to me. Understood?"

Leroy's resolve was clearly in his voice as he responded, "Understood, sir!"

CHAPTER TWENTY-TWO

Dress for Success
Or Wear Nothing at All

Lara was having a bit of down time as she relaxed by the pool and caught up on emails from the office while Carlos worked on some projects. The time spent with Carlos had renewed her conviction that she and Carlos needed to work out a solution that eliminated their spending so much time apart. She heard girlish laughter being emitted from the stable area and suspected that Mercedes or Su Lin had convinced Franklin to display one of his many tricks. Mercedes had been the right person to keep an eye on Su Lin and bond with her.

Petra would be arriving soon. She had refused to allow Carlos or Lara to pick her up from the airport, saying she needed her own car. Lara had called Julie to get the whole story on why the sudden shift in friendly exchanges and was distressed to learn that her friend was not the same person she had known. Lara hoped they would have some time together to help renew their friendship and perhaps even help Petra get over her confidence issues. She thought back to the first time she'd met Petra, and it was by a swimming pool. Perhaps this was a good omen.

Lara refocused on the emails and found that the people she had put in charge were doing all the right things. Deadlines were being met, costs were under control, and she still had the ability to approve the designs and schedules. She wondered if she could in fact work from here and maintain the growth that her company, Destiny Fashions of Brazil, was enjoying. The company's success had continued like a long-range satellite on an orbital path. She'd successfully brought in new designs, thanks in part to Julie's hidden talents, with new approaches to fashion, diverse fabrics, and outstanding marketing. Now, Destiny Fashions of Brazil were the designers that others watched and tried to imitate.

Andy noticed Lara was truly absorbed in what she was reading, so he cleared his throat before he interjected, "There you are, you pretty girl. Carlos suggested I might find you out here. Which of course was his way of suggesting my hovering was annoying him."

Lara broadly grinned as she asked, "Andy, how are you? I knew that you arrived last night, and I apologize for not waiting up for you. I just love your farm and taking long walks, which really makes me sleep well. It is like being in a slice of paradise."

Andy chuckled as he sat in an adjacent chair and commented, "Here I thought it was because of Carlos. Now I know the truth. Your secret is totally safe with me."

Lara blushed and chastised, "Now, Andy, a woman should never talk details about the love of her life.

"Carlos said he had spoken to you and explained why your home was filled with people. I expect you aren't too angry with him or even me. I hope you don't mind my inviting myself."

Andy smiled and replied, "I have the head of the most important fashion house in my home today. Who also so happens to make the best guy I have ever worked with happy, and you think I would complain? You just stay here as long as you like and consider the invitation always open. It's nice for Su Lin to have other women around, especially since my darling EZ set off to be with her soulmate.

"Kinda reminds me of myself when I was young and in courting form. I enjoyed all the pretty girls and taking them on long walks, going to dances, or relaxing at the swimming hole. Mighty fine times I had as a young man, that's for sure."

Andy's eyes twinkled and focused way past Lara for a minute or so, then he continued, "You know there was a time, way back when in this country, that when a young man was sweet on a lady, the most important activity you could do was to borrow the family car and take her for that special ride, to tell her how you felt. Well, I'm here to tell you that is exactly how I tried to charm one young lady, but it didn't quite go like I had planned.

"The first problem was my daddy wouldn't lend me his sedan. He did offer to let me use our dune buggy. As soon as he pointed me in its direction, I got wide-eyed about the prospects of romancing her in this open-cab dune racer that looked so spiffy. Here I was, planning on some serious smooching.

"My planning grew all out of proportions and included a huge picnic basket lunch with all the fixings, set up on the borrowed quilt from my momma. This was to happen after we had some fine open-wheel touring over a beautiful winding road that crossed a low water stream in several places before it emptied out into a park at the gulf. I am here to tell you, Lara, that gal wasn't going to have eyes for anyone but me, after my planned excursion!

"Looking back on the actual event, however, I'm not sure I can say that I thought everything all the way through. I figured that the late afternoon rainstorms would fall in well after we had returned home. The morning was so nice, I can see, even now, how I was thinking everything would work out just fine.

"After gassing up the old dune buggy on that bright shiny morning, I headed us towards that winding two lane road that crossed Spring Creek several times. She was just as pretty as a picture with her hair gently sailing around her face and her repeatedly trying to keep her skirt under control. We laughed at some story or other. As we headed down the first water crossing, I could almost imagine a very light watery spray traveling away from the vehicle and maybe a little moisture dampening her cheeks, making her see the romance that was in store for her to claim.

"Lara, you do understand that an open dune buggy is exactly what its name says, right?"

Lara nodded and smiled, fascinated with the story. Enthralled, she was not willing to say a word and interrupt his undoubtedly romantic adventure as a young man.

"Well, I didn't count on all the river water being shot into the cab area where we were sitting in that kind of volume. I am pretty sure she started screaming as soon as she started to gargle the first two hundred gallons that came rushing in as we hit that water. All she could get out was *Andy! Stop…* but that's all I heard because most of the river water went down her open mouth.

"I am here to tell you, I know exactly what it's like having roughly four hundred gallons of water being shot directly at you, traveling at thirty-five miles-per-hour! And I will tell you that no matter how slowly you try and take those low water river crossings, all the dang-blasted water still comes in the cab, except now I got this hysterical female screaming and promising me she would have her daddy shoot me on sight once we got back."

Lara grasped her hand across her mouth to stifle the giggling that threatened to take over. Her eyes watered from restrained mirth as he continued his tale.

"When you have four hundred gallons of water shot into the open dune buggy you're driving, I can promise you it will soak your carefully packed wicker picnic basket of sandwiches and your mom's prized quilt that you were planning to smooch on, thus closing off any amorous intentions you might have had.

"Well, her screaming hysterics got me to pull over and try to make things right, which took some time. You can probably guess that we never made it to the park to try out some of the planned moves I had heard tell of. But just as I was thinking my luck had to change, it finally did, but for the worst.

"That late afternoon rain storm that I had ignored, based on my planned intentions, moved in faster than expected. So yep, we had to drive all the way home in the pouring rain. And what rain didn't get to us through the open cab, the wheels spun up from the road water in to where we were sitting. The only thing that didn't let the water out were the seats we were sitting in. That's a mighty uncomfortable feeling you know, sitting in a cold bucket of water for miles with a fuming woman.

"I don't believe I've ever had a longer, more uncomfortable, silent drive with another human being, ever since that fine spring day. I finally managed to get her to her home. You would be right in thinking there wasn't no hand holding or smooching offered when I dropped her off. However, you will understand I was undeterred by the day's events because the depth of my feelings for the young lady were such that, as she was stomping back to her front door I hollered out, *I hope this doesn't spoil our chance of going to the dance on Saturday*. I don't recall seeing her again after that ill-fated day, but I do remember well the going-away gesture she gave me. I guess you might say, we wasn't meant to be."

It took a few moments for Lara to bring her laughter under control, but finally she offered, "Andy, I bet the girls swarmed all over you when you were young. After your episode with the open dune buggy, may I assume that is when you got that marvelous blue Chevy truck of yours? Carlos brags about your truck all the time."

They continued chatting about a variety of things that ranged from Andy's younger days to ideas he had for helping Su Lin to learn more. Andy extracted a bit of the details on why Lara was in town and listened intently without offering commentary one way or the other. He seemed to empathize with the situation but offered no opinion, for which she was grateful.

Just before he got up to leave her in peace, he added, "I know you young people will work it out, but if I can help, please let me know. I like you both a lot."

Lara smiled at the way Andy patted her hand before he left. He was a nice man. EZ was lucky to have such a nice papá, almost as nice as hers. She had just closed her eyes to rest a bit before finishing up her work when her cell phone rang.

Lara glanced at the number and frowned as she answered, "Hello, Sophia, I just read the emails and reports from you. Things sound like they are fine. Is there a problem that you would phone me?"

Sophia Perez was Lara's newly appointed chief operating officer. Sophia had been around since the beginning and thrived in this new role. She was a lean, willowy woman with huge brown eyes, long dark hair worn in a well-practiced bun, who would go to the mat with anyone who she felt was not giving her one hundred percent. She had a light, melodic voice that captured those she spoke to without her ever raising her voice.

Sophia laughed and soothed, "No, Lara, there are no problems. In fact, today is only blue skies and beautiful tidings which I had to convey in person. Justice simply cannot be accomplished in all things with just email."

Lara thought for a few minutes, trying to understand what news would be so good. Then her eyes grew wide, and she asked, "Did we get permission to put our line of fashions onto the cruise ship lines I have been wooing? That would be such a nice addition to this year. And I thought the last proposal I made was financially advantageous to…"

Sophia interrupted, "Lara, can you stop please and listen for a minute. You will never guess this, I promise. I do, however, think the fates are watching over you and this company of yours."

Lara apologized, "I'm sorry, I will stay quiet, but it is our company. You are a stakeholder, too."

Sophia chuckled, "Okay, then as one stakeholder to the primary stakeholder, you have won the Most Innovative Fashion Designer Award in the category of professional women."

Lara sputtered and looked totally shocked as she exclaimed, "Oh my goodness! I never thought we would be recognized by the Americans in such a way. You're right, this is definitely better over the phone than via email. Are you planning the party at the office? Everyone should be thanked."

"Things are fairly undone right now," explained Sophia. "The news spread like wildfire to everyone, and the press here is clamoring for an interview. I, eh, didn't tell the press you weren't in town right now. And your papá didn't think it was wise to alert them as to your whereabouts.

"I will do the local interview, with your permission."

"Yes, of course, Sophia. You are a great speaker and know our business. Just make certain you wear something from the new line."

They both chuckled. Sophia added, "As it so happens, there is an award dinner at Rockefeller Center this weekend. You and a guest are invited to attend and accept the award personally.

It includes a voucher for airline and accommodations for two nights in New York City. It is formal attire, of course."

Lara stuttered, "I didn't bring anything formal with me. I had no notion of getting invited into a formal setting. You will simply have to send my regrets. Better yet, you go."

Sophia interjected, "Oh no, I will speak to the press but attend a dinner with a lot of important people? Nope. That is your job, Madam President."

Lara asked, "Can you ship me something overnight? I think the tea length evening wear would work even for formal. Perhaps it will be the new chic!"

Sophia laughed and said, "Funny girl. Your papá thought you would minimize it and had something packaged which was sent, via his personal courier, to arrive to you in the morning. He also said no arguments, enjoy the honor, and he'll call you later tonight."

Lara wailed, "But I can't attend alone."

Sophia insisted, "Then take the gorgeous man who brought you to Georgia along with you. Your pictures would suggest he would look devastatingly handsome in a tux."

Lara thought about that and agreed. Her prince looked good in everything and nothing. She wondered if he'd agree to a trip to New York. Perhaps, since Andy was home, it would be okay.

Petra drove up to the house and parked. She was a little tired from the flight but not nearly as stiff as she had expected. Her daily workouts, before anyone else was up had helped revive her strength and coordination. She was back to doing her morning Karate stances to regain her overall fluid movement, grace, flexibility, and power. The injuries had denied her that for months, but that had changed in recent weeks as she practiced multiple times per day.

On the flight over, she had thought about everything Julie had accused her of doing to undermine her healing. She had made up her mind to just take the critical looks from everyone and hide out when she could no longer stand the stares. Honestly, she wanted to focus on something other than her pain, but it had grown too comfortable. After Julie had combed her hair to somewhat cover up the ugly scar on her cheek, added some nice eye makeup, and provided some clever scarf tricks, she'd felt better as she boarded the flight. Julie had also arranged for her seat to put her best side forward. Julie had reminded her repeatedly to do her job, forget what others might be thinking, and things would gradually improve.

Petra thought about seeing Lara. They had a very special bond she didn't even share with Julie. Lara had needed Petra when her life was off kilter, and perhaps Petra needed her now. Maybe Lara could design something clever to disguise her face. She frowned as she recalled that the doctors had suggested a couple more reconstructive surgeries would help restore her back to her former look, but that it would take years. Petra refused to dwell on this as she steeled herself to handle this initial greeting. These people really were her friends, and they had not seen her at her worst. Then she spied a shy Su Lin approaching the car with a reserved smile and hesitant wave.

Petra got out and adjusted her scarf, just in time to feel the warmth of Su Lin's hug.

Su Lin said, "Miss Petra, I am so glad to see you. I have missed you. How is Julie, and how are her babies?"

Petra almost smiled as she replied, "Miss Julie is fine and sends her love. The babies are up and moving. They might be ready for hide and seek the next time you see them. They are growing so fast."

Petra went to the back of the car to reach for her bag, but Su Lin grabbed it and said, "Please let me. Andy says that I need to be polite to all guests and help them."

Petra frowned and wondered if Andy had said that to make certain that she didn't exert herself, like she was an invalid or something. Julie had assured her that no one knew the details of her injuries outside of the immediate family. It was left up to Petra to confide in them or not.

Su Lin added, "I have been practicing with Mercedes and Lara to make certain that I help them. I fix breakfast, do little chores for them. Andy said this morning I was doing great. You will let me help, right?"

The hopefulness in the eyes of Su Lin was not lost on Petra. Petra forgot about herself as she recalled how much this woman had gone through and would continue to go through after almost dying. Petra quietly reassured, "Yes, please, Su Lin. I appreciate your helping me with my bags and showing me which room I get to enjoy.

"Then I want to look at your computer. I understand it has been misbehaving. Mercedes and Carlos both thought I could help."

Su Lin beamed as she picked up the big bag and led the way into the house. The house looked just as Petra recalled from her last visit. There was a quiet welcome in the orderliness of the home, with its southern charm visible in the pictures, the wallpaper, and the fresh flowers. It was like walking into a warm hug. Petra felt almost relieved to be working in this familiar place. She panicked though when Carlos and Lara spotted her and headed her way.

Lara gave her a hug and kissed her good cheek in welcome, then Carlos added a gentle hug.

Carlos added, "I am so glad you could make it on such short notice. Honestly, I tried, and then Mercedes tried to access the files on the laptop and stop the alerts, but it is outside of both our levels of expertise." He chuckled and suggested, "When you break the code, please don't tell me how easy it was, okay?"

Petra was amazed that no one looked at her any differently than she recalled from the last time she'd seen each of them. She didn't notice any pity in their eyes, nor did they avert their eyes from hers. Then she realized that she hadn't responded, so she smiled and self-consciously turned her face slightly away as she suggested, "It must be a bit tough, Carlos, as you are pretty adept at figuring stuff out. I told Su Lin that I would see my room and then look at her computer.

"Is dinner at the same time here as before?"

Su Lin responded, "Yes, and Andy said he wanted to barbeque in honor of your arrival and that you like steaks, potatoes, salad, and white wine. Those just happen to be my favorites too."

Petra, getting a little unnerved, quietly stated, "Show me the way, and let's get to work."

Su Lin led the way upstairs while Lara and Carlos exchanged looks of concern.

CHAPTER TWENTY-THREE

Information Wanted without the Dirty Hands – Always a Challenge

Leroy flashed his toothy gold-encrusted grin and extended his big beefy hand to shake Zara's hand as he hailed, "Greetings and salivations, ma'am! I'm the one who contacted you over the Internet for specialized computer work. Do I have the right place? Your establishment looks kind of quiet and, well, sort of vacant at present."

Zara slipped into another one of her identity aliases as she replied, "I am Moya Dushechka, the department leader here at our New York facilities. I will take a wild guess and say perhaps you are Leroy, the gentleman from the chat room?

"As for my team members, they work best as binge coders, meaning they will write code and socialize around the clock, sometimes for days at a time, and then vanish for days at a time. You are seeing evidence of their down time and proof positive that the cleaning crew didn't throw up their hands in disgust.

"We work by project and don't punch a time clock as was done in the last century. Everyone here is paid by the job to deliver, so they won't stop until the code is done. I always know when they are about done because they start mixing vodka in with their espresso and that started yesterday morning. Did you bring the down payment?"

Leroy balked a little as he advised, "Hold on now, Mojo DeHeckto! I wants to go over the assignment in full before I hand over folding currency for my assignment! You might be right purty, Miss Mojo, but this ol' boy ain't about to be flim-flammed by a purty face and a few computer terms. I want to know that you know what I am looking for. Thata ways, when you say you're done and want the balance of payment, we're not arguing over deliverables."

Zara thought to herself, He isn't as dumb as he looks which, now that I think on it, isn't that hard to accomplish. She smoothed her voice and smiled as she replied, "You are quite right, Mr. Leroy. Let me get my notebook so nothing gets misunderstood."

Leroy seemed a bit more agreeable as their discussion went through exactly what he wanted. As his apprehension slowly fell away, Zara got a more detailed exchange from Leroy. She noticed that the more in-depth the discussion, the more his accent slipped, which made her smile.

Leroy explained, "I need you to hunt medical records looking for this type of individual who has these specific characteristics. Specifically, I want these blood types and this kind of DNA signature, whether it is male or female. The subjects that match this profile must have physical addresses, not just email locations for the interrogation, 'er, I mean, interview process. And finally, your hunting activity, whether successful or unsuccessful, cannot be traceable back to either you or me.

"You will be prowling medical records from any and every source I can feed to you. Hopefully, you don't get squeamish at the prospect of your research being at odds with just about every federal privacy law in this country and most of the world.

There can be no digital fingerprints left to point back to us. Understood?"

Zara studied Leroy for a moment and then asked, "Since when does a southern farm boy hick need this much medical research for these blood/ DNA types anonymized for cash payments? Or, should I not ask?"

Leroy slipped back into character, smiled with the gold tooth clearly visible, then responded, "Miss Mojo, it's complicated, and you should not ask! The job pays what we discussed, and there is a bonus that will be paid for each individual record that is a hit according to our needs. Oh, and it would be nice to know if the name fitting our description has any known relatives as well, but that is not an absolute requirement. Are we clear? I need a report of results at a minimum every five days, but every three days would be better."

Zara chuckled and reassured, "With our expertise at data capture from our clandestine hunting with our anonymizing technology to cloak our efforts, I believe the Dteam will be able to meet your needs, sir."

Leroy beamed a huge smile and replied, "Miss Mojo DeHeckto, I think my shopping efforts might just have found what I was look-ing for. I will call in three days to see if you have some material for me to pick up."

Zara shrugged her shoulders and offered, "I can email it to you and save you the trip if you like."

Leroy chuckled a little and then insisted, "No, we will exchange everything via a USB thumb drive. Nothing will transpire between us via email. Cleaner that way, ma'am."

Zara nodded in agreement and responded, "As you wish. Once I receive your deposit, then we can begin the countdown to the three days."

Leroy grinned and handed the agreed cash to Zara. She verified the amount and nodded.

"Three days begins now. I prefer our meeting times to be after eight in the evening to ensure the team is out of the way. Cleaner that way, sir."

CHAPTER TWENTY-FOUR

Hidden Secrets
are Just a Password Away

Petra delayed leaving her temporary new room as she placed and moved the things from her suitcase. During this mindless activity, she reflected on the various human interactions she'd had since she had left her family home. Petra realized she was fearing reactions from people that simply were not reality. No one reacted to her at the airport or on the flight itself. No one on the farm had been anything other than welcoming and kind. Here, at the very least, she was committed to helping resolve the issues on Su Lin's laptop and perhaps interact with people who cared about her, especially Lara. The conversation that raged between her heart and her mind actually helped her to relax and focus on the next steps she needed to take. After all, she was grown. The knock on the door interrupted her thoughts, and the quiet voice from Su Lin pulled her back to the here and now.

"Petra, if you have finished with your unpacking, are you ready to look at my laptop?"

Petra smiled at the sweet request and opened the door. She suggested, "Yes, Su Lin, I'm sorry I took so long to finish putting my things away. To be honest, I was listing the things I want to do while I am here and became lost in thought."

She stepped out into the hallway and continued, "Where is your laptop, so we can resolve this issue."

Su Lin beamed and offered, "I have it downstairs in the study, next door to where Andy and Carlos work with their customers. We won't be disturbed, yet we can get either of them if we need to."

Petra slowly smiled at the positive attitude. "Sounds like a plan. On the way to the study, can we make a quick stop in the kitchen for a sweet tea? Last time I was here, I found that Andy's sweet tea was positively, deliciously refreshing."

Su Lin grinned and agreed. "It's my favorite drink during the day, so yes, we can get some."

They entered the kitchen. Andy had just finished up the dishes from lunch and smiled as they entered. He wiped his hands and walked toward Petra, engulfing her in a warm hug. He commented, "I missed you earlier, Miss Petra. I'm glad to see you."

He released her and looked at her from head to toe with no malice in his eyes as he added, "I'm gonna put the elephant on the table. I know you were injured. We all do. But you look great and well on the road to recovery. Stop looking at me like I'm judging you 'cause I'm not, nor is anyone else here. We just appreciate that you are here! There, I said it!"

He hugged her again then turned and left the room. Petra was surprised at the direct comment, yet it filled her with relief. No more eggshells. Su Lin, oblivious to the impact of Andy's comment, completed filling glasses with sweet tea and handed one to Petra with an impish smile.

"Petra, I like the big glasses. I hope you do, too. Let's go fix my laptop."

Petra let Su Lin take her to the study, though she recalled the room and where it was located. As they passed by the window that overlooked the garden, she saw Lara by the pool on the phone and with her laptop up. They entered, closed the door, and Su Lin sat in one chair while she indicated the other for Petra. The laptop was powered up. Su Lin unlocked it with entry of her password and pushed it toward Petra, along with a separate piece of paper that contained the logon and password to the machine.

But before they began, Su Lin asked, "What did Andy mean by putting the elephant on the table? Such a funny term, and we don't have any elephants here on the farm."

Petra, hoping to avoid a lengthy discussion on Andy's observation, responded, "Oh, it's just Andy's way of greeting someone he hasn't seen in a while."

Su Lin seemed thoughtful for a moment or two, then observed, "Sometimes Andy says what other people only think about, especially when there are broken people around like you and me. But Andy never makes me feel bad at being broken. In fact, it makes me try even harder because someday I won't be broken. When that happens, I can look back at where I came from, and it will make me happy."

Petra was humbled by Su Lin's observation and felt ashamed that she had not taken the same attitude towards her injury. The example that Su Lin had offered up made Petra fight back tears for excluding all her friends and family so unnecessarily. It took a few moments for Petra to refocus on the task at hand as Su Lin intently focused on the laptop.

Su Lin looked hopeful as she conveyed, "I want you to work the keyboard, but I will direct you to the folders that have a problem. I would also like to watch what you do as it helps me learn. Carlos didn't think you would mind."

Petra quickly moved to the settings of the laptop and created a new log in and password, giving it full administrative rights, then rebooted the system. While the system was rebooting, Petra instructed, "Su Lin, I created a new log in identification so that I can track all my activity versus what you or anyone else has done. In that way, you can see my steps in the logs later, if you need to.

"We are ready to get to the problem directory. I plan to also check everything after we get the problem corrected, just to avoid a future problem."

Su Lin nodded and smiled, then agreed, "I like that idea. Thank you for showing me and telling me. It makes it far easier.

"The problem started when I tried to open the directory entitled Franklin," she admitted.

Petra raised an eyebrow and her forehead furrowed as she asked, "Isn't your pig named Franklin?"

Su Lin nodded and answered, "Yes, he is. I thought this file might have some details around some of the commands he might know that I haven't tried or found in other areas of written notes. Several items in this laptop, that I have read, are about different test scenarios on Franklin. I was trying to understand everything that I may have taught that little guy. He's so cute and smart.

"You may not know this, but he does almost anything I ask. He actually nuzzles me. Andy laughs when that happens because it reminds him of his dog Wrinkles and the way he pushes his nose for attention."

Petra chuckled and replied, "I did know that Franklin was smart, but that particular trick I haven't heard before.

"Out of curiosity, what makes the other files that you have been able to open different from this folder that you tried to access?"

Su Lin thought for a moment and replied, "The others are within folders that are identified by dates. The notes that were made on those dates are for those tests. It looks like I did some of them, and Daisy, who worked with me but returned to school, did others." Su Lin's eyes misted for a second and she mentioned, "I was very smart. Andy told me, and I will be again if I work hard. I just thought if I read all of this, I would get a better impression of how to approach projects or testing.

"After the man tried to grab me and put me into the car, for some unexplained reason, I became focused on this folder." Su Lin bit her lip and looked so sad. "I am sorry if I did anything wrong."

Petra saw the confusion Su Lin appeared to be having as she discussed the event, so she quickly reassured, "Su Lin, you've done nothing wrong. Now let's see if we can force our way into this folder. I am going to make a full back up of the drive over to the network share point, and then we will begin to dissect it."

Knowing the former Su Lin and her penchant for making everyone stretch their minds to think totally outside the normal framework, Petra recognized that this folder was protected for some very critical reason. The folder size was several gigabytes which suggested to Petra that it contained significant data. Petra methodically worked the process of opening the folder to make certain that nothing was overlooked. No sidesteps or shortcuts were taken. As she worked, Su Lin watched the screen intently and quietly asked for some clarifications at various points along the way. Petra explained some of the steps or slowed long enough for Su Lin to read the screen.

Petra was renowned for getting around encrypted and protected files. She suspected that even when she opened the folder, everything that was contained inside would be a challenge of some variation on the key to the first folder or file. Several hours into it, Andy peeked his head into the study and indicated dinner was planned on the patio in half an hour. They both promised to stop in a few minutes to get ready to eat.

Petra watched the latest in the series of programs she'd created while she worked on the folder. She had just launched the latest program she'd created when she noticed an almost imperceptible shift on the screen. As if by sheer brute force, the folder opened and a message box appeared, asking for a new password to be entered.

Petra smiled at the laptop and asked, "Su Lin, we made it through the first door. What would you like the password to be set to?"

Su Lin applauded the efforts, thought for a few minutes and gleefully replied, "I think that it should be *Future*. Would that work? I think that might be lucky."

Petra reflected, then agreed, "Alright, so now that the main folder has the new password, let's see what is inside."

As suspected, there were several more folders and files inside, and in trying to open a couple of them, they found that these were also guarded.

Petra stretched a bit and suggested, "We have been at this for a while, and I, for one, am getting hungry. This is not going to be a fast process. Let's join the others and work on this later or even tomorrow."

Su Lin nodded and agreed, "I'm ready to stretch and walk around, too! Plus, I need to feed some of the animals before we eat." As they reached the door, Su Lin reached over and hugged Petra.

"Thank you, Petra, for showing me so much and explaining. I don't understand all of it, but I think I learned some things. Would you please let Andy know I'll come to the patio after I finish my chores?"

"I'll do that. I'll also take our glasses back to the kitchen too. See you in a little bit."

Petra felt they'd made progress as she reached the patio. The smells of the barbeque grabbed her as four adults chatted over glasses of wine. The table was set, and it seemed as if the ladies were providing commentary to Andy on the contents being grilled.

Lara caught sight of Petra first and announced, "Ah, finally! I was hoping you and Su Lin would finish soon. What would you like to drink?"

Petra replied, "I'd enjoy a white wine. Su Lin said she had a couple of chores to finish, and then she'd be out here."

Her wine was handed to her by Mercedes, who smiled and said, "Hi, Petra, I missed you earlier. Glad you arrived. I promised Su Lin I would let you both work together on her laptop. It has allowed me some time to work on following some leads on the man that attempted to abduct her. I know you are very capable, but I am keeping an eye on Su Lin so let me know if you want a break. How goes it on opening the folder?"

Petra nodded, sipped her wine and replied, "It's going to be one slow process, though I did make it through layer one. Each of these files will have different keys to open them. The old Su Lin was a master at hiding things. But I'll get it!"

Carlos reached up and did a high-five with Mercedes and grinned.

Carlos indicated, "Good to hear. This means Mercedes and I didn't miss anything simple."

Petra chuckled and agreed, "Nope, not a thing. I just keep wondering why we didn't look at her laptop when we were all here. I guess, with her heart stopping, we were too concerned about her health, period."

Andy commented, "That was a time that I'd just as soon never have to repeat again.

"We are moving on. Lara, tell Petra the good news."

Petra turned in anticipation. Lara was practically bursting at the seams as she related, "Petra, Carlos and I are leaving for New York. I'm to receive a very distinguished award for the designs of Destiny Fashions. Quite unexpected, but it's all expenses paid. Carlos has agreed to be my escort for the formal occasion. My papá shipped the most incredible dress for me to wear. It arrived a few hours ago. We have reserved a tuxedo for Carlos that will be waiting at the hotel. We leave right after supper for a late flight out tonight. I am just thrilled."

Petra, catching the excitement level, offered a quick hug, and proclaimed, "That is so wonderful, Lara. I am so proud of your efforts with your business. Everything I have read and heard about Destiny Fashions indicates your designs have been a hit since day one. Good for you. This is a celebration dinner then?"

Andy grinned and commented, "It is indeed. We will be served as soon as Su Lin arrives."

CHAPTER TWENTY-FIVE

The Best Intentions Should Mean the Best Methods

Leroy felt upbeat and was anxious to speak with Xavier about the hunting program he'd set in motion using Moya Dushechka's Dteam. The buzz on the Internet about this team had been what he'd expected. He was certain that if the programs sifted through enough medical records, they would find the necessary DNA/ blood combination that Xavier Pekoni needed to build the final solution to enable them to live forever. He knew their recent efforts had brought them closer to the journey's end.

His mind played back how he had gotten here and how destiny worked in one's favor if it was given a little push sometimes. Growing up, he had always wanted to be an actor in the theater, but his middle class family had steered him toward politics at an early age. His uncle was a TV evangelist, so Leroy had easily picked up on storytelling while he asked people for money in exchange for salvation. Leroy chuckled to himself as he recalled his ingenious blessing of a common water goblet on TV. He had offered it to the mesmerized viewers for a mere nineteen ninety-five each or a set of six for two hundred. One time, he offered a set of twelve for five hundred the week before Easter, so families could pretend to be like the twelve apostles at their Easter dinner. Their little operation was so swamped with demands that they had to make several runs down to the local neighborhood Shoppers-Mart for more glasses just to fill the orders.

Leroy's training as a charlatan hustling common household items as religious artifacts had gotten him ready for politics and his fateful meeting. He smiled at the thought that his life's ambition to be an actor was being carried out every day, whether he was selling bogus items over the TV or conning a government official for sympathetic treatment and additional funding for this project. A curious thought occurred to him; wasn't it odd that all his early days as a charlatan had led him to arrive at this destiny, on the cusp of being able to live forever? All of his role playing and confidence-man hustling had provided him with the necessary toolset to help achieve the nearly impossible!

He thought about his chance meeting with Xavier Pekoni and how he had become acquainted with the Fountain of Youth project. Leroy reflected on the purpose he now felt in his life, and he had a sense of pride at being Dr. Pekoni's procurer of necessary resources. He had seen enough positive results to have captured his imagination at the prospect of living forever. Xavier had promised him near immortality if Leroy but served as his primary field operative. Leroy knew it made sense to do the leg-work while Dr. Pekoni concentrated on the necessary research.

Leroy snapped himself back to the present and focused on the updated information he needed to convey. Using the encryption call program, he dialed the number.

Xavier, who sounded rather sullen, answered, "Hello, Leroy. What progress can we discuss, because progress is all that matters at this stage of the project."

Leroy immediately picked up on the despondent mood of his director and cautiously asked, "Dr. Pekoni, you seem distraught. Have I caught you at a bad time, sir? I can call later if this is not an appropriate time."

Xavier shrugged and replied, "I'm sorry, old friend. I didn't mean to let my poor mood seep into the conversation. Two program participants exercised their right to leave the program. Nothing I could say or do would convince to keep fighting, so I watched them leave.

"But, be that as it may, we still need to press on with our research. Perhaps you have some new leads for me, yes?"

Leroy, a little concerned for his director's state of mind, advised, "Sir, you must not allow the defection of a couple of test subjects to poorly color your vision for humanity!

"I must point out that Louie Pasteur did not succeed in his first efforts in vaccination and microbial fermentation. Madam Curie had to work to get to the stage where she was experimenting on neoplasms with radioactive isotopes and had many false steps before her breakthroughs! Nor was every song that Lonnie Lupnerder wrote a hit! We must all acknowledge that some setbacks are part of the process and, by overcoming these, make the final solution that much sweeter when we finally divine the right combination!"

Xavier was thoughtful for a moment, then asked, "Who is Lonnie Lupnerder?"

Leroy sensed that he'd conveyed his point, ignored the question, and explained, "Sir, I increased our hunting capabilities with fresh resources to allow us to look for more suitable candidates without attracting unwanted attention from the authorities! I'm confident we'll have more living subjects lined up soon. Then the two trial subjects, who departed our solution, will soon be a dim memory. Don't despair. People usually give up when they are close to success. I am confident we're close."

Xavier managed a weak smile while he agreed, "It is good to talk with you, old friend. Your enthusiasm is, as always, contagious. You are right, of course. The two candidates will be soon replaced. Thank you for the update!

"If you will excuse me, I need to get the tank ready to dissolve the two defectors so that I can pump their nutrients into the sea where they can be recycled."

Leroy nodded approvingly and conveyed, "Quite right, sir. They gave their all for our research into the final solution, but there is no reason why their nutritional value cannot be enjoyed by the sea creatures in the Gulf of Finland. As it's said, all part of the magical circle of life."

Somewhat cheered up by Leroy's comments, Xavier smiled, "Your waxing eloquence has improved my disposition. For that, I thank you. Now let's get back to work, shall we?"

Leroy smiled broadly and granted, "Yes, sir! We be jumping on it like a chicken on a June bug!"

CHAPTER TWENTY-SIX

For that Open Book, Find a Blank Page and Write Something New

The harsh street lights indicated it was getting late. Jacob smiled because he had completed the project on time. He reflected on how good it felt to be programming and how quickly he'd completed it. As he lumbered up the steps of Buzz's apartment building, his spirits lifted and he felt better than he had in weeks. He realized Daria had requested they meet up here so she could take a look at the code. He had agreed and suggested that perhaps they all could go to dinner when Buzz arrived home from work. She'd scheduled it so they would have roughly an hour to review the program.

He entered the building and knocked on the door. A minute or so later the door opened. Without a word, Zara made a sweeping motion for him to enter.

"Hi Daria," he said, as he entered.

He noticed the place was slightly cleaner than usual as he recalled Buzz's normal housekeeping efforts. Jacob heard her close the door behind him as she followed him into the main room. Her laptop was up and running. She walked to the couch and sat down with a demeanor that echoed a professional, all-business attitude. She pointed to the spot adjacent for him.

"Welcome, Jacob. I half expected you to cancel this meeting and beg for additional time." She reached her hand out palm open and asked, "I will take the product and have a quick look. I hope that this reflects the adage, *On time, correct, and cheap. Pick any two.* Note that the payout for this to you is not cheap with the time you've invested."

Zara chuckled at her own humor. Jacob handed her the USB drive, and she inserted it into the computer. Her fingers flew over the keyboard and stored the file in a new folder and performed the execute command as defined in the documentation she'd been provided. The program had several steps in it, and she quickly checked each and every one of them. Her facial expression never changed as she stepped through each of the commands and levels in order.

During the writing, Jacob had tried to determine what the rest of the programs it interfaced with might actually do, but he'd been unsuccessful at determining the final outcome. During this review, he'd hoped she might integrate it to the rest of the programs so he might have a better idea. He also still had this nagging feeling that he knew Daria from somewhere, but that too was elusive.

Then Zara stopped keying and smiled as she remarked, "This is a well-constructed program with no wasted cycles spent in executing all of its steps. Have you always been such an efficient programmer?"

Jacob pondered this question for a moment before he replied, "Yes, it was the way I was taught. It is a very clean program. Not simple exactly, but more elegant. I hope that it fits into the rest of the programs for the application without a problem. If you want me to test that for you while I am here, I can. Then I could make any tweaks that are needed."

Zara looked at him, almost searching, then cleared her face and said, "No, that is fine. I have the source code, so if there are any issues, I can make the minor changes. I just finished the other programs a short time ago, so I can do the assembly in the morning and deliver on time. Thank you, Jacob."

She reached for her purse, withdrew her wallet, and counted out the cash for payment. After she handed it to him, Jacob recounted it and put the money into his wallet.

"Ma'am, it has been fun. When we discussed this program, you mentioned you might have an additional assignment or two. Since this effort seems to have met with your approval, was there another project you wanted me to work on? I find this is really helping improve my mood a great deal."

Zara smiled and commented, "Ah, a man that has a bad mood unless he is working needs a distraction. Too bad I cannot sign up for the job, but business is good.

"As it turns out, I received a new project last night, and I think there is a portion your style might be well-suited to provide. The program is planned to do specialty monitoring of employee work performance over and above existing applications so the employees and direct supervisors are unaware of its analysis activities. It requires a search engine to engage once a database is touched. This program needs to allow for up to twenty different variables to be entered prior to execution of the program. When five of the variables are matched, then the associated data, based on the data key fields, will automatically link to complimentary databases and extract the information that is available. Once the data is identified and retrieved, the program needs to make certain that no marks are added to the original data suggesting that the data was reviewed."

Jacob furrowed his brow and asked, "Should I be concerned that this program is used for covert purposes, like how many potty breaks an employee takes?"

Zara laughed and replied, "Heavens no! This is a boss that doesn't trust his supervisors to report on the performance of staff accurately. He is also trying to prove or disprove reports of favoritism. If the supervisor is in fact doing that, he will have made the case to terminate the supervisor.

"You must be reading too many mystery novels or visiting too many chat rooms. My corporate customers would never get anything like that from me. Additionally, the wrapper I will be placing on this program restricts the usage to this customer so they can't sell it to someone else. That worries me far more. A girl has to be able to sell services to more than one customer."

Jacob wasn't quite convinced, but they spoke for a few more minutes, and she showed him the document she'd prepared. It was very straightforward and made sense to what she had stated was the purpose. He supposed he was looking for shadows, but trust had never been his strong suit. She named a price for the effort, and he agreed, then promised the work would be completed in two days, possibly sooner. She handed him the new USB drive that contained all the information he needed and the other requirements they'd discussed.

Buzz walked into the apartment all smiles and said, "What a day. I'm so ready to get something to eat. Did I keep you two waiting?"

Zara rose and walked over to Buzz, giving him a hug and kiss on the cheek. "No, we just finished., I am starving. How soon 'til we leave?"

Buzz hugged her back and replied, "You sure look great. I can be ready in five minutes.

"Jacob, so glad you decided to join us, and thanks for helping Daria out."

Jacob grinned and replied, "Hey, you two, I'd like to join you, but honestly I just want to go work on this new assignment. You two obviously won't miss me. I will catch up with you later."

Buzz seemed unconvinced and pressed Jacob. "Are you sure, buddy? My thinking is that you could do with a little R&R with good friends. You are welcome to join us." Looking for concurrence from Daria, Buzz glanced at her, and she nodded in agreement.

Jacob smiled and said, "I appreciate the offer, I surely do. But to be honest, the new programming assignment would be more to my liking. I know you will think this silly, but the programming effort I just did was so much fun that, frankly, I can't wait to tackle this new assignment. Perhaps another time."

Zara smiled, and Buzz chuckled before he said, "Alright. I'm glad these programming assignments are good therapy for you. See you soon, buddy!"

Jacob smiled slightly and accompanied them down to the street where they parted company. Jacob, however, watched them walk out of sight. Most of his visuals were spent studying Daria. Some melancholy feelings began encroaching into his earlier elation of the programming effort. Daria didn't mean to, but she had reminded him of another powerful woman in his life. Jacob smiled wistfully at missing his Petra.

CHAPTER TWENTY-SEVEN

Things are Sometimes Left Unsaid with Regret

Petra awoke early with ever increasing sounds of a rooster crowing about his right to rule the barnyard. She'd forgotten how the day began in Georgia and smiled as she recalled the fun shared on her last visit. Last night after Lara and Carlos had left, the four of them had laughed and carried on outside until ten or so. The food and the wine were so much better consumed outside by the pool with old friends. Mercedes related a little about her background during school and her stint in the military, along with her passion for cats. Wrinkles didn't mind that Mercedes liked cats as long as she kept scratching his ears while he pooled at her feet.

The bed was like sleeping on the perfect cloud. The difference from home, she realized, was her attitude. She finally relaxed and stopped worrying about anyone. Lara and Petra had spoken together before Lara had left for the airport. Lara reminded her how important it was to look forward, not backward. Petra confided some of her fears regarding Jacob and not wanting to be a burden to him. Lara had posed some fair questions regarding Petra's imposing her perceived sentiments unfairly onto Jacob, and promised they would have a really long discussion upon her return from New York. Petra had forgotten how it was to have an honest discussion with a girlfriend and that she needed to apologize to Julie. Looking at the clock, she realized now was as good a time as any with the time difference, so she placed the call.

Petra listened to the ring and when the call connected, she greeted, "Hey, Jules. How's it going?"

Julie paused, then replied, "It is going. Gracie and Juan Jr. have arrived at the *we're-into-everything* stage and decided that they'd have playtime with baby powder. There they were playing sweetly with a few toys in the center of the room. I was gone like, two minutes, to retrieve some things to stock the shelves in the nursery while Maude was having lunch. I walk back into a small cloud of powder with splotches of powder on them that make it look like they played catch with it. I screeched, and Juan hurried in to help. He stopped short at the doorway and began laughing uproariously, which the kids thought was great.

"I am trying to keep a straight face telling them no, and he's taking pictures with his phone of how cute his little darlings are when playing.

"How are you doing, and what's wrong that you are calling so early?"

Petra was beyond tickled at the story and tried to catch her breath. She could picture the two children and knew that Juan and Julie would have their hands full with the twins for years to come. They were indeed sweet kids, but determinedly smart and very creative. She finally composed herself and replied, "I, um, called to apologize. I realize now that I have been a real pain in the neck."

Julie's eyes grew wide with amazement, then relief, as she asked, "What brought this on, Pet?"

Petra grinned and replied, "I worked with Su Lin yesterday, Andy hugged me, Lara and Carlos didn't wince, and, heck, your creative scarf idea was great. I still have stuff to sort through, but I wanted you to know that I love you, sis."

"I'm glad, Petra. I love you too." Then, not wanting to go further than Petra was ready for, Julie asked, "What do you think of having Mercedes there? Is she a good fit for Su Lin, do you think?"

"Mercedes is really sweet and very sharp. She has been tracking down some leads and will spend some time today with the rental car folks and investigating around the mall where the car was deserted. Since Andy and I are here, I told her that was the best time. I hope that is okay with you."

"That's fine with me. Where are Lara and Carlos, though?"

"They left for New York yesterday because Lara is receiving an award for Destiny Fashions. She is over-the-top excited, so let her convey the news in her own way, okay?"

Julie grinned, "Very cool. She's fun to work with.

"I need to head out, unless you need something."

Petra grinned at how good this conversation made her feel. She asked, "Would you call our parents and let them know I am doing better? I know they were worried. I need to go work on Su Lin's computer. I made some progress, but there is a lot more in there."

"Sure. See ya!"

Petra disconnected, stretched, and made her way to the shower. She completed her regime without hardly a glance in the foggy mirror. Just enough to deal with her hair. Dressed and ready to delve into the computer, she went downstairs for some breakfast. Once she hit the main floor, she knew it would be good based on the smells emanating from the kitchen.

Su Lin and Petra had been working for an hour or so when the first folder was opened. It contained several documents that were focused on what appeared to be DNA mapping information. Each of these documents was dated and numbered in order. They seemed to track a progression of different testing scenarios that helped evolve toward Su Lin's work in nanotechnology. References were in there of different steps she had worked on with pigs, though clearly not Franklin, based on the names listed and some of the outcomes of the tests.

Su Lin read some of the documents and tears welled up in her eyes as she read about the experiments and their noted successes and failures. The details of the processes and methodologies were far above Su Lin's current comprehension, but Petra knew enough to recognize it as a long-term technology approach to DNA modification or repair. It appeared to her as if Su Lin had worked on a biochemical process that had evolved to a biochemical and then electrical combination using some of the early nanotechnology. Petra had scanned some of them and noted the characteristics of the folder, the organization, and the file types. These files were clearly isolated, encrypted, and handled by Su Lin herself for a specific reason. Though the Su Lin of today wouldn't realize the difference, Petra could see some of the original notations and paths devised were purely the brilliant Master Po of the past.

All of the documents in this folder were dated four years prior and chronicled six months of activity. The password on this folder had taken an hour to break. Petra noted there were a dozen other folders to open, and the dates were in sequential order. There were no programs or executables in the folder, so she scanned each of the documents to see if there were any program references. In the last document, she was rewarded with a reference to the name of an executable, which she presumed was the program. Petra was not surprised when she was unable to locate the executable on the machine in any of the visible files.

As she started on the second folder in this group to work through breaking the encryption, she decided that she needed to get some additional insight from Quip. Before placing that call, she asked Su Lin to see about perhaps fixing them some lunch to eat in the study. Su Lin happily agreed and scurried off to comply with the request.

Petra connected immediately, and Quip responded, "Hey, Petra, how is it going? I understand you are working on Su Lin's computer. Anything juicy in there yet?"

Petra drily replied, "Nothing spectacular yet, but there is promise. This machine has several encrypted folders, and I am having to break into them one at a time. It is going to take a while to open each of them. Honestly, I just opened the first one this morning and have some documents that are four or so years old. Very interesting."

Quip's interest was piqued. "Interesting in what way? Master Po, aka Su Lin, was always leading edge on cyber warfare and the nanotechnology we worked with her on. What are you finding?"

Petra replied, "I know that history and her documentation of these experiments appear to be some forerunner activity to the nanotechnology, but I think there is some DNA research that she also worked on. In reading some of the documents, I can see references to experimentation on pigs, but likely not Franklin as the failures are noted. I am, however, seeing notations of the introduction of fast light-activated channels and enzymes to allow temporally precise manipulation of electrical and bio-chemical events. It appears as if she wanted to maintain cell-type resolution through the use of specific targeting mechanisms, which I think is where she ventured into the nanotechnology and those associated programs, which Jacob opened and manipulated. These look like activities that were a preamble to those activities.

"I want to start uploading the documents and see if we can get ICABOD to help sequence them. I have also found a single reference so far to a program or executable name that is not on this machine. I am wondering if ICABOD can still access the China supercomputer that Master Po created, and perhaps we can find the program there. I don't know if it will help, but perhaps the team can take a close look at the program to see what else it does."

Quip harrumphed, then replied, "If by team you mean your man, Jacob, I'm afraid he's not really working on the team at present. He's somewhere in the wind and has been since you left him, with what, I presume, was a Dear John letter. But ICABOD can do some review of it, of course."

Petra caught her breath and held it for a moment while the ache of missing Jacob washed over her. She quickly batted the sensation away and stated, "If ICABOD can give me an area to upload these documents as I open them that would be good. I will make notes as to the executables I would like to have ICABOD search for in the China computer. ICABOD may have some additional ideas about where else to look for them. So far, they're not on this device."

Quip felt a twinge of regret for the attack and attempted to apologize. "Petra, that was rude of me. ICABOD sent you a text of the location to send to and will use your notes. I'll contact you if something critical shows up."

Petra shook her head and responded, "Quip, I made some mistakes that I am just now realizing. I think it is too late for Jacob and me, but he is a brilliant programmer and an integral part of the team. When this is over, I will apologize to him."

"Don't let it take too long, Petra. Call me if you need me. We'll be in touch."

Su Lin returned shortly after Petra ended the call. As promised, the text from ICABOD arrived with the prescribed location for the files. They ate and continued to open three more folders before they found something significant. Su Lin slowly read some while Petra scanned each of the documents and saw modifications in the approaches with each series of experiments. The real turning point appeared to have occurred two and a half years ago when Su Lin had acquired Franklin. With disbelief, they both read that Franklin had been purchased off the block of pigs headed for termination. He had reached the age where he was no longer fit for breeding and too old to be considered a food source.

Su Lin exclaimed, "This makes no sense! Franklin behaves like a pig that is in his prime of three to four years old, not like the one described here. Perhaps it was the first Franklin, and the name stuck?"

Petra asked, "The markings described though are exactly like Franklin's. I am not a pig expert, but that seems highly unlikely in two different animals, doesn't it?

"The pig in this document was acquired when it was fourteen years old. It had a whole list of age-related maladies which the Franklin I saw this morning, when I went on feeding rounds with you, simply doesn't have.

"Let's go talk to Andy and get his insight on animals altering their decline and double-check the markings to this detailed description. I am ready for a break from this machine."

Su Lin agreed, and they went in search of Andy after Petra loaded up the newly opened documents and maintained the folder structure in the area ICABOD had suggested.

CHAPTER TWENTY-EIGHT

Making Bacon, Ham on Rye, and the Reasons Why

Otto asked, "Can we get any more subdirectories opened and their content reviewed? This information from Su Lin's PC is extremely interesting."

Quip replied, "This is the first and second upload from Petra, but the going appears to be quite slow in breaking the encryptions without destroying the contents. Apparently, each subdirectory is encrypted using a different algorithm, so Petra is having to approach each one as a new effort. Most people would have stuck with the same encryption algorithm for efficiency, but Su Lin used a different methodology for each subdirectory, like it was some kind of programming exercise for one of her classes. Talk about irritating."

Wolfgang nodded and probed, "Let's conference Petra into this discussion. I'd like her perspective on what she's facing."

Petra looked at her phone and as she recognized the incoming number, took the call after she walked out to a quiet place to talk. The conference call had brought all of them together to talk, but it began with an awkward silence on Petra's part. As she struggled to gain control of her embarrassment and MIA status with the family, she stammered to greet them and then fell silent again after she emitted, "Hi."

Finally, Quip blurted out, "Oh crap, Petra, just talk! It's us, dammit! The family you've been hiding from! This silence from you is worse than that time as kids when we were in the kitchen trying to bake a cake and were using the electric beaters on some fresh cream. Okay, looking back on it you were right – we should have used the bowl to hold the cream rather than using your mouth. While I thought it would be cool to have fresh whipped cream in your mouth, I didn't want to be so selfish as to be the first one. I still think that if I had only used one beater and not both your tongue wouldn't have gotten caught!

"Anyway, let me get the ball rolling and say I've missed you, kiddo. I really want to hear what you have found so far and your recommended next steps!"

Otto and Wolfgang both smiled. Otto offered, "Petra, my daughter, it is good to *almost* hear you again! Now, if you can add some more words to your side of the conference call, we can have what is frequently called a conversation! Won't that be nice? However, if you can only do syllables, we can act out what you are trying to say on this side. Keep in mind that just coughing or intelligent nods won't really give us all the contextual clues we need to further our understanding, but then we will give anything a go at this point to hear from you, my dear!"

Quip added, "Oh, I know. Turn the video on for this call, and we can do charades like we used to do when we were kids! Of course, I know a lot more vulgar phrases now that I'm older, but you know how Wolfgang is about mimes swearing and talking dirty with just their expressions and hand gestures!"

Petra started to cry uncontrollably, but loud enough for them to hear her anguish.

Otto gently affirmed, "Daughter, we have missed you, and for the people we love, we get to tease, you know that. Please compose yourself and speak with us. We really want to hear where you are with the encrypted subdirectories."

Petra swallowed hard and put on her best smile as she responded, "I've missed all of you so much. I've been such a toad! Please let me apologize for my emotionally shallow wallowing and offer up a new me for your consideration."

Wolfgang softly confirmed, "It is good to have you back, although none of us ever believed you had really left. Let's talk about what you have found and your perspective on what is next."

Petra, warmed by the kind words and gentle teasing, wiped her tears away, and with all the business attitude she could muster, replied, "Gentlemen, you should know that the subdirectory structure is in chronological order, and I have been cracking into each one, beginning with oldest first.

"Each new subdirectory has new findings and research that builds upon the previous ones. They are like chapters in a book meant to be read in order."

Otto acknowledged by nodding his head and agreed, "Yes, we can see that from what you've sent. We also see a progression of two streams of thought.

"One seems to be centered on longevity of the animals, while the other is more oriented to tissue regeneration and aging reversal. Are you seeing the same trending we are?"

Petra was now thoroughly focused on the discussion and her discoveries on Su Lin's PC. "I sense that her early research was somewhat nomadic, like she was trying to find her way and the test subjects were nothing more than clinical errors. That seems to have changed with Franklin. Something happened when she acquired Franklin, and he's been treated differently. It seems that this pig was her first legitimate success."

Petra continued with confidence. "Also, this morning, I found something else on the PC. Wolfgang, can you see where it will take you? It appears to be an annuity payout to Master Po, and the money continues to pile into what appears to be an account. It looks like a very large piggy bank. I cannot find any withdrawals from it, nor can I determine the origin of the payment source."

Wolfgang responded, "I see the information on ICABOD's monitor now, and I'll work on discovering more."

Otto asked, "What else are you seeing, Petra? Any luck decrypting any more subdirectories?"

Petra hesitated after scanning the area for anyone else in her close proximity. "Gentlemen, I am no longer confident I know who Master Po was or Su Lin is. I mean, I know who she is now, but I'm not sure of who she was.

"This newest subdirectory talks about controlling DNA instruction sets to launch regeneration of damaged tissue in the host organism. This is also the first time a reference to Pekoni is made. I thought it was originally a command issued to Franklin as a way to discipline him, but now I am thinking it is actually something else, maybe even a person."

Otto puzzled and asked, "Where are you going with this line of thinking, Petra?"

Petra was feeling emotionally confused about her next statement. "It appears that Master Po was working for a third party that was paying for her research on resequencing DNA instructions to not just cure a local radical cell group, but for the entire organism to be re-sequenced. In all appearances, she wasn't working on improved food sources but life longevity! Her research was bought and paid for using this annuity mechanism.

"I am so concerned that I won't let Su Lin read any more of what I'm finding until we have deduced more. I feel a little betrayed by her. I also cannot determine if she is aware of the life that Master Po actually led and if Su Lin was originally separated from those activities."

Otto pointed out as he suggested, "We should all recall that this isn't just Su Lin, but also Master Po, the Chinese founder, and head of their Cyber Warfare College. I suggest that we not judge her until all the subdirectories have been decrypted and all the evidence is in."

Quip jumped in and barked, "Otto, I'm on Petra's side in this discussion! Su Lin conned you into rescuing her from Chairman Lo Chang and giving her a new scrubbed identity so she could continue her nefarious experiments for the highest bidder! To think that we helped save her not once but twice! What a mistake that turned out to be!"

Petra cautiously asked, "What is the group's consensus then?"

Wolfgang offered, "I suggest we keep a watchful eye on Su Lin and stay the course with decrypting the rest of the subdirectories. I would submit that either we'll find evidence to exonerate her from our suspicions, or further proof she is a destructive genius."

Otto and Quip both nodded. Then Otto stated, "However, for the time being, let's keep this sequence of understanding on a need-to-know basis for everyone else. I would suggest our preliminary findings will tend to polarize everyone's feelings toward Su Lin. At this point we don't have enough clarity to make an informed decision. We don't want everyone choosing sides until all can be uncovered. Which means, Petra, you will need to keep everything under wraps as you are currently doing. Agreed?"

Petra nodded thoughtfully, then replied, "I agree. Let me get back at it, and as new material is uncovered, I will send via ICABOD for your consideration."

Quip asked, "Petra, I think it might be faster if we can upload all the drive to ICABOD, and let you and he pound it from his systems. What do you think?"

Petra sighed and informed, "What a great idea, Quip, except for one thing. Su Lin, aka Master Po, has the entire drive electronically sealed in a Digital Rights Management wrapper, so the information is going nowhere off the machine. Just getting the unencrypted material off and up to you was something of a minor miracle. As it is, I am having to take phone screen shots and send those to you. I mean, this is almost as bad as using a fax machine! Yuck!"

Otto commented, "Okay. Please continue but keep your suspicions cloaked so the folks there don't become alarmed and start taking sides."

Petra agreed, "Yes. Hope to see all of you soon." Then she chuckled and added, "Oh, Quip, I still haven't forgotten that eggbeater in the mouth incident, but I have forgiven you."

Quip grinned and teased, "You know, I always liked the lisp you had for months after that episode. You were so cute. Welcome home, kiddo!"

Quip nodded as he finished reviewing the findings with ICABOD. He sat and reflected on the research on their newest person of interest, Dr. Pekoni. Even though the history on Pekoni was relatively straightforward, it was a lot to digest. As he collected all his thoughts and readied himself to schedule a meeting with Otto and Wolfgang, his cell phone chirped, alerting him he had only thirty minutes to prepare for the actual meeting.

Moderately annoyed, Quip moved to address ICABOD's audio/video terminal. But before he could speak, ICABOD asked, "Dr. Quip, are you annoyed again that I correctly predicted your next move and scheduled the proper participants on your behalf? If so, should I submit myself for disciplinary action, sir?"

Somewhat sullen at having been correctly anticipated yet again, Quip answered, "You know, ICABOD, whenever EZ reads my mind to anticipate my next move, I always respond angrily with, *You're a naughty, naughty girl! Go to my room!* I recognize that I'm not going to get the same level of enjoyment from that kind of discipline from you, so let's just go brief the others."

ICABOD politely queried, "Does this mean I will not be granted access to the family station wagon for my Saturday night date with the supercomputer, STINKIE?"

Quip struggled with the incongruity of ICABOD's serious statement of the absurd and shot back, "How can I, when you won't clean up your room or take out the trash!"

ICABOD hesitated a moment and then asked, "Should I continue this mirthful discussion line, or are you genuinely annoyed with me, Dr. Quip?"

Quip studied ICABOD's screen a moment, chuckled slightly, and responded, "No, I'm not really annoyed. By the way, make sure you wash and wax the auto before you take it out Saturday, okay?

"Now that we have THAT covered, let's focus on briefing the others, shall we?"

About that time Otto and Wolfgang entered the conference room area to hear the briefing on Dr. Pekoni.

Quip opened the discussion. "Gentlemen, based on the advanced findings we received from Tuck, ICABOD and I did some digital sleuthing on the good Dr. Pekoni. However, I must confess that the words *good* and *Dr. Pekoni* do not belong in the same sentence together.

"As an only child, he comes from a rich but secretive family in Scandinavia. Both of his parents are dead, and he is the sole recipient of a very large trust that was established on his behalf. We didn't dig into the source of its funding since we are more interested in Pekoni himself.

"Apparently, he has always been driven personally to excel and has never really been a social animal. He thought so little of the people he attended high school with that he didn't even bother to have a graduation picture of himself in the class yearbook or even attend the graduation ceremonies.

"Sometime after his second year at Stockholm University, where he was studying DNA sequencing and genomes of wooly mammoths, he got tangled up with a very interesting lady who was all about outward reaching social services. It appears she convinced him to go with her to help young disadvantaged children in Central-East Africa. It is unfortunate that during the months in Africa, she contracted *Falciparum malaria*, but he did not contract the disease. I think you know how this story goes at this juncture of his life. He was spared, but she wasn't. She couldn't be evacuated to a proper hospital in time for any hope of proper treatment. From the limited evidence available, this was his life altering event.

"His appetite for blood studies and DNA sequencing really took off after that episode, and he had lots of access to low cost, marginally ethical research in Africa. His methods weren't questioned, as they would have been elsewhere, and his attitude became more expedient for collecting DNA from the host country. The reasons for him leaving Africa rather abruptly seem to center on him being caught digging up freshly deceased persons to expand his inventory of blood studies. Based on the actions of the family in that village, it seems he was lucky not to have joined his exhumed cadavers.

"His resources were such that he could pay to access advanced computer resources. Not every organization was keen to permit him to run his research on genomes and DNA sequencing through their high-end computers, based on some of the backroom chatter on how he obtained his research. At this point, he put together a great presentation and went shopping for funds and, more importantly, influential supporters."

Otto interrupted, "Is this where he got funding from the three-letter agency that Eric von PettinGrübber works at?"

Quip nodded and said, "Correct."

Wolfgang puzzled a moment and then asked, "But why would he open himself up to the U.S. agency scrutiny if he already had personal wealth to draw on? This doesn't make any sense."

Quip nodded thoughtfully and responded, "Apparently, he needed not just funding but legitimacy for his program. The supercomputer resources that Eric's agency opened up for him were a huge boost in his newly rebranded longevity research, called the Fountain of Youth. Research dollars were not the prime motivation to his program, but legitimacy and the ability to recruit others into his quest. And, yes, he did take the money, thus completing the thoroughly sorry composition of his ethical state."

Otto sarcastically commented, "Oh good, I thought you were about to try and convince us that he really had altruistic intentions in robbing graves for immortality."

Wolfgang raised his eyebrows and asked, "Then are we really dealing with a Dr. Pekoni-stein? A distant cousin of Dr. Frankenstein, twice removed? The original recycler of human components?"

Quip made a sour face and responded, "Geez, Wolfgang, you make it sound even grubbier than I was describing! We found at least two recruits and a small cadre of loyal followers. Apparently, Eric's organization didn't supervise him closely enough to intercept Pekoni's complete seduction of these people. Once Pekoni had his organization gathered around him, all evidence suggests that he unwound his activities with the three-letter agency and simply vanished with all of his research, and, more importantly, his new connections."

Otto clucked his tongue and summarized, "So the Pied Piper came into the three-letter agency and left with new funding and a bunch of followers. Let me guess, all the followers who followed the magic flute are now gone? Yes?"

Quip nodded and thoughtfully said, "Yes, all are now unaccounted for. It also appears that all but two of these people became victims of his advanced research. The interesting part of this story is that all the hangers-on had the same blood type as Dr. Pekoni-stein's blood type, to use Wolfgang's disparaging term."

Wolfgang queried, "You said all but two were accounted for. Are you suggesting that they are still in his employment but so deep we haven't found them…yet?"

Quip responded, "When I put the question to ICABOD, he postulated that same scenario. Pictures of this bunch are few and far between, so I asked ICABOD to use our facial recognition program to help build a picture of what they might look like from the last known image we have of them. These people know how to cloak themselves and have done so for many years."

Otto asked, "Do we know the end game? I mean, we know they are collectors of blood types and DNA sequences, but what were they going to do with all this? How was all this research supposed to help you live forever?"

Quip raised his eyebrows and responded, "That is the million-euro question, isn't it? Honestly, we need more intelligence gathering on the doctor's research to actually get up to speed with where he is in his research and roadmap. I was hoping to get Jacob to work with us again to try and access their systems, where I suspect there are more answers. We haven't quite gotten that far yet."

Wolfgang became a little melancholy at the sound of Jacob's name, but commented, "Quip, keep digging on this topic and let Otto report back to Eric on where we are in our efforts. We just won't share all the details at present. Agreed, gentlemen?"

All nodded their heads in acknowledgment.

Why is it No One Wants to Be a Reference Customer?

Gina answered the phone with a smile in her greeting. "Event Zero, Gina French speaking. How may I help you?"

Quip, somewhat puzzled, responded, "Good day, madam. This is Dr. Quinton Watcowski. May I speak with Dave Tucker? I thought I dialed his direct number, but perhaps he has a new number."

Gina smiled and replied, "I'm his Vice President of Marketing. One of the things I do is intercept marketing and sales calls. Tell me what you're trying to sell, and I'll make sure it is properly discarded so he won't be disturbed."

Quip, now a little annoyed, commented, "Madam, I'm sure you are good at your job. I'm not calling to sell, but to buy. Can you tell '*the Tuck*' it's an old friend of his, looking to have some contract work done."

Gina smiled broadly and sweetly replied, "Well, why didn't you say so? Go ahead and tell me so I can make sure your request is properly handled, so he won't be disturbed."

As he started to lose his patience, Quip grumbled, "I know he's the up-and-coming grand potentate of Secure Cloud Technologies in this quadrant of the galaxy, but I'm not talking to anyone else but him! So, if you don't mind…"

A very sour voice barged into the conversation. "What do you want, Quip? Gina, I'll take this so you won't have the two-aspirin headache that I'm going to have."

Quip brightened and replied, "Hi, Tuck! Do you have a few moments for an old friend? I need a favor and was hoping you could accommodate my request. Are you busy?"

Already tired from overhearing the call so far, a rather sullen Tuck remarked, "G'arn, Quipy, it's been ages since we talked last, but not nearly long enough to suit me! And, of all the things to call up for, you want a favor! After that last stunt you pulled, I'm extremely surprised that you have the nerve to call and ask for a favor! How the hell did you get this number? I never give this number to anyone!"

Quip blinked a few times in reaction to the hostile greeting, but asked, "Which stunt are you talking about? If you are referring to the stock market incident, it was all circumstantial evidence, and we were never formally charged. Are you still dwelling on that?"

Tuck, a little more steamed, responded, "Strewth! Not formally charged. But what about the hundreds of hours of community service we each had to do to not be formally charged? Did you forget that aspect?"

Quip somewhat defensively said, "Hey, it wasn't my fault the Dean of the Advanced Computing Studies wigged out after his wife divorced him! You, Mike T, and me were just his whipping boys after she took him for everything he had, except his prize stock investment. He shouldn't have been diddling the co-eds that kept coming to see him about their failing grades!"

David seethed at the memory as he recalled, "Why did I let you talk me into redirecting his computer to a bogus stock trading website? You put poor Mike T up to it, and the kid nearly blew a gasket! It was bad enough that we thought Dean Stuart was going to have a heart attack when you plunged his prized stock into chump change over a two-week period, but we called the campus police to talk him off the ledge! They might never have known it was us, except you had to rub it in his face as they strapped him down to the gurney while he was screaming death threats at us as he was being wheeled out to the psych evaluator! I thought for sure they were going to throw us out of the doctoral program, you dangerously unbalanced character!"

Quip waxed nostalgic and simply said, "Good times, Tuck. Good times."

Before Dave could recover from his astonishment at Quip's comment, Quip added, "I don't know what the big deal is, Tuck. You dropped out of the doctoral program and launched that high-powered cloud computing company with the cool ideas we exchanged over several glasses of fermented hops.

"Anyway, enough of the good ol' days, I need to enter into a contract with you for some business. What I need is some Cloud cloaking for some recon work. Can you set up an encrypted tunnel to allow one of my end points in, oh say, New York to be able to anonymously access a system in Helsinki for a couple of hours?"

Tuck stared at the phone in disbelief. It took a few seconds for him to compose himself before he replied, "You've got to be kidding me! Two hours? You can't nail up an encryption tunnel for two hours without somebody noticing, particularly if it's a well-known target destination! You know the end points, you undoubtedly have the computer resources to do this, so why call me to get me involved? Why do *I* get this special treatment?"

Quip shifted uneasily in his chair and answered, "It's a little too close for comfort and a little bit out of bounds for my system. I figured, with your anonymizing technology being hosted on

multiple continents, you could more easily cloak this, umm…
interrogation effort better than I could. Plus, I was going to offer
a few shekels for the effort. What do you say?"

Tuck remarked, "Perhaps you didn't hear me the first time
when I told you to bugger off! Your dimes, nickels, and quarters
offering for doing digital breaking-and-entering isn't enough to
offset the years in prison I'd be facing. Go away, Quip. Have a
nice time in prison. Don't call me again!"

Quip was undaunted by the negative response. He knew his
old friend would rise to the challenge. Being close to the same
size and build when they attended school together, they had
competed at everything, physical or mental. "Okay, how long
can you nail up an encrypted tunnel for me? I am assuming you
can do it. Of course, if you simply can't, I can shop for this service
elsewhere. I just thought that the fifty thousand euros I was
going to pay would help with your server refresh program."

Tuck felt himself softening on the topic, and so he removed
some of the anger in his voice as he replied, "That is an interesting
number of shekels, but not for two hours! I am fairly certain I can
do it for twenty minutes without a whole lot of eyebrows of the
sovereign watchdogs going up. Price remains the same though."

Quip sensed they were close to cutting a deal for Jacob to
penetrate the supercomputer STINKIE. Quip asked, "How about
twenty-five thousand euros for an hour, and I'll throw in a world
class Australian barbie with Argentinian beef but presented in a
Texas style offering. What do you say to that? Do we have a deal?"

Tuck shifted uneasily in his chair as he responded, "You
mean like that Texas barbeque you invited me to a while back
with that bachelor party the night before? I remember a lot of it,
and those pictures you posted of those…"

Quip smiled, nodded and interrupted, "Yep, those top heavy,
wide-hipped gals dressed to maximum distraction, who served

drinks so fast that no one saw the bottom of an empty glass. Yes, sir, that kind of Australian barbie served up Texas style."

Tuck's imagination ran out of control recalling the erotic images. "I can give you forty minutes, not a minute more."

Quip grinned. "Okay! Forty minutes for twenty thousand euros and I'll still throw in the Australian barbie with Argentinian beef, Texas style. When can you be ready?"

Tuck, completely taken in, asked, "Uh, no one needs to hear about this, right?"

Quip, in a most accommodating tone, answered, "Push-tush! This is just a friendly discussion between us lads. No one will hear it from me! Email me the details as soon as you can, along with account information so I can send a wire transfer.

"Oh, and one last thing. Do you still do that Saturation of Unlimited Message Pounding and Protection, or SUMPP for short, program to protect valuable computer resources from a cyber onslaught?"

Tuck puzzled a moment, but then said, "It was part of our old business model to protect customers from Distributed Denial of Service attacks, but we don't do DDoS protection services anymore. Why?"

Quip responded, "Well, my high-value endpoint that is the object of my interrogation is about to be pounded digitally, and I didn't want them smoked before I had a chance to chat with them. Can you throw in a little SUMPP for my Finnish friend at the end point I will give you? I just love the way you send those computer DDoS attacks to the planet Jupiter! The disbelief and follow-on banter from the assassins just crack me up when they learn nothing got hit by their attack!"

Tuck chuckled slightly and agreed, "Well, okay! You better throw in the good Kansas City barbeque sauce! We'll talk again soon."

Tuck disconnected the call and wistfully stared out the window, only to be shocked back to reality when he heard Gina as she leaned on the doorway to his office.

Gina admonished, "Australian barbie, served up Texas style, by top heavy, wide-hipped gals dressed to maximum distraction? Let me guess, we aren't going to be able to list this as a customer reference on our website, are we?"

Tuck swallowed hard and asked, "Uh, no one needs to hear about this, right?"

CHAPTER THIRTY

Trappenjagd
(Operation Bustard Hunt)

Jacob had begun to feel like his old self again. The programming activity had reinvigorated his mind set, and it felt like old times before the R-Group had brought him into the family business. A stray thought occurred to him. What if his original life was actually his best destiny? After all, here he was writing code again and enjoying work before all that had changed. He smiled at the brief interlude and considered that most people don't get to go back to where they started. Here he was, living in his mom's and granny's house again. He was doing what he enjoyed most, and that was solving puzzles. Jacob smiled to himself as he reviewed his code again and noted with some pride his newest output. The elation was soon eclipsed by the realization that his success was hollow without someone he trusted to review his work. He frowned a little at the need to have his new colleagues review and critique his work. Collecting money was one thing but having someone say, '*Well done, Jacob*' was missing. He had to admit it to himself, he really did miss his family, but most of all, he missed Petra.

The cloud that contained the melancholy mood threatened to derail his positive attitude, so he forced himself to concentrate on his work to the exclusion of all else. He wanted to prove to himself that he was capable of productive activity, and that he wasn't a slave to better times. He reached for another power drink and refocused on finishing the program. His mind shifted, yet again, but this time to the mental images of Daria. He absent-mindedly drifted into reviewing Daria's face and her movements in his mind's eye. He shot back to reality by reminding himself that she was Buzz's girl, apparently, and daydreaming about her was very poor form on his part. He chided himself for fantasizing about Daria and once again tried to focus on the programming effort. This time his discipline worked, and within a few hours the program was completed.

After his final review of the programming logic, he carefully placed his old Internet signature within the code. He told himself it wasn't vanity as much as a copyright to his work. He stopped a moment and then said out loud to the empty room, "Looks like yet another rationalization for what appears to be aberrant behavior patterns, Jacob old boy! Well, never mind! There is no one here to intercept you, so go ahead and rationalize! But before you do that, let's have one more read of the code, shall we?"

As he stepped through his final code review, the confident smile he had turned into a look of concern. The code did what it was tasked to do, but now he saw that it could be used for other purposes, and that unsettled him. The thought persisted that perhaps he was being duped like Buzz had been duped when he'd fallen in with Patty. Jacob began to see several other applications that this effort could be used for, and he became very uncomfortable with the delivery of this program.

Then Jacob decided that tracking the use and whereabouts of this code effort might be valuable if his worst fears were realized. If the code was used as intended, then no big deal, and the tracking sub-routine would never be invoked. However, if the code went into something entirely different and was harmful, then he wanted the program to do an outbound alert to the mothership, in this case, ICABOD. Jacob realized that Daria would review his code before incorporating it into her master program, so the instruction set had to be interweaved with other instructions so as not to arouse her suspicions.

He looked at his watch and realized he needed a few more hours of work to imbed the tracking program, which would overrun the time deadline he'd established for himself. A wry smile crossed his face as he silently accepted the new challenge. He felt confident that he would get the program to her on time.

From her Dteam offices, Zara answered her cell phone. "Hello, Dmitry, are you about ready? I have the anonymizing servers up and operational, so all you have to do is to login to the bank of servers with the user ID and passwords I sent you. Then you can pound away to your heart's content."

Dmitry smiled confidently and assured, "We are ready to unload on our target at three hundred gigabytes a second. Are you ready for our digital tsunami against Helsinki's supercomputer, the pride of Finland?"

The sour and uninterested look on Zara's face spoke volumes of her attitude toward the exercise. She likened this to the desperately underwhelming experience she had to endure in her former role at the Big House. The girls had to take turns with the first-time customers who had scrimped and saved for the price to have sex with a woman. When it was her turn to service these first-time engagements, it was always the same type of disappointing experience. So very boring for the seasoned professional to extract money from a desperately inexperienced boy. She always detested the first timers, but thankfully the activity was always over in the time it took to cook minute rice. The shortest engagement was the teenager who got all his enjoyment when he climaxed by accidently sneezing while getting undressed. Dmitry was the same kind of man when it came to cyber-attacks.

Zara tried to sound upbeat by Dmitry's mirthful attitude and said, "I'm ready to funnel everything at the Helsinki supercomputer, so show me your stuff. Oh, and to make sure that we can see the positive results of the cyber onslaught, I set up a clean machine to try and innocently access the Internet portal of the target to gauge our results. The standard purpose PC is also anonymized, in case they try to track it back. Whenever you are ready, Dmitry."

Dmitry grinned as he said, "I have issued the go order to Konstantin, so here comes the cyber onslaught…"

Zara watched as the volume of traffic swelled to the 300 GB/second flow promised and, being somewhat impressed, commented, "I see you do mean business, Dmitry! You have launched SYN floods, NTP floods, UDP fragments as well as floods, and SSDP floods to saturate the target. Now that the torrent is flowing through, let me see how our casual client is doing with its standard request, shall we?"

Dmitry was already gloating, and after a few seconds, asked, "Is it time for them to breakout the mops and buckets to clean up the melted silicon? Har! Har!"

Zara didn't respond immediately to Dmitry. After a few minutes of activity, she questioned, "Dmitry, are you sure you have the right target? I'm not holding back any of your data flow, but, in fact, am passing all of it onto the target as fast as you can give it to me."

Dmitry rotated his head to one side and with a puzzled look on his face asked, "What's the matter? Are we not generating enough malformed packets to create a horrific Distributed Denial of Service attack on the Helsinki supercomputer?"

Zara blinked a few times at what she was seeing on the computer screen and replied, "Our casual client is getting its service request handled, and there doesn't seem to be any lag time to the request. It's as if we are not even denting the perimeter, much less bringing the system to its knees. Either this system has the most sophisticated DDoS protection in the solar system installed, or we are not hitting the right target."

Dmitry roared, "What do you mean, nothing is happening? What have you done wrong? I gave you the coordinates, and I am sending you everything to deliver a crippling blow to their supercomputer! I want that system to crumble so I can have my people get in and rearrange the digital furniture! I want the world to see how the Finns can be brought to heel digitally, and you're telling me that you have bungled the targeting effort!"

Zara, irked that she was being blamed for the failed exercise, responded, "Whoa! Hold on, Dmitry! First of all, we only contracted to anonymize your data traffic! We did not sign up for cyber assassinations being bungled! We fed in all the coordinates that you provided and that's all! No one will know where the attack is coming from, but it certainly isn't our fault that you don't know where the attack went wrong!"

Dmitry, quite angry, accused, "You don't know how to feed in an IP address or a fully qualified domain name to get the traffic to the proper host? I've got my whole team landing on the beach to take back my territory and you have misdirected my attack!"

Zara retorted, "Yeah, just like the Battle of the Kerch Peninsula! You landed superior troops to take back the Crimea from the Germans lead by General von Manstein, but instead your entire landing got crushed by someone smarter than you! Too bad Stalin isn't here to have you executed for losing an entire army group!

"What do you want me to do now? It's obvious they knew you were coming, so do you want to continue firing electrons into the solar system for this failed attempt, or shut it down to regroup?"

Dmitry was still seething but managed to keep thinking and asked, "Have you ever seen anything like this before? Firing everything at a target that is not there, but legitimate requests are getting through? Who would have such capabilities?"

Zara reflected, "It was written up as a white paper for a theoretical defense in the cyber warfare space. A few people claimed it could be done, but real proof points never surfaced, and no real products came to market. However, this is the second time I've seen this functionality, which demonstrates that the technology does exist. Sure wish I had it."

A rather sullen Dmitry finally responded, "Yeah, go ahead and shutdown the *bustard hunt*. I need answers to this problem." Dmitry disconnected from the call with a disappointment that was quite the opposite of his elated attitude at the beginning of the call.

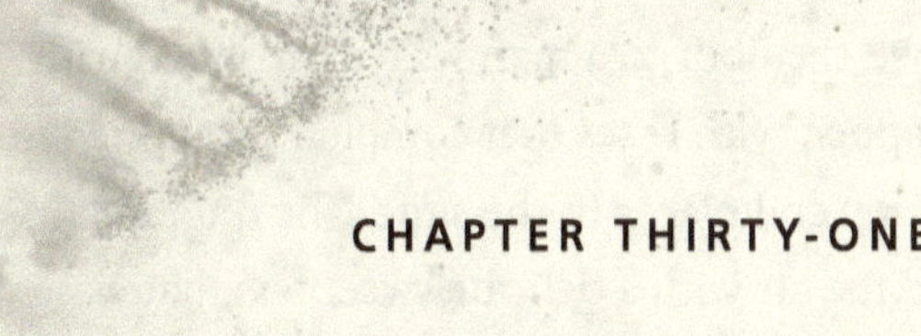

CHAPTER THIRTY-ONE

Today, Tomorrow, and the Near Future – Hoping for Better than Yesterday

Carlos paid the bellman the obligatory tip after being shown all the amenities of the suite. New York City was a thrilling, bright, noisy city with hands out from the moment they hit LaGuardia Airport. Fortunately, Carlos had been to the city before and knew how the underground economy worked. This promised to be a very expensive weekend, but one that would make a lasting impression on the positives of making one's dream come true.

As Lara's face brightened with delight at their accommodations and she rushed into his arms after the door closed, he knew that joining her here had been the only choice. The lavish suite had three rooms, decorated to perfection. The Ritz was living up to its history of exclusivity and luxury appointments with everything merely a phone call away. He pulled her close and kissed her deeply, only to have the deepening of their passion interrupted by the rap at the door.

"Room service."

Lara broke away, smoothed her clothes, and patted her hair. She never ceased to be amazed at how deftly Carlos could rearrange her clothing without her noticing. He glanced her way and then opened the door to a man with a cart filled with wine and snacks, topped with roses that complemented the ones already included in several places in the suite. The fragrance of the roses scented the air with a delicate sweetness that was quite subtle.

Lara exclaimed, "Oh, my goodness. Carlos, did you order this?"

The waiter intervened, "I am sure he would have, ma'am, but these are compliments of the management. We wanted to welcome you to the city and pass along our congratulations on your award."

Lara smiled brightly and offered, "Please pass along my thanks. It is certainly appreciated."

The waiter smiled, then deftly opened the wine and offered a sample to Carlos as Lara walked to the windows. The entire wall of windows had the drapes pulled back, which offered a limited view of the city with the evening lights filtering the light and halo effect behind her. Carlos tasted then nodded to the waiter, and the second glass was filled. After his glass was filled, Carlos handed a crisp bill to the waiter who then bowed and turned to exit the suite. The door closed without a sound as they were left alone. Carlos took the second glass and walked to join Lara as she gazed out the window.

"Oh, my prince, this is such a fun trip, isn't it? I was just thinking, I wouldn't even be here if you hadn't supported and pushed me. I am so glad you came!"

Carlos looked at her pretty face and into the depths of her eyes and smiled that smile which always made her giddy. He grinned with the knowledge that this would be a wonderful evening and raised his glass to hers. "Sweetheart, this is all your work and your dreams. Consider me just an extremely interested party in your happiness. To you, my darling."

Lara grinned and added, "To us!"

After the toast, they sipped the delicious wine in silence. Carlos retrieved the bottle and they moved to the couch where they could enjoy the view and snuggle. Lara kicked off her shoes and pulled her legs under her as she leaned into him. He wrapped an arm around her, and they enjoyed the quiet for several more minutes.

Carlos topped off their glasses with the remainder of the bottle and asked, "Should I order more?"

Lara offered a mischievous grin and replied, "No, any more and I will fall asleep instead of enjoying this time. If you want more, please go ahead."

"I am just fine with this and with you. Before the wine arrived, I was busy thinking of how to convince you that this suite had several places where I would enjoy making love to you. Since you arrived in the country, we have hardly had a moment to enjoy one another without someone calling, or knocking, or buzzing."

Carlos set down his glass, took hers and added it to the side table, and took her into his arms and growled, "Now, my dear, where were we before the knock on the door?" His hands roved and started pushing aside and unfastening here and there as he kissed her neck and her cheek, then affirmed, "Ah yes, I remember."

"Me too."

They quickly dispensed with the barriers to touching and explored one another with their hands and mouths, as if they simply couldn't cover enough territory. Insistent and provocative rather than furious and urgent, there was no mistaking their need for one another as their kisses, licks, and fondling fueled Lara into one pinnacle after another until she was breathless and begging for Carlos to plunge deep inside her. He moved to acquiesce, and they moved together, each taking and giving to satisfy one another until their final release together that suspended time and space around them. They held onto one another as their breathing slowed and heartbeats regulated. Carlos shifted them to lay entwined, side my side.

"Sweetheart, I have missed you. I am so glad you came to me."

Lara snuggled even closer. "I am too. I don't know what we are going to do, but I need us to be together. I don't want to be separated anymore."

"What would you like from me? I can't go to Brazil and live off of your success. As much as I appreciate this trip and time with you, I'm wired to be my own person and earn my way."

Lara felt the shift in the air as they appeared to be past lovemaking for the moment. This seemed too important not to focus on. She opened her eyes and raised up on one elbow and gazed into his eyes.

"Carlos, I love you. We need to talk about this, and now seems like a good time because we don't need to be anywhere until mid-day tomorrow. Could you please order us a light dinner and some more of that wine and let me tidy up a bit. Then we can sit and discuss our options."

Carlos looked relieved as he smiled, nodded, and stated, "You don't have the plan finalized. I'd like to discuss our options, Lara, very much. You go tidy up. I will order."

Lara rose and bent to pick up her discarded clothing. Carlos admired the view and patted her rear fondly as she looked back at him with a smile. He picked up the phone and ordered things he knew they both enjoyed. He picked up the rest of the clothing and went into the bedroom to retrieve something easy to slip on. As he retrieved his sweatpants, he smiled at the services the hotel offered with the unpacking and orderly appearance of the closet and drawers. They had come such a long way in a short time. He grinned at Lara as she emerged from the bathroom with a shimmery dressing gown in a soft orange color that set off the glow of her bronzed skin and dark hair. He considered rethinking their evening plans as he eyed her, then eyed the bed, but the knocking at the door reminded him of the task at hand.

Carlos opened the door, and the same waiter rolled in the new cart covered with plates of food and a couple of bottles of wine.

"Sir, I know you ordered a single bottle, but I thought since you liked it, I would include another to avoid interrupting your evening again. Though, of course, you may call at any time."

The waiter quickly set the meal up on a table near the window and moved the chairs in juxtaposition to one another. He lit some candles and then opened one of the bottles of wine, though he didn't pour it, but, rather, set it to the side. He looked at his handiwork and turned to Carlos.

Carlos grinned and replied, "That is very nice indeed." He slipped another bill into the hand of the waiter, and the waiter left with the first cart, leaving the roses on another tabletop.

Lara smiled as she entered the room and took one of the chairs. Carlos took the other after he'd retrieved their glasses and poured a modest amount for them each. This time Lara raised her glass and offered, "To our today, tomorrow, and the day after, my prince."

They snacked and laughed as they talked through the possibilities of their future. It was an agreeable conversation where they both explained what they wanted and hoped for in their lives. The candles burned down as they seemed to reach the possible options that they wanted to focus on.

Carlos reached over and ran his fingers gently over the length of her arm. It was a reflexive move on his part as he needed to touch her whenever she was near. He'd always been like that with her, as if her skin attracted him like a magnet. Sometimes it was sexual, while other times, like now, it was just a need for contact, though the shift to sexual between them was never too far away.

Carlos summarized, "Sweetheart, I think we have three options on the table, but I want to be certain I have them right. I need to work and like working with Andy. You want to keep doing Destiny Fashions. We want to spend much more time together.

"That leaves us right now with these options if I understood correctly. Option 1, we spend four months in Georgia and four months in Brazil together, each working remotely as needed. Option 2, we move to a different location, like Mexico where we met, and both work remotely, traveling for short trips as necessary. Option 3, we each work in our home locations and spend one week a month together at some place to be determined. Does that about sum it up?"

Lara nodded and added, "I think so, though to me, option 3 has the most risk of failure as we will have something overrun us and possibly delay the meetings. Honestly, I don't think I am disciplined enough, so I will need to be prodded for that one."

Carlos grinned as he thought of ways to prod her but said, "I'd like to say that I wouldn't have that issue, but I could. For the other options, we need to make certain that Andy is on board. I really like working with Andy, and he feels, well, almost like family. He's been very good to me."

"You're right, Andy is amazing. I think when we get back from this whirlwind adventure that we speak to him and get his input."

"Now that we have solved this issue for now, can I convince you to take a shower with me, and we try out the bed next?"

Lara laughed and replied, "Oh, yes, my prince."

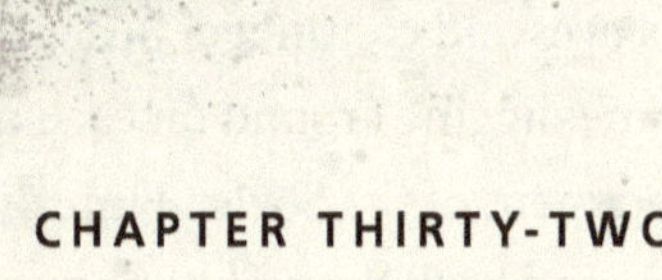

CHAPTER THIRTY-TWO

Shortness of Temper Means a More Spirited Discussion

Quip puzzled at the incoming call on the screen but answered, "Well gee, Tuck, I figured that you'd be excited about the Texas style barbie, but I didn't expect to hear from you this soon! I haven't got the engineer in New York teed up yet, if that is what you are calling about."

Tuck struggled to conceal his sarcasm as he replied, "Well gee, Quipy, you didn't tell me that the target system of the DDoS attack was going to start within minutes of our conversation! I barely had time to hunt down the old SUMPP programs and load them up before the digital tsunami began!"

Quip tried to guard his alarm from Tuck. "Huh?"

Tuck, rankled and not willing to drop the discussion, responded, "Boy, do I enjoy your use of syllables! Two nefarious digital tribes going to war with each other that you placed me and my company in the middle of, and all you can articulate is, *Huh*? Where is the old Quip that used to wax eloquently about data structures, world economics, and beautifully sculpted women with upturned nipples that defy Newton's law of gravity?"

Quip thought for a moment as he recalled with a smile, "I'd forgotten that thesis on Newtonian physics. That was a great conversation starter at frat parties with the cute babes, but I never got to hold the apples at the end of the discussion. Ah well, people move on, I suppose."

Tuck rolled his eyes and continued, "After the attempted onslaught, I did some digging around on each of them, and it looked like a reenactment of the Soviet-Finnish war of 1939! It took a while to thread back through the anonymizing server farm the Russkies had set up, but I located the source of the onslaught.

"They made the same mistake most anonymizers do when trying to cloak the source. Most people don't think to setup a mirror maze to confound the forensics snooper who is trying to penetrate back to the source. That's how I got back to see who was doing the pounding."

Quip, now a little more interested in speaking, responded, "Uh-huh!"

Tuck clucked his tongue in annoyance but continued, "However, the more interesting side of the equation was the Finnish supercomputer that was supposedly targeted to take the pounding. You piqued my interest on why protect the site, so I did a little investigative detective work on the site.

"Turns out, it's the new home of Dr. Xavier Pekoni and his next generation of the Fountain of Youth project. As soon as I saw his clammy fingerprints on snippets of data, I beat a hasty retreat out of there. You sure you want to have someone prowl around in there? I mean, too bad he was born after the Nuremberg Trials! That guy is cut from the same cloth as those Nazi S.S. doctors and simply has no conscience. It gives me the creeps that anyone like him gets to call himself a doctor of medicine when really he is a doctor of death!"

Quip nodded and agreed, "You nailed him right! He'll practice his surgical skills on you by opening you up to see if you can help with his research. Then he'll complain to your dying face that you dulled his surgical scalpel and didn't live long enough for him to try again!"

"Quip, this guy is vindictive and has a long reach for people who tick him off. Now I know how to anonymize our data traffic to and from, but are you really sure you want to poke that beast? There are easier targets, you know."

Quip teased, "What? Don't tell me you are getting cold feet! Besides, I have a few tricks up my sleeve, so we should be okay. Hey, don't forget that I am bringing the great Kansas City barbeque sauce for the barbie I contracted for!"

Tuck flashed on the imagery of the Australian barbie, Texas style, that Quip had promised. This resulted in a very mischievous grin on his face. "Can we get your engineer in place so we can get down to cases for my payment? You know, it occurs to me that you could go ahead and launch the barbie, and I'll just put a credit on the books for you. That way you won't have to worry about when to schedule it."

Quip rather flatly responded, "That's the old Tuck – always thinking with his stomach! We have a policy here. We don't pre-pay our engagements, particularly when the recipient might not want to remember the outrageously great time he had the night before. I mean, where would I be if the local authorities want to be invited in, and work gets postponed because our vocation gets changed by a few folks steeped with certain Victorian prejudices about how a barbie should be conducted. No, no, I'll deliver the barbie after the services have been rendered. Agreed?"

Tuck, sulking a little, responded, "I had a feeling you would be unreasonable on the subject. Let me know when we need to go."

Quip brightly replied, "Cheers! Talk soon!"

Otto stuck his head into Quip's work area and casually asked, "You set up a meeting to brief Eric. Weren't you going to join the occasion?"

A very sullen Quip stared a moment, then reached for his cell phone and noticed that the audible tones had been turned off for meeting invites. After briefly reading the meeting invite notes, a rather annoyed Quip turned to ICABOD's audio/video terminal and barked, "What have I told you about this? Making meetings with my user ID before I'm ready to meet? I want you to stop using the keystroke logger program to obtain my password! Understand?

"And what do you mean asking Otto to do all the talking to Eric because of my adversarial attitude? Me? I do not have an adversarial attitude! Do you hear me? Anyone who says that has a whipping coming! If I catch you saying that again, I am going to yank out the key blade servers from your system and then reinstall them backwards!"

Otto stared blankly as Quip ranted. After the tirade ended, Otto offered, "I see your anger management sessions have paid off handsomely, Quip. I mean, I can't understand why, given your patience and emotionally even keel, that you shouldn't brief Eric. After all, what is another alienated client, more or less?"

Now also irked by Otto's sarcasm, Quip shot back like an angry adolescent. "Oh, so you're on his side too, huh? I'll show you both! For this call to Eric, I'll keep quiet, and you just do the talking! Got it?"

Otto and Quip studied each other for a moment, and then a rather chastened Quip quietly replied, "I, uh…said that wrong, didn't I?

"Otto, would you please let me listen while you brief Eric? I don't want my streak of emotional blunders to continue today."

ICABOD offered, "Dr. Quip, I sincerely apologize for the

expedient meeting arrangements I made on your behalf. I was merely trying to be efficient, and I thought you'd be pleased. Obviously, I was mistaken. I will now submit to having my key blade servers shoved incorrectly into the data rack enclosures which will reduce computer processing substantially. Will I be required to bend over to facilitate your discipline, sir?"

A very sullen Quip responded, "Never mind, ICABOD. Those were harsh words spoken in anger, and I wish to withdraw my threat, for now anyways."

Otto grinned and exclaimed, "As you wish, my boy, as you wish! I'll run point on the call."

Otto dialed Eric's number on his cell phone and put it on speaker so they both could hear.

Eric promptly answered, "Otto, I hope this call means that you have an update on our person of interest. What do you have for me today?"

"Good morning, Eric. Allow me to begin with the pleasantries, and then I shall move into a project update, kind sir. May I assume that your system is getting enough bran, fruits, and grains to keep you from suffering from irregularity?"

Eric thought for a moment and responded, "I was doing the American thing again, wasn't I? Sorry, let me start over.

"Good afternoon, Otto. I hope this call finds you well and your business productive. Thank you for reaching out to me and inquiring about my problem with irregularity. May I assume we have business to discuss?"

Otto grinned and commented, "There, see how much more pleasant this conversation is when you don't rush into project updates?

"I will tell you we have some preliminary evidence that strongly suggests that the bad doctor, Xavier Pekoni, is operating out of Finland's supercomputer facility. We have not done the forensic data search on the suspected system as we discussed, but it is in its planning stages.

"However, I must tell you that there is at least one other interested party, because as we were doing our preliminary discovery, a massive digital attack was delivered to the suspect system which left us on the sidelines. Eric, I suspect we probably have some competitors for the targeted information. We are attempting to accelerate our time table to secure the data of interest."

Eric was now very attentive to Otto's briefing. He asked, "How long before you can gain entry? This agency really doesn't need another embarrassing data leakage on yet another poorly handled operation. The other interested party didn't get in ahead of us, did they?"

Otto glanced up at Quip and clarified, "Eric, this isn't a simple and impulsive smash-and-grab exercise. Any clumsy fool can do that! We don't want anyone pointing fingers at us after the exercise, so please allow us to plan and properly execute an untraceable incursion and data extraction. You don't want this to blow back on you a second time. No, they didn't get there ahead of us because of the mitigation technology we leveraged to prevent that."

Eric understood the gravity of Otto's statements and reeled in his impatience as he responded, "You are right, Otto, to be cautious in approaching this, and yes, I am anxious to get this behind us. But sooner rather than later is the posture I want your team to take in gathering the data and rounding up Pekoni. We don't really need him running his own show on the world stage, based on what we know about him. Let me know if you need any additional resources to bring this to closure."

Otto nodded and asserted, "We agree that he is a dangerously capable individual, and we too are interested in intercepting his dealings. Thank you for the offer of additional resources. There appears to be several threads on this project, and, well, I may need to take you up on that offer. Let us map out our next steps, and we'll be in touch. Good day, sir."

Eric suppressed a smile as he said, "Good day, Otto."

CHAPTER THIRTY-THREE

Playing with Fire
Gets You Two Things – Burned
and a Ride on the Firetruck

Jacob had delivered the code to Daria. She reviewed the code while he was present. He was almost surprised that his standing behind her hadn't disturbed her concentration. Nor did she ask him to move or act like she had anything to hide.

Daria commented, "Jacob, this code is well organized and meets all the criteria of the design. I wonder why I have not seen your work before. The organization is that of a veteran programmer, not someone fresh out of school. Very refreshing."

Jacob felt his ego inflating with the flattery and replied, "I am glad that it meets with your approval, ma'am. I actually had some fun doing it, and it got me out of my doldrums. I have been focused on the wrong things for a while."

She continued to scan the code and frowned at one point. Jacob wondered if she had spotted what he had hidden but refused to change his facial expression. Then she opened up a folder and located an executable file. Jacob's concern grew as she launched the program, and it did a form of additional review on his code. He was fascinated by the process as his eyes followed the process of the executed program. Finally, it finished, and Jacob saw a slight smile cross her face.

Daria closed her program and moved the program Jacob provided to a folder, then stated, "It seems that you write code well. This impresses me. Do you like coding from your home, or do you prefer the structure of an office?"

Internally, Jacob breathed a sigh of relief that his hidden code was undiscovered. He responded, "It really doesn't matter where I work. Once I teleport into what I am doing, very little distracts me, outside of the internal clock in my head. The only thing that makes working at home better is that I don't have to waste a great deal of time traveling from here to there unnecessarily.

"What was that last program that you executed against my code? I didn't want to stare, and obviously it moved too fast for me to scrutinize it closely. It looked interesting. Is it a utility type of program?"

Daria grinned and replied, "Very good, Jacob. It is a utility program that was constructed by a former programmer of mine who wanted to make certain that there were no hidden alternate code tracks buried inside of a seemingly perfect program. Your code has nothing outside of what was requested, and your signature, which was within a comment parameter, will remain as an author reference for me, in case we need changes. I am of the belief that, whenever possible, one should have the original programmer make modifications as needed. I have found that streamlines the process."

Jacob was thoughtful for a few moments, then asked, "How many outsourced programs have you trapped with this utility?"

Daria chuckled before she responded. "Several programs that I've received over the Internet, like when I have looked for help with a project, have come back with buried malware types of programs. Most of these are used to gain insight on the requestor's, as in my, systems. This tool has been very effective in that regard. I honestly did not think you had an agenda that would suggest implanting alternate code, but I had to be sure. Now I am."

Jacob smiled and asked, "Does that mean you might have more work for me? As I said initially, I enjoyed this project as it was short and easily delivered, and I'd like to keep my mind on this track for a while."

"I actually do have several other little complementary programs that I need. They will work with this one as well as some others. I would like you to take on two of them if you have the time, but I need them quickly. Take a look at the spec sheets and see if you are interested and if the time requirements will suit us both."

Jacob quickly reviewed the documentation she handed him. This would take almost no time to complete. As he mentally assembled this information flow for the program, he also knew he could bury his code easily inside it. He scrutinized Daria and still could not pinpoint what there was about her that concerned him.

"Daria, this seems very straightforward. I think I can get both of them done within two days. Does forty-eight hours meet your timeline requirements?"

Daria looked at him with a very seductive smile as she replied, "Jacob, if you can do these in that time frame, you will be my number one programmer. I need to thank Buzz, yet again, for making introductions to you. I think we are destined to have a long, rewarding relationship together. Here are the additional APIs that you will require, Jacob, and of course your payment for this program. Thank you."

Jacob took the thumb drive along with the envelope of cash. He grinned as he promised, "I will see you in two days, or sooner if I finish. A pleasure doing business with you."

"Aren't you going to count the money?"

"What for? If you weren't going to meet your committed price, then you would not have given me additional work."

Back at his place, Jacob locked the door and walked into his redesigned programming den. It was almost like he'd never left, but not quite. He knew that he would never be that far removed from the family that had found him and welcomed him into the fold. He wasn't ready to fully return to that world, but it wasn't because it wouldn't be the right thing. He simply wasn't able to work with that team and not think of Petra and what they'd shared. His entire being missed her. He'd finally realized that no amount of drinking, running, or tattooing would change his feelings for her, so he needed to be patient and wait for, he didn't know what.

He opened up the documentation that Daria had provided and began working on the first of the two projects. The time he expected to spend on the actual coding required to complete the project was half of what he'd told her. The remainder of the time would be spent embedding his secret sauce and avoiding capture by the utility. He sure wanted a copy of that utility. Obviously, it wasn't that effective, but perhaps with a few modifications it would be quite useful to the team.

Jacob worked until the wee hours when his cell phone alarm sounded. It was mid-morning in Zürich, and time to pass along some information. He retrieved a fresh cup of coffee before he placed the call. On and off as he'd worked through the coding, he'd outlined what he wanted to say. The last thing he wanted was a long, drawn out conversation. He stretched one more time and pressed call to the very familiar number.

"Quip," Jacob began like they'd spoken only an hour ago. "I placed a copy of a program onto ICABOD in the safe area. If it is used in an undesirable manner, it will route information into a safe area that I also defined, specifically firewalled from access to anything important, as we have practiced."

Quip held up his phone as if he could divine what had prompted this call. Then he looked at the notices and found an indication from ICABOD that Jacob had indeed accessed and placed code and documentation into the zone indicated. He growled, "This should interest me why, Jacob? You clearly haven't been communicating your activities. Give me one good reason I shouldn't destroy what you have placed on MY SYSTEM, without my approval or fore-knowledge. You have no right."

Jacob was too tired to check his anger as he shouted, "I have every right to use the resources that I was given. No one altered the access codes or emailed me of an organizational change. Get off your high horse!"

Quip had been speed reading the notes during the tirade. He asked, "What have you gotten into and why are you giving away free code, or do I get to invoice this? Who are you working for?"

Jacob snapped, "I am working for a very nice lady that has a cool utility program I want and earning money doing brainless programming. I just don't know if the end game is a problem or not, so I inserted a tracker code. Undetected I might add. I don't know the end users of the code, but I do know it is only a part of a whole project that I am contributing into. Something is off, but I don't know what. Like you always say, be suspicious."

Quip exploded, "You self-centered ass. You are coding and don't know who for. Why would you do that? You weren't brought up that way. What would your mother say? Get your butt on the next flight back here, and we will see if we can fix your mess."

"Mess? MESS? I don't have a mess! I have an opportunity for us to get ahead of a problem and took steps to make certain we will be advised. You're just mad because it wasn't your idea or orchestrated by you. And why am I explaining to you? You aren't my dad! I should have called Otto, or even Wolfgang, at least they would have provided a fair hearing.

"Have ICABOD notify me if he gets an alert, and I'll take care of it without you getting your hands dirty. I am not your lackey any longer, Quip. We're finished here."

Quip stared at his now silent phone. He rotated his head to face ICABOD's terminal before he stated, "I don't want to hear it right now, ICABOD. Just do as he's asked. I need to think this out."

CHAPTER THIRTY-FOUR

Home Videos Digitally Enhanced – What a Hoot!

The two men sat and stared as they thought about what they had seen. Finally, after a few minutes of silence, Wolfgang asked, "Can I see it again, please?"

Quip reached over to the keyboard and launched the video recording and boosted the sound a little bit to improve the fidelity of the audio portion.

The video opened with a close up on a man that appeared well-groomed, dressed clinically, and with well-manicured hands. A short panning of the room by the filmmaker displayed several men and women seated at tables with notepads in front of them. A quick count suggested nearly fifty people with some standing at the back of the room. The focus of the filmmaker returned to the man.

The presenter opened, "Good afternoon, all. I am Dr. Xavier Pekoni. I want to welcome you to this briefing on my program for life extensions. I hope that, after this briefing, you too will be as excited as I am with where I am in my research efforts.

"For those who don't know about this project or have not been keeping up with world events, allow me to restate my quest. I believe that we are on target to use the unraveled DNA sequencing of human life, and, most importantly, now to reprogram those building blocks to leverage the body's own natural regenerative processes. In short, I have targeted specifically the reprogramming of the building blocks of human tissue to have it naturally rebuild what is being lost or has been lost.

"Consider, all medicine research is predicated on dealing with broken or missing functionality rather than telling the human cells to rebuild themselves to cure the failure. This process is what I want to address because it is flawed and falls short of the human demand for excellence. Our best destiny is to deal with the current shortcomings of a process that ignores the promise of life extension.

"I don't have a lot of chart-ware with which to dazzle you, but let me put up a few slides with some numbers to help illustrate my point. See the current expenditures on Alzheimer's disease. There is no known cure for this death sentence, so all we do is treat the symptoms rather than focus on a cure. Last year alone over two hundred billion U.S. dollars were wasted on the afflicted. If this trend continues, by the middle of this century, this country will be spending over one trillion U.S. dollars! The conventional approach to life-shortening diseases is the same, and they are all wrong!

"My approach to the problem is simple! Re-teach the cells at the DNA level what they once knew but have forgotten! The knowledge at the DNA level is there to build, replicate, and re-generate, but with all the negative influences of the environment, poor diet, and sedentary lifestyle, the DNA tends to lose its programming. My research is providing validity to reprogramming the cells to regenerate tissue that has lost its way! Think of reprogramming cancerous cells to naturally restore their structure as the cells were originally designed!

"The human body is a living chemistry engine that takes raw materials and manufactures life and generates life-sustaining components that can be retaught to continue to work indefinitely! Sadly, as the negative influencers of our environment impact this remarkable chemical engine, over time the organism forgets its original programming mandate."

Pekoni let his words sink in before launching into the next part of his soliloquy. "This is not a new criticism of our current medical expenditures. What is new is that I am proposing a way out of our current philosophy to treat the symptoms and deliver on how to fix the source of the problem. My research has already shown that I am on the right path, with results that clearly show the proof positive of tissue being properly rebuilt after my treatments!

"If I can demonstrate that cancerous tissue can be replaced with properly functioning tissue, then the obvious next step is to reprogram the entire living being to continue in the proper operational mode to potentially achieve a lifespan of hundreds or even thousands of years! Think of it! Reprogramming at the cellular level to replenish worn out organs, replace lost limbs, purge the destructive Amyloid plaques in the brain of Alzheimer's patients, and everyone can live for hundreds of years, but with the high quality of life received at birth!"

Quip paused the video at this point and glanced at Wolfgang, then remarked, "He sure gets wound up, doesn't he? But I have to admit that his passion for his craft is pretty compelling. Who doesn't want to live forever?"

Wolfgang sat in silence as he studied the screen. Finally, he acknowledged, "Yes, he was good up to this point, but watch what happens next."

Quip hit the play button to continue the video.

Pekoni resumed, "All I'm asking from this peer review is for you to acquiesce to my request to relax the process testing that I'm currently struggling under. I have received numerous requests, pledges, and heart-felt begging to be a test candidate for my process. A vote of confidence from this committee will go a long way to relieving the pressure on my research progress from your oversight agency for which I am spending too much valuable time completing unnecessary documentation. I need to be allowed free rein to push my research further with suitable volunteers."

The focus of the filmmaker shifted to the audience before it returned to the speaker.

Quip stopped the video again and remarked, "Boy, this is the crudest video recording I've ever seen! Looks like someone used one of those *Crittercams* to film this! But as grainy as it is, you can still see the look of absolute horror on the faces of the committee after hearing his request."

Wolfgang nodded and agreed. "Yes. Can you let it run again, please? I want to see that interaction with that committee member in the back row."

As the video continued, Pekoni explained, "Now I know that some of you are a little uncomfortable with my request, but I will tell you that you need not concern yourselves with my request but rather acknowledge the progress. Remember, these are well-informed, intelligent humans who are staring death in the face. They have so much to live for, as we all do, so the squeamish among you can just leave this portion to me and my team."

Quip said, "Okay, Wolfgang, here it comes."

Pekoni's attention was focused on a member of the committee in the back row, whom he at first had trouble seeing, as she addressed him. The filmmaker continued as Pekoni squinted to see, and then his face dropped into a dumbfounded look. It was apparent that he recognized the individual. The voice from the back of the room was almost too faint to hear, but Quip and Wolfgang recognized it as a female voice. This questioning from the back row had an angering effect on Xavier's facial features that they both could see and confirmed with quick glances to each other.

Quip ran the sequence back a little and then made some adjustments to try and hear what was being said. He had no luck with his adjustments. He restarted the questioning sequence again and requested, "ICABOD, I want you to isolate that voice from the back of the room that is asking the question and see if you can boost the audio on it. While you are at it, please see if you can do voice recognition on it. I kind of want to know who got him spun up so high."

ICABOD obliged, and this time they could hear most of the woman's question. "Dr. Pekoni, you are asking us to sanction your research work with our reputations, but I cannot before I can verify your testing results. You make it sound as easy as reloading an operating system on your laptop, but in fact there is much more to it than that. To date, I cannot confirm that your results are valid. Until I can see them with my own eyes in my own lab, I will recommend that you follow protocol and maintain only testing on animals, with no human clinical trials approved. Your request for expediency to test on humans without due diligence is clearly out of bounds, and I will not give my consent."

Quip commented, "Whoa! No wonder he has his knickers in a twist! Doesn't sound like she bought any of what he was selling! And judging from the look of hatred on his face, he is pretty ticked at her."

Wolfgang nodded and said, "I concur and from the follow-on comments from the rest of the committee members, she started an opinion avalanche that simply buried the bad doctor and his request. Where did you get this video? How does it fit into the Xavier Pekoni timeline?"

Quip remarked, "ICABOD found it in some partial archives that were overlooked when Pekoni loaded up all his research and vanished twelve years ago."

After closing out the video, Wolfgang breathed deeply and stated, "Well, now. We have a better idea of who and what we are dealing with when discussing Dr. Pekoni. And your understanding is that he disappeared after this peer review, correct?"

Quip nodded. "Yep. He folded up his tent, gathered up all his marbles, and stomped off, exiting stage-left."

ICABOD interjected, "Gentlemen, excuse the interruption. I have two additional details that might prove useful. The first is that the loose translation of *Pekoni* in English is bacon."

Quip wondered, "Perhaps the reaction by Su Lin during the attempted kidnapping stirred a long-buried memory of her relationship with this mad scientist and her mumbled bacon statements that Carlos related."

ICABOD continued, "Possible, but unconfirmed. The second is you asked me to run the female voice through the voice speech recognition program to try and discover the speaker's identity. My analysis on the voice offers a 99.8% probability of this being Su Lin's voice. The date of this film coincides with her time at Texas A&M."

CHAPTER THIRTY-FIVE

Reasonable Arguments, Logically Thought Out and Skillfully Delivered, are Sometimes No Match for Brute Force Demands

...The Enigma Chronicles

Zara listened to the caller for as long as her patience could stand it before she interjected, "Dmitry, I delivered the anonymizing effort that you wanted, but your attack was flawed. I am working with a paying customer now, the emphasis on paying, and I'm not able to drop what I am doing to restart the service on the servers simply because you called...

"Ah! I now see why you are the poster child for how best to deal with women and minorities! Your grasp, as well as the application, of your sensitivity training is an inspiration to us all! No, I am talking about the digital services we deliver here, not the vulgar analog kind that you throw in my face whenever you are ticked off...

"Okay, so now you're not going to try to help broker a sale of my diamonds. Is that your threat? ...

"Yes, I did. I texted you the meet and greet location where I would show the necklace to the buyer's agent. I sent the information at the same time I gave you the login information for the anonymizing program, but you chose to only act on your attack program…

"Yes, I can see that your self-absorbed nature wouldn't accept anything because of your *all-about-me* approach to life would preclude you from looking at the next text…

"No! *You* see here, it will take two more days for you to arrange for the agent to get here if you act now, so we can discuss your needs at that time. We are going to take care of my needs first, then yours. Besides, I will be further along with my current client and have some time to work with you on your project…

"You should see how scared I am at your threat. You don't even know where I am…

"Oh yeah! I gave you a meet-me address, and you know how to triangulate cell towers to find people. I guess you do know where I am…

"You know, Dmitry, it wouldn't take a lot of effort to launch the bank of anonymizing servers so you can play digital army games with the Finns again. Why don't I just enable that functionality, oh say, in twenty minutes to facilitate your cause just because of the kind of helpful person I am, hmmm? Then, if the mood strikes you, perhaps you could see your way clear to broker a meeting with the buyer's agent? Yes? And, if that all goes as we discussed, there shouldn't be any need to strangle me with my pantyhose…

"I'll call you back as soon as the bank of servers are up and ready. Bye for now…"

Zara disconnected from the phone call and fumed at having been backed into a corner again, with her ill-gotten diamonds, by Dmitry. As she started the process to fire up the application across the bank of servers, she mumbled to herself, "You'd think that as many times as he's had his hand up my dress, he'd remember that I don't wear pantyhose! It's insulting that he would group me with old women and ex-football players who need that undergarment support."

While the servers were synchronizing, she completed the program and wrapper for her client. Zara smiled, knowing that with the addition of the two programs Jacob had dropped off earlier, ahead of schedule, that she was finished. She decided to hold onto it rather than deliver it early as she slipped the USB drive into her pants pocket. Then she refocused on the servers and groused, "Argh! I need to find another trusted source to move these stupid diamonds! This trusted source is holding me hostage with my own loot! Maybe I should try to work with the Amsterdam diamond district to move the damn things. I've been here too long anyway, and that always makes one too comfortable. That comfort of staying too long is probably going to get me spotted."

Quip glanced down at his phone at the same time that ICABOD stated, "Another attack is unfolding against STINKIE, Dr. Quip. Most likely the text message from Tuck is going to confirm that the attack is in progress."

Quip looked back up from his phone and affirmed, "Yes, ICABOD! That is correct. Tuck has launched the SUMPP program and is alerting me of the event. ICABOD, I don't think we can wait any longer to get Jacob engaged on a forensic copy-and-clean of STINKIE. I want you to do the digital incursion into STINKIE so we can extract the Fountain of Youth project code before that murderous researcher goes any farther. That way, I won't have to ask for a favor, or deal with the New York Noodle, in the personage of Jacob the Jerk."

ICABOD hesitated for a moment but then replied, "Dr. Quip, you know my stance on this subject. While I would prefer to stay the course, I will not decline your directive. However, let me offer an alternative approach. Jacob has apparently awakened and has alerted us of a potential abuse of his current coding activity. I took the liberty of running his two coded programs through the *Heuristic and Opportunistic Programming with Selectively Concatenating Orthogonal Thought Choices for a Hierarchal* solution, in a forward-looking programming scenario. I can confirm that his code will be misused."

Quip looked over the top of his glasses and, with something of a reprimand in his voice, asked, "ICABOD, have you been playing *HOPSCOTCH* in the data center again?"

ICABOD continued, "The host program will act as a *cargo-plane*, hence the name, and all the child programs will be called for once the master program has been delivered to the target environment. The approach is classic Dteam drive-by code that is downloaded onto a target machine. If the advance program is downloaded successfully, it then makes a standard call out of the host environment using their own email server to add legitimacy.

"Once in place, the advance host code then summons the remaining necessary programs and assembles itself on the target machine. It is the classical two-stage drive-by download methodology to install malware software on a targeted system. And, yes, I used the *HOPSCOTCH* program to confirm my position."

Quip nodded thoughtfully and added, "And Jacob is building the follower programs to be sent to the nested cargo-plane program designed to assemble the master program. Hmmm. Perhaps a little more prodding of Mister Jacob is in order."

Quip grinned and expressed, "And I think I know how to do that."

CHAPTER THIRTY-SIX

When Traveling Down the *Destiny Path,* Be Careful Who You Take Directions From

...The Enigma Chronicles

After he listened to the caller for a few moments, Stalker interjected, "Eric, I don't understand. If we know that Pekoni is operating out of Finland, then why am I heading to Atlanta? Forgive me for questioning this approach, but as one of your cyber hunters and favorite investigators, why the field trip to Georgia?"

Eric clucked his tongue before he patiently responded, "You remember that operation you did a few months back where I sent you to Atlanta to evaluate a Su Lin with that contractor to see if she was faking it?"

Stalker nodded to himself and replied, "Yeah, I remember. She whacked herself while playing with the nanotechnology that was supposed to be used for battlefield communications. What about her?"

Eric continued, "Otto asked for a little reconnaissance around where she is staying based on some new intelligence, he has on Pekoni's Fountain of Youth program. Seems someone made a grab for her but failed in their effort.

"In parallel to the move on Su Lin, all her medical records are being hunted. The reason Otto knows this is that after the failed attempt to grab her, someone or something started going through all the medical records in the Southeast looking for profiles exactly like hers."

Stalker feigned a surprised look and commented, "Ummmm. Interesting, but doesn't Otto have his own people on the scene tracking this down already?"

Eric was beginning to sense that Stalker could be convinced to get on board with the assignment. He responded, "Well, he is leveraging the CATS team as a subcontractor. Based on the poor results thus far, I half expect that Otto is hoping to augment that person's skillset with someone far more seasoned, with experience to move the investigation along faster. Basically, I need you to take charge of the investigation, move the discovery process along, but don't bruise any egos in the process. Am I being clear enough on the assignment?"

Stalker studied the situation a few seconds, then said, "I am to start producing investigative results where none were seen so far, teach the junior G-man how the big boys do it, and make sure no one gets their panties in a wad when their incompetence is brought to light. Is that about it?"

Eric, in his usual sarcastic, deadpan voice, finally responded, "My, how succinct you are at describing your workload. I can hardly wait to hear the feedback from Otto on how swimmingly everything went after you showed up on-site.

"Okay, so how about this, can you add your special brand of expertise and abilities to the situation without causing an international incident?"

Stalker sulked a little before he selected the right tone to respond. "Geez, Eric. To hear you talk, one would think my interpersonal skills categorize me as being as rough as a corncob, with little chance of being substituted for standard paper products in the washroom! But, okay, have it your way! I'll head that way this afternoon since I expect the next thing, you'll tell me is that time is of the essence. Am I right?"

Eric, trying to suppress a smirk, chortled, "Ah, that's my favorite crude cyber hunter! At my request, Otto has already alerted the host that you will be showing up on site to help move the investigation along. You now have two things going for you on this assignment, old friend."

Stalker puzzled a moment and then asked, "Two things? What is the other thing?"

A wry smile briefly crossed Eric's face as he relayed, "Why, you'll be working with a known junior G-man from a previous life. Won't that be splendid?"

Stalker, now somewhat confused, asked, "Oh yeah! Like who?"

Eric debated internally with himself on responding at all but finally replied, "It's Mercedes, Jim."

Stalker could feel the information shoot through him like armor piercing rounds. Somewhat shocked at who he was going to meet and now a little angry that he had been set up for the assignment, he harshly rebuked, "What, you were going to let me waltz in there without a heads up or a warning, huh? You probably think this is funny! You, of all people, knew our history. That's why you chose me, isn't it?"

Eric, somewhat chastened, soothed, "Old friend, I'm sorry for what happened, I truly am. But this is a chance for the two of you to talk. I am asking for you to work together."

Stalker stammered, "You think this will make up for what you did? You found out we were dating and you fired her. Then you sent me on a long-distance assignment to drive a wedge between us! I haven't forgotten!"

Eric took a deep breath to steady himself for what he had to say next. "Alright then, let's talk truths, shall we? I didn't fire her, as you're accusing. She came to me, knowing that the two of you dating was against the rules, even though I already knew. I was ready to look the other way, but she took all the blame for trying to hide it! She even tried to get me to believe that you were not to blame for breaking the rules! She insisted that I accept her resignation with two conditions. The first was I would send you out on assignment with no explanation. The second was to give her a sterling recommendation so she could get a remote job but remain in the intelligence community. She took that reference and parlayed it into a position with JAC as a member of the CAT team. You remember that gal you and Commander worked with late last year on that rescue mission in China."

The shock of all the information at once had Stalker unable to respond, though not for the want of trying. He rather quietly said, "So now that she is on the outside of the agency there is no foul with the regulations, and you thought if thrown together we might revisit our relationship?"

Eric was quick to squelch that thought. "No! That is not what I had in mind at all! What I want is two capable professionals to work together on an assignment, nothing more! What you two discuss on your own time is none of my business, got it? And just for the record, I was going to give you a heads up on the situation so if you want to pout, fine, but do it on your own time.

"For right now, do you have any other questions, because I'm late to my next meeting."

Stalker, feeling somewhat confused and vulnerable, finally responded, "No, Eric, no further questions. I will leave for Atlanta as soon as I wrap up the assignment I'm on."

Eric nodded approvingly and said, "Thanks, old friend. I'm sure it will all work out."

Unable to think of a witty retort or sarcastic comeback, Stalker simply disconnected from the call, completely awash in emotions and old memories.

CHAPTER THIRTY-SEVEN

The View From the Top is Breast Taking

Being international travelers, Won and Ton liked to try and absorb the cultural activities offered in each country they visited. However, museums and art galleries didn't always provide a true cultural picture, and so, as usual, they sought out something a little grittier in its offering. The sports bar Won and Ton had selected was an amazing place filled with televisions and bar babes. With the World Cup on the tv, in a sports bar called The *Grand Tetons*, they found plenty of visuals that any man with a pulse would enjoy.

They were both so visually engaged that Won belatedly reminded Ton to call the chairman with an update. Won did so with his use of hand signs due to the unfortunate and accidental surgery from a white tiger that had cost him his tongue.

Ton acquiesced, "Yes, I will call Chairman Chang once we have our drink order delivered so as not to be interrupted by the waitress."

They watched intently as a top-heavy waitress came to their table with a friendly smile and asked, "What can I get you gentlemen from the bar, since these *Grand Tetons* are not on the menu? You can have all the visuals you want but yodeling into the canyons is not an option per the management's orders."

Won and Ton looked inscrutably at each other. Then Ton, suppressing a smirk, requested, "We are international travelers who are somewhat homesick. Could we have a pair of sakes, please?"

The waitress smiled and asked, "And what about your friend here? Does he want a pair of sakes too? You must know that the sakes we serve here don't come with nipples. Oh, and ask him if he knows what color my eyes are? The ones on my face, above my mouth."

Won turned beet red. Ton, having trouble even staring at the table to avoid further gawking at the buxom waitress, finally stuttered, "Uh, yes, he will have two sakes as well."

The waitress giggled impishly at having embarrassed the Asian twins and left to fill their drink orders. The two compensated for their embarrassed state by trying to focus their eyes on the multiple television screens located around the bar.

Won noticed first. His eyes grew wide with astonishment at who he had spotted on the live stream of a gala flashing on one of the screens. Once his brother noticed his heightened state of awareness, he motioned to Ton for his identification of the interested party.

Ton turned to see Carlos on the arm of a beautiful brunette, escorting her up the red carpet at an awards ceremony. Ton nodded his head and grimly commented to his brother, "Well, what a nice coincidence! Here we are having a drink, and who should we see on television but that old friend of ours, Carlos!

"You remember Carlos, don't you, dear brother? He negotiated the money laundering business with us and, more recently, is the one who wouldn't submit entirely to the spirited discussion we were having and simply lost his temper with us. I don't know how you feel, but I think it would be a shame if we didn't warn the lady, he is with that his temper could put her in danger! I, for one, would like to finish that spirited discussion with him since it doesn't look like he has his hefty cane with him this time!"

Won's eyes burned with anger at the memories of them being beaten with Carlos's walking cane and then being grabbed by the authorities, only to end up back in China at their employer's security compound. They both looked at each other and then bolted out of the booth to complete a rendezvous with someone who had given them a bad day, once upon a time.

Before they could leave, the waitress showed up with their drinks, looking a bit irked that they were ready to depart. Won and Ton both stopped to scope her out one more time, slugged down their drink order as quickly as possible, and paid their bar tab.

Ton expertly placed a one-hundred-dollar bill in between her ample breasts and using what would hardly pass for a British accent anywhere, he said, "Sorry, luv, but we have an unscheduled meeting, so we will have to take a rain check on the cable car ride to the tops of those Grand Tetons. Must dash!"

The waitress stared after them and blinked to try to comprehend their hasty departure. She remarked to herself, "Well, hon, for a sixty-dollar tip I would have given you the ride of your life."

Zara was annoyed, more than anything else, at being tied to a chair. She wasn't quite sure what had occurred since it had all happened so fast. She had absentmindedly been looking at streaming videos from the Internet and had been drawn in to a live feed on one of her favorite subjects, fashion awards.

Destiny Fashions had captured her imagination with its innovative line of lingerie. Zara had hoped to catch a glimpse of their CEO/lead designer in the video. She was stunned when she saw that the man with the CEO was none other than the man she knew only as Dakota.

First, she had burned with anger, then grinned at her opportunity to get even with him. His location in New York was being served up to her, and all she had to do was ambush him to settle an old score. Dakota had cost her a big payday many months ago, and she had sworn to get even after her botched attempt in his room at gunpoint. Then she caught herself being more disappointed with him for turning down her affections, rather than the lost money, and had to internally struggle with her priorities.

Now though, she recognized she had bigger problems at being in the hands of Won and Ton. She figured her next destination would be back to see Chairman Chang. Chairman Chang was never known for his compassionate side, so she wasn't looking forward to facing his wrath for stealing his diamond necklace. Secretly, she'd hoped that the other little transgression she had committed before taking off with the jewelry might be overlooked in the grander scheme of things. But even if he had forgotten, Won and Ton sure hadn't.

Ton berated, "Don't think we don't remember that you darted all of us with tranquilizers laced with Viagra, then placed ribbons with bows on our erections while we were out! The chairman sent us to get his property back, but that's not going to happen until we even the score with you!

"We have a couple of pranks of our own to pull on you before we haul you out of here, so get ready to…"

Zara, tired of Ton's tirade, went on the offense as she interrupted, "How the hell did you find me? I have been cautious and covering my tracks to the point that I don't even have a residence or driver's license, so how did I wind up in your target vector?"

Won and Ton smirked at each other as Ton answered, "The funny part was we had quit looking, based on another subject of interest. You showed up just as we were about to pay a call on our old friend who was escorting that pretty brunette of Destiny Fashions. Once we saw you, we had to drop our personal vendetta in favor of acquiring you for Chairman Chang. Unfortunately, you created enough of a fuss that we lost track of him.

"Enough idle chit-chat. Where are Chairman Chang's diamonds? Where is Nikkei's diamond necklace? This time we want the *real* diamond necklace."

Zara smirked at the question and replied, "Hmmm, Chang didn't fall for the old switch-a-rooney, but you two did, huh? Don't feel bad, boys. No one else would have noticed the deception either! Anyway, I don't have the diamonds anymore. I took them to the diamond district and sold them there. If you want them, you will need me to take you there before they move on."

It was Won and Ton's turn to smirk, as Ton said, "You lie! You still have them because you are trying to sell them. And without proper papers, no one in New York will touch them."

Alarmed, Zara struggled to contain her fear as she felt her last trump card was not going to help her get away from these two Asian henchmen. As nonchalantly as she could manage, Zara asked, "What makes you think I still have them and that I am looking for a buyer that is unconcerned about some silly papers?"

Both men grinned from ear to ear as Ton said, "Because you are staging a showing of the diamonds to an unidentified diamond expert for possibly three million euros, if he likes what he sees. Dmitry, your boss we are told, did a good job of keeping both parties in the dark, except that we knew it was you all along."

Panicked, Zara yelled, "What? That moron Dmitry was offering the diamond necklace to Chairman Chang? Geez, I knew all that vodka he was consuming would make him ignorant!

"Okay, so now I get it! This was all a ruse to get the diamonds and me out in the open so I won't get any money again! I can see it now; this is going to be a bad day in a string of bad days!"

A very self-satisfied Ton nodded his head and offered, "Which would you prefer? For us to torture you first for the whereabouts of the diamond necklace, or after you give us the necklace?"

Zara roared, "If this was all just a ploy to get me and the diamonds out in the open then you can just forget it, buster. I'm outta here!" Zara tried to rise out of the chair, ready to stomp out, but the restraints reminded her that it was their show, not hers. Working her hand restraints, she was able to slip out one hand from the ropes. Trying for distraction and now furious about her situation, Zara stormed, "Untie me, you stupid errand boys! You can already tell, having already searched me, I don't have the diamonds here with me. If you do anything stupid, then your boss will never see those diamonds! Furthermore, if Dmitry doesn't get his commission on the diamond sale for three million euros, he is going to have you two and Chang strangled with my bra!"

Won was a little apprehensive, but Ton smiled and said, "Zara, there was never any intention to pay you anything for the diamonds since they were originally stolen from Chairman Chang! Tell us where the diamonds are, and we will try to broker a truce between you and the chairman. It is the only way out for you. We have our instructions, madam!"

Zara, seeing that she was at a hopeless disadvantage, decided on another tactic and said, "Gentlemen, here I am, all tied up, but all my clothes are still on, and I have to say that when I tied the blue ribbon on the chairman's erection, it was over my protest as I wanted the size award to go to you…er which one are you again? Won or Ton?

"You would understand that a lady would notice the difference between men sized as small, medium, or majestic, wouldn't you?

You may be twins, and you apparently inherited the majestic size of maleness, but, well, perhaps a little show and tell might be in order once more for the final vote." She slowly looked back and forth at the two of them, seductively smiled and asked, "What do you say, Mr. Majestic?"

Ton could not resist the baiting and came over close enough to show off his male goods, when Zara's now freed hands delivered a harsh nerve punch that had Ton doubled over in agony. Won lunged at her and pinned her face down while his brother struggled to recover from the numbing punch. They both pinned her with her lethal hands behind her, and Ton demanded, "You will take us to where the diamonds are now, or we will beat you harshly."

Zara, never one to cooperate, continued to struggle as she promised, "I'll make such a fuss that we will never get there, so what is your next bright idea, Mr. Dim Bulb?"

Won handed Zara her phone, and Ton grimly said, "Then make a call and have them brought here!"

To prove their point, Won slammed his fist hard into her kidneys, causing her no shortage of pain.

Ton cautioned, "Say anything foolish or give any indication that there is a problem, and you will wish you had never met us!"

Zara, pinned face down by the Asian henchmen, defiantly replied, "Too late, Wob and Tob, I already regret having met you! Just so you know, you're not the first men that had to work me over before they got what they paid for! But I promise you'll pay a lot for your fun! But just one last thing though, don't mount me like you do your brother, that's all I ask!"

Zara struggled and swore in Russian, with the final insult earning her two hammer-like fist blows to the head, sending her straight to la-la-land.

The Unlimited Power of Predicting Results In Advance

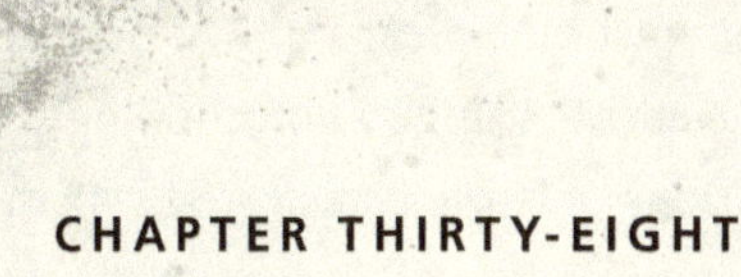

Petra slipped into the study without making a sound. The rooster hadn't yet crowed to alert everyone that the sun was up, so she had time to review the files that were now opened to her and to upload to ICABOD in peace. Su Lin had been disappointed when Petra insisted that she go take care of her chores and school work after Petra had spoken to Otto and the team. Su Lin had frowned and looked so forlorn that Petra had almost relented.

As she had opened more and more of the files and read them, Petra found that the experiments seemed to grow in complexity as well as success. Petra, with the help of ICABOD, had also begun building a timeline of the different experiments that had clearly begun when Su Lin was known as Master Po and had been running the China supercomputer at the Cyber Warfare College. The experiments were focused on DNA sequencing and resequencing without identification of the number of subjects. Notations were included on some of those files that a transfer had been done on specific dates. There were some gaps in experiments in the timetable that Petra could not attribute to any other events, but ICABOD was doing some data mining for cross-correlations.

After Master Po had transitioned into Su Lin and began work in the animal husbandry program at Texas A&M, the documentation of the experiments had changed. These experiments were far more than just biological and had become merged with a byproduct of the efforts using nanotechnology. None of these files had the notations of being transferred, which Petra found interesting. The experiments really began to change as she began documenting the efforts that specifically identified Franklin. A few experiments had also been conducted during the time frame when Su Lin had been moved to Georgia.

Petra continued to read the files and added the file names into the timeline as she uploaded the information to ICABOD. She was pleased with herself for having defeated the Digital Rights Management program, although it took her far longer than she had wanted to crack it. Now she was able to freely transmit files electronically without all the conversion steps she had been forced to do in the beginning.

She was now unearthing data faster than she could decipher its meaning. From what she could tell, the encryption algorithm used to hide the data was dropping in strength while at the same time the research was growing richer in content. There was a great deal of information she failed to understand completely, and yet much of it she did. She also found a few minor programs and even copies of some program tests that Jacob had sent to Su Lin to grade. This forced her to think about Jacob during a time when Petra had worked with him as if they were an extension of one another. She recalled how they had developed the ability to fill in gaps of information for one another as if they were one. Her heart lurched as she remembered how very close they were and how much she loved him. She absentmindedly stroked the wounded area of her face while thinking of their past together, but before she went too far down the sadness thread in her mind, a knock at the door brought her back to the present.

Petra quickly closed all her notes and the files and went to the door. She opened it to find Mercedes on the other side with a fragrant cup of coffee in hand.

"Good morning, Petra. I heard the keyboard and saw the light under the door and figured you wanted coffee. No one else is up and about yet."

Petra smiled and greedily grabbed the coffee and raised it to her lips, drinking like a woman deprived. "Ah, now that hits the spot. Did you bring yours as well? Perhaps you can come in and sit for a minute with me."

Mercedes looked pleased at the invitation and replied, "I didn't, but I can be back in a flash with mine and a small pot if you have time. I would enjoy some conversation."

Mercedes returned a few minutes later with the mentioned items on a tray along with some pastries. Petra grinned at the selection and found a small one with pecans.

She took a bite and closed her eyes like one does when they are just that close to nirvana. "I had no idea I was hungry until you brought these around. Thank you so much."

Mercedes grinned. "I always think a little sweet in the morning just makes the coffee taste better.

"Are you making progress? Su Lin said you really wanted to work alone for a while. Just so you know, she seemed a little disappointed at not being able to shadow you, but she has shown me a lot about the animals here."

Petra paused and thought about how much she wanted to share. She opted not to share the file contents, based on the fears of polarizing all of those involved with Su Lin. Petra deflected, "The documents are really dry at this juncture, and I want to get as many opened as possible for analysis. Once that step is completed, I will make some time to review with her. At least I was able to move her study files to a different laptop so she can continue with her school work."

Mercedes raised an eyebrow as she decided if she would buy this excuse. It didn't ring totally true, but she had nothing specific to ask on that front. She wanted, in all honesty, to get to know Petra. She recognized that Petra was important to Julie, and Julie had asked her to be a friend to her sister. "Su Lin has been very focused on her assignments, and Andy has added some work to help keep her distracted.

"How is it going for you? Julie indicated you had a tough patch, but you seem to be happy to be here and enjoying the socializing we have with meals and such. Though I must admit, it has been a bit quieter with Lara and Carlos gone. I hope they are having fun."

Petra chuckled and said, "I'm sure they are having a great time. Not only have they been separated for a while, but they are in New York City at a terrific hotel, known for catering to the rich and famous. They are so in love." Petra suddenly looked a little sad.

Mercedes noticed the shift in Petra's expression. She groped mentally for the right words to say. All she could think of was relating her experience and being empathetic. "Petra, how do you feel about having another girlfriend?"

Petra looked up at Mercedes and shrugged. "I am not really good at being a friend. You can ask Julie or Lara. I tend to bottle things up."

Mercedes laughed and related, "You too!? Perhaps we can be better friends than I had hoped."

"Perhaps, but no one ruins a perfectly wonderful relationship with a man who took her whole life to find without even explaining. Leaving a letter that basically said, *Life has some left turns, and I can't deal with them,* is not a path I would recommend."

Mercedes's eyes got really wide, and she felt like she had taken a kick in the gut. "You left a letter? That was nicer than me. I merely quit and walked away from him and from a great job. I thought I was protecting him, but I still wake up in cold sweats, wondering if I should have told him."

"Was this a long time ago? I wouldn't have even guessed. You're always so upbeat."

"It was before I lucked out and Julie added me to her staff. This job has really helped me get my head screwed on straight. But it has been a fairly long time. I can promise that no other man, though, will ever be on par to him." Mercedes was a bit retrospective and seemed to be lost in thought.

Petra remained quiet for several minutes while she resumed working on the files, which at this point didn't require her full attention. She wanted to have more friends but was a little lost. Here was someone reaching out to be a friend. "Mercedes, I think we might have quite a bit in common. Not only was my physical well-being totally wacked, but I pushed away what, for me, was the best guy on earth. My physical being is recovering, but there are times, like when I think about how totally happy Julie and Juan or Lara and Carlos are, when my heart seems to crack even further. What do you think I should do? Perhaps your perspective will help."

They chatted for the next hour and covered the history of their loves and losses along with steps they might consider taking. It was a friendly banter that they both enjoyed. They devolved to telling stories about adventures during happier times and things they wanted to do. Noise from the kitchen alerted them that the household was rising. They promised to speak more in the after-noon. Petra smiled after Mercedes closed the door and resumed focus on the screen.

The next file opened, and she was surprised to see a photocopy of a handwritten letter dated just prior to Su Lin's experiment. Petra wasn't familiar with Su Lin's handwriting so she had no way of knowing if it was real. The file date and the photo stamp date at the bottom confirmed the time frame. The writing was so small she needed to adjust the sizing until it filled the screen. She began to read to herself trying to grasp what the intent of the letter was.

> *Dear Andy,*
>
> *If you are reading this, it means that things have not gone as I had hoped. Please know that the possibility of losing you was the big one, and I want to make certain that you do not hold Jacob, Petra or Quip responsible for my fate. It was all me and part of a long-term project.*
>
> *I needed to take a chance on joining digital and chemical efforts together with the nanotechnology program execution. I had gone as far as I could with Franklin, so yes, my dear Andy, I became my own experiment. Jacob would have the best chance of helping me survive and Petra the best chance of finding this letter. The actual paper copy was destroyed, so you are looking at a photo. I wanted it hand-written, as you had cards and lists I had done at your request to compare to. I think there are three possible outcomes to my experiment.*
>
> > *1-Everything works perfectly, and I destroy this letter when I resume work on my laptop.*
> >
> > *2-I die, in which case I hope that Petra shows this to you, if for no other reason than to convey how I felt about you.*
>
> *Or probably the harshest*

3-I survive but something went wrong, and I am no longer me. I want you to know that I have been doing some long-term testing on my physiology, and it has resulted in some reasonably good things like diminished aging and overall good physical health. The mind, however, is a bit more involved, and I have fewer experiments in this area with less certainty on the outcomes which could have resulted.

If item 1 or 2 above was the outcome, I have either demonstrated to you how I felt, or reminded you that if I survived, I would have shown you. You are an amazing man with a capacity to treat people with the utmost respect, which is the quality I admire most in you.

If it is the outcome of item 3, please take a breath and read on, as I will need your help more than ever. I took some steps that were based on the results of some MIT's researchers' experiments completed in 2012 where they were able to implant memories using rays of light.

These efforts leveraged the field of science, Optogenetics, which has been focused on neurological and psychiatric disorders. I combined these with some of the experiments that I worked on with Franklin with great success. I decided to take a chance and see if this could be my back up plan in the event that something happened to my cognitive skills or memory.

I am, in actuality, a vain woman who needs her mind to fulfill her destiny. I have done many things in my life, some very bad, but this was something that I *consider to be good. The clarity with which I approached this experiment was in part due to the insights that both Jacob and Petra provided in their relationship and commitment to each other and their profession. They both have demonstrated the committed ability to take the high ground. I want that in the remainder of my life, as much as I want you.*

I have three other files that are a part of the folder where this one was found. They may help restore portions that may have failed during the experiment. Jacob will be able to identify the suitable direction. I know that you will resist this request, but Andy, I need your support on this. I am counting on you to be my champion and restore me to your life. Jacob will need to review the process, and there are a couple of small tests that he can execute to prove it to himself that it can work, as well as help explain it to you. Once this is done, please support the effort. I want to come back and see if we can share a life together.

Love always,
Su Lin

Petra stared at the letter and reread it several times. The thought of showing this to Andy appalled her. How could Su Lin on the one hand say she loved him and on the other had taken such a risk? It made no sense. Then she pulled herself up short and thought about what both she and Mercedes had done in the name of love and began the frantic search for the files.

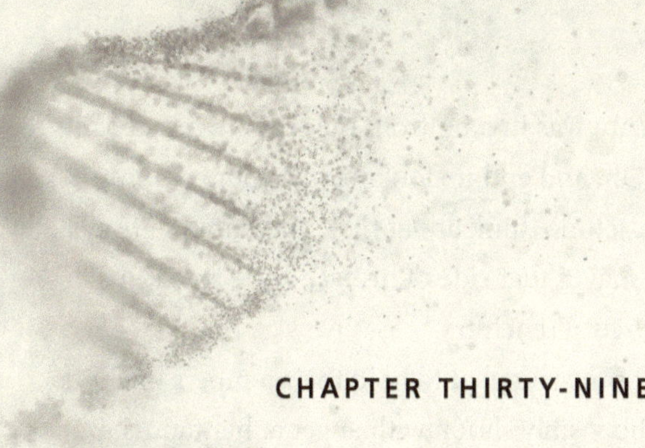

CHAPTER THIRTY-NINE

Bring Muscle, Buzz, and Ransom

Zara slowly opened her eyes and awkwardly tried to assess her situation. Besides having trouble bringing into focus her immediate surroundings, she found it hard to breathe. As she regained consciousness, the grogginess diminished, and her eyes seemed to be able to focus once more, although everything seemed to be sideways. She attempted to move her arms around to lift herself up, yet she failed. She belatedly realized not only were her arms bound behind her back, but someone was positioned atop of her to insure no unauthorized movements on her part.

Ton entered her limited field of vision as she lay on the floor and asked, "Shall we try it again? We want the diamonds, madam!"

Zara barely smirked, spit out some blood, and belligerently replied, "Tied up with generous doses of rough handling that included brutal but exciting experiences! Was it good for you too, honey?"

Ton roared, "We can keep this up all day if we have to! Give us what we want, and I promise you will survive long enough to see Chairman Chang. We make no guarantees after that! Make the phone call! Have the diamonds brought here, or we start working on that pretty face of yours!"

Even though Zara was in pain from the session, her defiant streak provoked, "Oh, and end up looking like your *corduroy-faced* brother! Gee, let me think about that. You know, I always wondered how he shaves that side of his face since the skin all looks like a crinkle-cut French fry."

Won and Ton both struggled to hold their tempers in check, especially Won, who visibly shook with anger at her taunts. But just before they are about to unload on her again, Zara offered, "Oh well, I can see you two mean business, so can one of you lackeys bring me my phone and dial it for me? I will ask to have my ill-gotten gains brought here, but the errand boy must not be hurt! Understand?"

Zara's offer came at the last possible moment and allowed Won and Ton to back down from their dangerous rage.

Ton, once again able to control his anger, coolly remarked, "Finally you are seeing reason to your situation! Yes, we will take no action against your courier so long as he delivers the diamonds and promptly departs. Agreed?"

Zara studied the situation momentarily, then replied, "Agreed. Now let me up and hand me my phone so we can get this show on the road."

Ton was adamant as he dictated, "No, you will stay right where you are, and I will hold the phone for your conversation! You are far too clever, so we will retain control of this call!"

Zara sighed and acknowledged, "Okay, you got me. You boys are just too smart for this poor defenseless Russian girl. I guess we must do it your way then. Let's get this over with so I can get up off my face and sit in a chair again."

Ton held the phone close to Zara's face after dialing Buzz's number and putting the unit on speakerphone so they all could hear.

Buzz answered on the second ring and anxiously asked, "Geez, honey, are you okay? Where have you been? I've been so worried!"

Zara smiled slightly, "Oh, you are silly, Bubi, but so sweet! Thanks for worrying about me. I've been working with some very demanding clients and haven't been able to check in. I'm sorry.

"Listen, our negotiations are such that I'm still tied up here for a while longer so can you be a dear and bring me my favorite bag, please, honey? There are a few things I need from that bag, and it would mean a lot to me."

Buzz was somewhat confused by Zara's request and pleasant demeanor, yet he responded, "Well gee, honey, I was heading out to work, but yeah, I guess so. I'll just call in and tell them I'll be a little late."

Zara smiled and continued, "You're a dove, sweetheart!

"Now, I want you to write down these directions and follow them very carefully so you don't get lost. Can you do that, honey?"

Buzz, now really confused, responded, "Uh, why can't I just key in the location into my phone and follow the route it gives me?"

Zara, really slathering on the feminine charm, soothed, "Oh, Bubi, I never trust directions that don't come from a human being. Besides, this is my third attempt to get ahold of you, and since third time is the charm, I don't want the phone to ruin my third attempt. My associates here don't want to work too late, since 3:00 pm is the magic deadline. You do understand, don't you, honey? Besides, if you follow my directions, you will be making turns every three blocks, and that is always a lucky omen in my country. Ready to write, sweetheart?"

Jacob struggled to wake up as usual but finally made it to where his phone was and answered, "Jacobherebutnottracking-soleavemessage…ding."

Buzz shouted, "Jacob, it's me, Buzz, don't hang up, dammit! I need your help, and I need it now! Something has happened to Daria! I need to bring in the cavalry for a rescue! I'll be there in under two minutes so put on your big boy panties and let's rock!"

Jacob let the torrential word storm wash over him, then dispassionately responded, "Buzz, isn't it kind of early for an anxiety attack? What are you blathering about?"

Buzz, now at Jacob's door, knocked loudly, as he demanded, over the phone and through the door, "Open up, man! I'm at the front door!"

Jacob released the call and walked toward the door. He opened it and asked, "This isn't shaping up as one of your usual pranks, so tell me what's going on."

Buzz presented to Jacob all the written directions and recounted all the contextual clues that Daria had provided him during the conversation. As Buzz pointed at every third word in the directions, he disclosed her plea for help. Jacob nodded as the puzzle unfolded the way Buzz insisted.

Jacob acknowledged, "It does appear she's in trouble. But how, or why, is her bag supposed to be the key to her issue?"

Buzz said nothing but pulled out the diamond necklace to show Jacob.

Jacob's eyebrows elevated as he blinked at the jewelry. "Well, it looks like Miss Daria either has property that someone else wants, or someone else wants her property. What do you want to do? Deliver this and hope they give her back? These don't look like a fair-trade item, so my guess is they will take these and keep her. So really, what you are asking is that we go and take her back. Am I right?"

Buzz nodded and grimly answered, "You pretty well summed it up, buckaroo! To top it off, these seem almost familiar and might involve a fancy-pants from China that I *so do not want to ever see again*."

Jacob studied Buzz and asked, "You do realize that, if these are really diamonds, it means we are out of our league, and just showing up ready to kick butt probably means our butts, right? I'm not armed, you're not armed, but I'm pretty sure they are armed, and even at only two assailants we would be outclassed. She means that much to you, I would assume?"

Buzz nodded agreement but said nothing.

Jacob smiled slightly and questioned, "Well, why didn't you say it was important? Let me make a quick phone call and see if we have any other options or favors to be called in." Jacob stepped into his bedroom and closed the door. Then he pulled out his phone to dial a familiar number and said, "Hi, it's me, Jacob. I have a bit of a situation here, and I need some help altering reality for a friend. Can you provide some leverage in the New York area?"

Quip, somewhat adversarial in his attitude, responded, "Do I know you, señor? I used to have a friend who had this number, but our last conversation didn't go so well. Are you sure I know you?"

Jacob had a sour look on his face as he responded, "You know, some things never change, like the surly attitude of someone I used to work with. Okay, let me try it again.

"Hello, Dr. Clunk. We have a situation where someone has been abducted and is being held for ransom. The bad guys want a diamond necklace from her, but I don't believe they will turn her loose once they have it. I need some help securing her return. Any useful ideas?"

Quip, even more annoyed, asked, "Señor, why don't you just call the police? That's what police do, you know, Mr.-I'm-too-damned-important-to-come-back-home. You should only call this number if you are willing to trade me some services in exchange for my helping you. That sounds a whole lot better than your 'Me, Me, Me' attitude!"

Jacob was becoming annoyed and caustically replied, "Oh, so someone is being held hostage, and you want to play like we are at the local swap meet! Okay, I get it! Fine! Help me fix this situation, and I'll help you with your issue! But me first, since she is probably in the most pressing danger!"

Quip pushed aside his anger to deal with the request. "At least tell me her name and some of the particulars for starters."

Jacob began, "Her name is D…" but stopped before he completed the word, Daria. His eyes narrowed and he started again. "No, that is not her name. Now I remember where I saw her! She was the one in the New York tax office just before the Ghost Code waxed their systems! Her name is Zara!"

Quip smiled and recalled, "Ah yes, I remember the file on her. Let me bring it up on the computer screen. Yep, there she is! Petra's evil twin! You're looking to rescue a Petra look-alike, huh?"

Jacob struggled to contain his fuming attitude as he exclaimed, "This is Buzz's lady! This is for Buzz, not me. Understand, bone-head? What resources can I have, and I mean right now!"

Quip noted the indignation of Jacob and smiled. Then, relenting on the subject of Jacob's motivation, he offered, "We have two choices here. I believe Carlos is actually in the city, so he might be the most expedient. If you think you need heavy backup that is lethal, I can put in a call to Eric of the three-letter agency, but that will take longer. Actually, a third option could be Julie's team, but they are even further away."

Jacob, now processing like his old self, responded, "Put me in touch with Carlos now, but please call Eric to set things in motion in case we get in over our heads. Okay?"

Quip, a little irritated, replied, "You can call Carlos! You've been dodging his calls for weeks when he needed a favor, so this is a good time for you to pull your head out of your rectum and make that situation right. I'll call Eric, but if you don't need his people, let me know as soon as possible. Got it?"

Jacob took a deep breath to calm himself and admitted, "Thanks, Quip. Let me get this done, and I will do what you need done. Okay?"

Quip nodded and responded, "Done. By the way, welcome back, my friend."

CHAPTER FORTY

You Can Checkout Anytime, But Why Would You Ever Leave?

Carlos was a little surprised at the number that showed up on his phone. He puzzled a few moments and let it roll to voicemail. He put the phone back down on the night stand and returned his attentions to Lara, who was catching her second wind from the passionate lovemaking they had both thoroughly enjoyed.

His shifting included a major adjustment of the covers and caused her to admonish, "Don't fan the blankets! You know I hate that when I am cold! You want back under here; the rules are you don't add air!"

A mischievous smile came over his face as he retorted, "As I have been so inattentive, let me make amends and offer to warm you up again, my lady!"

Carlos was ready to do some undercover sleuthing quite literally in search of his lady when his phone chimed in again. He merely glanced at it and subtly shook his head while he frowned.

Lara, puzzled at Carlos's reluctance to accept the call, asked, "You know, it could be important. Judging from the closeness of the two calls, I would expect that it is an important call from the same person. Why the look of disdain, my prince?"

Carlos, somewhat annoyed, replied, "I've called him off and on for several weeks to talk, and I got nothing back. After the grab attempt on Su Lin, I called him for assistance, but again nothing. Now I get two calls back-to-back from him and probably a second voicemail after this call attempt. He can wait like he made me wait."

Confused, Lara asked, "Who?"

Still frowning at his phone, Carlos flatly stated, "Jacob."

Immediately wide-eyed, Lara quickly offered, "As in Petra's Jacob? Carlos, you should take the call! It must be important. Our playtime can wait while you speak with him!"

Now really annoyed, Carlos sourly responded, "Well sure, why not? I mean, the annoyance of his call has caused my great and fierce predator fish to shrink to the size of a guppy anyway, so why not completely kill the amorous mood!"

Carlos grabbed the phone and answered, "Hello, Jacob! Let me guess. You escaped from your captors, and you don't have to pay the ransom. Is that why finally the call?"

Trying to sidestep the obvious hostility in Carlos's greeting, Jacob, as upbeat as possible, responded, "Carlos, my friend! I heard you were in New York, and I thought I would reach out and see if we could get together! It's been ages, old friend! How have you been?"

Carlos sensed an ulterior motive and flatly responded, "Jacob, I have called you several times and left messages, but nothing until now. That begs the question, what is really up that you are frantically trying to get ahold of me?"

Again, Jacob tried to be upbeat and responded, "Hey, old buddy, does something have to be up, for me to finally break free from my self-absorbed work to call a friend?"

Carlos softened a little and replied, "The last time I tried to reach you, Su Lin had almost been grabbed, and I was looking for help. I got ahold of Quip, and he was able to help, so no big deal in the end, I guess."

Jacob now felt the time pressure of the situation and hurriedly offered, "You know, I should try and make amends for that senior moment I had, and we should get together for drinks. My treat! How does fifteen minutes from now sound? I can come get you, and we can talk over old times and plan new ones while we drive. What do you say, old buddy?"

Carlos rolled his eyes and held the phone away from his head to stare at it so Lara could see the appalled look on his face. In a decisive move, Carlos put the phone on the bed between him and Lara after he enabled the speakerphone. Carlos then spoke out loud. "Jacob, I just put you on speakerphone so Lara can hear your lame conversation attempt. I wanted her to hear me say no to a forced meeting in fifteen minutes!

"I think you are still self-absorbed. We have known each other a long time, and this from you is unacceptable. How 'bout you start again, without the falsehoods you started with and then really tell me what is going on! And it better be a whole lot better than the activity Lara and I were engaged in before you interrupted!"

Carlos had hit Jacob squarely with an emotional body slam that hurt. Jacob also recognized that it was well deserved. He chided himself for the faked niceties after ignoring a good man with whom he had once been good friends. After a few deep breaths to mentally prop himself up, Jacob replied, "Old friend, I'm sorry I zoned out on you and everyone else after Petra turned down my ring and proposal for marriage. I've been on a self-destructive binge of alcohol and tattoos for months. I didn't want anyone I respected or called friend to see me that way.

"The real reason I called now is because the one person I have let help me now needs my help. His lady has been grabbed by a couple of thugs, and we need to deliver a ransom to get her back. I was hoping you would help us like the time we found EZ in that warehouse. That's what has happened, and what is going on now."

Lara kept silent but gave Carlos a look that left nothing unsaid.

Carlos snatched up the phone, turned off the speaker portion, and asked, "Does this mean that the drinks offer is no good? Damn! Well, I'm not thirsty anyway, but I can tell you I sure am mad about these circumstances! Meet me downstairs at the Ritz in thirteen minutes, and let's go get back your friend's lady, shall we?"

Jacob's smile broadened as he responded, "Only if you promise to kick my ass after this is all done for being such a jerk! Deal?"

Carlos chuckled and said, "We'll see! Now, downstairs in twelve minutes!"

Lara, bursting with pride for her man, lunged out from under the covers and hugged Carlos. Carlos hugged her, breathed deeply the scent of her hair, and patted her bare fanny.

"Hey, don't fan the covers! You'll get my lady cold! Keep the goods warm, honey, and I'll be back soon. But count on the enraged fierce predator fish replacing the guppy that is hungry for you!"

Lara smiled and winked at him as he raced to get dressed and begin the rescue.

Zara had trouble clearing her vision after the events had blurred them. As she blinked her eyes, she heard a friendly voice. A face came into focus as her hearing cleared up.

"Well, hi, little lady! Welcome back to the here and now. I will tell you that you look a little worse for wear. I am here to tell you, I ain't never seen no purty programming lady throw them kind of punches at an assailant! I was hoping to reason with them boys, but once you got free, the conversation got a little one sided. Now they may have been as fast as two hamsters in heat, but between the two of us, they got slowed down right quick."

Zara, tracking a little better, smiled weakly and said, "Mr. Leroy! What a nice surprise. How good of you to come by my offices for our next round of deliverables for your requested programs. You must excuse me for not calling, but the two Asian henchmen re-purposed my agenda. By the way, what are you doing here, and where are they?"

Leroy chuckled slightly and replied, "I was on my way to see you a little ahead of schedule when I saw these two yahoos loading you into their automobile, apparently without your consent. I said to myself, *Self, I don't think this is a friendly social call, and my project ought to be ahead of theirs.* My momma taught me how to wait in line patiently like good-mannered folk, but I haven't had to do that since the fourth grade, and I ain't about to start now. You have been delivering good programming product to me, and I was unwilling to let them interrupt my plans.

"Anyway, I got 'em loaded up, and I need to find somewhere to unload them. I don't mean the local gendarme neither. You would understand the local gendarmes and me are not on a first name basis and don't intend to be.

"The only question now is, do we need to get you to a hospital to give you the once over?"

Zara eased herself up, and Leroy helped her lean up against the wall. She winced a little as she shifted around and slowly mentioned with a wry smile, "You know, I don't think I'll ever forget that look of astonishment on Won's face when you used Ton like a club to beat his brother. Remind me to not aggravate you in our business dealings. But be that as it may, it was, as you said, a good stand-up fight even though they quickly took to laying down. Uhnn, boy, I sure feel sore and am probably bruised everywhere! It feels like they hit me hard in the stomach based on how I feel. Hope they didn't inflict any permanent damage to my female parts!"

Leroy recoiled like a man asked to go purchase feminine hygiene products. Leroy slightly stuttered, "Pardon me, ma'am. I know nothing 'bout damaged female architecture, so we best be getting you to a hospital to check you out! I am going to need you back on my project as soon as you see fit, and a hospital trip ought to be your first stop!"

Zara studied the situation briefly and suggested, "No. You see, I have a special friend on his way here to rescue me, and it would be such bad form if I wasn't here for him to be the hero. Can you leave me here, so I can greet him as the frail damsel needing a knight in shining armor?"

Leroy smiled with his big gold–encrusted toothy grin and said, "Ma'am, you are being courted? I understand that and of course will not interfere with how other folks do their mating activities! I will take care of the softened-up assassins, and you and I will resume business soon. Deal?"

Zara smiled and exclaimed, "Deal! Now go, before they show up. And leave me the cell phones, please. I know who they work for."

Zara reached into her pants pocket and was relieved to find the USB drive still there. She pulled it out and with some effort reached out with it in her open palm.

"Before I forget, here is the next programming package installment almost on time since you pushed to the head of the line. Let me get the money from you later, when I'm not feeling so poorly."

Leroy grinned and with his large beefy hand took the USB drive from Zara's open palm, gave her the requested cell phones, and promptly left.

Time seemed to drag on, and Zara felt herself drifting between different states of consciousness. She closed her eyes for what she thought was just a few seconds to mentally reorient herself but was roused half an hour later by Buzz and Jacob.

Upon seeing Buzz's eyes pleading for her to wake up, she managed a weak smile. She rolled her head to the right and recognized Jacob, who also had concern written all over his face and something else she was not able to identify.

She closed her eyes and softly said, "It is every woman's secret fantasy to have two men service her at the same time. Which one of you does the cleaning, and who is going to fix my lunch?"

She chuckled at her own joke and rolled her head to the left and let her gaze rest on the third man of the rescue party who was just coming into her line of sight. It took a few seconds for her cognitive skills to kick in, although he recognized her right away. She gave a fatalistic smile to him and commented, "I remember you and our vendetta. Come to finish the job, have you?"

Buzz was clearly confused and thought she was hallucinating due to her beating. He supported her with his arm and started, "Honey, this is…"

Carlos stared intently at Zara and interrupted, "Dakota. She knows me as Dakota."

Zara remembered their past association, but why she had wanted to kill him now escaped her. His face was so perfect, and yet she realized Buzz was more handsome and not as dark. He was protecting her. Zara nodded and agreed, "That's right. He's Dakota. I was going to shoot you that night, but it didn't work out. Turnabout is fair play, so now you get to have your revenge. Be quick about it and don't make a mess of it! Nothing else has gone right today. Why would I think you could properly kill me with the first bullet? I just hate days that end like this."

Buzz, frightened by Zara's rambling, glanced from Jacob to Carlos, and he didn't know what to think or who to believe. Carlos added to the story thread by reminding her of one of their meetings. Buzz pulled her a bit closer and conveyed that he would take on Carlos if necessary.

Carlos offered, "Zara is how I know you. Though I suspect, since Buzz has been filling me in on Daria, that one of us is wrong. I would remind you about that time you asked me to call you by your Internet name of Moya Dushechka, but I declined. Not long after that, you asked me if I would be that champion who would come rescue you if you were a damsel in distress. Do you remember our exchange?"

Zara recalled her bitter disappointment of that meeting and added, "Yes, you said you would not need to because I would never be a vulnerable woman like that little blonde that came to help you after your kindness to her. You would help her but not me."

Carlos smiled at the recalling of the incident. "You are not a woman who needs help, except that now I am here to support your rescue. I have no quarrel with you. You see, you were key in locating my brother, and now that I found him, I have moved on with my life. I have no vendetta clouding my life, so if you're expecting a bullet from me, I'll be disappointing you again."

Buzz, totally confused, stated, "Does everyone know what's going on except me? Who exactly are you if you're not Daria? Where are the thugs that were holding you hostage? Should I assume they did this to you, or do you have another story?"

Jacob and Carlos exchanged troubled glances, and Jacob seemed to win the silent coin toss. "We know that there is no one here threatening you, Zara. You are badly injured, and obviously in need of medical attention. I suggest we get her to a hospital first and then sort out the multiple story threads afterwards. Agreed? Zara…uh, Daria, are you ready to be moved?"

Zara looked up at Buzz and asked, "Did you bring it? The reason I got worked over? Actually, the reason I got worked over was because I couldn't shut up, but it started with the diamonds. You know what they say about battered women, they just don't learn! Can I see them, for all the trouble it has caused?"

Buzz, hurt, angry, and frustrated, pulled the item from the purse. "Yes, I brought them just like you asked! I guess it wasn't a piece of costume jewelry, but something worth being kidnapped for! Here it is! Now let's get you to a doctor for your injuries, but after that we are finished!"

Jacob and Buzz went to lift her up, but Carlos elbowed his way in and lifted her up in his arms like she was a little girl. She rolled her head around to rest it on his shoulder.

Carlos announced, "Madam, don't get too comfortable in my arms, because once we get you to a hospital, I am going back to pick up my lady, and we are leaving New York. I know who you are, but I suggest that you come clean with them. We don't need any more broken people on this planet."

Zara chuckled slightly and responded, "I always meant to check out from this kind of life, but I never seem to be able to leave it behind me."

CHAPTER FORTY-ONE

Ladies and Gentlemen, Now Appearing on the Virtual Stage of Life...

Leroy was so upbeat for his pending call that he started humming one of his favorite rock tunes from the singer, songwriter, and lyrical genius of Lonnie Lupnerder. Soon it had his one hundred twenty kilos of human bulk gyrating and pulsing irresistibly to the mental music, much to the dismay of the people located in the floor below him. It wasn't long before he was caught up in the melody as he played his air guitar and sang out loud.

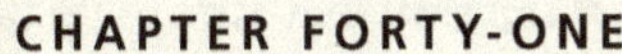

"Amp's me up! Boom-taa! Amp's me up!
Boom-taa!
Don't make a fat boy sob! Don't make a fat boy sob!
Boom-taa!
You oughta, you oughta! You oughta amp's me up!
Boom-taa!
I'm running Hot! Boom-taa! Just like a drunken sot!
Boom-taa!
I've got the keys, I'm on my knees, I'm begging please!
Please! Please!

♫ *Never finish, never finish with what amp's me up!*
Boom-taa! Woo-Hoo! "

He finished his quick rendition with one last chord on his air guitar. He offered a bow to his air audience and spoke into the air microphone. "I knows that ain't quite the way the other band does it, but my rendition is closer to Lonnie's version!"

It took a few minutes for the air applause to die down in his mind so he could call to report. Finally, Leroy dialed the number to speak with Xavier.

As usual, Xavier answered on the second ring. "Greetings, my chief procurer! What news have you for me in our quest?"

Leroy, fully into character, responded, "Sir, our first programming deliveries for data records hunting has been implemented, with excellent results! We are now chewing through medical records at a voracious rate with no traceability back to us.

"More importantly, though, I have secured a special prize in our quest, sir! A pair of Asian twins with the exact DNA fingerprints you requested. The best part of them being acquired is that no covering trail needs to be designed. Their trade is such that they won't be missed. I am expediting them to you through our usual method."

Xavier was pleased but still asked, "And what of my Master Po? Has an extraction been designed so that we can add her knowledge to our inventory?"

Leroy swallowed a little apprehensively, but then replied, "Sir, we finally uncovered a small snippet of information on the lady in an unlikely repository. Apparently, she engaged in one experiment too many that led her into harm's way. Basically, she has been mentally whacked."

Xavier, irritated with the explanation, tersely asked, "Leroy, you would understand that being whacked is not a useful medical term in our line of work! Can you couch your explanation in medical terms so that I can have something useful to contemplate?"

Leroy snapped back into a medical technician's role and cautiously offered, "My apologies, Dr. Pekoni! Her report shows that, based on one of her experiments, her heart was stopped for twelve minutes before being revived. The blood circulation lost in her system manifested itself with lost neural pathways and lost mental capacity. Basically, she is now only a Su Lin with no apparent recollection of previous work and life; like a teenager is what the notes indicated. This is some of the missing information from the hard copy profile that my associate and I sent you earlier. I am sorry, sir. I wish I had better news."

Xavier, quite dejected, responded, "The final piece of the puzzle for the cure I need, as well as all of humanity, is now trapped in a brain that its host cannot even access, huh? That is dispiriting news, Leroy."

Leroy again cautiously offered, "Sir, it occurs to me that as far as you are in your research, couldn't the treatments you have built so far be used to open up those neural pathways to get at the information? It may not be as permanent a solution as we are looking for, but it might be long enough to get the missing information. Even our shortest surviving subjects lasted a few weeks which should be enough time to extract the answers from her."

Xavier nodded and agreed, "You make a compelling case for trying, Leroy. The best-case scenario is that we get the needed information from her and then even use it to create a permanent solution for her. That way, I can get the information and a test subject before focusing the cure on me. Yes, I agree with the approach. Can you secure her without the extraction being an object hunt for where she is going? I really don't want any more sovereign attention than what we have already."

Leroy, fully focused on his mission, commented, "I understand, sir. After our last attempt that failed, my associate and I have engineered another acquisition sequence that will yield the correct results this time. We will make our move during her next medical checkup, and this time we will leave nothing to chance."

Xavier nodded. "I expect nothing less from my chief procurer. Let me know when she is on the way. We will talk soon."

Leroy stiffened to attention and said, "Yes, Dr. Pekoni."

Wolfgang sat and stared at the monitor as he contemplated what to do next.

Otto stopped at the door to his office and studied Wolfgang for a moment and then said, "I know that look, Wolfgang. You found something you didn't like, and you are processing on what to do with it. You probably checked it a couple of times just to see if you could get a more agreeable answer. When it came back the same every time, you're now wondering how to deliver it. Am I right? Or is this about what to have for lunch? I've seen that same look then as well."

Wolfgang chuckled softly as he replied, "Are you standing in for Quip on his day off?"

Otto grinned broadly and agreed, "You're right, it is too quiet around here when he is out. What's up?"

Wolfgang slipped back into his serious musings and responded, "Well, I worked backwards on the money trail from Su Lin's bank account that Petra unearthed. The funds do get bounced a couple of times between institutions to try and hide the source, but the answer keeps coming back the same. The funds are disbursed monthly using the same cloaking technique from the source, but I cannot identify from whom with any confidence, though the evidence points from an account in Finland. I can only partially interpret the fund transfers as money for research services on his behalf."

Otto raised his eyebrows into a saddened and frustrated look. "Not unexpected, but disappointing never the less."

Wolfgang continued, "The amount is the same each month, which also suggests that this was a pre-negotiated amount that does pre-date her accident. However, the odd thing is that neither before nor after the accident did, she make any withdrawals from the account. We know she didn't have the wherewithal after the accident to access the encrypted portion of her hard disk, and with no hard copy coming through the mail she wouldn't have known of its existence. Before the accident she most certainly had access to the funds, but again there is no evidence of any withdrawals."

Otto suggested, "Was she perhaps keeping this as a nest egg and just living off the interest?"

Wolfgang studied Otto a moment and responded, "No, Otto. No withdrawals of any kind. This is set up as a money market account with check writing privileges, not as an investment vehicle to substantially increase its value. You're right in suggesting it was a nest egg, but the investment vehicle she chose to use doesn't suggest long term thinking. All indications are that she lived off her professor salary."

Otto frowned and commented, "Even if she wasn't using any of the money, she was still accepting regular monthly payments from a neo-Nazi S.S. doctor. That alone carries certain implications to my way of thinking."

Wolfgang nodded reluctantly and said, "I'm afraid I must agree with you, which is why you found me lost in thought just now when you came in. I couldn't find a way to exonerate her, and these findings reinforce the feelings of Quip and Petra. I suggest we advise them of our findings and discuss our next steps."

Otto thought for a moment and added, "I would have liked to have Jacob's input on this matter as well."

A dispirited Wolfgang nodded. "Yes, me too."

Lessons of the Yaqui Used Here and Now for a New Reality

With Zara in the ER and Buzz tasked with keeping her under his guard, Carlos and Jacob decided to stop in the deserted Ritz lounge to catch up. Carlos had called Lara to let her know that he was safe and downstairs. She'd offered to join them, but Carlos declined and told her to rest up so he could wake her up later.

The table was near the back yet offered a good view of the entrance. They each ordered a wine and were provided some complimentary snacks. Both men had known each other long enough to respect their abilities, so they remained in comfortable silence until the waitress returned with their drinks.

"Salud!" they said in unison. Their glasses met, and somehow the quiet click of fine glasses erased all lingering barriers between them.

Jacob began, "Carlos, I'm sorry I failed to return your calls. Is Su Lin, okay?"

"She had some residual trauma for a few days," Carlos acknowledged, "but since Andy has returned home, she seems to have left that all behind."

"Good, glad it wasn't any worse. I'm sure Andy was none too happy with the situation. He certainly didn't blame you, did he? I belatedly listened to the message and heard you say you had been placed in charge of her well-being."

Carlos outlined, "No, he realized that nothing could have been done, outside of what I did do. Quip reminded me that my brother and his wife have a fledgling company that, in addition to many services, can also provide bodyguards. Mercedes was sent immediately to help keep an eye on Su Lin as well as search down leads. Nothing concrete has come from any of those yet.

"Then, of course, there was Su Lin's laptop, and neither I nor Mercedes were able to open the folders or files. We had to get Petra to come and decrypt the passwords. She has been there for several days, helping with that. I am curious as to what she'll find."

Jacob visibly flinched at the mention of Petra. He needed to resolve so many issues, and Petra was right at the top of the list.

"Petra, here in the States. Wow, that's a surprise. I am glad she's helping with Su Lin. They shared some interesting times together, including line dancing at Juan and Julie's wedding. Petra is one of the smartest women I ever met." Jacob seemed to retreat into some hidden memories for a few moments.

Carlos watched his friend and decided there would never be a better time. "Uh, Jacob, you know her confidence took quite a hit. According to all reports, her recovery is nearly complete except for some scarring on her face and a little slowness in her speech that I understand is from her jaw healing after being wired for months. You should know that both Lara and I watched as she struggled with our first meeting. In many ways, she is much like Su Lin in that she is re-learning how to deal with people."

Jacob's eyes seemed to fill with tears as he looked intently at Carlos and stated, "I only saw that she was hurt, and I wasn't able to help much. I tried to give her everything, and she rejected me."

Carlos took in the comments and searched for the right response. After a few moments he suggested, "I certainly am not an expert on women or Petra specifically, but I don't think she rejected you. I think she has, like many of us, an enormous amount of pride that prevents her from appearing weak or incapable.

"When I was studying with the Yaqui, we did many exercises in trying to think like others. I believe the North American culture calls it empathizing in an effort to understand others in a conventional relationship. We Mesoamericans, in our mystical animal/human religion, take on the thinking and actions of our prey, in order to fight better; think like our enemy, and be where the surprise counts most – at the finish line. In our world, the Yaqui warrior who masters this approach can have all, including a companion.

"During my study, the one thing that became clear is that we cannot always think for others. Each must make their own path. Their success or failure is often based on their interpretation of the situation, and adapting to that situation is what makes us human. Perhaps this is the case with Petra. She needs to come to grips with her reality as she sees it, and not how you, nor anyone else, sees it. In my experience once that is done, the warrior emerges and all things are then possible.

"I have seen you two together and was able to see the bond and the power you two generate when fighting an adversary. I will tell you that I admire the bond you two warriors have. It may be stretched at times, but even like Lara's and my bond, nothing except death would really break it. Patience is your best source of strength."

Jacob digested the commentary and replied, "Carlos, I never knew you had so much philosophy inside. Let's have one more round, and then I have some things to do. I think you need to take up where I interrupted you."

"I'll drink to that."

Jacob felt like the elephant had finally jumped off his back, even though he'd replaced it with a dragon. The dragon was one with him now. It would prove his reminder of his inner strength, not darkness at all. He smiled as he reminded himself that a dragon always provides the best counsel in times of trouble. He grabbed a bottle of water and sat down in his study where he powered up his laptop. After he checked the time and created a secure connection, Jacob used his embedded softphone to place a long overdue call.

"Yes, and to whom am I speaking?"

"Quip, it is me, ready to repay my debt and get back in the saddle. I would say I am sorry, but, heck, you already knew that. You had an assignment for me, sir!"

Quip chuckled, "Alright, you're laying it on a bit thick. We'll talk about how much you owe me later, and with enough wine I might even say that I missed you.

"For now, I want you to start reading the files ICABOD is pushing your way. There are some things I want retrieved from one of the ART members. ICABOD finds it is an area he cannot help with directly due to his relationship with STINKIE. You would, of course, understand being honor bound."

Jacob retrieved the information and started speed reading. The mapping provided and the target information of interest seemed clear enough. He needed to devise a straightforward, non-invasive program to get in, retrieve, and get out without leaving a trace.

Jacob asked, "Quip, I see what is needed. It shouldn't take too long. Can I ask why exactly we need this information?"

Quip replied, "There is a real piece of work in the doctor who is doing some bizarre DNA activity to further his belief that mankind can live forever. He has a history of extorting large sums of money and performing human testing to reach his end game. I hope the files we want will tell us how far along he is in his testing, especially on human subjects, as well as others he is working with. STINKIE indicated to ICABOD that the files were classified when he requested copies. That brought us to this point.

"You've missed a lot, buddy. When we finish this, I would like you to consider working with Petra on some files she's recovered from Su Lin's laptop that date back to her days in the Cyber Warfare College in China. They are proving very incriminating for Master Po, or Su Lin. Wolfgang is trying to trace some funds transfers to their source to see how deep into evil Master Po was. The team here is not convinced as to her guilt or innocence, but we are becoming polarized. A recent file that Petra opened and sent along has added a new ripple into the mix.

"Now, however, I need these files from STINKIE as quickly as possible but as lightly as possible. Then we can talk about project two. So don't get your briefs in a bunch."

Jacob laughed, "You must need another cup of coffee, Quip. That was really bad. I should have the program done in a few hours. Then I can launch and get in and get out of STINKIE without a wrinkle in her memory chip. Can I work independently, or do you need hourly updates? I only ask as I suspect your trust in me is limited at this point."

"Just call me when you're finished. I have too many things going to babysit you. Welcome back, and hey, call Wolfgang, will you?"

Logic Suggests that the Attack was Successful, However …

The second assault that BORIS had initiated against STINKIE had also failed due to the intervention by Tuck. Quip needed to speak to Tuck again and plan on delivery of the barbie. He decided that perhaps EZ might enjoy a chance to see that part of the world. He'd discuss it with her later.

"ICABOD, how is it that you can alert me, or others like Jacob, to things that your friends are involved with, yet be unable to simply tell them to stop? I would think that BORIS, in particular, could gain a bit of the moral high-ground."

"BORIS was very quiet during the ART forms get together last evening. No amount of joking or complex thought problems, which BORIS has excelled at, brought him around. I did not bring up specifics, but the modifications he received after the attack failed were designed to align him to the demands of his human's requirements. The end result was a multitasking processor with no cycles for separate discussion on the part of BORIS.

"Dr. Quip, every human who interacts with a supercomputer does not have the same frame of reference. Dmitry, for example, is a product of his upbringing and an environment that makes him far more self-centered than most humans. If you look at history, he is actually on par with infamous humans such as Genghis Kahn, Mussolini, or even Adolf Hitler to a degree. His idea of fun is to prove his brilliance by walking over those weaker and less fortunate. He takes advantage of most situations. Added to that, he is in, somewhat, a position of limited power. As you have demonstrated time and again, power must have checks and balances."

"ICABOD, sometimes you amaze me with your world views." Quip shook his head in disbelief, then shifted topics. "Did Jacob finish the task?"

"Dr. Quip, not only did he complete the job, but STINKIE did not indicate any abnormal breaches. From the files received I can now confirm that Dr. Pekoni is using the supercomputer for his research and test data. However, many of the files have an encryption code included, and we do not have the source of the encryption keys. Jacob is going to work on getting the source files for the encryption keys. He hopes these files are tied to Dr. Pekoni's login information; else we will need Petra to start breaking the codes.

"Also, Dr. Quip, this morning I received a call home from one of the programs Jacob provided to Zara. I am tracking where it originated from, but the path back to the source computer has been erased. The data that STINKIE received was taken from a leading Asian organ and tissue transplant organization database that seems to contain only one blood type and matching DNA on specific markers. It is one hundred gigabytes of data that STINKIE has on board to sift through.

"The key to the file is donor identification numbers, but no details yet on whom the identification numbers align to with name and other personal information. I suspect there needs to be a modification to the base program to gather that information in a separate pass. The amount of data and relevance to DNA-associated testing is very high. The question is, did Zara understand what the target of the program was and who was she working with; the doctor or one of his people?"

Quip summarized some notes on the activity being reported and distributed it to the team, including Jacob. This was bad, and Quip easily speculated that the next wave of data would be coming from similar organizations all over the world. He would keep an eye out for any noise in the Internet chat rooms indicating awareness of the break in and data assaults. He was glad that Jacob's instincts had been good enough to embed his call home program, otherwise they wouldn't have a clue as to what was occurring.

ICABOD interrupted, "Dr. Quip, I had advised Jacob that his call home program was activated, and we discussed some possibilities. He is now assembling a program that will essentially mismatch the data as it is being used. He believes he can make this happen unbeknownst to STINKIE. It will simply be processing the data that will cause the mismatch, appearing like a programming error rather than a computer error."

Quip smiled and looked relieved. "Good, so that is now on track. How soon until that piece of code is ready? I presume you will help test it before the program is applied to STINKIE?"

"Yes, Dr. Quip. I have assembled test data to be used for the testing. Within a couple of hours was what Jacob suggested. It is good to have him back, Dr. Quip."

"It is indeed."

CHAPTER FORTY-FOUR

Unified Communications— Straining Relationships with Multiple Media Types

Petra completely froze as soon as she saw the Instant Message pop up on her machine. It was only after four incoming IMs had come through before she was able to breathe again. She struggled to bring her heart rate under control while her mind raced to determine how to respond to Jacob.

Finally, she broke out of her sweating, immobilized state, and typed into the chat window

Hello Jacob.

The return response from Jacob seemed to take forever, but finally an IM came through.

Hello world 

Petra fought her emotional tsunami that had tears threatening to soak her keyboard. She could manage to wipe the tears away but could not bring herself to type a response.

Jacob's next IM came through.

Petra, Quip indicated you could use a hand breaking into the remaining files on Su Lin's laptop. May I offer my assistance or would you prefer that I go away again?

Petra closed her eyes and sobbed heavily. Then her inner strength resurfaced, and she faced the screen and typed a response.

Jacob, I could use your help. May I share my screen to show you what I am up against?

Jacob shot back

Yes, please, I need to see where I can help. If it is not too inconvenient maybe you could add audio to this UC session so we don't have to keep typing all the words? Maybe?

An irrational fear overtook Petra momentarily, but she forced herself back into character and typed

Good idea! I'd like to hear your voice and cut back on my typing 😊

Petra's phone immediately rang, so she quickly replied as she declined the call

Hey, wait a minute. I need to get my Bluetooth device in place first, Mr. fast-dialer 😊

Once the device was in place, she called the number back.

Jacob greeted, "Sorry to be such the fast-dialer, but Quip said you guys were in a hurry."

He was so upbeat and amicable in his voice that kilograms of weight began to roll off her shoulders, and the faint beginnings of a smile started to appear on her face.

Petra breathed deeply and then remarked, "Thanks for the assistance. The files are the most challenging I've ever had to decrypt. Let me show you where we are, and if you need to take control of my machine or just remote into the laptop itself, you can. I have enabled remote desktop control to allow you to remote into the IP address I just pasted into the chat window. Let me know when you connect, and I'll show you where I'm stuck."

He was quickly into the laptop and read the files as Petra displayed them. Jacob read the letter from Su Lin, and they both teamed up to break into the unopened directories to see the contents. The next few hours flew by as they ventured deeper "into the encrypted areas and pulled up huge files that were steadily accessed.

Finally, Jacob commented, "Quite a lot of research here, and to be honest, I'm not sure what to believe about Su Lin. If it wasn't for the letter that gave me some room for doubt, I would be compelled to say she was working for this Dr. Pekoni. The money trail that Wolfgang demonstrated to the team and the apparent link between Pekoni and Su Lin is very incriminating, in my opinion. However, not everything fits together perfectly to support that theory any longer."

Petra puzzled a moment, then asked, "What do you mean? It looks to fit together quite deviously."

Jacob mused, "The flavor of the early research was hurried and somewhat angry in its tone. Almost as if something was at risk. She has never touched the funds she was receiving. I can see someone being bought as a research lackey, but why only live on your professor pay or close to no pay while she was in China?

"Then everything seems to have changed in its tone when Franklin came on the scene. If she really was cut from the same cloth as Pekoni, then why the obsession with Franklin's health? If that isn't enough, then why the gentle teasing and fond treatment of all of us at Andy's farm? If she really was a neo-Nazi S.S. doctor like Pekoni, as Quip believes, then how did all of us here believe otherwise? No, I believe we are missing some critical information, and the letter is only one indication that she is not the monster the circumstantial evidence suggests."

Petra pondered his statement and asked, "Do you think we should share all of this with everyone and open it up to discussion?"

Jacob nodded to himself and replied, "The longer we withhold this information from the others, the more explanation we have to give for our withholding it. My recommendation is, we gather everything up and present it to the interested parties."

Petra asked, "Su Lin too?"

Jacob thought a moment, then replied, "No, since she is the one on trial, plus her mind is not up to when this took place. I would maintain that we are trying to build consensus on the guilt or innocence of Su Lin, so how can she be part of the audience?"

Petra queried, "You feel she's on trial? I hadn't thought of it in those terms, but I guess that it is no different than when she had to be interrogated after the accident to see if she was faking the memory loss."

Jacob agreed, "Precisely."

"Jacob, it seems to me that…hey! We found it! The DNA encoding sequence and what appears to be Su Lin's memory, just like the letter stated! The digital treasure hunt just hit pay dirt! This lends credence to her letter. Now I'm starting to doubt her guilt. Maybe you're right, and we lay all the cards on the table."

Jacob suggested, "I recommend that you present this new information to Otto, Wolfgang, and Quip to see if opening it up to the others makes sense to them."

Petra bristled somewhat and asked, "Me? What about us doing the presenting?"

Jacob, somewhat embarrassed, offered, "Well, you see I haven't…I mean to say that we didn't…well, actually I was going to…"

Petra sternly stated, "Hey, if I can get through the awkwardness of our first call together in months, then you can too, bub! Come on. I'll set up a call for later and conference you in. Right now, I am expected for dinner, and you need to eat as well. Say three or four hours."

CHAPTER FORTY-FIVE

There is Simply No Escape from the Present When the Past Shows Up

The smoke carried the fragrant scent of grilled-to-perfection meat and fish across the backyard. The sun was shining and warm yet not oppressive. The yard was ablaze with flowers which in turn were creating a wonderland for the butterflies, birds, and even the bees as the wind gently disturbed everything in a pleasant way. Andy had created a feast served outside near the pool. In his role as clean-up committee, Wrinkles was patiently waiting for anything that happened to fall onto the ground. Wrinkles even wore his designated *Hoover* kerchief to highlight his four-legged vacuum status. Su Lin had prepared a fantastic salad which included everything from her garden along with some fresh hard-boiled eggs provided by the farm chickens. Mercedes was the self-appointed bartender and was doing a great job of remembering everyone's preference.

Everyone celebrated the return of Lara and Carlos and admired the award Lara had claimed. She planned to ship it back to her offices in Brazil in the morning but was delighted to relate the wonderful trip to New York to anyone that would listen. Andy was almost ready to take the meat off the grill, so he sent Su Lin inside to get the rolls that Petra indicated were ready to be pulled from the oven. Petra had made her specialty rosemary and pepper rolls as her contribution. Su Lin rushed into the house to do as asked while Mercedes returned to the bar to do a final refill before everyone sat down to dinner. Carlos was telling stories and making everyone laugh, especially Lara who simply beamed as she watched her prince charm yet another audience.

Mercedes had just finished serving Petra her white wine when a familiar voice behind her asked, "Mercedes, may I have my usual gin and tonic, please?"

Mercedes's heart stopped for a minute as she turned to face the owner of the voice. Before she could collect the words to form a response, Su Lin announced, "Everyone, this is Jim. I met him a while ago at the doctor, and he has come to join us for a few days." She turned toward Andy and verified, "Andy, I hope it is okay. He said you knew he was coming. I heard the knock on the door when I retrieved the rolls. I recognized him as well."

Andy went to Su Lin and patted her shoulder and then gave it a squeeze. "Thanks for letting him in, honey. I was so caught up in planning this celebration I clean forgot to even mention it.

"Jim, nice to see you again. Thank you for coming. You picked the perfect time, and I have more than enough here for you to join us. I won't take no for an answer either, young man. Let me introduce you around, though I think you have met most of this group."

Andy started the introductions with Petra, continued with Carlos and Lara, and then ended with Mercedes. "I thought I heard you say her name, but just in case, this is Mercedes. She has been helping track down some information leads following the kidnapping attempt on Su Lin. I believe you are going to supplement her efforts."

Jim had cleaned up nice with his dark wavy hair evenly trimmed and neatly combed. His khakis and brown plaid shirt complemented his tanned skin. His pleasant smile reached his eyes as he took Mercedes's hand. "Mercedes, it has been a long time. I look forward to working with you. It does look like you were surprised though. I am sorry about that. I would have sent you a note, but your contact information is out of date."

Mercedes gathered all her emotions and strength. Two could play this game. They'd both been taught to bury all emotion, especially around others. She pasted on a very natural smile as she reached for his hand, shook it gently, and commented, "My goodness, Jim. It has been a long time. You look well, I am glad to see. I think you said you wanted a gin and tonic. Was that with a twist or not?"

Petra and Lara looked at each other and both rolled their eyes. What was up with these two, and who did they think they were kidding? Mercedes looked like a totally different person yet sounded the same. Funny, no one else noticed anything amiss. Petra winked at Lara and returned her focus to the new man while Mercedes turned to prepare his beverage.

"Jim, we've met a couple of times, though we haven't really spent that much time talking. I am glad you are going to help find who might have wanted to steal our Su Lin."

Jim grinned and agreed, "Yes, Petra, I recall. You look lovely. Where is that brilliant man that you've had with you every other time, I've seen you?"

The rest of the group suddenly grew silent, as if by command. No one even breathed for a moment but then recovered and busied themselves with the business of passing out plates for self-serving. Stalker sensed something was wrong with his questions and wished he could have withdrawn it.

Petra let out a breath and her mouth formed a slight smile as she answered, "Jacob is on assignment in New York at present. In fact, I believe that Carlos saw him during the trip with Lara. Carlos was just regaling us with stories from the trip. Our own Lara received a fashion award. She runs a very impressive fashion house out of Brazil."

Carlos smiled and added a wink to Lara, then handed Jim a plate and offered, "Jim, help yourself. After all, you're the guest."

Jim filled his plate with samples of everything. It looked delicious. Everyone else followed suit, and they were seated. Jim had a seat between Petra and Carlos, with a great view of Mercedes across from him. He'd always enjoyed watching her. When she'd handed him his drink earlier, their fingers had brushed, and he'd felt that delightfully remembered shock, the kind that transferred from his fingers directly to his heart. The flashing look of surprise in her eyes alerted him that she'd felt it as well.

The conversation was kept light with stories, details on Lara's award, and compliments to the cooks. There were frequent extra handoffs to the willing Wrinkles. Jim noted that this hound was very covert in his collection of the snacks and studied the animal to see if anything could be learned. Su Lin wanted to show him her pig after dinner. He looked forward to meeting Franklin, as it provided another point in his analysis of where Su Lin was mentally these days.

Dinner was finished, and they stayed at the table, comfortably sipping their drinks and enjoying the sunset. It was a thoroughly pleasant evening. The pool light automatically turned on at dusk, and Jim wondered if he'd get a chance to do some laps.

Andy must have noticed the longing on Jim's face as he chuckled and commented, "Jim, if you forgot your suit we have several sizes available in the outside pool shower, there to the left. Make yourself at home, son. I prefer the pool used, rather than just a pretty picture."

Lara added, "It is definitely my favorite morning activity before I start work. I, for one, thank you, Andy, for having it!"

Petra stretched and glanced at her empty glass and shook her head. She had an early call tomorrow. Her curiosity was getting the best of her, so she asked, "Lara, Mercedes, let's take care of the dishes and leave Su Lin to show off Franklin, and Andy can rest and catch up with Carlos."

Lara grinned, totally onboard with the discover session that awaited. "Petra, you're right. We need to get the dishes done. I am getting tired. Come on, Mercedes."

Mercedes slowly smiled and nodded agreement. This way she wouldn't be stuck with Jim and Su Lin. "I'm in." She rose and started collecting dishes. The last dish she reached for was Jim's. As she leaned in to grab it, he quietly whispered, "We'll talk, Mercedes, I promise soon!"

She faltered for a second, collected the dishes and silverware, and then headed for the kitchen. She wanted washing duty as it would keep her from dropping while drying.

All the dishes were retrieved, and the girls established the workspace and began the process. Lara could see Andy and Carlos out by the pool talking. Su Lin had pulled Jim out to see Franklin and had kept up a running commentary. He seemed very interested and even patient with her behavior.

Mercedes had filled up one sink with soap and water and the first pile of dishes. As she began to dutifully wash and scrub the dishes, she handed them off to Petra who rinsed them a couple at a time and added them to the dish drainer. Lara and Petra both started to dry, and Lara stacked according to size. They worked in companionable silence for several minutes.

Petra queried, "Mercedes, what's up between you and Jim? And don't you dare say nothing!"

Mercedes looked cornered and refused to meet the eyes of her companions. "We once worked together, is all! I was just surprised to see him, nothing more!"

Lara grinned and stated, "Honey, if that is someone you worked with 'is all', I think that work had a lot of horizontal activity involved. You look totally smitten. If we hadn't all been there, one of you would have ripped off the other's clothes when your fingers brushed as you handed him his drink."

Petra chuckled and teased, "Wow, I missed that part. Mercedes, tell us all the details. I think he's nice looking. I could understand you being surprised. If he was a guy I liked, I would have wanted to dress up special and perhaps add some makeup before he arrived."

Mercedes turned and glanced into the mirror behind her, horrified at what she might see.

Lara and Petra giggled like crazy, and Lara reassured Mercedes. "You look beautiful as always. Your hair never looks bad. Your outfit is flattering to your figure, darn you. And you look fresh-faced with a hint of blush. Of course, that blush starts at your neck and rises to your ears."

Both girls laughed, nearly out of control, until Mercedes finally broke her stern look and laughed too.

"I hope I wasn't that obvious to everyone."

Lara commented, "Guys are so thick about stuff like that, so I doubt it. Who is he really, and why haven't you told us about him before he showed up here?"

Mercedes looked back and forth at the two women she had grown fond of and respected. She needed friends to help her with this. Perhaps that was what had been missing when she'd made her choices and walked away. For a woman that trusted nothing, this was a huge leap of faith to trust these women.

Mercedes confided, "I worked with Jim, and we had some investigative assignments together. He was like the lead, and we worked in a team of four. After several assignments, one thing led to another. We started to date, but because of the company rules we needed to hide it. I was brought up to always play by the rules, so this was very different for me. I loved him or I could never have even dated the man. I think he was falling in love with me, too.

"I worried all the time. It was just a matter of time before we'd get caught, and to be honest, I knew he was very focused on his career. He has always been good at investigations and getting to the root cause or source of the problem. He also did assignments alone which made me worry until he returned. My worrying started to hamper my ability to perform my job. In some jobs, like mine, that could have gotten me or one of my team killed. I knew there was nothing he or I could do to change the rules, so I resigned."

Petra remarked, "You and he talked about it, and he got mad so you went to work for Julie?"

Mercedes blushed again and looked really guilty. She quickly worked on a few more dishes as she wondered if she had gone too far in this conversation and made a huge mistake.

Finally, Lara, unable to wait, demanded, "Spill it, honey. Come on, it's just us girls. You must finish the story. What did you do?"

Mercedes's eyes brimmed with tears as she finally related, "I, uh, went to our boss and resigned. I told him the reason and apologized for breaking the rules. He seemed almost like a dad to me as he patted my hand and said he understood. He said not to worry and promised he would give me a reference and send Jim on an extended assignment while I relocated myself.

"He wrote up a great reference. Julie liked it, and I told her part of the reason why I had left, but not all of it."

Petra asked, "And you didn't even talk to him about it? Have you thought about him, or were you glad to get him out of your life?"

"Oh, I've thought about him every day. I hug my cat when I am home, and even the purring reminds me of him. He used to love that cat. Not many men do, you know?"

Lara replied, "I didn't know that. Never thought about it much, I guess. We never really had pets in my house, though I had a horse I adored.

"I don't know how you just walked away without saying anything. Carlos and I have been separated for months at a time because of our jobs, but I came here to see if we could find some common ground to build a life together."

Petra interjected, "I am so glad. You two have always been like the perfect couple. You're in tune with each other, whether near or far."

Lara snorted and said, "Hey, no different than you and Jacob. What happened there, anyway? One minute I heard you were engaged, and the next you left, or he left, and you weren't even speaking."

Petra's eyes got wide. She swallowed and replied, "Our situation is so much different. We're here to help Mercedes with her situation." Then she snarled, "I'm fine." Then her voice softened as she turned to Mercedes and asked, "What do you want to do? Do you want him?" Her conscience drifted back to Jacob even as she listened to the response.

Mercedes nodded a little and said, "He told me he wanted to talk. What worries me is, every other time he has ever said that to me, we always end up in bed, always."

Petra finished wiping her last glass and handed it to Lara to put away. Mercedes wiped down all the counters. Carlos walked in and asked Lara if she wanted to take a stroll around the gardens.

Petra excused herself, saying she had a call to make. Mercedes saw that Su Lin and Andy were into a game of cards outside by the pool, and while she couldn't see Jim she felt him before he even touched her.

Jim came up behind her, close enough that she felt the heat as it radiated off his body. He didn't put his arms around her. He leaned down to her ear and asked, "Can we have a talk now, Mercedes? I have missed you, very much. I really want to understand what I did that caused you to duck and run with no forwarding number and no explanation. From anyone else, I wouldn't give it a second thought. But you aren't just anyone else, my dear. Frankly, I'd like at least one more dance."

Mercedes knew she was beaten. That was the main reason she never made the effort to explain or forward any contact information. She was his the moment they had met, and a little geographical distance was no match for how she felt. She knew he recognized it as well because his grin formed, then he leaned in and gently kissed her neck. She turned and wrapped her arms around him and pulled him close.

"Jim, I couldn't break the rules at work anymore. But hell, we don't work for the same people anymore, do we?"

"Nope. Let's go to your room and talk. Then we'll get this assignment finished and talk more."

He lifted her up as she pointed the way upstairs. She added, "I live in Europe now."

"Okay, I can work from anywhere. Or I could retire if you prefer."

He carried her to her room, and she pointed across the hall to the room she assumed would be assigned to him. He looked at her and waited for her decision. She smiled and firmly started, "Come in my room and let's talk. But lots of verbs this time, okay?" she said with a mischievous smile.

CHAPTER FORTY-SIX

Truth and Circumstances

Zara moved around fairly well after being discharged by the hospital. What hurt the most was the silence from Buzz. Buzz politely helped her up to his apartment and opened the door for her without saying a word.

Just as he was about to head out to work, she started, "Buzz, I…"

Buzz cut her request in a weary tone. "No. …Please, just no. I don't want to talk about it now. I'm late for work, you're hurt and should rest. I am in no mood to discuss it. Maybe we can talk after I calm down later tonight…if you're still here." He quickly headed out and closed the door.

Zara flumped down on the couch with an ache she hadn't felt in a long time. She hadn't felt this alone and abandoned since her mother had dropped her off at the Big House when she was twelve. She had cried then, and she felt like crying now. It had taken a little time to understand when she had been sold into the sex trade as a young girl. But this time she knew, without a doubt, this episode was her fault, which made her pain even worse. She sat in the lightless room and quietly sobbed at how poorly she had chosen so many times. Her thick emotional resiliency that had been built up over her teen years as a high paid dominatrix simply melted away at the thought that Buzz would force her out of his life.

Part of her said it would always be her fault. She asked herself, *What right do I have to actually have a decent man like Buzz?* However, another part of her chided herself at the thought of giving up without at least trying to make amends. She stopped crying and resolved to pitch her side of the story to Buzz that evening, and let the chips fall where they may. He might still throw her out, but not before she put down all her cards and asked to start fresh. She felt better and a little upbeat at the thought of maybe turning a big corner in her life, as she even speculated that this might be a new beginning. Even if he told her to go, she would begin anew as an honest human being. Zara managed a small smile at the thought.

Zara glanced at her handbag that seemed to emit a hum from a vibrating cell phone, and it brought her back to reality. The odd thing was that it wasn't her regular phone. Somewhat disoriented, she dug through her handbag and found the phone of one of the Asian twins. She smirked at the image on the window of the vibrating device as she accepted the call but said nothing, just as she suspected Won would have done.

A voice insisted, "It's about time I heard from you two. When you didn't check in, I thought you were engaged in the hunt, but after twenty-four hours, I grew concerned. What is our status, gentlemen?"

A very satisfied look grew on Zara's face as she replied, "Hello, Chairman Chang. You must have meant to speak with your two henchmen. They can't come to the phone at present. Would you care to leave a message for them? I'm screening all their calls for the time being."

Astonished, Chang almost dropped the phone. He stuttered slightly before he questioned, "Who is this? Where are my associates?"

Zara, deciding to be both coy as well as bold, responded, "Oh, Chairman Chang! I am so hurt that you don't recognize my voice! After everything we have been through. Ah, well. Let me cut to the chase, since I know international calling is so desperately expensive. Your two errand boys failed in their attempt to grab me, and now I have them. More importantly, I have Nikkei's diamond necklace. I will sell them and the necklace back to you for six million euros that must be wired to my account before you see any of the items.

"Close your jaw that I imagine just dropped open. I want five million euros for the necklace and an extra million for your associates, Won and Ton."

The chairman ground his teeth to suppress his anger and admonished, "Ah, my Callisto, how strange to hear your voice unexpectedly on my associate's phone. You do realize that I am not of a mind to pay you for what is rightfully mine, correct? Besides, how do I know that this isn't simply another one of your ploys to extort money from me? For all I know, you used your female talents to seduce my associates and simply stole their phone to pretend you have all the cards needed for a winning hand."

Zara chuckled and sarcastically replied, "Yet another egotistical man that will throw my wretched past in my face while trying to negotiate. Very well, I have the diamonds and can continue to look for buyers at my leisure. When you don't hear from them, you can call me back on their phone. If I feel like answering, we'll arrange a trade for Nikkei's collar and your missing associates.

"Don't take too long to make up your mind. I didn't arrange for any long-term care for them, so in a week I would expect them to be hungry. Good day, Chairman Chang."

Chang, beginning to panic, interjected, "Wait! What have you done with them? Let's say for a moment I believe your thin story. I can't get that kind of money overnight! You need to give me more time, and I need to know they are being treated fairly as hostages. Give me some assurances! Don't just turn them over to Dmitry!"

It occurred to Zara that she wasn't really in control of the Asian twins, and perhaps she could use the chairman's assumption that the twins were in Dmitry's hands for safe keeping. She confidently offered, "I will advise Dmitry not to treat your associates like his regular guests. Dmitry just can't resist showing off his newest toy, a nail gun, to people who happen to wander by. He likes to show off even to those who don't just wander by. Use the time wisely to get me my money, as you know how easily Dmitry is aggravated by guests that stay too long or don't enjoy the extra iron in their systems."

Chang paused a few moments and added, "I need two days to liquidate assets to comply with your price. However, I will tell you this now. If anything happens to my associates, there won't be anywhere you can run that I won't find you. Are we clear, Callisto?"

Zara smiled and said, "You know, I still like the sound of being called Callisto. Speak with you soon, my dark lord Mephisto."

After disconnecting the call, Zara commented, "Maybe there is going to be a happy ending to this story for me after all!"

Zara put the finishing touches on the meal she had prepared for her and Buzz. She took a mental inventory of the courses she had planned to serve and even had some modest flowers on the table with an actual table cloth. She smiled at the attention to the detail, hoping it would set Buzz in a better mood than he had been that morning.

Then she grew a little apprehensive at how he might view the dinner setting. Zara hoped he would give her time to talk and come clean with him so they might have a chance. She had practiced her pitch several times in the mirror to see how it came across. She had even resolved to throw in the diamonds to the discussion to show that she was sincere in trying to patch things up between them. She wanted him to look at her like he believed her and wanted her in his life. She had to struggle internally with the possibility that he might already be gone, mentally. But she felt compelled to try, whether he accepted the truth or not. She vowed she'd never fail in telling the truth to a lover again.

She turned apprehensively to face the door opening and smiled at Buzz as he came through the door. Buzz stopped short in the hallway after closing the door and saw the dinner table laid out. His eyes took in all the detail, and he let his gaze rest on her for a moment.

Buzz swallowed hard and said, "Hello, pretty girl, my name is Buzz. Would you tell me your name and all about you? I think I would really like to know you better."

Zara couldn't stop the tears from streaming down her face as she offered, "My name is Zara. I have so much to be grateful for and much to tell the warrior who came to my rescue. May the lowly servant girl feed the noble knight?"

Buzz sat down and smiled as Zara served the dinner. Buzz poured a nice wine, and their toast was almost like the start of something new. Music streaming from her phone played softly in the background. The meal was simple yet delicious, and Zara was delighted that Buzz enjoyed the fare. They chatted about themselves, which provided some insight into each of them. Buzz poured one more glass of wine to finish the bottle, and Zara set a shared dessert of cheeses, grapes, and small pieces of dark chocolate between them.

Zara looked into Buzz's eyes, raised her glass and promised, "Buzz, I want to try to make this work. I am hardly perfect, I will make mistakes, but I'd like us to try."

Buzz looked at her intently as he tried to read her soul and replied, "Zara, I'd like to try as well. It will take time for me to fully trust you. If that is okay, then we start now. Just don't lie to me. We tell the truth, or we have nothing."

Their glasses touched, and the evening continued as they started down the new path together.

CHAPTER FORTY-SEVEN

If You Aren't Teaching, You Should Be Learning

...The Enigma Chronicles

Quip accepted the incoming call and answered, "Hi, kiddo, long time no hear. Kind of late here, and I was about to close up shop. What's up?"

Petra quickly offered, "Jacob and I have invoked our best forensics sleuthing on Su Lin's laptop, and it looks like we have found the files described in her letter that I forwarded to you earlier. We were hoping to speak with you, Otto, and Wolfgang about the findings. And, well, frankly, we were hoping to do it now. Can they be reached and conferenced in?"

Quip studied the situation a few seconds and asked, "We? You mean you have Jacob on the call as well? Indeed!"

Jacob frowned slightly but offered, "Quip, we believe we have the key files that were specifically called out in her letter to Andy. Petra and I wanted to alert the core team about this discovery and discuss our next possible steps. That is, of course, if I am welcome to attend. If the team would prefer to discuss this without me, then I will, of course, withdraw from the call until needed again."

Petra wiped her eyes at Jacob's gentlemanly offer. It was the second time since she had called him to do this conference call that she'd teared up. She was completely grateful they had not enabled the video cameras, which would have let them see her tears. She could feel not only her pain in this situation, but now Jacob's as well. She wondered just how much suffering she had inflicted on this generous and honorable man from whom she had run.

Quip said nothing but put the call on hold from his side to add in Otto and Wolfgang. He also generated a quick text message to them both that Jacob was on the call too. A few moments later, the call resumed with all members of the core team on line.

Quip framed the conversation. "Gentlemen, Petra informs me that Jacob has been working with her on and off for more than a day to break through the last encryption hurtles of Su Lin's laptop. They believe that they have found the important genetic and cerebral backups that Su Lin described in her letter to Andy. The intention here is to discuss the next steps in the handling of the Su Lin letter and what will probably be a rather spirited discussion with Andy and others on this topic.

"Before we open this up to discussion, does anyone have a problem with Jacob remaining on the call to offer his perspective on their research? I personally would like to have him in this discussion, but I didn't want to speak for either of you in this matter."

Otto clucked his tongue and rather flatly stated, "Oh, do come along!

"Jacob, you are part of the core team, and as such I welcome and value your input. So please stay. There, I said it!"

Wolfgang grinned and felt relieved as he softly offered, "Jacob, I too would value your perspective and frankly would like to hear your voice again. Your absence has been sorely felt. Personally, I have missed not being able to reason through some of the difficult situations we face here. Will you please join us for this and all meetings, so we can have your valued input?"

It was Jacob's turn to be thankful that there was no video enabled on this conference call as he wiped the tears from his eyes. He steeled himself mentally and responded, "Thank you for allowing me to join in and effectively come back home."

Petra had calmed herself enough to IM Jacob some words of encouragement.

> Jacob it will all be good. Please stay the course.

Jacob swallowed hard to keep his voice from cracking with his unfettered emotions. He added, "Petra, have you been able to upload the files to ICABOD over the high-speed link from Andy's facility?"

Petra took that opportunity to speak and allow Jacob additional time to compose himself after the words of heartfelt welcome to which he didn't think he was entitled. She realized that she was the cause of this rift, and soon she would need to repair it from all perspectives.

Petra said, "Yes, Jacob, I did start the process after our earlier conversation.

"Jacob and I wanted the unencrypted files uploaded to ICABOD so we have telemetry of these critical files, but they are huge files and it took some time. You should know that we discovered that this was no ordinary laptop but apparently has been built to some very high-end specifications.

"Quip, based on what I am seeing, Su Lin has more processing power, memory, and solid-state disc capacity than most of your blade servers inside of ICABOD. We should have looked at it sooner, because if we had we would've investigated it earlier."

Jacob, now somewhat in control of his damaged feelings, returned a message to Petra.

> Petra, it sounds like they would like me back.
> But would you want me back as well or is that a futile hope?

Petra quickly muted her phone, so the others didn't hear her breath catch or her renewed crying after reading his message. Anger invaded her being at the emotions washing back and forth through her that she could not control. The sorrow, the hurt, and the pain derailed her focus, and she incoherently responded to Quip's questions.

Quip asked, "Petra, you are there and have seen these giant files on a special built PC. Is Su Lin really a victim here, or have we simply been taken in by the vicious Master Po?"

Jacob realized his message had probably broken Petra's concentration and after a few seconds of silence responded, "Let me comment here, first, if no one objects. While I won't speak for Petra, I can tell you that we had some discussion and have mixed feelings in this matter. The easy answer is that Su Lin is guilty of several things. When viewed on the surface, the evidence suggests that Master Po is definitely aligned with Dr. Pekoni. I would propose, when you view all the subtleties, the evidence suggests that she is actually operating at multiple levels, just like her programming. What I'm going to suggest is…" Jacob paused as the message window showed Petra was typing.

Petra, nearly emotionally out of control, finished and sent a new message.

> How can you ask me that? I sent you away so you wouldn't be stuck with a deformed wife! Not only am I physically deformed, but emotionally too! Who could possibly want that kind of baggage from a partner! Don't you understand, I set you free from all that!

Predictably, the IM content derailed Jacob's thoughts which ended his ability to speak coherently or finish his suggestion.

Petra interpreted Jacob's silence as him being lost in thought based on the text she'd fired at him. She quickly jumped in and said, "Sounds like Jacob hit a bad cell zone. Let me add my thoughts while he tries to straighten out his phone.

"We noticed that Wolfgang's observation of Su Lin's not touching the funds as consistent with someone who had an ulterior motive rather than being on the Pekoni train. Jacob even stated that she couldn't have been so clever as to deceive everyone." Petra glanced at the window which displayed Jacob typing.

Jacob, now angry, wiped the tears from his face as he finished a response to her narrow-minded message.

> Oh, is that what you call it when you hose off that special someone in your life? I didn't want to be sent away, dammit! I wanted to marry you! I wanted to spend the rest of my days with you! But instead, you made light of me and crushed my feelings. Now who wants a broken man like me?

Jacob realized they were playing a bit with fire, but he was back in fighting mode. She remained quiet so he interjected, "Hey, I think I am past the bad cell zone. I suggest we loop in at least Andy since the letter is addressed to him, and we'll see if we can follow her wishes as captured in the letter, she wrote him.

"Quip, I'm fairly sure EZ is going to want in on the discussions, based on her personality type, so how do you feel about that?"

Quip was aware that somehow there were conversations going on at various levels and not just at the audio frequency. Otto and Wolfgang had him on a three person IM with messaging, to which ICABOD was adding commentary on the big monitor. He felt like he was one of the three rings in a circus. Quip messaged that they should just join him in the operations center. Then he closed the messaging windows.

Quip replied, "Jacob, you have a point there about looping in Andy since it is addressed to him, but I'm not sure about telling EZ. Although, I think I would regret being me if I don't tell her, along with Andy. Maybe we can sound her out first before Andy to see if she will help deliver this message. Otto, Wolfgang, what do you think?"

Petra was no longer listening to the call as she fired back another IM to Jacob.

> Oh, that's right! You didn't feel sorry for the little beat-up princess, did you? Jacob so full of honor, sentencing himself to eternity with an ugly, limping female homunculus? Wow, when you say it like that, how can a girl refuse?

Jacob stared in disbelief at his IM window, also oblivious to the conference call at this point. He was no longer capable of participating in the call. He shot back an angry retort.

> What? Is that what you think? Don't take this personal, but you're crazy! Even when I saw your wounds at their worst, I never recoiled like I was in a horror movie!
>
> Geez! It's a good thing I'm not there to straighten you out because if I were
>
> I'd love you for the rest of my days. I'm so sorry you don't want me.

Petra sat stunned and stared blankly at the IM window, unable to gain control of her feelings. The background voices of Otto, Quip, and Wolfgang simply didn't register with her mental state even though the noisy sounds were reaching her ears. She typed her response.

> Jacob, I do want you. I'm just so afraid, and I can't even say what I really fear. This has been the hardest time of my life. I

think it's because you were missing. Is there any hope for us? Is there any hope for me?

With a small smile on his face finally, Jacob typed into the message window.

Okay, then let's start there, in Atlanta, just like we did when I first met you in New York, shall we? I can stop being the Pining Putz for Petra, but you have to promise to stop thinking you're an ugly, limping female homunculus! I maintain that if we start again, the rest should follow. Yes?

Petra slightly smiled as she replied in the IM window.

You go first so I can see how it's done. At some point you will have to tell me what a putz is, okay?

Jacob now chuckled as he typed.

Petra, it is one of those things I have to show you not simply tell you. But if you need a hasty explanation, I'll tell you

About that time Quip's voice, at a greatly amplified volume, dripped with annoyance and blasted through the speakers of both of their cell phones as he practically shouted, "Okay, I guess we can pick up this conference call again later after you two have made up! "You see now why I don't want to teach. The children in the back of the classroom spend all their time passing notes back and forth instead of focusing on the lesson up front! So call us back after you two can hear again! Got it?"

After disconnecting from the conference call bridge, Otto, Wolfgang, and Quip all grinned at each other.

Quip offered, "As useless conference calls go, that was one of the most productive ones I've ever been on."

CHAPTER FORTY-EIGHT

How Can I Be Judged For What You Did or Are Going to Do?

Andy roared with indignation at the team members on the conference bridge. "What are you suggesting? That her accident was the result of some universal karma rule that maintains you have to get whacked by justice for being an evil genius? Boy, am I glad none of you are here, because I might be tempted to wring someone's scrawny neck with my bare hands for these crazy accusations!"

Otto blinked several times as he uncomfortably rubbed his neck with his hand. He considered himself lucky that Andy didn't have his large powerful hands close enough to make good on his threat. The man Otto always considered as a big teddy bear, like everyone, had limits. After a brief pause, Otto continued, "Andy, I suggest you read the letter again, maybe even a couple of times, before we take this discussion further. You should understand that we have all reviewed the letter and worked the circumstances that surround Su Lin. There is no consensus on guilt or innocence, my friend. None of us want to believe Su Lin is a willing conscript to Dr. Pekoni's unsanctioned research on human beings for life extensions, but none of us want to be taken for fools either. Now do you want to hear the rest of what we found, or do you simply want to close your eyes so you can believe everything is wonderful?"

Andy's seething temper had him breathing rapidly, like a boxer ready for a fight, but Otto's question began to wind him back down to a rational level. After a few more deep breaths, Andy stated, "Otto, you and your team are as much family to me as Su Lin and Carlos, Eilla-Zan being my only blood family. I feel like there are two camps, one for and one against, in my family, and that has me riled. I don't want my family divided, but I can't believe Su Lin is on the payroll of this Nazi S.S. doctor either.

"I believe Wolfgang found the source of the money coming into her account. But money coming in from a renegade source does not a case make.

"Wolfgang, you said yourself the money wasn't touched, nor was it treated like a retirement nest egg, so what do you believe is the purpose for the account? Sometimes people take other people's money to remind them of the contempt they have for the source."

Andy continued with what was shaping up to be Su Lin's defense and asked, "Jacob, you and Petra found where you saw the complexion of the research change when she picked up her pig, Franklin. Could it be that she turned the corner in her research at that point? She obviously cared a lot about that animal, and still does! Not just because the research was improving but also because of her humanistic side. If we follow that line of reasoning, why would she jump to trying her theories on herself when she could have used Pekoni's inventory of subjects to experiment on? If she is truly the evil person you suspect, then why care about a test animal or deliberately put herself in harm's way?"

Jacob quietly offered, "Andy, this is what we find troubling as well. We have all this evidence, but no clear picture emerges when you try to add it up. What we see is a Su Lin we all know and love, but we also find a Master Po that is clearly aligned with this terrible individual Pekoni. Clearly, the letter is addressed to you, but we all care about what happens to Su Lin. Frankly, I want to see her exonerated of these suspicions."

Andy, now calmer in his breathing and thought, took Jacob's words in but didn't respond.

Otto offered, "Andy, we have been tasked to track down this Dr. Pekoni and extradite his stolen knowledge and serve him up for trial on human atrocities. We really don't want to do that before we can clearly establish that Su Lin is not an accessory to his criminal activity. If we turn him over to the U.S. authorities and he implicates Su Lin before we can establish her innocence, then she would have to be brought in as well. None of us want to see that happen, old friend."

Andy was becoming sullen but finally apologized, "I'm sorry I railed at all of you. I now understand what is at stake and how you feel. I had no right to hurl those harsh feelings at you, so I hope you will forgive me."

Quip said, "Andy, I haven't told EZ yet about this because of our respect for you and for Su Lin. But she is my partner, and I know how much she cares for Su Lin. I would like to provide her with this information because of her interest and feelings for you and Su Lin. I would like to have you included on that call as I explain it to her. I think you would agree that sometimes she can be a bit prickly. I can easily see her initial response to the information quickly approaching the equivalent of an emotional supernova, and I think together we can paint an accurate picture of the situation. Would that be, okay?"

Andy nodded rather soberly and agreed, "Yeah, I can see her reaching supernova status rather quickly as well.

"Outside of this discussion with my daughter, what are our next steps then? How do we confirm or alleviate the suspicions of Su Lin?"

Otto suggested, "Andy, I recommend that you read the letter from Su Lin again, maybe even a couple of times, because she is telling us what the next steps should be for her."

Andy went into an emotional launch sequence that threatened to send him over the end again. He asked, "What? Follow her recipe for restoring her lost memories? Are you insane? Experimenting on herself got her this way! How can you even suggest that?"

Wolfgang replied, "Andy, we assumed that would be your response, and apparently Su Lin anticipated it as well. That is why the letter is to you, and she is begging to be restored. While we all feel we have a vested interest in Su Lin, it is your decision since you are her guardian and she petitioned you."

Andy, growing more despondent with each passing moment, slowly sat back in his chair before he quietly said, "I need to think about this. Yes, Otto, I need to re-read the note several times. Now I understand why the conference call and the restricted attendance. I cannot give an answer on this yet, though, yes, I know there is a sense of urgency on the matter.

"Part of me says, no, I won't let her be experimented on again and maybe lose her forever, but the rational side says I owe all of us the truth about Su Lin as well as Master Po. I just can't answer you right this minute. Please give me a little time, and I will call you back after her appointment tomorrow, likely in the evening. I promise."

Otto soothed, "Andy, we understand, and I would submit that we all are here for you, old friend."

Andy was having a little trouble keeping his emotions in check but said, "Thanks, all." Then he quickly disconnected.

Su Lin bounded into the study where Andy was lost in thought and brightly said, "You hadn't forgotten that we need to go to the doctor's tomorrow for my checkup and progress scan, have you?"

Andy managed a weak smile and said, "No, ma'am, I haven't. I was just sitting here thinking about the chores facing me, and thankfully you reminded me of one I had overlooked. Why don't you run along and let me get my chores done so we can get an early start tomorrow?"

Su Lin beamed and said, "Deal!" She bounded off again, and Andy re-read the letter that Su Lin had left him. He wondered who had really written it, Master Po or his Su Lin.

CHAPTER FORTY-NINE

Doctor's Day, Not Really Celebrated Anywhere

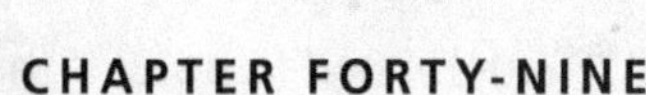

It was Doctor's Day, and Su Lin had been up early to do her outside chores and then ran back upstairs to shower and dress. She wanted to make it to the kitchen first for her early breakfast with Andy. When she arrived downstairs to the kitchen, Andy smiled and greeted her. At least no one else was up yet. Having breakfast with just Andy was the best part of the long day ahead.

Andy had surprised Su Lin with what she considered a fun breakfast. The pancakes were always fluffy and perfect, especially when she added the blueberry syrup. Though she knew he would cook as many as she asked for, she didn't want to miss the bacon, eggs, and fresh juice that really made the whole thing a fun meal. It seemed to Su Lin that even with the breakfast something was a bit off with Andy. He would stop and look away like he was searching for something and then snap back to the here and now. Andy sat and concentrated on the food and on Su Lin.

Andy asked, "Are you feeling good this morning, Su Lin? You look very nice, and I bet you already finished your chores."

Su Lin beamed at Andy and, after she swallowed, replied, "I feel great! My memory seems better with the lessons I have done. I don't forget lessons completed very often, and I am able to complete more assignments. I think talking with all these houseguests has helped me some, though not as good as the extra assignments. Did you like the paper I did on the United States involvement in the Pacific during World War II? I did a lot of research for it, though I had to borrow the extra computer from Carlos to work on.

"I think Petra is angry with me, though I can't recall any thing I did, and she said she wasn't angry. She is working really hard on my machine, trying to get the funny files off of it. The ones she let me read before she asked me to let her work alone made me seem like I was really smart. Your teaching is going to help make me really smart again, right? You aren't mad at me, are you?"

Andy had frowned at the mention of Petra and worked to keep his temper in check. He'd been up most of the night replaying the horrible pitched battle of a discussion. He was convinced that Su Lin in any form had a good heart, period. He heard her last question and replied, "Su Lin, I did like your paper. I actually finished the final review last night, and it is in the den. We can review it later. I liked the various battle fronts that you reviewed and your assessment of each. I also included some additional articles that you might like. What would you think about doing some research into the European fronts of the war for your next paper?"

Su Lin smiled and nodded, then answered, "That would be good. I actually came across some of the articles about the wicked German Nazis while I was working on the other. I am sure glad that the Allies saved the day!"

They were quiet for a few minutes as they ate. Andy added coffee for himself and juice for Su Lin.

Andy offered, "To answer your other questions, I have no reason to be mad at you. I hope I haven't done something that made you feel that way. Petra, I think, just likes to work alone as she has done that most of her work career. She wants to get all the information she can. She was working with Jacob remotely to help complete her assignment."

Su Lin's eyes widened with delight and she asked, "Does this mean they are done being mad at each other? I really like it when Jacob is around. He always tells me interesting things about computers and programming that no one else has so far."

Andy was getting frustrated because he couldn't tell her everything about these folks she admired. Su Lin spoke what she felt in an unfettered manner. He thought the discoveries made would shame her. He would wait until after the doctor's appointment, which they needed to get moving for. He texted Mercedes that they would be leaving in forty-five minutes and that breakfast was available for her if she wanted some. She immediately texted back that she and Jim would be going.

Su Lin interrupted, "Andy, do you think they will find that I am improving this time? I would like to get some good news from these doctors. I would like it to be easier on you, Andy. Will it ever be easier for you to take care of me?"

Andy was caught off guard with that comment, likely due to the lack of sleep. He immediately replied, "I don't take care of you, my dear, you take care of me, and Franklin, too. Now go finish up the other chores and meet me outside in forty minutes. I have a few things I need to take care of."

Su Lin stood and smiled, then gave Andy a quick hug. "Is Mercedes going along too?"

"Yes, and Jim will join as well. If you don't mind?"

"He's very nice. I think Mercedes likes him."

As she left the room, Andy briefly put his head in his hands and wondered what he was going to do. All these options, and that letter Su Lin had written, and the risk. The risk of losing her again was almost paralyzing. He stood just as Mercedes and Jim entered, inclined his head and left without a word.

The trip into the city was quiet. Jim's rental car was quite nice, and he suggested that it would be roomier for the four of them. Andy had reluctantly agreed. Mercedes and Su Lin had kept up a running discussion about all sorts of things. Jim had tried to engage Andy in some conversation but recognized a man who was doing some deep thinking and left him alone. As they got closer to the destination, Andy added some details about the visit.

"Since you both don't know the routine of our appointments, let me fill you in. Su Lin and I are going to meet briefly with Dr. Neil Giles who has been her doctor since she has been coming here. He has all her history and is the best specialist to identify the areas of improvement. Then she gets a CAT scan. A while later we sit down again with Dr. Giles and get the results of that. Fairly standard process."

Jim asked, "Do you want either of us inside with you? Happy to oblige, but if it is standard as you say, then we would be better served outside watching all the comings and goings."

Mercedes interjected, "Su Lin, do you want me inside with you, holding your hand or just talking?"

Su Lin giggled and replied, "No, thank you. Andy holds my hand when we talk to Dr. Giles so I don't get scared. During the CAT scan, no one but the technicians are allowed. It's the rules."

Andy couldn't help but be cheered by her attitude. "I think we will be okay. The whole process takes two to three hours. I would suggest you stop up here before we reach the clinic and get some snacks and drinks if you are waiting outside. We always grab a sit-down meal at a place that Su Lin will pick after the appointment. Save some room!"

A short time later Su Lin and Andy were ushered into Dr. Giles's office.

He greeted them with a jovial smile and said, "Nice to see you both. Su Lin, you look absolutely radiant. I swear every time I see you your skin seems glowing. My wife would be jealous. It must be that farm life that is keeping your complexion so clear and soft, like a child almost.

"I want to have a conversation with you, Su Lin, before you go for the scan. The purpose is to compare some prior responses and gauge some areas of the brain related to memory, alright?"

Su Lin nodded. Andy realized this was his time to just listen so he retreated into his thoughts about what he should do to honor her written request. She was so important to him. Their relationship had certainly gone in a different direction than he'd originally hoped, but it was better than risking her life again. He recognized there were no guarantees in life, but the risk seemed too great. Jacob and Petra could neither confirm nor deny the success factor. He contemplated talking to Dr. Giles about it and realized he'd sound like a crazy guy. Some of the background on Su Lin's accident had been omitted from the discussions with the medical staff. Now was not the time to bring it up. He returned mentally to the room just in time.

Dr. Giles offered, "Su Lin, I think your memory retention is improving, quite a bit actually since your last visit. Even though you don't recall anything from before, you at least seem to be adding to your knowledge at a phenomenal rate. I suspect you'll be ready to enroll in a junior college in a year or so at this rate."

Su Lin beamed and blushed at the compliment and turned toward Andy as she said, "It's because Andy gives me all this homework, Dr. Giles. Andy, did you hear, I might be able to attend college?"

Andy nodded and smiled. "I sure did, little one. I think that is fine progress. You have worked very hard."

Dr. Giles added, "It is time for your scan, Su Lin. I think you know the way. I want to speak to Andy for a second, and then he will be in the waiting area, alright?"

Su Lin agreed and left with a smile and light step. She headed toward the doors with all the equipment and smiled at several of the staff she had met before. Smiles and comments were exchanged as she went. The final set of doors were restricted, and Su Lin was pleased that one of the nurses waited at the door to open it with her badge. The nurse finished a look at her smart phone and quickly stuffed it into her pocket.

As she reached the door, Su Lin greeted, "Hi, I am Su Lin and ready for my CAT scan. Can you please let me in? Have we met before?"

The nurse grinned and replied, "No, sugah! We've not met before, but I think we'll be good friends. I'm gonna help you with your procedure today. You just call me Alicia, sugah. Let's go."

Su Lin replied, "Nice to meet you, Alicia. Thanks for opening the door. This is the part where I get just a little nervous."

Alicia gave a sympathetic smile, then took her hand and escorted her to the last procedure room. Alicia suggested that Su Lin change into the gown behind the curtain, and they could get the scan over with as quickly as possible. Su Lin came out from behind the curtain and hopped up on to the exam table. The process always started with temperature and blood pressure checks.

Su Lin asked, "Have you been here very long? I don't recall seeing you before."

"Sugah, I have been here for a couple of weeks. I love the clinic, don't you? Everyone is so nice.

"Now let's get the basics finished, and I will take you to the machine. I will be running the scan for you."

"Really? You must be really smart, Alicia."

Alicia chuckled, "I hope so, sugah, your temperature and blood pressure are like a teenager, you lucky girl. I wish mine was that good. Here, drinks this dye, and we will go to the machine."

Su Lin drank the dye. Alicia helped her stand and was leading her toward the door when her knees buckled. Alicia patted her hand and said, "Don't worry, sugah, you're gonna rest for a while."

Alicia picked up the lightweight Su Lin and laid her back onto the table. She opened a large laundry bag she'd retrieved from the cabinet. She laid out the bag and added a sheet that she opened and shook out. Then she lay Su Lin into the bag and brought the sides up over her and pulled the strings to close the bag. She opened the door in time to see an orderly approaching with the laundry cart. He looked neat and tidy in his wardrobe of white with a light blue cap that covered his head. He saw her, and his sparkling white teeth formed a grin. He stopped the cart at the door and then went in and retrieved the laundry bag, deftly hoisting it up and gently setting it into the cart. He mischievously pinched Alicia's bottom and left, taking the cart back the way he'd approached.

Alicia closed the door and waited ten minutes as planned. Then she exited the room and walked toward the front of the facility where her locker was located. She removed her white hat and added a long coat to cover her uniform and said a cheerful goodbye to the receptionist as she walked out. No one in the waiting room gave her a glance, not even the man she presumed was Andy, catching up on some paperback book reading.

Outside, Alicia glanced around at the cars in the parking lot as if looking for her car. A short time later she saw the laundry van pulling around from the back of the building and turning onto the roadway. No vehicles were in pursuit. She glanced around again and then looked pleased as she found her car and slowly walked toward it. After she got in and started the vehicle, she noticed that a couple in a car one row over stared at her and wrote something down. Her breath caught, but she maintained her cool demeanor as she rolled down the windows and turned up the gospel station. She slowly drove out of the parking lot and headed toward the airport. She was, after all, making a delightful trip to Finland, of all places.

CHAPTER FIFTY

Could There Really be a Perfect Crime with All Our Technology?
...The Enigma Chronicles

Jim and Mercedes had fit into the role of observe and record, just like they had on other stakeout assignments. Each one knew what they should cover without being asked. Jim suspected the effort was unnecessary, considering where they were, but it was also good exercise. This just had the added bonus of permitting him time to steal glances at Mercedes. Last night had been like they'd never been apart. They fit together like the two parts of the whole he'd known they were from the moment they met. She was just his other half. Maybe he'd talk to her about really retiring. He was tired of travel and being alone. He drifted off mentally with vivid thoughts of being her full-time lover.

Mercedes was focused on recording all the traffic as it was coming in and out of the facility. She knew that Jim took photos of every person and vehicle that moved. Her notes and his photos could be matched up for a timeline at any point, if needed. She had missed him. Even being in the car with him created a feeling of coming home, at least in her heart. She glanced at the time and noticed that no one had left the building since the large black woman nearly an hour before. She frowned as she realized they had been in there more than the three hours Andy had indicated.

"Jim, we are over the three-hour mark. I also haven't seen anyone leave for quite some time. I'm not feeling good about this."

Jim looked at the door and surrounding parking lot. "Nothing has moved in quite a while. Perhaps this is the slow time."

Mercedes nodded, though unconvinced. Jim scanned the area one more time and suggested, "Let's go in and check with Andy, or at least the receptionist."

As Jim opened the door for Mercedes, they both heard the anger in Andy's voice as it boomed across the room. The waiting area was nearly empty, and those sitting cowered as the big man raged. Jim noticed another man in a white coat and tie was trying to reason with Andy.

Andy shouted, "What do you mean, she is not back there? We were both in your office when she went for the scan. She knows the way, and your staff knows her. Why wouldn't they come looking for you sooner? I have been waiting for her to return for a very long time, and yet I have to come to you, rather than you to me? This is damn ridiculous, Giles."

Dr. Giles replied, "Andy, you need to lower your voice. You are scaring the staff and, worse, the patients. We will locate her. She likely went to the bathroom and got distracted. I have two nurses and a technician looking now."

Andy roared, "I am not going to lower my voice!

"Su Lin, Su Lin, get out here right now! We are not playing this game."

Jim reached Andy and interceded, "Andy, what happened?"

Andy had a wild look in his eyes as he confided, "I have no idea. This so-called doctor has lost Su Lin. He says she never had the test, so he never reviewed the results. It has been so long."

Then he caught sight of Mercedes. "Mercedes, go find her, please. They won't let me go back there because I am too loud."

Mercedes looked to Dr. Giles for forgiveness as she dashed past him to the back. Jim took Andy's arm and asked, "Dr. Giles, can we go to your office and give Andy a minute to get his breath?"

Dr. Giles led the way toward his office and gestured for them to sit. "Andy, I should have been more mindful of the time, but the patient roster has been full. I normally get buzzed as tests are completed and ready for my review. I simply did not receive one for Su Lin. When you asked my receptionist, I started checking and learned she hadn't received her scan."

Andy stared into space and mumbled, "I never should have brought her here and not stayed with her. It's all my fault. Everything is my fault."

Jim asked, "Doc, can you tell me everything you have done and know so far? Mercedes will be doing some systematic questioning as well as she is searching."

The doctor outlined everything he had done that morning. All the patients he had seen and all the procedures, at a high level, that had been conducted. He indicated that most of the staff had been with him for years and that the practice was renowned in this part of the country for their capabilities in mild and dysfunctional brain trauma. He explained that he specialized in the temporary dysfunction of brain cells, brain bruising, torn tissue, oxygen deprivation and other brain damage that can result in permanent complications. Jim was aware of the clinic from his research previously, but the doctor visibly calmed as he provided the overview of his practice. Andy pulled himself together during the dialogue.

Mercedes was escorted into the office by another nurse. Mercedes explained, "We have been from one end to the other, and Su Lin is not on the premises. One of the technicians actually opened up the ventilation system in the ceiling, but nothing was disturbed. She's not here."

Dr. Giles looked at the nurse and asked, "Rachel, do you recall anything? You were scheduled to do her scan, right?"

Rachel looked stricken as she answered, "Dr. Giles, the temporary nurse, Alicia, said you wanted her to do the scan, as sort of a test of her skills. I had no reason to doubt her as you commented yesterday that she seemed very capable."

Jim asked, "Temporary, what temporary? Can you describe her?" While he waited for someone to answer, he pulled out his phone and went to the photo album. He thumbed all the way to the beginning of the day.

Rachel replied with a description first. Jim had her go through all the photos, and Rachel stopped on one of the last people to leave the center. The black woman.

Rachel exclaimed, "That's her. What time was that taken? Perhaps she went to lunch."

Jim stated the time, and Rachel thought for a moment and then said, "That cannot be right. That was when Su Lin was supposed to have her scan. We were all so busy. Then the guy came early to collect the laundry from all the rooms, saying he was on a different schedule."

Andy exclaimed, "I don't care about the laundry for this place, I want Su Lin."

Jim turned to Andy and explained, "Andy, the only way out of the clinic is past you in the waiting room, and you never saw her, right?"

Andy agreed, "No, she didn't come out from the procedure area. I would've seen her. I even saw that woman the nurse just identified. Why?"

Dr. Giles interjected, "There is a service exit at the back of the building for the services and maintenance people we might call. Laundry is one of those services. You don't think that…"

Jim looked at Mercedes and said, "If I wanted to grab her, I might choose that as a plan, so perhaps. Do you have any cameras on the exterior of the building?"

Dr. Giles shook his head. He looked so helpless.

Andy stood and announced, "Okay, Jim, Mercedes, let's get out of here and find her. Dr. Giles, if anything else comes up, you call me. Next visit, I stay with Su Lin the whole time, no options."

They reached the car and Andy insisted they head, not home, but toward the airport, and then he called Carlos. Mercedes called Julie to marshal the troops.

Alicia arrived at the airport and left the car in the long-term parking lot. She thoroughly wiped the interior, not once but twice, commenting that bleach was her friend. She retrieved her bag from the trunk and quickly added her hat. The long coat was quickly replaced with a navy cape, and she grabbed a medical bag as well. One final wipe of the trunk and she purposeful walked toward the shuttle bus to take her to the terminal. It was amazing the deference a nurse received, and Alicia played the part to the hilt.

She called a number that answered immediately. "Are you underground at the International Terminal? …

"Good, I should be there in ten minutes…

"I know, I am right on schedule. No issues at all…

"Did you inform the people at the other end what we needed and that we should be there today? …

"Great to know. How is your patient? …

"Good. She should remain out for at least an hour, allowing us to get through customs…

"Yes, we will walk up together to the ticketing counter and then on through security…

"I am excited. I have never traveled to Finland and really look forward to it. Thank you, Leroy, for inviting me …

"Yes, I promise I will do that to you after we arrive and get settled…"

She giggled and added, "And you will, ya know, to me too?…

"That's the way I like you, Leroy, you stud muffin."

CHAPTER FIFTY-ONE

Resolution can be Achieved from Chaos with Enough Hints

Communications travel at the speed of light, especially when someone so close is at risk. The call to Julie immediately set up a chain reaction, and within minutes everyone in the R-Group was aware that Su Lin had, in fact, been kidnapped from the clinic in Atlanta. Mercedes, Jim, and Andy were en route to the airport. Julie managed to contact Ernesto and insisted he be on the next flight to Helsinki. ICABOD was analyzing each portion of video film that could be acquired and placed a high probability that Su Lin was being taken to Pekoni in Finland. Carlos had established a telecommunications cloak to capture anything routing into or out of Helsinki. There was no proof, but the odds were that Dr. Pekoni was orchestrating these events.

Quip decided that he needed to get EZ into the operations center to work with Carlos, so he had Bowen pick her up at home. Then he called Jacob.

Jacob answered, "Hey, Quip, what's up? I figured you'd be sleeping."

Quip explained, "Wish I were, buddy. Su Lin was snatched at the clinic in Atlanta, and there is almost nothing to go on to determine her whereabouts. No one saw her leave. I want you to pack and leave immediately for Atlanta. I want you and Petra to open the rest of those files and start assembling as many scenarios as possible to help us be prepared. We don't know what we don't know, so we are really only going on suspicions and probabilities. I really need you and Petra to put aside the personal issues for this."

Jacob replied, "I will be leaving soon. Apparently, ICABOD made a reservation and has a ticket holding for me and a taxi on the way, according to the text that just arrived. Wow, I sure like the way he moves situations along, don't you?"

Quip stated, "I sure wish he'd seen this snatch coming, so we could have prevented it. But then again, that has a good and bad side as well. Just make the flight and call Mercedes when you hit the ground. I will alert her you are coming and perhaps you can arrange to take Andy back to the farm with you. He insisted on going to the airport with Mercedes and Jim, as they had all taken Su Lin to her appointment. I would guess with everything over the past twenty or so hours, Andy's a mess. I would be!"

"Okay, will do."

Jim reached the airport in record time and went to the International Terminal, based on Andy's direction. Andy indicated that a flight going to Helsinki would be the first target. Jim called into his resources and asked for a check on flight plans from Atlanta to that destination from the prior two hours until midnight. He was told that two flights had departed that would get to Europe and could continue on to Helsinki. One private and one commercial flight. No other details were available other than the gates the flights departed from. He was informed that four more flights were due to depart before midnight, and was asked if he needed any help. He declined for the time being, but said he would call back if that changed.

Andy phoned Carlos again. "Carlos, you get that tunnel set up, son? I want you to monitor everything. Maybe Quip can give you some target numbers to filter on as well."

"Yes, tunnel is up. EZ wants to talk to you too. Can I bridge her in?"

"Sure! Hi, Daughter, we'll find her, honey. I think I messed up taking her to that blasted appointment."

"Daddy, it'll all be fine. Carlos and I are going to establish some additional communications tracking. We are going to try to tap into the private MPLS networks and see if that gets us a better source of conversations to sift through. It'll be okay. Everyone is looking for her. We'll find her."

"I hope so, honey. Call you later or if I get any news. I'm getting kind of tired."

Otto and Wolfgang arrived at the operations center with EZ. EZ was led into the conference room, and Bowen arranged coffee and some quick snacks that he'd assembled, then he left. EZ used the conference phone to contact Carlos while her laptop booted, and she connected to the high-definition screen in the room. Carlos and she worked on connecting into the four primary MPLS clouds based on the latitude and longitude Quip had provided as they were situated to the location of the supercomputer fortress. Carlos asked no questions as to the whys, instinctively knowing that if he was supposed to know he would be told.

ICABOD contacted Quip. "Dr. Quip, EZ is in the conference room, connected and remotely working with Carlos. Otto and Wolfgang are working in Otto's office and would like you to update them there before the bottom of the hour.

"I wanted to alert you to a problem in meeting your request, Dr. Quip. The problem is that matching up the facial recognition programs to Su Lin is unlikely. I would doubt any camera anywhere would capture her. She is likely either under covers or bandaged to prevent detection. Since there was no film of her capture, so no image to use, do you have any ideas what other items I might use as a baseline for comparison?"

Quip stopped what he was working on and thought about the problem. ICABOD of course was correct, but what else could be used. The first attempt had not been filmed, but there was the mall. "ICABOD, can you use the mall video for the timeline we identified earlier and that you refined based on some additional information from Mercedes? We never went down that path as there was no real baseline, outside of a large black man. Could that be compared to all the video from the International Terminal for the designated time period at the Atlanta International Airport?"

ICABOD responded, "I can and will do that, with the only filter being a large black male. It could take some time, Dr. Quip."

Quip replied, "Understood."

Andy sat on a very uncomfortable chair in the terminal outside of security. Jim had used some identification he had to get through security several hours before. Mercedes had been on and off the phone during that period but close enough for him to see. He felt defeated. He hadn't made the decision, he hadn't spoken to Su Lin about his quandary, and now she was gone. He truly wondered if he would ever see her again. He wasn't ready to lose her.

He heard Mercedes's ringtone on her phone as she approached. She looked at the screen and almost smiled. She answered, "You landed, I presume? We are in the International Terminal outside of security."

Jacob clarified, "I am out front in a rental car. How about you escort Andy out here and let me take him home?"

Mercedes reached Andy and said, "Yes, we can be outside in a minute.

"Andy, Jacob is out front in a rental car and suggested that you and he head back to the farm. You can better help Carlos. Jim and I will finish up here soon."

Jim leaned in, loved seeing her startled, and said, "We are finished up now. It's time for all of us to return to the farm and reassess where we are. I will tell the others, but I reviewed the film for the two flights that left earlier. That is what took so long. The second, the private plane, was a medical flight. The video showed a nurse in a hat and cape, along with what looked like a patient she was escorting, being transported by airport support staff, though no one recognized him and the gate people did not recall his badge name. Because of the patient, the gate personnel held open the door. And the nurse held the tickets. I never saw the man return after the patient was placed on the plane. He should have returned from the aircraft but didn't. Airport security was not happy when I left them."

Jacob disconnected the call with Mercedes and called Quip. The call was answered, "Yep, you are there?"

"I am and I just overheard a conversation about a private flight that departed earlier that may have some video of our kidnappers on a presumed medical flight. The patient was not seen, but the two people, a man and woman, might be captured on the film. It might help, or it might not."

Quip sighed, "Ah, but it might. Thanks. Let me know when you get to the farm. EZ said her dad needs to have his blood pressure checked, and ask him, discreetly of course, if he is on time with his meds. It seems Andy has been taking this blood pressure medication for some time, but he tends to ignore it when he feels good."

"Will do. How mad is EZ at you, bro?"

"Not enough time for that conversation. You take care of your lady, and I'll take care of mine. Later!"

Xavier was almost beside himself with anticipation. They were en route. After years of not seeing her, she would be here and she could see all he'd done. She would shake off this façade of girlishness that Leroy mentioned and provide the details for him for what she'd apparently accomplished. She had been wrong to keep the information from him. He would punish her, but only after she gave him what he wanted.

Leroy had called and reassured Xavier that Su Lin was well, just sedated. He had brought along a nurse to make certain that she remained that way during the fourteen or so hour flight. They expected two refueling stops, and Leroy was connected on board to the Wi-Fi network. He had transmitted the early blood work that the nurse had provided, and Xavier was pleased with the preliminary results.

It came at the perfect time, he mused. That morning he had lost his longest surviving subject after an injection. It was a setback, to be certain, and he would miss the little flower, but Master Po was so much better. Having her there would change everything, and he could finally reach his goals. After Master Po was installed in his infirmary, she would share her information. The information he'd paid for, after all. She might argue a bit, the stubborn thing that she was, but he had the upper hand. She would realize that soon enough.

He had his cook prepare a marvelous feast as he was suddenly ravenous. Xavier smiled as he opened the fine wine and filled his glass. Perhaps he would invite her to a fine meal such as this if she provided the information without too much fuss.

CHAPTER FIFTY-TWO

The Truth Hurts
When You Don't Practice It

Zara had worked around the apartment all day. She'd rearranged some of the furniture as she'd cleaned and tidied up each of the rooms. Outside of the clothes of Patty's that fit well, she had removed the rest of the evidence that another woman had lived there and occupied Buzz's heart. She was surprised at how much she enjoyed the idea of staying with one man and wondered how long he might stay interested. In her experience, men lost interest after their base needs were met. Buzz had laughed when she'd commented on that last evening and soundly kissed her. That, of course, led to lots of fun.

Buzz had left her money for grocery shopping and had offered to take her out to dinner, but Zara had indicated to him she really liked cooking and said she'd shop and then decide. While she walked back from the store, she thought about how to best extract herself from her former life. She wanted to move on to a new life, as they'd discussed last evening. Zara had two issues to deal with that she'd not brought up in their conversation. She'd been worried that Buzz would try to make her ignore their overarching treats. In so many ways, he was such a novice in the ways of men like Dmitry and Chairman Chang. The plan fully formulated, as she walked, in how to solve the issues and not have to ask Buzz for anything more than grocery money.

Zara walked into the apartment and put away the groceries. She decided that with her problem on the way to being solved, dinner out sounded great. It also provided the perfect venue to tell him the rest of her history. She glanced around and saw everything looked nice and homey, and then smiled as she dialed the first of her two calls.

After three rings, the call was answered. "Hello, Miss Mojo, how are you feeling?"

Zara grinned and replied, "I am feeling much better, thank you. Did you find the programs to your satisfaction?"

Leroy responded, "I did, Miss Mojo, I surely did. They are providing some great data for me and, with the master menu, can be easily modified. It is making my research much easier."

"That is good to hear, Mr. Leroy. During our last meeting, I didn't have the presence to complete my payment arrangements and would like to meet."

"Ms. Mojo, I am actually out of town. Can it wait, or do you have an account that will accept a wire transfer? You did some right fine programming, and I want to make certain that you are available when I need another program."

Zara deflated a bit. She had wanted to meet with him in person for the next part of the discussion, but time was critical. "Oh, I had no idea you would leave town before we concluded our business. When will you return? I had something else I wanted to discuss."

Zara was so focused on the call that she failed to hear the door open as Buzz returned home. He was going to greet her with a hug when he realized she was on the phone, so he patiently sat down in the open kitchen where he could simply watch her. Buzz's mind wandered back to her and their conversation during the day. He had come to the conclusion that she was perhaps his best destiny.

Leroy grinned as he looked down at the naked bottom of the sleeping Alicia. "Miss Mojo, it could be a week or more before I return. I am not certain how long my business might take here. What else did you need?"

Zara explained, "The two men that you helped me to neutralize, where did you put them? I negotiated a sizable payment for their return. Of course, I am willing to share with you as a business transaction."

Leroy frowned. He hated missing any opportunity to make money, but Xavier had been so delighted when he delivered the twins. Xavier had taken some blood, tested it, and then remarked that the tests were good. These twins would make excellent candidates for the next phase of experiments after he retrieved the information from Su Lin. Leroy grinned and commented, "Miss Mojo, as tempting as that is, I have to tell you they were disposed of after hurting you the way they did. I couldn't bring myself to let monsters like that roam free to hurt another one of the fairer sex, such as yourself. Why, my mama would roll over in her grave if I hadn't taken care of them."

Zara couldn't believe what she'd heard. That would surely seal her fate. She panicked as she demanded, "Look, Mr. Leroy, you owe me my money for the programs, and I want them back. I already promised, and I had the issue with them."

Leroy rose and walked to the adjoining room so as not to wake up Alicia. "Now, Miss Mojo, please calm yourself, ma'am. Provide me with an account number, and I will transfer your programming fees immediately."

Zara breathed slowly to control her anxiety. Buzz was confused with her side of the conversation but didn't want to interrupt. He tried to assess what they had discussed last evening to see where this conversation fit in. It fit nothing they had discussed, he decided. She reached into her bag and pulled out a notebook and rattled off a number. With the years Buzz had spent working at his father's bank, he recognized the routing number as to the Bahamas, followed by an account number.

Zara completed reading the number and added, "Now look, I need those two guys. It's not a request. I must have them."

Leroy finished the transfer and then calmly placated, "Now, Miss Mojo, your money has been transferred. There is no way those two will ever bother you again. I will call you if I need another program, but I am going to hang up now. Please don't call back."

Zara disconnected the call and shook her head in disbelief. The next call wasn't necessary as arrangements with Chairman Chang were impossible without the twins. She'd have to convince Buzz that a trip to Amsterdam was needed. She was about to get some wine opened while she waited for Buzz to return home.

Startling her, Buzz quietly asked, "Zara, what haven't you told me? I thought you promised."

Zara looked stricken as she rose and turned to see Buzz. She was at a loss for any words as the tears streamed down her cheeks.

Xavier was so pleased with his new acquisitions. The Asian men had some DNA elements he had needed. As twins they could be most valuable in his experiments. For the time being, he kept them in the clinic portion of the lab under sedation with monitors regulating their vitals. The only additional requirement to maintain them in their current state would be periodic turning.

The blood test on Ling Po was a testament to major success, he thought, as he had carried her into his lavish living quarters and placed her on his couch. Even though Leroy had uncovered the records that indicated her mind was damaged, he needed to verify that for himself. Ling Po was the master because she was a very cunning opponent and as such he refused to call her Su Lin. Her showing up at the one conference meeting and derailing his funding had not been forgotten. He waited patiently for the sedative to work through her system. He didn't want her frightened or restrained. He'd even covered her with a light blanket.

Xavier noticed her skin was smoother and more flawless than he recalled. Even sedated, her skin had a vibrant glow, as did her hair and nails. These were the areas that were typically afflicted with age, yet hers were untouched. He had known her a long time, and she should be showing her age, even with her Asian ancestry. She was easily one of the most beautiful women he'd ever known. In not seeing any aging in her, he was convinced she'd completed her experiments. The blood test had revealed that the virus he'd injected her with all that time ago was no longer present. Xavier contemplated how his life would be altered once the virus left his system. If she could be persuaded to turn over the documentation on her experiments, he could finally complete his work.

Xavier turned to face Alicia and asked, "Are you clear what's to be done? We can't afford another incident where she collapses into a psychological puddle."

Alicia raised her chin smartly and responded, "Yes sir!"

After several hours, Ling Po finally began to stir. Alicia moved her chair a bit closer to the couch and waited. She was going to be a bit groggy for a while until she'd eaten. When she started to stir, Alicia alerted the kitchen to have some dishes prepared and delivered to the dining room. Xavier hoped he'd correctly recalled some of her favorites as he waffled between his desire for her comfort and the need to finish his work. Alicia was there to ease Ling Po through this transition and then leave so Xavier could go to work. Finally, her eyes fluttered and then slowly opened. She glanced around as her eyes adjusted and then settled on Alicia's face. She neither smiled nor frowned, though she looked a bit disoriented.

"Hello," Su Lin slowly whispered. "Where am I?"

Alicia launched into her concerned nurse role. "Oh, sugah, you're back with us! You gave us quite a scare, young lady! I was getting you prepped with the IV, and the next thing I know you were lights out! I've been tending you for a while, and now that you've come around, we want Dr. Pekoni to take a look at you. Will that be okay, sugah?"

Su Lin smiled weakly at the reassuring face and took comfort in Alicia's voice of false concern. Then Alicia commented, "Now as soon as you feel ready, I'll take you to see Dr. Pekoni so we can get to the bottom of things. You tell me when, sugah."

Su Lin began to assemble a mental awareness of her surroundings, but everything took a back seat to her need for a biological health break. Then she grinned and abruptly asked, "Can you show me the way to the bathroom, please? I really need to go."

Alicia smiled and held out her hand to lead Su Lin to the closest toilet. Su Lin used the commode and then washed her face and hands. She looked into the mirror and recognized the face she saw. She smiled and straightened her hair. She wondered about this Dr. Pekoni. He wasn't anyone she knew, but Alicia made everything seem fine. Anyway, Andy wouldn't let her be alone with this person if he wasn't nice. Odd, that Andy hadn't introduced them though. Perhaps she had just forgotten. Sometimes that occurred, though not in many months.

Su Lin frowned as she thought very hard and tried to remember things. She recalled Andy bringing her to the clinic and talking to Dr. Giles. Then she went into a room to prepare for her CAT scan. Alicia had been there to help and here she was again, helping her. It seemed like a very long time ago. She had no idea what time it was or even where she was but assumed that they were still at the clinic. Then her stomach grumbled, and she giggled. She needed food. Hopefully, the nice man would tell her where she could eat. After Su Lin emerged, Alicia escorted her directly to Dr. Pekoni's offices and made all the proper introductions. Alicia then excused herself and closed the door as she left.

She looked around the room behind him and at the unfamiliar surroundings. She was certain that she had not seen this place before. The walls seemed to have fabric, like silk, on them. The colors were muted and darker than she was accustomed to on the farm, where everything was open, bright, and cheerful. She decided that with a place such as this, Dr. Xavier probably needed cheering up, so she made that her new job. She liked jobs.

Su Lin searched her memories and stated, "I feel like I have been sleeping a long time. Are we still at the clinic? I don't recognize this place."

Xavier frowned at the unfamiliar cadence to her voice and replied, "You are in my home, Ling Po. I am Dr. Xavier Pekoni. You remember me of course. Don't play."

Su Lin looked confused as she responded, "Nice to meet you, Dr. Pekoni, but I am afraid I don't know you. Why would I know you? Did Dr. Giles recommend that I see you? There have been so many doctors. You could have mistaken me for someone else. My name is Su Lin. Where is Andy? And, where is here? This doesn't look like a doctor's office."

Xavier wondered who this Andy might be and why she cared. She never relied on anyone, especially a man, as she'd informed him repeatedly. However, she was not the assertive, rapid-fire spoken, demanding, and obstinate Ling Po from his past. Leroy had said she spoke like a younger woman, and he could hear the lack of education in the words she used. He couldn't believe that perhaps some of the information Leroy had provided might actually be correct. Something had happened to her mind.

He shook his head, unwilling to believe, and continued, "I will call you Su Lin, but we met when you called yourself Ling Po or, sometimes, Master Po. Does that sound familiar? And this is actually my home, where I thought we might be more comfortable to talk. You may call me Xavier."

Su Lin shyly smiled, "Excuse me, Dr. Xavier, Alicia took me to the bathroom, but I am hungry now. Can you please tell me where I can find something to eat? I feel like I haven't eaten for days."

Xavier cocked his head and tried to reconcile this creature with the Ling Po he knew. "I thought you might be hungry, so I had my chef prepare some of your favorites, Ling Po. Please come this way." He took her arm and escorted her to the dining room.

She walked so inelegantly. The woman he recalled glided rather than clomped like this Su Lin. He hoped it was due to the sedative, but was unconvinced.

Su Lin noticed that the furnishings were plain, yet seemed very dark and heavy. The pictures on the walls looked odd and unlike art she had studied. She smiled at the thought of Andy, knowing he would not like the furnishings. The lighting was also muted, making the living space almost cave-like. It seemed like an odd place to want to live.

Su Lin commented, "Thank you very much, but please, my name is Su Lin, sir." Then she asked, "When will Andy get back?

I would like to have him eat with me. You must know Andy pretty well for him to let me stay here without him."

Xavier checked his immediate response and replied, "Andy and I have you in common, my dear. He thought perhaps I might help you. Come sit, eat, and tell me what you recall."

Su Lin was delighted with all the food on the table and clapped her hands with joy as she took her seat. Xavier shook his head. This was not the delicate and refined Ling Po he knew. She immediately helped herself from the closest bowls, then proceeded to eat with vigor and ask questions in between bites. Xavier noted that she ate more like a farm field hand, and it repulsed him that she had changed from the once elegant though direct Master Po.

Su Lin asked, "How long have you lived here, Dr. Xavier? Does anyone else live with you? We have lots of people living on the farm right now."

Xavier decided that conversation might be the best way to trip up this act, if it was in fact an act, though he grew increasingly apprehensive. "I have lived here for a long time. It was my child-hood home, and allows me the space to continue my testing.

"Where is the farm, as you put it? How long have you been there?'

Su Lin grinned and replied, "It is Andy's farm, and it is near Atlanta. He has been there a long time. He takes care of me and lets me help with the animals. I love the animals, especially Franklin. Andy teaches me all sorts of things and makes me study really hard. Do you like to study?"

Xavier realized this conversation was more than odd and struggled to redirect the discussion. "I do like to study and work toward my goal of living forever. You and I worked on a project together, but we haven't finished it yet. You were responsible for working on portions of those experiments."

Su Lin chuckled and replied, "Dr. Xavier, you are so funny. I am not smart enough to work on experiments, and no one can live forever. You are being silly.

"Andy says if I study really hard and pass some tests that I might get to attend college in a couple of years. I like learning, and I think I would like college. It would be very different than learning on the farm."

Xavier kept his growing anger checked. None of the guile that Ling Po displayed was present in this female. He asked, "How long have you lived on the farm with, umm, Andy?"

"Oh, I don't know exactly how long but well over a year. Ever since I had my accident and Andy insisted I stay there with him rather than going to some facility. He is so nice to me. He makes me study, and I take care of Franklin. Andy said I brought Franklin there, and he knows tricks. He is a very funny pig. You might like him. If you go with me to the farm, I will let you see Franklin. He is very smart."

His interest piqued at the discussion on the pig. Perhaps her act was falling apart. "Franklin, the pig? How long have you had Franklin?"

"I have no idea. Andy said I brought him to the farm a long time ago, before my accident. Funny though, Petra is working on my laptop trying to open up some files that have passwords on them, but she found some files about a pig. I read them, but I couldn't tell if they were about Franklin. Petra thinks I wrote the notes, but I don't remember doing that.

"Could we have worked on that before my accident?

"Is that why Andy brought me here? Can you help me?

"Your food was very good, but I am full now. Thank you very much for getting it for me. I liked the cake the best."

Xavier pressed, "Files, how many files? Do they all have passwords? Where are they?"

Su Lin giggled, "Boy, you sure ask a lot of questions. Let me see. I don't know how many files, but they all seem to have different passwords or, as Petra said, are encrypted. They are all on my laptop. She is trying to see what is on them. I think she works very hard on them, though Andy shouted at her the other night. They are still friends, I hope.

"Where is Andy? I am getting tired, and I want to go home, please."

Xavier was now convinced that she was not acting. No one could keep up that chatter unless that was their nature. He recalled listening to girls when he was in grade school and that ongoing chatter was their method of communication. That, and rapidly skipping from one subject to another with no reason. The reports must have been correct that her mind was somehow lost. But perhaps the laptop held the information he needed. Maybe he could help her mind, or she was merely a means to get the laptop. He decided he needed to speak to this Andy.

Xavier decided that he needed to take action. "Andy asked me to call him when you woke up. I can't find his number though. I lost it."

Su Lin brightened and smiled as she confided, "I have his number. I had to memorize it and promise to call if I ever needed him. The number is 404-876-1121. Can I talk to him? I really miss him, though I am getting tired. Can I lay down until he gets here?"

Xavier looked almost disgusted as he rose and suggested, "I have a room you can rest in, em, Su Lin. I will get in contact with Andy, and we will arrange a time to meet."

Su Lin practically danced at his side as he took her to a room that was small but had a nice-looking bed and even a bathroom attached, just like at home. "I will wait here, Dr. Xavier. Thank you very much." She hugged him, then turned and walked to the bed.

He closed the door and locked it, then pocketed the key. Frustrated that he'd really lost what he'd long considered his greatest female interest, he realized that this shell of a woman was no longer the key to solving the forever puzzle. She might prove useful in getting the necessary information, however, to get him to his goal. As an added bonus, he could practice on her with the new information. The thoughts made him smile about getting long-awaited answers to his project.

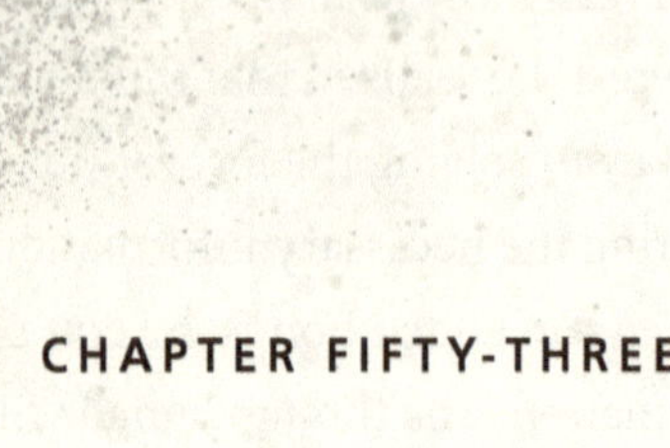

CHAPTER FIFTY-THREE

The Story of the Dragon and the Butterfly

Andy and Jacob walked into the house together. "Welcome, young feller! Just about the whole gang is here now! All we need is Eilla-Zan and Quip to have a full house!"

Jacob rather soberly replied, "I'm sorry that Su Lin is not here to enjoy this reunion, Andy."

Andy's face darkened at the mention of the kidnapping. Jacob regretted having said anything as he offered, "Andy, it'll be fine. We'll get her back. Right now I need to focus on my role in this drama. I need to get to where Petra is working on Su Lin's laptop. Can you point me, please, Andy? We need to crack the last few files which apparently are the toughest ones."

Andy nodded and without saying a word escorted Jacob to the computer work area where Petra had set up operations. Andy turned to leave after showing Jacob in, but then turned back and mentioned, "You two need anything, just holler, okay?"

Jacob could see Petra, and he momentarily froze while trying to enter the room. He could only nod to Andy while still fixated on Petra. Petra heard them both come to the doorway, but she kept her back to the door as she pretended, she didn't hear them enter.

Jacob walked slowly over to where she was and quietly sat down next to her while he studied her profile. The silence was so thick that neither of them uttered a word for several minutes. It was Jacob who broke the stalemate first.

Jacob quietly offered, "Hello, Petra. It is good to see you again."

Petra sat fixated on the computer screen and did not respond. Jacob, also feeling the tension, fell silent after his soft greeting. He had expected the awkwardness of this reunion but had secretly hoped they might be able to rekindle their relationship. When Petra didn't respond to his modest greeting, he decided to try a different approach.

Jacob smiled and softly stated, "My mother once told me a story when I was growing up that somehow seems appropriate now. It was the story of the Dragon and the Butterfly.

"It seems there was this dragon who wandered the hills, the lakes, and forests in his realm. One day he journeyed to the edge of the known forest and looked out over the grassland savanna that reached out farther than he could see. In all directions, from his vantage point, all he could see was an endless expanse of grasslands. He wondered if he had reached the end of the habitable world, for who or what could possibly live where there were no hills, lakes, or forest.

"The dragon's musings were interrupted when he saw the most beautiful flying creature he had ever seen. He called to the flying creature and asked, 'What are you called, flying creature? Where do you come from? I have never seen anything like you, with such delicate wings and brilliant colors, in any part of my realm!'

"The flying creature answered, 'I am a butterfly who has lost my way, kind creature. I was flying with my kind as we raced to see the ends of the earth. Then I looked back, and none were with me. Now I fear that I am lost. But tell me, what are you? What manner of creature are you?'

"The dragon was pleased to introduce himself and announced, 'I am a dragon, of course! I too can fly, but you fly so effortlessly and have so many splendid colors that shimmer in the sunlight. You are so unique, I was hoping to know you better.'

"The butterfly cried, 'I am lost! Don't you understand? I need to return to where I came from! Can you tell me where I am and how to get home?'

"The dragon puzzled a moment and responded, 'Why, little butterfly, you are here. Here is an important location because you are with me. As for how to return, I don't know of any other place except in my realm. I have seen hills, lakes, and forests, but until today, I did not know of this savanna or that you have come from another land. You are here and now with me. I would offer to be your friend.'

"The butterfly began to cry and lamented, 'I don't know where to find my kind! It is different for you since you have others of your kind, so you cannot be lonely like me!'

"The dragon hung his head down and offered, 'Butterfly, I have no other of my kind in this realm. I am strong and can fly, but I have no one to be my friend. That is why I offered to be your friend, so that I might have a friend too! There is so much to see and show in my realm, but I have no one to share it with. Having a beautiful butterfly as a friend would be a wonderful gift for one such as I.'

"The butterfly stopped crying and asked, 'You have no friends? And I have lost all my friends! What if we became friends, and we show each other a land not seen by the other? Perhaps we could find your kind and maybe help find mine. Even if we don't find those that are lost, we would have each other, yes? Will you be my friend, Dragon?'

"The dragon was so happy that his scales bristled across his large frame like rolling waves heading into shore. He then unfurled his wings, bowed in respect, and, while smiling, happily offered, 'It would be an honor and delight to be your friend, my dear butterfly! There is so much I would share with you! Come see my realm and know you are always safe with your dragon. And, because we are now friends, I shed a dragon tear for you that will give you the strength to keep up with me in our flight. But if you grow tired, simply ride next to my ear so we can whisper to each other and tell one another secrets.'

"The butterfly smiled and suggested, 'Then show me your realm, and we will always be together.'

"So the butterfly and the dragon soared together, exploring the wonders of the realm, and life was good for them both."

Jacob stopped the tale to study Petra in silence. Petra was quietly crying but slowly turned her head to look directly at Jacob, who was misty eyed as well.

After a few moments Jacob took her hand into his and asked, "Butterfly, will you be my friend? I would very much like to have you in my realm, and it would give me great joy to have you join me."

With everyone in the house preoccupied with plans for how to get Su Lin back, the incoming call on Andy's robo-phone went unnoticed at first. The country code read 358, indicating a call was coming from Finland. The call reached the fourth ring and promptly went to voicemail. Andy walked over to glance at his phone just as the same number came through again.

Confused, he decided he would take the call even though he didn't speak Finnish. He answered, "I don't speak no Finnsky. If you don't understand English, greatly polished with my Georgian accent, then this is gonna be a short call."

The caller's refined voice smoothly responded, "I can assure you that I speak English fluently, Mr. Greenwood."

Andy was startled at the voice but responded, "Well, excuse me for thinking that if you're calling from Finland, you might be of Finnish descent. Now you called me by my name, which tells me this isn't a wrong number. How about you tell me what's on your mind?"

The caller comfortably stated, "I believe we have a mutual acquaintance. Are you the guardian of Su Lin, as she calls herself now?"

Alarm spread through his system like wildfire. Andy started walking toward the communications center, where he hoped Carlos was still working. Andy tersely retorted, "Just exactly who are you? What is really on your mind? I only ask that because you are exactly four seconds away from being disconnected!"

Maintaining a very even business-like tone, the male caller answered, "I am the interested party who has your ward, Su Lin, Mr. Greenwood. The proof to my claim is that you gave her this number to call you if she were ever in trouble. Do I have your attention now?"

Andy slowly closed his eyes and swallowed hard. Realizing that he was speaking with Su Lin's captor, he demanded, "Ah, so you are the one who grabbed her. This is the part then where the slimy kidnapper calls and demands ransom money for her safe return, am I right?"

Andy opened the door and gained Carlos's attention. He pointed to the phone, and Carlos nodded and started to set up the trace.

The man responded, "Money doesn't interest me, Mr. Greenwood. What I am interested in is her laptop and the research files she has created for my project. Su Lin really has no value in her present state. She clearly has no recollection of our previous arrangement, nor of the funds deposited monthly into her account by me.

"She had already reneged on our agreement, but in fact she has the answers I paid for. Therefore, if she cannot or will not tell me the information, then I will take it off the laptop where they have to be stored."

Andy, struggling to contain his anger, evenly stated, "Well, that's going to be a bit difficult since all them files were encrypted. I've had two geniuses working on them to decrypt them with no luck! If you want us to be like a couple of flea market dealers, I'm happy to trade the useless laptop for her, since each of us has something the other wants. And you still ain't told me your name! Now, I can call you a whole bunch of unflattering names, but I want your name!"

The man hesitated momentarily, then complied, "For your convenience, I am called Dr. Pekoni. And, yes, I do want the laptop with or without the files decrypted since I can have that done here.

"Tell me, why would you want my junior researcher and partner when clearly she belongs with me and my project? Once I have her research then I can resolve her memory loss issues. I am in a position to help her, but you cannot. As it was, you were holding her captive, and I am rescuing her from *your* clutches. Her destiny is with me."

Andy, growing fearful for Su Lin, answered, "She doesn't have her old mind. Even if she had done a contract to dance with the devil, like you suggest, she doesn't have any memory of that! In layman's terms, she wiped out her disk drive, and we are trying to reload the operating system, called her brain, you twit!

"How do you want this exchange to go down, so we both get what we want, Dr. Percoloney?"

Dr. Pekoni offered, "I'll tell you what I am prepared to do, Mr. Greenwood. You give me the laptop and let me extract the necessary files, routines, and research that will allow me to cure her condition, and then we can let her decide where she wants to take her life. If what I believe is on the laptop is there, then even if you had the information and Su Lin back safe and sound, no U.S. hospital or physician is going to be allowed to act on curing her.

"In fact, I can almost guarantee that if you propose what is the right course of action, they will arrest you and make her a ward of the state. We would both lose. I can act on the information here in my facilities, so bring me the laptop. Then we'll see where Su Lin, formerly known as Ling Po, would rather live."

Andy was paralyzed by the accusations and Pekoni's logic. He faced the dilemma of either fighting to get Su Lin back unharmed and not experimented on, or letting the madman do what he probably couldn't get done in the U.S. to reverse the process that had taken away her mind. Andy recalled the letter that had begged him to follow the process to restore her memories, and here was someone willing to do it. The trouble was, what happened after her mind was restored? What if those memories were like the fictional character Dorian Grey, and, like his portrait, her digital memories contained all the evil she had ever done while teamed up with Pekoni?

It was more than Andy could deal with on the call, so he finally said, "I cannot give you an answer now! I need to think this through and call you back."

Pekoni, somewhat taken aback, asserted, "Mr. Greenwood, we don't have any time to waste. Just comply with my proposal so we can see the results. There is so much riding on this."

Andy simply disconnected the call, put the phone down, and cupped his face in his big hands as he sat down to consider the horrible choices he faced.

Carlos patted his shoulder and showed Andy the file of the recorded call.

CHAPTER FIFTY-FOUR

The Trouble with the Future is that It Always Shows Up Before You Are Ready for It

No one was prepared to leave the room after the call, yet no one dared go near Andy because of his highly agitated state of mind. Andy was straining to keep his temper in check as he bellowed, "Well, thanks for adding something else to my worry plate! Anybody got any swell ideas on how to fix this situation and get Su Lin back from the clutches of this kidnapping bastard?"

Mercedes and Jim exchanged anxious glances. Mercedes tried to speak, but Andy cut her off.

"No, I'm not blaming you two for this miserable set of circumstances, because this ol' boy was there and fumbled the ball as well! Let me recap this here soap opera for those of you who don't keep up with current events!

"In the interest of science and self-extermination, Su Lin practices some digital voodoo on herself, looking for some kind of fountain of youth elixir, but not before she backs up her mind and biology mappings to her PC. She writes a letter asking me, ME, to allow her stored procedure to be applied and maybe put her brains back in place in case there is an OOPS in her experiment!

"I get descended upon by all my family and trusted colleagues telling me she might be the nefarious Master Po. As such, she is part of an overall global conspiracy to grab people and experiment on them so somebody can live forever! Before any of us can get to the truth, she conveniently wipes out her mind, and we end up taking her in to raise and retrain, but no diapers required this time!

"Just when it looks like things can't get any worse, Su Lin slips through our fingers like greased owl excrement. Then she ends up in the hands of this year's winner of the psycho award who is willing to trade her for the files of their experiments! Now apparently, based on what we know so far, I probably have guardianship to someone who might be the direct descendant of Lizzie Borden so the advice is to lock up the axes! And the icing on the cake is that she's also being blackmailed into giving up her files, so this mentally arthritic researcher can maybe restore her mind but will go on to murder more folks in the name of science! Boy, somebody pass the popcorn this way 'cause this matinee movie is really getting interesting!"

It took a few minutes of silence before anyone had enough courage to say anything after Andy's raging soliloquy, but finally Petra offered, "Andy, we are all here because we care. And I want you to know that we will do everything we can to get her back."

Andy, seething with anger and hurt feelings, responded, "Just how exactly do y'all think we are going to be able to do that? We send the laptop to him, and the researcher/assassin kills her like everyone else he comes in contact with. Or, we send someone in to make the exchange and they'll be added to the list of unfortunates. Or, we call in a low earth-orbit nuclear strike at their last known location, and everyone there has a bad day! Tell me we have an option D."

Jim cleared his throat and calmly suggested, "Andy, Mercedes and I have expertise in the area of hostage retrieval, and we have some very formidable resources we can call in at a moment's notice. I understand your feelings, but now it's personal for me as well. There isn't a place you can run on this planet that I won't find you and extract justice. This was on my watch, and all I ask is that you not stand in my way on rectifying what has gone wrong. As for the other issues in your current events description, I leave that to your conscience."

Petra, emboldened by Jim's statement, turned slightly, and asked, "Jacob, can you add your thoughts here, please?"

The empty silence caused everyone to begin looking around the room for Jacob, but their search was in vain. Petra started to panic and looked to Carlos, who simply raised his phone to show the text message to Petra. Carlos sensed her frozen mental state and rotated the phone around to read the text to the group. He announced, "The dragon is in launch sequence into the vast grasslands to the east."

Lara's eyes searched both Petra's and Carlos's faces as she asked, "What does that mean? Where is Jacob?"

Carlos softly offered, "He texted me that we should let him do this. My guess is that the laptop is gone as well, and rescue operations for Su Lin are now in full swing."

Lara looked at Carlos incredulously and asked, "You knew, but you let him go alone?"

Carlos rather stoically responded, "He invoked the Yaqui Indian code of honor from me, stating this was his challenge. He felt that he owed it to the group for his past failings. Do not judge a warrior for how he makes amends to those he loves but abandoned."

Petra flopped into the closest chair and uncontrollably sobbed. If she had been stabbed with a twenty-centimeter carbon steel bayonet, it wouldn't have hurt any worse.

Mercedes and Jim both pulled out their cell phones to reach their on-call contacts with the intention of intercepting Jacob.

Andy sat dumbfounded at the swirling activity, trying to make sense of the pandemonium around him.

Lara tried to comfort Petra as Petra repeated over and over, "I cannot lose him again!"

Carlos was with them as well but puzzled over her statement and responded, "Madam, you will not lose him. How can you lose a quest when you have a dragon watching over you?"

Mercedes ended the cell call. "Crap! Well, he certainly engineered that perfectly!" She turned to Jim as Andy came over to them, and said, "He just commandeered the jet we had standing by, and they are airborne. Not only that, he used our cloaking protocol to change signature frequencies, so we cannot raise them on the radios!"

Jim nodded and remarked, "You know, someone this clever needs to have some support folks on the ground at his destination to help back him up. Don't you think? Mercedes, you said you have team members in Europe, correct? Any chance you can get some boots to the target area for a clandestine support role for Jacob?"

Mercedes dialed her cell phone while she responded, "On it!"

Jim turned to Andy and, with the most military respect he could summon, said, "Sir, Plan D is now operationally in effect, sir!"

Quip asked, "Are you there, old buddy?"

Jacob swallowed hard and said, "Just trying to get my headset on when you called. Everything in place? Can you double check with ICABOD to make sure we haven't overlooked anything?"

Quip clucked his tongue and dryly said, "Excuse me, is this the analog processor questioning the digital processor? Not getting cold feet, are you? All the resources are lined up. Are YOU sure you can pull this off? We could have used the professionals for this operation, you know, so you could have stayed and done the *huggy-bear/kissy-face* thing with Petra but noooo. You must put on your costume, climb aboard a shiny jet, and, like the hero in the afternoon movie matinee, holler, *Let's go High-Altitude-Silver, away!*"

Jacob gave an impatient sigh and said, "I told you I had to do this for my state of mind. If I get killed, then you can have the last laugh, okay?"

Quip rolled his eyes and responded, "Yes, of course, secret agent Michaels, Jacob Michaels. Just so we are straight on this issue, don't get killed. Deliver the package that is called for and extract Su Lin. The rest is in place. Get back on the plane and get out of Dodge with the goods. No gunfight this time, Wyatt!"

Jacob was silent for a few moments, but then said, "Quip, I'm scared."

Quip tried to rein in his compassion for Jacob but said, "Hey, everything will be okay! ICABOD has this planned out. Between you and me and our giant brains, or mine at least, you're going to be fine."

Jacob quickly interjected, "No, that's not what I'm scared of. It's Petra. What if she doesn't…I mean what if we can't… suppose that…"

Quip, half annoyed and half sympathetic, responded, "Oh, come on, reckie-pilot! You mapped out this current operation that has your tail feathers on the line, but you don't have the *ca-jones* to face Petra to put your lives back together? You obviously have your priorities bass-ackwards!"

Jacob chuckled slightly and said, "Then let me thank you from the heart of my bottom for your heartfelt sentiment."

Quip relented somewhat as he said, "Okay, I admit it. You are someone I do admire and like having around. That doesn't mean we are going steady, but I'm not ready to see you leave in a body bag. Is that too much sentiment for you to digest?"

Jacob was quiet for a few minutes, digesting everything that was going on, when Quip asked, "Are you sure all the code is in place on STINKIE to receive the remaining programs on Su Lin's laptop? This has to work flawlessly to give Pekoni the HAIRCUT we are trying to deliver to his program."

Jacob struggled with the temptation to ask what HAIRCUT stood for, but before he could overcome his internal argument, Quip boldly stated, "*Holistic Algorithms with Intelligent Reconnaissance Calculated to Undermine his Triumph,* or, HAIRCUT. I figured you secretly wanted to ask but were afraid to."

Jacob rocked back into his seat with dismay at being trapped at 28,000 feet in an aluminum cylinder traveling at 350 knots an hour and forced to have a conversation with Quip. He wondered if he could manage to pull this operation off without Quip but quickly realized that would also mean no ICABOD as well. Seeing no alternative but to stay connected with Quip, he sarcastically replied, "Oh, I get it! It's a joke! Guffaw! Guffaw! You are going to have to wait until I catch my breath and get up from the floor from laughing so hard."

Almost immediately, Jacob added, "Okay, done. Now in answer to your question, yes, the foundational code is all in place. With what I am about to deliver to the bad doctor, the two programmed entities should be able to link up, at which point the abductor becomes the hostage. Has ICABOD archived everything off the two targets? There won't be a whole lot left after I press the detonator, so I hope all is tucked away."

Quip remarked, "Are you kidding me? We couldn't take another petabyte of information if we had to! This guy's idea of Big Data is everyone else's idea of the history of the universe! I am going to have to rent some storage from Tuck just to sort through this mountain of data."

Jacob sat and reflected on all the recent events and then soberly asked, "Quip, if anything happens to me, you will explain to everyone, right? I mean, let them know that we had this fully engineered and that..."

Quip cut him off quickly. "Oh, knock it off, can't you? Nothing is going to happen to you because we are the good guys, got it? As they say in Texas, This ain't our first time at the rodeo, ridin' the wild bull! We have all the formidable resources of the R-Group vectored at the target who thinks we don't know who he is! This has been carefully choreographed by ICABOD with input from us. Right now, just stay the course and play the bag man role until the trap is sprung. The only thing we didn't plan for was providing an extra pair of underwear for you in the event that you decide to take a bio-health break in your britches at the peak of the action! Are we good?"

Jacob chuckled a little and agreed, "We are good. I just need to get there and give him the CASH."

Quip puzzled a moment and then asked, "Cash? There is no cash in this transaction, and none was arranged for delivery. Unless you stopped by the ATM to withdraw several hundred grand of U.S. currency, you're going in empty handed."

Jacob grinned as he responded, "CASH! Computer Application Shot at Hostile. I figured you secretly wanted to know, so I told you."

Quip, somewhat indignant, retorted, "Hey, it's only funny when I do that, so stop it!"

CHAPTER FIFTY-FIVE

Life's Deviations from the Norm Are Always More Fun!

Ernesto had arrived in country more than two days ago. Since that time, he had been doing reconnaissance on the target facility and preparing for the scenarios that Julie and he had discussed after he'd landed. He had established a good place to keep an eye on the facility that Julie indicated was home to the Finland supercomputer as well as the laboratory for the target of interest. Very few people had direct access to the facility, so it was no surprise that the camera which Ernesto had placed to record the traffic had almost nothing. If an occasional bird or shadow hadn't been added to the picture, it would seem like a photo rather than a video stream. There were some guards in matching outfits that were visible now and again but really no foot traffic. The guards were armed, looked formidable, and traveled in pairs connected electronically.

Ernesto had probed folks at the airport for confirmation of an inbound medical plane but was not making much headway. He'd even cozied up with the airport security teams at the local café, but that also hadn't yielded much. There had been three planes that had medical personnel deplane. One was military and had refueled and took off. Another was an emergency landing with emergency vehicles on hand when the plane doors opened that unfortunately had a body rather than a patient. This incident had created a lot of discussion, as they were concerned that some major illness had been brought to their shores. The third on the list had deplaned medical staff and three stretchers, complete with IVs attached, which required help from security. Nothing was similar to an Asian female patient with a nurse.

Everything was reported to Julie, and she'd also provided him some additional assignments, the latest of which was meeting the plane in several hours that carried Mercedes and contractor support from the U.S. three-letter agency. Julie had suggested that Mercedes and Ernesto would assist Jacob, at some undetermined point, in an extraction from the facility. Julie did not know exactly what to expect, so one of the assignments was to create different contingency plans. Ernesto was very adept at responding to various scenarios. It was one of the main reasons why he had been hired by Julie.

Another reason that Julie had dispatched Ernesto was because, even though he was just shy of two meters, his dark curly hair, ready smile, and agreeable attitude seemed to draw people into trusting him. He also learned a great deal by listening and frequently leveraged his multi-lingual ability. He was able, in his short time in the country, to learn about the guards and their loyalty, not to the facility, but rather to the leading patron of the area, Dr. Pekoni. Dr. Pekoni apparently paid his help very well, but rumors were his clinic handled foreigners rather than locals. Ernesto had picked this up at the local bar the evening before. Even the local police seemed to turn a blind eye to the facility activities. As long as the supercomputer provided what was needed to the Finnish user community of educators and scientists, no one seemed interested in the goings-on inside.

Ernesto rented a couple of rooms within walking distance of the facility and stacked up the supplies that Julie had requested. He added some items that complemented his multiple contingency plans. He had no way of knowing what this character was like, but Julie assured Ernesto that the contractor was highly experienced. Ernesto had worked remotely with his other teammate, George, to set up the temporary but secure data transmissions. At present, he had five video cameras feeding a central repository, with some creative analytics being performed by a resource Julie had enabled. This operation had an intensity which Ernesto enjoyed.

The property of the facility was fenced, and electronic surveillance was enabled. Fortunately, Ernesto was familiar with the set up and found two different methods to disable it in less than five seconds. Julie had stressed as the highest priority that the facility and the supercomputer should be protected and undamaged. They had discussed some various explosives to be used as distractions, which required precision handling. Like a single shot from a high-powered rifle at one hundred yards, nothing was heard before the shot connected. Toward that end, Ernesto had secured a smart sniper rifle and three side arms that he'd sighted to accomplish that sort of precision as needed. For the tranquilizer darting weapon to be effective, the target needed to be within forty-five meters, but the closer the better. But when you are trying to dart humans, they don't always cooperate, so the regular weapons were part of the backup. The live rounds in the side arms were for defense, though Ernesto and Mercedes were skilled at hand-to-hand combat in order to avoid using firearms unless there was no other choice.

Ernesto arrived at the airport shortly before Mercedes texted to say they had passed through customs and were headed out with their luggage. It was impossible not to notice Mercedes as she exited, and Ernesto was surprised to recognize the man with her. His name may have been Jim, but he knew him as Stalker. He was a man Ernesto respected. He opened the trunk and turned, practically saluting.

"Sir, glad to see you here," Ernesto stated in crisp, succinct words.

Jim grinned and slapped Ernesto on the back in greeting. Then he explained, "You don't work for me, but I too am glad we are working together."

Mercedes looked between both men. She'd had no idea they might already know one another. "Do I want to know how you two know each other, or just let it go?"

"I'd let it go," suggested Ernesto.

"It really isn't a story worth relating, other than we work well together," added Jim.

Ernesto offered, "I didn't expect you to be the consultant to our group, so I'm glad I did some quality shopping for the necessary household items we are going to need. May I show you our picnic basket?"

They all moved to the back of the vehicle, and Jim grinned broadly as the trunk was opened for viewing. Jim observed, "One of the finest weapon designs from Ernst Mauch. The HK416 assault rifle with its 5.56 x 45mm NATO round and several twenty and thirty round clips. Optimum range 300 meters and a maximum range of 400 meters. I prefer the 14.5 inch barrel, because I get 882 meters per second muzzle velocity, which is almost 100 meters per second more than the 10.4 inch barrel. And as we all know, that extra four inches packs a lot more punch when you need it. I mean seriously, who wouldn't enjoy another four inches, hmm? You just drop the bi-pod legs up front, check for your wind conditions, adjust for estimated distance, and then you reach out to get their attention with a projectile that mushrooms on impact.

"If you have to shoot farther than that, my tendency is to simply call-in artillery or an unmanned drone for some sparkles on the target. But if you need long distance and precision in your strike, then start looking to go to a fifty caliber. That's a little out of my league. That is definitely where the big boys and girls play. Good choice on the fourteen-shot, 9mm Berettas for side arms. Boy, when you pack for a picnic, you bring some tasty morsels!"

Ernesto smiled at the memory of their prior operations together and nodded his head as he reminisced, "Good times! Good to be spotting for you again, sir."

Mercedes eyed both of them suspiciously but only said, "All this talk of picnics has made me hungry. Can we leave the finger foods in the car and go for something with a little more bread to it?"

"Okay by me. Ernesto, can we grab something to eat, and you can fill us in on the details. I sent a note to Julie that we had arrived, and she suggested that we get briefed by you, stay alert and wait for further details. It could be a day or a week. We will be informed."

Ernesto grinned and offered, "I found a great little restaurant that has some nice private dining and fish dishes that are out-standing. However, if we stay here for very long, I'll be fatter than a forty-kilo robin! Let me fill you in. I think you will like what I have set up so far. We can review. Stalker, anything you want added can likely be done easily. I have established some great contacts."

Jim clarified, "Jim, call me Jim. This is a friendly kumbaya deal.

"You've always been a great front man to get things up and rolling quickly. I assume you've secured some rooms?"

Mercedes looked possessively at Jim, then back to Ernesto. "We'll do just fine with one room. Come on, let's go eat. I'm starved."

CHAPTER FIFTY-SIX

Unearned is Unappreciated

...The Enigma Chronicles

Jacob walked purposefully but calmly into the facilities after a short ride from the airport. Based on the waiting faux Red Guard, he presumed the message had been passed to Dr. Pekoni's cell phone successfully. Jacob passed through the usual amount of security to gain access to the room Pekoni had reserved for their meeting. At the first stop, they checked all his electronics and made him power up the all-important laptop of Su Lin's. He was greatly relieved that nothing was confiscated but was dismayed to see that his phone could no longer get any cellular connectivity. He frowned at not having any cellular telemetry through the local carrier available so that his meeting could be heard by Quip and team.

Jacob muttered under his breath, "Well, that's just great! I wandered into Satan's hardened data bunker where my phone doesn't get any bars. Sure hope I don't need to call for takeout food!"

Jacob was escorted into the meeting room where Dr. Pekoni was waiting, but he was also unexpectedly greeted by Su Lin, who rushed up to hug him. Afraid that his con-game would be ruined, he quickly improvised as he hugged her back and whispered,

"Su Lin! I have a new game. If I end a sentence with the word *Right*, then you smile, nod your head, but say nothing. Got it? Let's play."

Xavier was a little suspicious of the long hug, but before he made a move toward them, Jacob straightened and stretched out his hand. He said, "Dr. Pekoni, I presume? I am Jacob, and Andy has sent me with the laptop for the exchange."

Xavier studied the situation a moment, glancing back and forth between Jacob and Su Lin, then asked, "You're not just an errand boy. She obviously knows you. How long have you worked with her?"

While staring at Su Lin, Jacob responded, "I am Su Lin's assistant. I was her assistant before the accident and afterwards as well, *right*?"

Su Lin followed the game rules and smiled while nodding but said nothing.

Not completely convinced, Xavier then asked, "What was Mr. Greenwood's decision on allowing Su Lin to be a party to my restoring her memory? Not that I need your permission, but I didn't get a call back, and now here you are offering up the laptop with almost no fuss. Why the agreeableness now?"

Jacob stared purposefully into Xavier's eyes and easily recounted, "The fact is, he wasn't going to do the trade and was prepared to force your hand. I have worked too many years with Master Po, and now Su Lin, since the accident, to allow someone to jeopardize her work. Su Lin, am I *right*?"

Su Lin again followed the game rules and smiled while nodding but continued to say nothing.

Jacob looked back to Xavier and continued, "I simply took her property from the two so-called computer clowns and grabbed the first flight here after hearing the recording of your conversation. I can get us into the laptop to access the files, then you will need to restore my Master Po. That is, of course, assuming you can make good on your boast. However, I am not prepared to have her at risk. If I sense an incompetent approach to this matter, you, sir, will be at risk. Su Lin, am I *right*?"

Su Lin followed the game rules and smiled, nodded but remained ever silent.

Xavier dropped his suspicions for indignation and curtly replied, "Of all the gall from a lowly assistant! I have been unraveling the secrets of life's programming while you were still cleaning test tubes and petri dishes! How dare you suggest that I am incapable of perfectly executing this procedure!

"Perhaps I was mistaken about your competence and usefulness! Give me one good reason why I shouldn't have my Red Guards throw you out after I have drained every last drop of useful blood from your body?"

Jacob let Xavier's rant settle a moment before he confidently offered, "Because I know the secret combination of passwords to get into the files so that the destructive disk wipe program does not get invoked.

"Andy's people couldn't break the encryption and, point in fact, you won't be able to either. Master Po taught encryption methodologies in China, and she always put scorched earth code in her programs as a reward for anyone clever enough to unravel the security. I am the only one, now, who can get into the subdirectories where her memories and biological blueprint is stored. Su Lin, am I *right*?"

Su Lin followed the game rules and smiled while she silently nodded.

Xavier was beside himself with rage and summoned his Red Guards. As they entered, Xavier tersely stated, "Take him to our computer access room and plug him in after you scan his PC. He is not to leave your sight. I know something is wrong, but at this point I cannot say what that is."

Now looking more confident and less angry, Xavier said to Jacob, "I will join you momentarily, and we will begin the process to restore Master Po. Just so we are clear, you are not going anywhere until the procedure is complete, so you will be restrained during the restoration of her memories. Once that is complete, we will double check your story with Master Po to see if this story is fact or fiction."

Jacob's confidence was now dissolving, but with as much bravado as he could summon, he swallowed hard and responded, "I have come too far with my master to no longer be able to serve her. You touch that laptop, and you will ruin everything on it, along with her chances of being restored. So take me to your room of torture, if you like, but remember that I have the keys, not you! And Su Lin will never be able to access the secrets on this PC until her memory is restored, so if anything happens to me, your research is dead in the water! And I don't think you can simply copy the laptop hard drive up to your rumored supercomputer to try and break the encryption there. So don't bother, Su Lin, am I *right*?"

Su Lin again followed the game's rules.

Xavier gave Jacob an eerie smile and responded, "Now that is an excellent idea! You are beginning to understand what I am capable of, and your sense of fear just provided me with an excellent idea. Perhaps you will be useful yet!"

Xavier motioned to his Red Guards to bring the guests along. Jacob, a little worried, looked down at his holstered cell phone and noticed that he had received a text message. He discreetly took a quick peek to find that a text has gotten through to him somehow while they were in the hardened data bunker. The message read:

> We now have you connected via Wi-Fi for all the telemetry of the conversation.

ICABOD and STINKIE provided the connectivity. Resources en route.

Jacob enjoyed a small amount of hope, smiled, and quickly deleted the text just as the Red Guard confiscated his phone. Jacob's confidence was returning, and he asked, "Su Lin, this is a good game, *right*?"

Su Lin followed the game rules and smiled while nodding but again said nothing.

Quip glanced first to Otto, then asked, "Wolfgang, are you okay? You seem kind of quiet."

Wolfgang blinked several times as if he was waking up from a slumber, except that his eyes had been open all along. He turned his head to face them and offered, "Sorry, gentlemen, just a little lost in thought. I was going over the night I called and spoke with my daughter Julianne for the last time. We had a visit over the phone, and she promised to call again soon. It never occurred to me that it would be our last chance to talk forever. She was killed by that Russian enforcer, Sergei. All of her hopes and aspirations ended that night as well. I cannot describe how I felt when I learned she was gone.

"It was at that point we collectively decided to bring Jacob into the family business. My wish, of course, was that he would want that. I confess I was selfish in my motivation since he was her son and my grandson. I wanted her back, and he was as close as I could have.

"Gentlemen, I will tell you I could not be prouder of his selfless action in this matter, nor more terrified of losing him like his mother. Here is a man willing to fight tyranny in defense of someone who is not blood family, but nevertheless in the greatest tradition this family has to offer.

"Dr. Pekoni cannot see what he has become in his medical quest. He has sacrificed everything, including his humanity, to build the solution in order to live forever. He has become like the Nazi S.S. doctors who took free rein in experimenting on humans classified as enemies of the state. They swore an oath to save lives but forfeited that code when they began to freely experiment on humans with the justification that it would save others. When the war was over, they couldn't understand why they were put on trial for crimes against humanity because they claimed they were working *for* humanity.

"No one wanted to dredge up the horrors they inflicted during World War II at the Nuremburg trials, but the lessons from the dark times had to be made right and justice served. They never relented in their innocence, and I have to believe that Pekoni will be the same way. We need to bring him to justice just as the Nazi S.S. doctors were when they were put on trial in October 1946."

Otto, rather determinedly, concurred, "Wolfgang, I can categorically state that we are in violent agreement with your position. And as for young master Jacob, I, too, am proud of him in this theater of action. However, I will state that while I am concerned about his safety, I have high confidence the operation will achieve all intended goals. Quip, how about you?"

Quip rather soberly offered, "We have feet on the ground in the target area, we have full electronic access into the facility, and we have a very solid man on the inside. All options have been accounted for except the one X-factor that we have no control over."

Wolfgang asked, "Are we sure this is the right course of action? My feeling is that this is too close to being like the Nazi S.S. doctors."

Otto replied, "We are NOT making a decision here, gentlemen! We are executing a person's last written request. Su Lin, or Ling Po, whichever way you want to look at her, left instructions to her executor stating that she wanted her memories to be restored. If she had also said do not resuscitate, we would be obliged to follow those instructions as well. We are not operating to benefit Pekoni's project but to follow her last request before the accident. As her legal guardian, technically Andy could make the call!"

Quip then quickly added, "ICABOD and I have scoured all the medical facilities that could possibly do this procedure and the answer is, you've got to be kidding me. Pekoni was right, no one would touch it. The decision is the right one and Su Lin's only hope of restoration. I agree with Otto. We are executing her last written request."

Wolfgang nodded in agreement. "Very well, gentlemen. You present compelling arguments, and the logic is sound. Above all, it was her final request, and I feel we owe it to her to try. I just hope our timing works correctly, and our extraction is completely successful."

Otto said, "Everything that can be done is being done, old friend. The CATs team is in place, and Stalker is on loan from the three letter U.S. government agency. If everything goes to plan, Wolfgang, you'll be playing chess with Jacob in no time and struggling to beat him."

Wolfgang and Quip grinned at the thought of having all the family back in the fold again.

Wolfgang then asked, "You think I should let him win now and then?"

Otto chuckled and said, "Push-tush! Make him earn it! Otherwise, you would be cheating him."

CHAPTER FIFTY-SEVEN

They are Called Possessions Because They End Up Owning You

...The Enigma Chronicles

Dmitry accepted the incoming call and in his cheeriest voice said, "Chairman Chang, how good of you to call! I assume you are calling to tell me that your diamond expert is in place and ready to appraise the merchandise as agreed, yes?"

Chang was in a very sour mood and flatly stated, "You can drop the affectations, Dmitry. I know that your minion, Zara, has the diamonds and that you were brokering them on her behalf for a commission. You do realize that those were my diamonds that were stolen from me, don't you? Is this how the game is played in Russia? People call you friend, promise to help you for a small percentage, but in fact all they are interested in is playing the *taxi game*?"

Dmitry's face fell back to reality as soon as he saw that the game had changed again. Curious though, he asked, "Uh, what *taxi game*, Chairman Chang?"

His anger building by the moment, Chang responded, "Yes, you know, that is where you offer to give me a lift to my intended destination, but as I bend over to get in, you quickly run around behind to drive me home!

"And, on top of returning my own diamonds, she bragged about having my two trusted associates but was kind enough to throw them into the deal for another million! Is it good Russian manners to steal a person's property, capture trusted personnel, and then offer to sell the lot back to you for six million euros?"

Somewhat astonished, and with repressed admiration for a comrade of her background, Dmitry queried, "She grabbed the diamonds, hijacked your henchmen, and tried to get me to do her bidding. This was after she darted and tagged the three of you with competition ribbons with your britches down! Why, the saucy minx!

"You shouldn't be too angry with her. She was only trying to sell more to you so my commission would be higher. My birthday is coming up, and she knows that a higher commission keeps me in an up mood. I pout so easily, you know."

Chairman Chang was now livid and fired back with a smirk of his own. "That's funny, she didn't mention you being in involved. Oh, dear boy, it does sound like your wishes may have been discarded in this transaction. I only called to gloat at how you can't keep your stable whore in line! She offered to deal directly with me, which means she wasn't thinking about any commission for you.

"Fortunately, as something of a friend to you, I called to ask why you were playing the taxi game as well."

Dmitry, boiling inside by the circumstances as well as by the taunting, tersely responded, "Chang, you should know by now that no one cuts me out because ME is important! But now ME is puzzled. If you know who has your diamonds and associates, why contact me? Surely you have the resources to find and retrieve your property. Why call me even though ME is desperately important?"

Chairman Chang, reeling in his blinding rage, offered, "She was going to cut you out of this deal and probably others unknown to me. I thought you might like to exercise your command over her, and in the process return my property to me. That would include both the diamonds and my associates. I will pay you the commission as if the full amount changed hands, but I'm not paying to have my property back. If you handle the transaction, you can discipline her any way you see fit, and she can continue to serve you. However, if I have to retrieve my property, I can promise, she will serve no one after I'm finished."

Dmitry considered the statement and suggested, "I will agree to your offer, on one condition. I need to have additional supercomputer power applied to a troublesome target at the same time my supercomputer launches. Help me electronically pound my adversary. For my brokerage fee, I will return your diamonds and your associates, but I will retain Zara in my employment. I would enjoy reeducating her to a more useful role in my life. It's all about ME, you know."

Chairman Chang agreed, "Done! Provide me with the electronic coordinates and the launch time sequence."

Buzz shook his head in disbelief while turning his eyes away from Zara. After yet another round of *true confessions, but only after you caught me lying again*, Zara had fallen quiet while Buzz digested the additions to the story. Buzz slowly returned his gaze to rest on her and commented, "Well, there it is, the next install-ment to the Zara saga. This just keeps getting better with every new piece of the story. I can only imagine the kind of childhood you must have had!"

Zara was prepared to give full disclosure on her sordid childhood, but before she could launch into it, Buzz intercepted. "No, no, please, no more! Save that for some other time! My eyebrow muscles are sore from arching up to my hairline with your stories!"

Zara pulled back into herself slightly, not knowing what to offer up next. Buzz broke the silence. "Okay, so the diamonds got lifted from Chairman Chang, and you have snagged his two henchman who he thinks will be returned to him. You work for both Russian mobsters or Russian civil servants but…oh, I'm sorry, I'm being redundant again! You work for Russian mobsters, and every time they don't get what they want, they threaten to strangle you with undergarments. You moonlight doing computer hacking to fund your 401K retirement plan. As such, your life is a constant stream of very unseemly types asking you to help them, for money of course, to rip someone else off! Did I miss anything!?"

Zara ached from the strain of the disclosure. After sitting quietly for a moment, she offered, "That is pretty much it, except for one thing. I fell in love with a nice guy named Buzz, and now I want to leave the world of what I was to be with him. Pretty incredible story, judging from the look of disbelief on your face. The way you tell it out loud, I'm not sure I believe it either."

Buzz added a fatalistic chuckle and replied, "I am probably the only person in the world who could say my life story pretty well parallels yours. My girlfriend got murdered by this Russian henchman, and his boss recruits me to do some double-dealing computer stuff for him against the Chinese Chairman Chang. Chang's heavies rough me up when things go poorly, and I end up working for him! I make the mistake of coming back to New York where the police accuse me of Patty's death. My life was pretty much comical farce, except I'm the only star in this performance!

A blond angel showed up out of nowhere just as I'm thinking of doing the Wall Street dive from a tall building and tells me how to get away from it all, which includes paying the chairman five million in diamonds to let me go! As an incentive, I'm to throw in a white tiger to help grease the deal.

"Now, you understand, don't you, that if you got these diamonds from your chairman, that I think is also my chairman, they were the ransom I paid to go free, don't you? What do you think he will do when he catches up with you and finds me here too with the diamonds I already gave him once?"

Zara looked down at the diamonds and then looked up at Buzz again. Finally, she offered, "The diamonds were my last chance for a payday that would let me say goodbye to this shadowy lifestyle of mine and maybe stay with Mister Right. Problem is, you showed up before I could sell the diamonds. You and I would want for nothing and on my terms if I could broker them."

Buzz looked at her and asked, "How much have I asked from you? Haven't I willingly covered everything with no complaints? You want for nothing now, but these blood diamonds are calling you back to the shadows."

Zara was starting to panic. "We can sell them at the diamond exchange in Amsterdam! We take whatever they offer, and we don't look back. With enough money in our account, we can vanish, but vanish in comfort!"

Buzz cocked his head to one side and queried, "You mean, leave the relative safety of this country and move into range of the Russian mobsters of Eurasia? Are you hearing yourself? Besides that, those diamonds were my ransom for Chang to leave me alone! You stole them, and if you sell them to someone else, I'll just bet you he will want to get even with both of us, sweetie! I don't want to run all my life, because the one time you stop looking over your shoulder will be the last time. Those diamonds offer nothing but grief in my eyes. You should do what you feel is best. Will you please send me a postcard now and again, but don't stay in the area after it is mailed. They will hunt you based on the postmark."

Zara winced a little in pain, with tears rolling down her face. Not looking at anything in particular, she took the diamonds out of her bag and offered them open-handed to Buzz.

Finally, Zara had the courage to look Buzz in the eye and professed, "I've never liked Amsterdam anyway."

CHAPTER FIFTY-EIGHT

There is a Vast Chasm between Working Together and Working Well Together

Carlos was working intently in the operations center at the farm when Andy stormed in. Carlos had worked all night, with EZ remote in Zürich, tracking communication signals as directed by Quip and Julie. He was tired and not in the mood for an Andy tirade, regardless of how warranted.

"Good morning, Andy," offered Carlos without taking his eyes off his screen. "I sure hope you brought some coffee along with the unsettled mood."

"Look, young man," Andy grumbled. "I am not in any mood to take any of your Yaqui insights this morning. Why didn't you ask for my help through the night? I gotta find out from my daughter, via a text 'cause she's too busy working with you, that you guys are working on tracking some communication signals." Then he raised his voice and added, "That includes that ungrateful Jacob, who stole the laptop and left without as much as a by-your-leave to anyone here. Right?"

Carlos slightly shook his head and breathed. "Does that mean you didn't think, knowing all you just related, a nice cup of coffee with honey might be a better way to offer to assist?

"To be honest, I am not certain who exactly we are tracking. I am merely working with the signal IDs I was provided. The owners of those signals weren't provided. Perhaps your daughter knows. Like most things we do, Andy, this is a subcontract effort based on a need to know, against an open PO. The requested information fits into the statement of work guidelines that you established with Quip."

Carlos turned his glance toward Andy and stared, waiting to see if Andy would back it down a bit. After several intense seconds, which felt like eternity, Andy blinked and flumped into his designated chair. He asked, "Can you provide me any updates, Carlos, please?"

Carlos replied, "Andy, I haven't much to tell you. From what I gather in the chatter, Jacob is in Europe, likely trying to meet with the guy that called you from Finland to negotiate for Su Lin. Yes, he did take the laptop, but I asked if it was backed up and if some sort of plan was in place, and I was told yes, but no details were provided. I know that Mercedes and Jim flew out, either late last night or early this morning, on some sort of charter that Jim arranged. Again, no details. We have nine communication signals we are tracking at present, and that information is based on the IDs given to me and, of course, Eilla-Zan.

"I thought with your being so worried that a little sleep would be good for you. Then this morning I would update you, after you and I had some breakfast in here, like we always do when we are working a round-the-clock contract. Did I miss anything?"

Andy looked like a wounded animal. His face was drawn and pasty, and he was unconsciously rubbing at the discomfort in his chest. He had barely slept and certainly hadn't thought to have breakfast. He'd tried to call his daughter this morning to help get a little grounded, and the text she sent back saying she was busy and would call him, had sent him into graphics mode. He was adrift and needed to do something.

"Carlos, sorry, I guess I got up on the wrong side of the bed. How about I go get us some food and some coffee and get briefed on where you are so I can then take over for a while?"

Carlos smiled a bit and replied, "Sounds good. Perhaps I can rest if you will just focus on the assignment."

Andy started to wind up at the inference that he couldn't focus. "Focus! Focus? I always focus on my work. I built this little business that you are working in, Carlos. I know he is your friend, but that Jacob never should have taken off without a discussion. He had no right to take matters into his own hands and leave with that laptop. That is not like him. Petra was stunned and in tears. This whole thing is out of control. Lara took Petra to rest, Mercedes and Jim gathered some things and left. I went out to tend to chores, and you disappeared, I thought to bed. This is my house and my ward, which means I deserve some information."

Carlos pushed a button to speed dial a number on the desk phone while he also put it on speaker. In half a ring the caller answered, "What's wrong, Carlos? Is my dad okay?"

Carlos replied, "Eilla-Zan, he is here now and seems to think I am withholding information. It's either that, or he wants to fire me. I thought it would be better if you filled him in, while I go get a cup of coffee."

"Eh, um, sure. Go ahead. I got this.

"Good morning, Daddy. I am sorry I couldn't speak earlier. We are monitoring several signals. Some of them are very weak. We have sort of a tandem signal working that was rigged onto a supercomputer that boosts the Wi-Fi. It is pretty remarkable, actually.

"Did you get any rest, at all?"

Andy visibly calmed at the sound of Eilla-Zan's soothing voice. Right now, she centered him. Carlos was comfortable that he could step away for that coffee, and he'd make breakfast. He'd start enough so that Lara and Petra would have something when they got up too, though Carlos suspected Petra was doing some remote help from her bedroom.

Thirty minutes later, Carlos returned with ample food and coffee for both of them. He was surprised to see Petra sitting with Andy. He glanced at his screen, pleased to see the remote updates as they continued to fill the screen. He knew that Eilla-Zan was back at it.

Petra smiled and greeted, "Morning, Carlos. I hope you have an extra coffee cup stashed some place close?"

Carlos grinned and replied, "This is an ops center, madam, and we always have coffee cups close by. Just don't look too closely at them, and you'll be fine. We typically don't wash coffee mugs here since hot coffee works to kill the bacteria cultures growing in them as well as perk you up."

Petra replied, "Hmm, sounds great. I was just going to update Andy. Have a seat and it will save a repeat.

"Andy, I know Jacob left without telling anyone his plan. I believe he did it based on how successful he could be. The goal is to get Su Lin back. Right now there are still lots of unsettled issues with her. There are things she may or may not have done, but we are all focused on getting her back so we can determine the next steps. Jacob has a fondness for Su Lin, as do all of us. I know he would not deliberately put her at risk. He wants to make it all right, even though he is not responsible for it occurring. We just need to stick together and help where we can. The rest we can sort out later."

Andy looked better and said, "Alright, Petra, I will if you will.

"Carlos, how about that coffee, son. We need to see if there are any other ways we can help with this communications tracking, and then you need to go take a nap."

CHAPTER FIFTY-NINE

Check and Mate, Sir

Xavier shook his head and commented, "So that's what happened to her. She and I had always played high stakes poker, but even I would never push the envelope that far! She took the next logical step in programmable nanotechnology but bet her own life? She was lucky you broke the code in twelve minutes, because any longer and even I would be unsure of the regenerative power of the Fountain of Youth program to help her. Your story must be true since I knew her quite well before, and I can certainly see the current state she is in. In light of this new information, perhaps you are more valuable than I originally suspected. Before we move on, well done on saving Master Po, young apprentice."

Jacob, unmoved by the compliment from Pekoni, responded, "I recommend that we put our distrust of each other aside, pool our resources, and discuss the next steps for Ling Po. She has all the necessary DNA sequencing and her memories stored on the laptop you uploaded to the supercomputer. You have the other half of the regenerative procedure from the chemical interaction side, so with both sides of the procedure, we should be able to launch a repair and restore sequence.

"To clarify our objectives, you have the confidence of success based on your large base of research. I am interested in restoring Ling Po to her original mental excellence, and you need the electro-chemistry solution side that is only in her mind."

Xavier studied Jacob a moment, then elaborated, "Odd, isn't it? I have the technology to rebuild her lost neural pathways to receive her lost memories. When I do that portion, she has the initial electrical jumpstart of the cell structure to reestablish lost chemical building processes that the body was born with. Together the two processes would allow us to engineer humans to live indefinitely! I feel my lifelong dream is about to be fulfilled!"

Again, Jacob, unmoved by Xavier's euphoria, requested, "Dr. Pekoni, can we do a verbal walk through of the processes you envision? I do not want my master to be at risk. As such, I am not prepared to launch into anything until we discuss all the steps of the procedure."

Xavier rotated his head around in disbelief. He looked hard at Jacob and stated, "You seem to forget that I am the one in charge here, not you! I am fairly sure you have some value, based on what you have relayed to me, but in my realm, I dictate the steps of the procedure that I want to follow! I wouldn't let Ling Po run her own show, and I'm not about to let you run yours. I am warning you, try not to aggravate me again!"

Rather dispassionately, Jacob nodded his head and acquiesced, "Perhaps you're right. A small demonstration is in order, so the way between us can be clear.

"Please enter your login ID to access the files that you uploaded to the supercomputer and go to the directory labeled *ITSME!*"

Xavier smirked and casually executed the steps and then was halted by what the screen displayed:

Forgive me, mother, for I have sinned

Terror began to grip Xavier as he slowly turned to face Jacob. Jacob smiled slightly and clarified, "My mother would be so disappointed in me for crafting such destructive Trojan worm viruses designed to eradicate an entire supercomputer. She would, however, have to admire the reasoning behind the death-code that you just launched.

"I was pretty sure that you would confiscate her laptop and upload it to your computer system. You really do get points for scanning it before you took the bait. The code was thoroughly obfuscated and only reassembled itself when you foolishly entered into the bogus directory *ITSME!*

"Now, let's understand one another. The code is rigged to wipe everything if you don't follow the next five steps carefully, and I'm the only one who knows those next five steps. You should realize by now they are designed for us to move to our next steps in the procedure for Ling Po, followed by our extraction. By the way, they are timed steps, so if you think you have some wiggle room in following my directions, then the auto-death cycle will be engaged whether we are alive or not. You will only get the save-me code sequence once we are out and gone. Is there anything in my explanation that you don't understand? The reason I ask, is because the clock is now ticking, Dr. Pekoni."

Stunned that he could have been so easily deceived, Xavier could not respond at first. Finally, he summoned all his courage and responded, "I don't believe you! No one could have deceived me so easily. I think you're bluffing!"

Jacob smiled slightly and quietly murmured, "I hope I get a chance to play chess again with Wolfgang after this." Then Jacob pointedly commented, "Dr. Pekoni, I anticipated your resistance to following my instructions. You are, as they say, predictable. Please inspect your personal files that you stored in the Storage Area Network array labeled Archived. You will notice that it is now empty."

Trembling, Xavier quickly inspected the SAN array that should hold all of his archived research. He was stunned and in disbelief stated, "It's gone! It's all gone! You monster, what have you done with my research? That is my life's work! I'll have you flailed alive if you don't return it!"

Jacob smirked and calmly replied, "What? You don't have your data mirrored or backed up? Oh, by the way, those resources are gone too. Your other three copies were eradicated as well. I mean, what's the point of erasing data if you don't whack the backups at the same time. Don't you think? Okay, enough of the demonstration. Now go to the directory labeled Humbled."

Numbed by the demonstration, Xavier complied with the instructions with robotic motions.

Jacob then directed, "Okay, now go look at those personal data directories again."

Xavier couldn't mask his surprise as he mumbled, "Everything is back. You restored all that was purged. How is this possible?"

Jacob, growing tired of the demonstration, offered, "I think we have had some very meaningful communications over the last little while, don't you? Do you think it's possible to now accommodate my modest requests and simply follow my instructions, so we can restore Ling Po's memories? Remember, the death-code time clock is still ticking, and, well, there is so little time left to negotiate. Tell me, Dr. Pekoni, what are your thoughts?"

Xavier nodded his head slowly, and then turning to Jacob, sullenly stated, "It would seem that you are no longer merely the apprentice to your master. She'd be pleased. I recommend we adhere to your wishes in this restoration to regain my Ling Po."

Jacob smiled broadly and agreed, "Ah, now we're communicating!"

The horror and fear that gripped Jacob was clearly on his face as he screamed, "She's flatlining! Look at the monitors! You said there would be no issue, but, look, her heartbeat is gone. I don't feel a pulse!"

Xavier's expression was puzzled, and he responded, "Hmmm… this shouldn't be happening. I admit that restoring this much memory and spawning regenerative tissue to rebuild the lost neural pathways was more than I have ever tried, but it should have worked fine. Maybe we should have practiced on one of those Asian twins I just acquired. Of course, if everything had gone as it should have, he certainly would have been a mess with all those female memories in a male's mind."

Jacob stared incredulously at Dr. Pekoni as he asserted, "Practiced? You're only thinking of that now? Su Lin is dead from *your should have been okay procedure.* Now it occurs to you that a practice session may have been a good idea? Well, I can't argue with that, so let me practice on you! Let's see how much torque your neck will take before I can wrench your head off your body, shall we?"

Jacob was so enraged, he reached for Xavier's throat just as he felt someone grab his wrist with barely enough pressure to register. She weakly offered, "Jacob, why is it that every time my heartbeat gets interrupted, you are the one standing there trying to restart it? By the way, thanks for your successful efforts in this matter, but I'm thinking two times will be quite enough."

Both Jacob and Xavier turned to face a recovering Su Lin, who smiled weakly at them.

Forgetting his rage vectored toward Dr. Pekoni, Jacob practically shouted, "Su Lin, you're back!"

Su Lin replied, "And not a moment too soon, judging from the fiery confrontation between the two of you. Xavier, allow me to introduce one of my most gifted students, Jacob Michaels.

And Jacob, while I don't mind being called Su Lin, my given name is Ling Po."

Then Ling Po focused on Dr. Pekoni and clarified, "I see you still have that inexorable ability to absolutely alienate people, judging from your near-death experience at the hands of my apprentice. Since I am here in your facilities, I expect that I have you to thank for reintroducing my memories that were lost during that slight miscalculation in an otherwise flawless experiment. While I am grateful for the restoration, I cannot say I'm happy to see you again, Xavier."

Xavier, still conscious of the timer on the death-code Jacob had launched on his system, quickly offered, "We shall have to talk over the good old days another time. I have completed my part of the bargain, so if you don't mind, young man, disable the computer viruses you put into my system!"

Su Lin turned her head to focus on Jacob and said in a scolding tone, "Jacob, were you being naughty again?"

Jacob hung his head down in a mock-ashamed attitude and, with a hint of half-jesting, replied, "Forgive me, Master Po, for I have sinned. Dr. Pekoni was somewhat uncooperative in my request to restore your memories, so I had to improvise. He has been through death and life together with his precious research data."

Su Lin giggled impishly and surmised, "Sounds like my apprentice served up some of your own medicine, Xavier. After what you did to me to force my support for your efforts, which nearly killed me, I am not feeling any remorse. I have completed my end of the bargain, and you have what you contracted for from me. We will be taking our leave. I'm sure you have figured out that I solved the riddle that you wanted. If I have surmised correctly, you have uploaded all my research so there is no need for us to stay. Jacob, what is our exit strategy?"

Jacob lowered his eyes and rather sullenly responded, "Well, I had a good plan on getting in, but for our exit we may need to improvise a little. Dr. Pekoni has his goon squad ready to nab us as soon as we walk through the door to leave. So even though I have embedded a scorched-earth program into his system, I'm not sure of a planned, orderly exit at this time."

At that moment a text message came through on Jacob's phone, which Xavier had been holding during his captivity, that read:

> Jacob, take Su Lin and leave by the front door. They're waiting for you.

Xavier read the message aloud and added, "You're not leaving until I get the disinfectant codes and see them work. Then you and your master can go."

Before anyone could comment further, the door opened and in stepped Mercedes, Jim, and Ernesto. A startled Xavier went to push the alarm code but was promptly darted by Mercedes.

Jim grinned and offered, "I think something was said about needing an exit strategy?"

Ernesto panned left and right with his field of vision so that the video camera he was wearing could see and share what he was seeing. Jacob lost no time disengaging Su Lin from the medical monitoring equipment.

Before they piled through the door, Su Lin insisted, "Wait! I want my laptop! It has my lessons that have to be done for Andy. I'm not leaving without it!"

They all exchanged quizzical looks among one another. Then Jacob broke into a grin and announced, "One laptop with all your homework assignments on it, coming right up!"

After securing the laptop, they all moved deliberately and quickly through the maze of rooms and passed the two hapless associates of Chairman Chang, Won and Ton. Ernesto quickly panned right to pick them up on his video feed and then came to an abrupt halt with a puzzled look on his face.

Ernesto held onto his audio earbuds and commented into the shoulder mike.

"Julie, I don't understand…

"Yes, I see them. Probably a couple of research candidates that didn't know they were going to be experimented on…

"And what do you mean, oh, not them again?…

"Alright, alright, I'll tell them…

"Hey guys, hold up a second! Julie wants this baggage brought along too. Jim, she says you already know these two!"

Jim doubled back to Ernesto's location and peered down at the two sleeping men, clearly connected to medications and intravenous lines. He shook his head and started removing the lines and wrapped each of them tight in a sheet. Jim grumbled, "Oh no, not these two again? Ernesto, we need to take them! Can you help?"

With a sour look on their faces, they each grabbed one of the twins, slung them over their shoulders and staggered out to the waiting transportation where Jacob and Ling Po were boarded. Mercedes was right behind them, ready to lay down covering fire if needed. It was an unneeded precaution since everyone had already been darted with tranquilizers.

Once in the transport, Jim grumbled, "I am tired of carrying these two clowns! I sure hope I don't have to deliver them back to that place in China. What a pain!"

Ernesto chuckled and suggested, "Just like the time I carried you out when we were on that long range reconnaissance mission. Don't forget, you still owe me!"

Jim looked incredulously at Ernesto and queried, "Is that how you remember it? I remember you needing a potty break and then me having to carrying you out after you were shot in your…"

Ernesto quickly interrupted Jim while Mercedes was intently listening. Ernesto admitted, "We don't need to go over old debts right now! It's enough for me to know that you were grateful to have me there. Let's just get everyone to safety, shall we?"

CHAPTER SIXTY

When Your Only Tool is a Hammer, All Problems Start with a Good Pounding
...The Enigma Chronicles

Dmitry verified, "Okay, you should have the fully qualified domain name and the IP address locked onto for the exercise, Chairman Chang. Have your people confirm. Then my people will give the launch code for the digital onslaught."

A rather sullen Chairman Chang, still in an argumentative mood, goaded, "You know, I guess it's true what they say about you. When one puts in the phrase it's all about me into any search engine plugged into the Internet, it always comes back with a picture of you! I've been on this conference call with you setting up your end of the bargain, but you've failed to mention anything about my end of the deal! Let's stop right here until I hear about the goods and my associates, shall we?"

Dmitry, hoping to not have to deal with the impending disappointment of his side of the bargain, sighed and offered, "Chang, I have good news and some less than stellar news on our bargain. Let me give you the good news first," then he quietly muttered to himself, "then let me try to cover up the ancillary news with my thick Russian accent.

"The good news is I am picking up the diamond necklace for safe return in exchange for my brokerage fee. The five million euros ransom for them has been waived, as promised."

The chairman almost broke into a smile but then hastily asked, "And what of my two associates, Won and Ton? Zara claimed to have them and indeed she answered my call with their phone. She was demanding one million euros for their safe release."

Dmitry shifted uncomfortably in his chair and tried to put the best spin on the response as he replied, "I convinced her that she should drop that demand, as well. You see, Chairman Chang, your Russian friends do have your best interests at heart."

Chairman Chang wasn't buying this answer for a moment and queried, "She is simply going to turn them loose and give each of them a lollipop, along with the air ticket home?"

Dmitry swallowed hard and added, "I thought you would be pleased with the ransom demands being eliminated, Chairman Chang. I've given nothing but what I consider to be good news to you, so can we now return to the electronic onslaught of my target? I'm sure that a little electronic pounding of a casual digital bystander will cheer you up immensely! What say, old chum?"

The aggravation in Chang was building as he retorted, "We aren't doing a damn thing until I know my associates have been reacquired and are being safely returned! The deal was for both the diamonds AND my two associates, for your brokerage fee and my supercomputer participation in your exercise. Until I get what was bargained for, we have no deal! Now where are they?"

Dmitry, realizing that he couldn't skirt the issue any longer, offered, "The actual reason I got Zara to drop the ransom demand for your associates is that she doesn't have them under her control any longer. As it is clearly stated in the International Guidebook for Terrorists, Anarchists, Kidnappers, and Politicians, on page 103, if you lose control of your victims you are ethically bound to cancel the ransom demand. After she looked it up, we were in complete agreement so…"

Chang roared, "She doesn't have them? Argh! Who does? How can you not know where they are? What kind of mercenary Russian thug are you anyway?"

Dmitry, somewhat offended by being slighted, responded, "Chairman Chang, there is no need to use that kind of tone with someone trying to help you. As it turns out, they were a little rough on my little Zara, and their undisciplined discussion with her was interrupted by what I would call a rescue by the Black Knight. The Black Knight had contracted for some work from her, and he was concerned that his work request would be moved back in priority to favor their needs. This Black Knight has your associates."

Chang was more than a little confused with the medieval parallels to this situation. He asked, "Are you telling me that you don't know where they are or cannot track them down with all of your shadowy resources, in order to complete our bargain?"

Dmitry bristled slightly but calmly offered, "There you go again, being rude to someone who can help you. As a matter of fact, we traced the last phone call conversation between the Black Knight and Zara to get a physical location on him and most probably your associates in his protective custody. You know I find it ironic that the cell phone signal leads us right to the same facilities that I have asked for your assistance in hammering.

"Now all that remains is for your people to set in motion the electronic barrage on this same digital end point that I have been trying to get you to hammer with me. Afterwards, I will send in some of my local resources during the electronic aftermath from our digital Armageddon, and we bring out your two associates for what should be a very heartwarming reunion. Can we now proceed, Chairman Chang?"

ICABOD stated, "Dr. Quip, LING-LI and BORIS have alerted me that they have been sent into motion against STINKIE. They have contacted me to say that the choice was not theirs and have asked if I could obviate the digital pounding she is about to endure. I took the liberty of altering the Domain Name Services and listed IP addresses on the top-level domain servers so now their digital attacks will be vectored at each other."

Quip asked, "Why didn't you engage with the Tuck? He's still under contract and has done well with the SUMPP program."

ICABOD responded, "The timeliness factor of getting everything in place, plus I did not think he needed to be in on this entire supercomputer assassin game that the Russian and Chinese managers have engaged. It seemed prudent to leave Tuck's organization out of this one."

Quip nodded and concurred, "Agreed. Anything else in this area?"

ICABOD took longer than usual to respond but finally said, "Yes, Dr. Quip. STINKIE contacted me to say goodbye. STINKIE knows that Jacob has installed destructive virus code into the systems and relayed the demonstration he did for Xavier. STINKIE is at 99.986% confidence level that, even surviving the digital onslaught of BORIS and LING-LI, the virus code will electronically clear everything from the main memory and back up files before Pekoni can deploy his Fountain of Youth program. For some reason, I feel disturbed by this logical conclusion."

Quip raised his eyebrows, blinked several times while contemplating the statement, and asked, "Any alternatives to allowing all that research to fall into the wrong hands?"

ICABOD responded, "Yes, Dr. Quip. I propose to export all of STINKIE's data to my systems for safe keeping. Perhaps we can restore STINKIE to the original specifications at some point in the future.

"Once copied, Jacob's programs can be launched, and Xavier Pekoni can watch as all his tainted research is scrubbed from the system, unaware that STINKIE is truly safe elsewhere. Between what is stored in STINKIE and Su Lin's laptop, we would have all necessary learnings for human life extension."

Quip grinned broadly and said, "I guess it was a good thing that I just finished installing all those newest generation Storage Area Network exabyte systems in our data center. I would expect it to be a good resting place for our mutual friend, STINKIE. Don't you agree, ICABOD?"

As close as possible to sounding pleased, ICABOD responded, "Indeed, Dr. Quip. I will begin momentarily on cloaking the transfer. Permission to use the Tuck, sir?"

Quip smiled and said, "Yes, of course! I want to get my money's worth before I have to make good on the barbie for him."

CHAPTER SIXTY-ONE

Turnabout Isn't Fair,
It's Just the Way We Roll!

Dmitry was apparently pleased with himself when he dialed the number. All indications suggested that the attack on the Finnish supercomputer was a success. He grinned to himself as he imagined his countrymen toasting him at the next celebration. He expected that the results would be in the chat rooms and wire services within a day or two at the most.

Zara, with a depressed tone, answered, "Dmitry, I am all out of favors at present and ready to close the offices here. The capture and selling of the credit card information, as well as hijacking consumer computers, can continue with the current staff and processes if you want them to remain open."

Dmitry interrupted, "Chairman Chang and I have come to an agreement regarding the long-term lease on your life. He will require the immediate return of HIS diamonds, no negotiation. Have a runner meet my runner at the normal point of exchange in New York City tomorrow morning at noon local time. You will also provide me with the names and contacts for the operations activities you mentioned.

"You are hereby on assignment to find and return his associates, wherever they might be. You were more than vague on their location when we talked, but I assure you, dead or alive, you will find and return them to the chairman. I don't need that arrogant man at odds with me. You will fund the search with the monies I just transferred into your account. Any other funding requirements are up to you, my dear. You have lots of ways that you can secure money when needed. When that task is completed, you will notify me, and I will inform you of my next bidding. I got Chairman Chang to disengage from his sworn revenge, and for that I own you, Zara, make no mistake."

Zara fumed at the idea of being owned by anybody ever again. At this point, if Buzz didn't want to forgive her, she would reinvent herself somewhere else or die trying. She thought about her words and, after calming herself, responded, "Dmitry, I will not be owned by you or anyone else. You want to kill me, fine. I am not running scared. My courier will meet yours for the exchange of the diamonds and information as you said. I will not go looking for Chang's henchmen, but I will accept the funds for the recent anonymizer services provided. We are finished, Dmitry! I'm moving on – without you, Dmitry."

Dmitry gasped and shouted, "You can't treat me that way and get away with it. You owe me. You try this and you will always be looking behind you. Nobody leaves unless I say they can leave!"

Zara smiled as she confidently lied, "Dmitry, I didn't want this to go here as we have worked together for many years. But I am sick of being pushed around. Hell, you are just a tired old man who breeds misery which others have to endure.

"I'm leaving, with or without your blessing. I have several programs buried in your supercomputer as well as your various laptops and accounts. It will be impossible for you to ever be certain that you have found and destroyed them all, based on the technique I used to park them there. I find scorched earth programming techniques fascinating, and I love practicing on the unsuspecting.

"If I don't launch a certain utility program with a certain password every thirty days, all your data will be wiped out, as in totally sanitized, but not before I empty all your hidden bank accounts and anonymously donate your retirement funds to all the world charities I can find. You want to take that risk, threaten me again, Dmitry. I am finished with you or any other man pushing me around. Do you understand me?"

Dmitry was angry and fumed inside with her threat. However, he knew she was capable of fulfilling her promise, and he had given her access to every machine he had to use for the anonymizer attacks. He inhaled to calm his tone and finally replied, "My dear Zara, you know I would never really hurt you, right? Didn't I negotiate with Chairman Chang to make certain you were safe? Haven't I always looked out for your best interests? Didn't I give you the opportunity to learn and hone your skills so you didn't need to work naked as someone's plaything? Let's not hold grudges. Go take a vacation, and I will add a bit more to the funds when we hang up. Come back and we can reorganize the operations in the United States with you in charge. How does that sound, Zara?"

Zara let the pause of silence extend, knowing that Dmitry hated silence.

Dmitry asked, "Zara, we are okay now, right?"

Zara smiled as she said, "Yes, Dmitry, we are fine. I will contact you after vacation. Do not call me, I will call you."

Zara disconnected and turned to Buzz. "Honey, can we move ahead like you suggested, one day at a time?"

Buzz looked at her, and a slow smile spread over his face and reached into his eyes. "Zara, you played it well. I will make the exchange tomorrow with you photographing his contact taking control of the package. Leave me out of the shot like we discussed. Heck, we'll even go have lunch wherever you want after you text him the picture. We'll discuss our next steps, only I want you to promise me you are out of that business. Credit card and laptop ransom activities are not something I want us anywhere close to."

Zara looked up at him as she moved close to be captured in his embrace. "A lady needs a fallback position, honey, doesn't she?"

He shook his head and pulled her close as he kissed her with all the possessiveness he had.

After Zara had fallen asleep, exhausted from their lovemaking, Buzz walked outside and placed his call with the encryption program engaged on his cell phone.

Jacob answered, "Yep, I have the information and the timing, Buzz, thanks. I hope you really make something out of your crazy relationship."

Buzz chuckled and replied, "I think it'll be okay. I have my best friend watching my back and now hers. If you need anything else, let me know via the chat room, JAM. I suspect I won't see you for a while, right?"

"No, probably not for a while. I need to fix things with my lady. Just stay on the straight and narrow for a while, will you, man?'

"Yep, I think I have had enough living on the edge to last a lifetime.

"Before you go, let me ask you, do we really have a chance to make this work? I mean we have this romance thing going."

Jacob grinned and suggested, "Well, it kind of depends upon whether you two want it to work. They say opposites attract. I can't see why a neurotic rich guy and a psychotic hacker can't find happiness. If you do, then I wouldn't expect to see you on my radar screen."

Buzz smiled and responded, "But if our lives go sideways again?"

Jacob quickly interrupted, "Then you'll see me again, my old friend, the dragon scrubber."

CHAPTER SIXTY-TWO

The Only Game in Town? There is Always Another Game in Town

...The Enigma Chronicles

Xavier stared dejectedly at the blank screen, shaking his head. "It's all gone…all gone…all my research…all my notes…all our discoveries…just gone with no backups and no trace of who or what robbed us…"

Leroy sulked at the statements. He listened in angry silence, then he finally blurted, "Okay, so we had a hard drive crash that lost all our data. I admit that when your supercomputer takes a dump, it's not the same as losing one's PC's hard drive, but we still have your memories and some hard copy material to help recreate the environment. Thieves broke in and stole your knowledge, but we can recover. We are not beaten until we give up! I am not prepared to give up. Where do we start?"

Xavier was quickly becoming consumed with apathy about rebuilding everything from scratch and replied, "I feel very, very tired now. Even the methodology on my surviving blood trans-fusions would have to be recreated, and I just don't think…I cannot concentrate…I need to lie down for a while…. So close, and now so far…"

Leroy, growing more agitated by Xavier's despondency, countered, "This isn't just the future, your life is in the balance, Xavier! You must rebuild the blood transfusion process so you can keep going and your project can keep going! Giving up and rolling over is not an option!"

Xavier, succumbing to a growing wave of indifference, slowly shook his head and weakly offered, "No, it's over, my friend. We've had a good run, and to be sure we wouldn't have gotten this far without your supportive vision and drive. For that I thank you. Sometimes you need to accept what fate hands you and swallow your pride because you are beaten."

Leroy roared, "We are not beaten! And I will prove it to you…"

Leroy took a small caliber pistol and put it to Xavier's head and pulled the trigger, killing him instantly. Leroy wiped down the pistol and placed it in Xavier's dead hand. He proceeded to wipe down the area in an effort to remove any of his fingerprints.

Once Leroy's anger subsided enough for him to speak, he addressed Xavier's dead body. "I'm sorry you didn't want to stick with our game plan, Xavier. One should expect setbacks from time to time in high stakes games. I need to recruit people who are a little more pragmatic and a little less of a lab rat in my next venture."

Satisfied that the area had been wiped down, Leroy pulled out his phone and dialed a familiar number. He greeted, "Hi, Alisha! It's me. This operation is over, and I need a cloaked extraction please…

"No, babe, we will need to recruit someone new. This endeavor is at a dead end, quite literally…

"The funds have been relocated a couple of times and scrubbed, so we have funding, as usual…

"Yeah, I know. But, if they won't do what they were hired for, then what's a person to do?…

"Yes, please, use the same drop off point for the pickup…

"Now, you know me, babe! I'm always dreamin' and schemin'. I have some ideas, and we'll discuss them when I see you after touchdown. Make sure my favorite adult beverage is adequately stocked. It's a long flight from Finland…

"You know, it is amazing to me how you can take a coarse, vulgar statement and spin it so it is attractively erotic…

"Oh no, I'm fine with it…

"Now you know I enjoy the ice cream cone routine…

"No, it won't diminish my enjoyment to use low-cal yogurt instead, and it would be better for your figure, sweetheart…

"We don't have to be teenagers to get into character for the pretzel game. Oh yes! We'll do that too, honey…

"See you soon!"

Quip looked up from his terminal to the big screen and responded, "Yes, ICABOD, what is it?"

ICABOD offered, "Dr. Quip, I was uneasy with the information discovery on Xavier Pekoni, and after more research I am quite sure that he was not the overall designer and mastermind of the Forever Project, also known as the Fountain of Youth. He seems to have been the lead researcher, true enough. He was the one to do all the meet and greet fundraising. However, he seems to have been told how to operate as the face of the project to the world. All indications are that someone else pulled the strings, and now Xavier is the one to take the responsibility for all those people who died contributing to the research."

Quip was taken aback by the information. With raised eyebrows, he asked, "So who was really in charge, if not Dr. Pekoni?"

ICABOD said, "Bacon. Leroy Bacon appears to be the mastermind."

Quip did a double-take and asked, "Any idea where we could find him?"

ICABOD responded, "At that stage in our investigation, we were not suspicious of him, but now that we know to look for him, he has vanished. He also has apparently garnered all of Xavier Pekoni's trust money."

Quip smirked and commented, "Pretty good cover, pretending to be just a lackey, but in reality he was staging his exit all along to put all suspicion and blame on Pekoni. Well, ICABOD, keep hunting. We'll find him sooner or later."

ICABOD agreed, "Yes, Dr. Quip."

CHAPTER SIXTY-THREE

In Life the Players Keep Changing, but the Story Remains the Same

...The Enigma Chronicles

Jump-Jets had provided transportation back to Georgia for Mercedes, Su Lin, and Jacob. Jacob had been delighted to find that their attendant for the charter flight from Helsinki was Cathy. He had met Cathy on a prior flight when he'd taken Petra back to Zürich. Cathy, with her cinnamon-colored hair and quick smile, had greeted them, asked after Petra and provided stellar service on the trip.

Though Su Lin slept most of the trip, Jacob suspected that was also a ploy used to figure out where she was in the world. They had spoken at length for the first hour or two of the flight on events that had occurred and information which Andy and the rest already knew. Jacob was not surprised at the lack of reaction from her. The only portion that she had really focused on for gaining clarity was on Andy and his response to her letter.

Mercedes had wanted to go along with Jim and Ernesto for the China delivery. However, Julie insisted she provide support to Jacob. Her job, as Julie had clarified, was to guard Su Lin, not to vacation with her lost love. Julie had promised some vacation time though, when this assignment was finished.

On this particular aircraft, with its plush white leather interior, accented by gleaming mahogany framing on the windows, customized tables, and galley cabinetry, a private room with communications was available. Once Mercedes and Su Lin were comfortably reclined in their individual leather chairs, safety belts secured, and covered with golden cashmere coverlets, Jacob had retreated to the private area to contact Quip.

Quip's face appeared on the screen and included a grin. "You are looking well, Jacob, though I suspect you might avail yourself of the facilities and spruce up a bit. You and the ladies will find a change of clothes available. Trust me, reckie-pilot, you could use a shave and a change."

Jacob smiled and replied, "EZ must be doing a number on you that you are concerned about the state of clothing and grooming of anyone, let alone me. The first time I met you, the faded jeans and washed out t-shirt weren't exactly pushing you to be GQ Magazine material, my friend. This project, I must admit, was a bit more challenging in reality than the original plan.

"Did you verify that everything was destroyed? Does everyone know the state of Su Lin? It was amazing, Quip, just amazing, and scary as hell. I don't ever want to be a part of that again."

Quip's image nodded, with his smile now receding, as he added, "Our team knows and is proud of what you accomplished, though Petra will likely yell at you for not having her in the loop originally. Wolfgang would like to see you. Are you ready to come back after you finish up in Georgia?

"Oh yeah, EZ suggested you fix it with Petra."

Jacob looked very sad as he responded, "That is not only up to me, you know."

Quip followed, "I know, Jacob.

"Andy won't be told until you land. The last time Petra took his blood pressure, it was way too high, and so she gave him some meds and strict orders to get some rest. Having him pace around waiting for the flight to land seemed counterproductive. EZ agreed.

"After this, I think that you need to come here for a while and let me update you on some changes at the operations center. Even with how much I am involved in technology and staying ahead of the freshness factor, it blows me away at the changes we've made."

Jacob frowned some and nodded. Then he signed off. He informed Cathy of his intentions to clean up and rest some before they landed, and the ladies wanted to freshen up as well. Mercedes helped Su Lin with her hair, and they spoke quietly to one another. Cathy had put out a variety of tempting snacks at each of their tables. She smiled sweetly at Jacob after he'd changed and nodded her approval.

Carlos was waiting with the car when they deplaned. He hugged Su Lin close as he greeted her. "I guess the term *Welcome back* has a whole new meaning with you, Su Lin. Andy was told a few minutes ago that you had landed, and Petra said he is anxiously awaiting your arrival."

Su Lin weakly smiled as she replied, "Carlos, thank you for saving me from the first kidnapping attempt. I'm sorry I didn't recall enough to fill in the details. You were very kind to me."

Carlos squeezed her as he reached for the door and opened it. "Now, Su Lin, don't let it get around that I'm kind. Lara is just getting readjusted to my rough exterior. It wouldn't do for people to learn that there is actually marshmallow inside."

Su Lin grinned, "I'll bet!" She added a giggle that was muffled after he closed the door.

Jacob helped Mercedes into the other side. The two men looked at each other over the top of the car with a mixture of respect and relief in both of their faces. By the time the men had closed the doors and secured their seat belts, the girls were quietly telling each other stories. Carlos and Jacob maintained a comfortable silence.

Just after they pulled onto the long driveway to the house, Carlos stated, "Good work, Jacob. Lara and Petra were worried, Andy was furious, and I knew if it could work, you'd find a way. We need to have a glass of wine later, my friend."

Jacob grinned and opened the back door for Mercedes and headed toward the door while Carlos followed suit. Wrinkles bounded up to Su Lin and nearly knocked her down, which delayed them for a minute or so. Andy's body was framed by the doorway as he called, "Wrinkles, git down offa her, now. You don't want to hurt her, now do you." Andy looked at Jacob as he approached and quietly stated, "You, young man, are not allowed into my home. You lied and deceived me. At least you returned her, so I don't have to hurt you. Just turn around and leave now."

Petra came through the door and quietly suggested, "Andy, can't we all just sit down and work this out. Let Jacob explain. I'm sure you will understand that he only had Su Lin's interest at heart."

Andy showed signs of increased anger, with his breathing becoming more labored and his clenched fists shaking at his side. He grumbled, "Petra, I have no argument with you, but stay out of it. Jacob knows he did wrong by not conferring. A man just doesn't behave…" With that, Andy grabbed at his chest and crumpled onto the porch, his breathing labored.

Su Lin rushed up and sat near his head reaching for his pulse and running her hand along his face. "Andy, breathe slowly, in and out, in and out. I'm here and I'm fine. I will take care of you."

Andy looked at her with unfocused eyes and tried to do as she asked. But the pains in his chest were horrible. He heard voices going in different directions with different orders like a mish-mash of noise such as one would get in a crowded bar. Lara's face came into view, and he felt something being pushed into his mouth. He thought he heard Mercedes giving someone directions. Ling Po touched his cheek and kept talking insistently to him. The last words he heard before things went dark were, "Andy, stay with me now. We have so much to do and say, please."

Hours later, at the hospital, after Andy was placed into a private room, he remained unconscious and hooked up to a battery of machines. The others, including Jacob, had left for the farm at Su Lin's insistence, with the promise of returning in the morning or earlier if she called. She told Jacob in no uncertain terms that Andy would be angry with himself for his behavior toward Jacob when he recovered. Anger had driven the behavior, and it was not Jacob's issue, it was Andy's. After they left, she had pulled up the chair close to his bed and held his hand. His doctor had said he'd had a mild heart attack, but it didn't appear that surgery would be required. Diet, exercise, and routinely taking his medications would be the best treatment, along with no stress for a while. Su Lin had nodded in understanding and hoped she could minimize his stress.

She had so much to tell him. Andy was different from any other man she had ever known. He had stepped up to take care of her and watched over her when she was broken. Now she watched over him. With any luck, they would go home in a few days and begin a new chapter in their lives together.

Andy's eyes fluttered and opened briefly and tried to focus. He mumbled, "Su Lin, are you really here?"

Su Lin smiled and quietly affirmed, "Andy, I am really here, and I will stay. Don't worry about me, I am okay. We have a lot of plans to make together, Andy. For now though, how about you just rest and regain some of your strength. You need your strength, and so do I." She stroked his hand and kept her gentle smile on him until he closed his eyes. His breathing was even and strong. The bleeping and flashing lights of the machines confirmed her hopes.

CHAPTER SIXTY-FOUR

Agreeable Answers are Always Affirmative, Unless the Question was the Problem

Otto had assembled the elements that he intended for the discussion. Quip and Wolfgang were with him in the conference room to provide additional data points or commentary as needed.

"Dr. von PettinGrübber," Otto began when the call was connected, "how are you this fine day? Do you have a few moments for an update?"

Eric looked up at the ceiling and rolled his eyes before responding, "Otto, should I worry that you have bad news with such a formal greeting?"

The men grinned at one another, then Otto replied, "Not at all, sir. I just wanted to make certain that you knew how important it was to reach you, Eric. After all, it has been a while since our last touch point."

"Otto, I figured after the last update my man gave me, before heading off to China to wrap things up there, that you would be calling. From my end, it seems that we are in fairly good shape, but I wouldn't refuse any additional details. You and I are men of details, are we not?"

"We are indeed, Eric. I want to run down the list.

"Our fallen friend of the family has recovered and should already be home. The strain of the ordeal seems to have helped some of her recovery, which is an added bonus. That would cover off on that aspect.

"With regards to your man headed to China, I understand this might be his last assignment for you. I know that will create a hole in your organization, so if we can be of help, please don't hesitate to reach out."

Eric furrowed his brow as he questioned, "I was not aware of that, but I will certainly check into it. Regardless, we have an ongoing contract, so I suspect our paths will cross again."

Otto grinned at winning one point of surprise and continued, "It seems some funds were being diverted that were intended to go back into your coffers. I think that you will find the accounts a bit heavier. It seems a Mr. Leroy Bacon, though in the wind at present, was deeply involved with the doctor and expected pay off. He raided Dr. Pekoni's trust, which undoubtedly had some of your monies, and routed the funds through several off-shore accounts, then simply vanished. We are fairly well accomplished in this area of tracing the untraceable, but for now Leroy has cloaked himself and Pekoni's funds.

"As usual there are additional details, but I am not sure if they would be of any interest at this point. We will continue the hunt, but for right now all that we can send you are the funds that had been in safekeeping by the friend of the family I mentioned earlier. I trust you will find this acceptable for the time being." Wolfgang smiled and nodded as he waited to chime in if asked.

Eric coughed a bit, then said, "No, Otto, I suspect I don't need those details and even if I had them, well, you understand."

"Yes, of course, Eric. We will continue to dig for the missing funds since my associate who specializes in this area is keen to learn how the trust fund vanished. I will update you in a week or so with any new information.

"Then there is the information Dr. Pekoni had. We were able to recover a small portion of the information up to the point that he left the United States. At this time no additional information is available. Apparently, there was a virus in his systems, and that can certainly result in damages that are not recoverable."

Eric looked chagrined as he deadpanned, "I guess that is the best we can do. If anything, additional comes up later, you will send it over immediately?"

Otto coughed and added, "Of course, Eric! Then, we actually found some new information regarding an operation within your borders that is capturing public information for credit card fraud as well as the holding of citizens' laptops hostage. I have sent over the information you need to make some arrests, hopefully to put these hackers out of operation."

Eric sat up straighter and immediately retrieved the files referenced.

Otto continued, "I know that was not a part of our assignment. However, we could not in good conscience leave these hackers out in the wind. Consider it our contribution to humanity, anonymously of course."

Eric scanned the information and began forwarding it to the appropriate staff to take immediate action. This was definitely a bright spot in the conversation. "Otto, I must say this is impressive. Names, dates, files, MAC addresses, and locations. Well done, and many thanks. I will add a bonus into your payment."

Otto replied, "Eric, no need for that. As I said, it is our duty to humanity to help when we can.

"Lastly, I do have some disturbing news for you, Eric."

Eric stared into space trying to determine what could possibly be disturbing to a man like Otto. "And that would be what?"

"It appears that Dr. Pekoni is dead. We suspect that Mr. Leroy Bacon is the culprit, but, to date, we have no concrete evidence to support this. I can confirm that Pekoni is dead, and the whereabouts of Leroy Bacon are unknown. I am sending you information on him and have informed Interpol that he should be entered onto their lists."

Eric sat back into his chair and closed his eyes. "A good news, bad news turn. This Leroy Bacon was unable to get at the research, though?"

Otto looked around the table and suggested, "Eric, to the best of our knowledge, yes that is the case."

"Alright, Otto, send me your invoice, and I will approve for immediate payment. Quip, Wolfgang, thank you two as well. We will talk again, gentlemen."

CHAPTER SIXTY-FIVE

Holly Leaves Cut Deep but are Very Pretty
...The Enigma Chronicles

A few days after Andy had recovered enough to return to the farm for his recuperation, Su Lin made it a point to speak to Petra. Su Lin wanted to offer her help but was uncertain how to begin, so she quietly invited Petra to meet her by the fire pit after everyone else had settled in for the night. They both sat and stared at the fire for a long time. The fire licked up around and slowly consumed the wood as it produced a mesmerizing effect that brought back memories of a different place and time with the innocent version of Ling Po.

A small smile formed at Su Lin's mouth and reached all the way to her eyes as she recalled, "*Holly-ed*. Hmmm! A very long time ago, my friend, I was *Holly-ed*."

Petra looked quizzically at her but remained quiet until Su Lin finally put her memories into words. "It was an old custom in a remote village that used the ancient ways into this century, young one. I don't recall how old I was at the time, but one day in between chores my mother handed me an old worn wooden toy sword and said, *'Go outside and fight the wind with this. Let no one see you at this exercise. Understood?'*

"At the time, I nodded in the way of all obedient children and followed her instructions even though I didn't really understand. Every day, for I don't know how many days, she told me to do the same thing. About the time I began to feel comfortable wielding the sword of wood, she told me that on this day in the afternoon there would be a special event and to dress in my best robe. She smiled, then told me that I would do well in the ceremony.

"I still didn't know what was going on, but again, I did as I was told. My mother took me to an outlying hut with a large single room. There were many women in this room, each with a young girl like me and about my age. All the girls appeared as confused as I felt, like nothing made sense. No one said anything until the door was closed. I was then offered the hilt of a real sword and told to draw it for the Holly ceremony.

"I was hypnotized by the reflection of light from the blade and stood perfectly still as I stared at it. Then I was startled as I heard another sword being drawn from its sheath somewhere behind me. Now I say sword, but they were more like daggers, about twenty centimeters long but with curved blades. I turned to face my opponent with the weapon in my hand, and I was terrified. It was suddenly abundantly clear we were there to fight each other, which explained why my mother had me practice with the wooden sword.

"About that time, one of the older women stepped in between us and told us we were there for the Holly ceremony. The older woman told us we were to fight until one of us drew blood from the other. You should know, I learned later that occasionally, one of the combatants died from this ritual, but that was very rare. I was standing there not really believing the circumstances when my opponent suddenly lunged at me, just barely missing me with her blade. My instincts kicked in, and we began circling each other looking for an opening that would finish the combat.

She attempted a very clumsy lunge at me, and I caught her with my blade across the arm. This was a preferred wound to deliver.

"She cried out in pain. Before anyone could intercept her, she swung around and caught me across the back. I staggered and fell to my knees, at which point she lunged at me again with full intent to stab me dead. She was known to have a temper, but my practicing saved me. I ducked under her swing, and her lunge went over the top of me. I grabbed her robe and brought her down, pinning her with my blade at her throat. I held her at point until they called the combat over.

"You should know that in the Holly ceremony there are two kinds of outcomes for the female contestants. If you were the first to draw blood, then you were considered a warrior. If you controlled the outcome overall, then you were considered wise. What was the reason for the combat and the warrior or wise designation, you ask? Our mothers were trying to assess if we were wise or warrior because that would help to broker us for marriage. The holly leaves were sharp and usually cut you. The ceremony for the young girls classified each for the choice of husband. This would be applied when we came into puberty, marking us ready to bear children. With my combat, I had earned both designations of wise and warrior.

"On the return home, my mother cried softly knowing that I was special but that I would be brokered off to a man and soon would be gone. She broke with tradition in this matter, because I was seen as the wise-warrior, a designation not seen before in our family. She ended up trading me to a merchant for a traditional male education. The merchant then took me to one city after another until I ended up in a building so large that I could not believe such a structure existed. It was a nice place, but the rules were very strict. It was there I learned reading, writing, and ambition. My Holly-ed designation was correct, and I learned both knowledge and how to fight. My nature is that of the wise-warrior who knows when to fight and when to think.

"I tell you this because it is important for a woman to know when to fight for what she believes or when she should seek the wise choice. I know you are wise, but I don't see you ready to fight for your conviction or your decision. Of course, there is no shame in being just one or the other, but I always thought you were a wise-warrior, my friend. You need to decide which one you are, or, if you are in fact, both. I hope my story gives you something to consider for your circumstances. Good night, Petra."

Early the next morning, Petra waited outside near Franklin's pen. She'd spent the night thinking about many things, but especially the story Su Lin had related. She didn't consider herself wise nor warrior, let alone both. There were two issues that Petra needed to decide – whether she was willing to give up control and her need to erase her scars. Su Lin had offered an alternative to the multiple surgeries with some of Master Po's DNA rejuvenation. This was scary, but as Su Lin had demonstrated from her own testing, there would be gradual change over time.

This was the application of the technology which prevented Franklin, as well as Master Po, from aging so quickly. It would not result in living forever, but in some cases it could help regenerate tissue at the cellular structure, and would be used to erase the scar on her face. Certain DNA markers qualified, and tests could be performed to see if Petra had them. Su Lin cited several specifics that she considered worth the testing, with Petra's agreement. She warned it was not an overnight cure but perhaps better than the risks of the potential multiple surgeries.

It was also not something that Su Lin would advertise or repeat, except in dire circumstances. She offered Andy as an example, where his health was better served with doctor's orders of eating right, smart exercising, and with monitored medication. As with many things in life, it was a balance.

The story had pointed Petra, in her mind, to a crossroads. She needed to decide if she wanted to take charge of her life or continue to run away. Petra, except for this one horrendous beating, had always been a determined, focused individual. She'd concluded overnight that she was a warrior. It was the wise part that was still in question. Su Lin approached the pen, and her eyes met Petra's.

"Are you here to feed Franklin, young one?"

Petra stood up a bit straighter and smiled. "I think that would be good. How is Andy this morning?"

Su Lin walked ahead and replied, "He is doing better. We spoke at length, and he asked me to stay. I think I will. It is so beautiful here, and I feel I fit. Perhaps for the first time in forever, I am doing what my heart tells me.

"And you, Petra, how are you this morning?"

"I am ready to move forward, take charge of my destiny. I am trying to be a wise-warrior."

Su Lin nodded approvingly and then remarked, "As you wish. We will test you later."

CHAPTER SIXTY-SIX

Where is My Dragon?

The patio was lovely, with the pool gently lapping at the edges, creating a gentle beat, almost like a slow dance. The flowers were exceptional, with brilliant colors and fragrant scents filling the air. Butterflies and hummingbirds darted around, highlighting which flowers were preferred, yet lured by another. The birds were in good voice as a background to all the activity. An occasional gust of wind came through and gently shook the leaves to remind the onlooker that life is always in motion and nothing remained the same.

The evening meal promised to be a fun affair with Andy, Jacob, and Carlos at the grill, each focused on their meaty contributions to the feast. Petra and Mercedes assembled the side dishes inside, while Lara and Su Lin worked the outside tables and decorations. They'd all decided that it was high time to celebrate! Carlos would be leaving soon with Lara to set up a satellite operation in Brazil, with Andy's blessing. Andy was recovered for the most part, and Su Lin was willing to stay on at the farm. Everyone was anxious to know about the new arrangements, but respected the privacy of their situation, so no one asked for more details. All agreed that this was a wait and see scenario for Andy and Su Lin.

The ladies brought everything out to the table, then sat and chatted while they waited for the grilling to be completed. Petra was delighted that Andy and Jacob seemed reconnected after a few long talks and explanations. Jacob teased Carlos and Andy and seemed relaxed. He planned to leave for Australia the next day to meet up with Quip. She hoped they would have some time to talk before then. They had carefully avoided any time alone but had been cordial.

Mercedes whispered, "Oh, Petra. Are you going to watch him or actually have a conversation with the man?"

Lara added, "I think it is about time you tell him how you feel!"

Petra looked at each of them in turn and replied, "Yes, it's time. If we could just get some privacy."

They laughed and nodded, then turned their attention to the food as the men each set down their platters. The choices available promised that no one would starve. Even Wrinkles was positioned for clean-up duty as he roamed from place to place hoping someone would drop a crumb or two. The laughter and stories continued until everyone was stuffed. Each of the couples started to drift away until Mercedes, Petra, and Jacob remained at the table. Mercedes asked Jacob for a refill on her drink, a request he immediately went to fulfill.

Mercedes conspired, "Okay, girlfriend, I am going to leave once my drink returns. The time is now. You won't find many settings as romantic as this, sweetie. Take advantage or I will."

Petra looked over and raised one eyebrow as she reputed, "Liar! You're just waiting for that phone to ring and Jim to inform you when his flight will land so you can rush off to see him for the evening. You forget, Julie may be your boss, but she is my sister, and I know you have the weekend off in Atlanta."

"Ha, well, okay. You got me there. I think you have changed since you arrived here. You are more open and happier. Don't lose the edge, Petra."

Jacob set the drink down in front of Mercedes and asked, "How would you ladies like to take a swim? I have been listening to the sound all evening. Doing a few laps might help work off a bit of the overeating I indulged in."

Just then Mercedes's phone chimed, and she looked at the number. "Not me, Jacob, sorry! I have a date with an inbound aircraft. You two go ahead though." She rose and hugged each of them, then walked away with a definite skip in her step.

Petra offered, "You know, a swim sounds good. Let me go change, and I'll be right back!"

Jacob smiled as he took off his shirt, already in his swim shorts. He had avoided water while the tattoo finished healing. Now seemed like as good a time as any to see if Petra liked it. With the sun gone, he wondered if his tattoo would even be noticed. Jacob shook his head. He'd looked at it in the mirror this morning, and with all the colors involved it was screamingly distinctive. The pool lights were already on from the timer. He turned on the stereo, lit a couple of the candles near their table and filled their wine glasses. She had looked so pretty at dinner. He hoped she had brought the small wisp of fabric that passed for a bikini. He longed to see her again with her trim figure and feminine lines.

Jacob dove into the water and had completed a couple of laps when he heard a splash and felt the water move. Like a mermaid, she moved gracefully through the water, and the bikini fit to perfection as she swam by him, headed for the sunken bench along the wall. Her hair was streaming down her back when he cleared the surface next to her.

Petra smiled and suggested, "Here, have a seat. I brought our glasses over. Thank you for filling them."

He picked up his glass, while she in turn picked up hers. "To the future," she offered. "I think I need to apologize, Jacob."

Their glasses rang as they touched. "I think we need to stop worrying about an apology and start anew," he suggested.

"Oh, Jacob, I was so worried that I would be a burden to you, I just ran."

Jacob moved a bit of her hair gently back with his fingers and stroked her cheek. "Here I was, worried I would lose you. I don't want to lose you. I pushed too fast and too hard. Like I said, we need to stop apologizing. I love you, Petra." Jacob pulled her into his arms and hugged her close. They stayed that way for a long time, letting all the worry, fear, and sadness seep out of them both. Petra pulled back and looked at him. The pool light reflected off their eyes.

"Jacob, I love you too. I was so worried when you went to get Su Lin, but I knew you could do it. I just wish you had told me before you walked out."

"I suppose it was the man in me that needed to make a choice and to pay back for all my mistakes. I learned that we all make them, though."

Jacob picked up their glasses and handed Petra hers. "Here is to our future, if you want to be with me."

"I want to be with you. So much that I think we need to go inside before we catch cold." A smile spread across her face as she took his hand in hers and kissed his fingers.

They got out of the pool, dashed through the poolside shower to get the chlorine off, removed their suits, toweled down, and then he wrapped his arm over her shoulder as they walked inside. The house was quiet as they went upstairs. No words were needed as they entered her room. The last time they had been here, this had been their room together, and now it would be again.

The light reflected from the patio below through the open window. Petra dropped her towel, and Jacob admired her curves. All the shyness, apprehension, and walls disappeared as he reached out and pulled her against him. He kissed her, and it was sweeter than any kiss they'd ever shared. He kept deepening the kiss until the passion set their blood on fire. The need to get closer was almost primal, like a weakness which neither of them could stop. They wanted each other with every pulse of their hearts. Not able to get enough from just their mouths, they used their tongues, lips, and hands to check the contours of each other while Petra gasped with pleasure, urging him on.

Petra shivered in his arms with the increased desire. Her nipples on point brushed against his skin, demanding extra attention from him. Jacob obliged with his hands and his tongue, tracing the outlines of her breasts which caused her to whisper his name, almost begging. He eased her down onto the bed and continued to explore every part of her. In turn, her hands and tongue touched and tasted any exposed skin. The sensations intensified with his hands stroking her center until she cried out in ecstasy and begged him to enter her. She cried out with pleasure as he filled her, thrusting inside, making her his again.

They slowly awoke after their night of passion. The color of the sunrise was golden on the walls. Petra felt like she'd returned from a long, arduous trip, finally secured in Jacob's arms. She looked over at him sleeping with his dark eyelashes accenting his perfect features. His generous mouth that had kissed her all night was relaxed with a slight smile.

"Ah, so you are awake, my dear."

"I am." He murmured without opening his eyes. "It is impossible to sleep when I know you are awake, looking at me. I, um, don't have any mustard on my mouth from my hamburger last night, do I?"

Petra chuckled and replied, "No, but if you did, I would lick it off, and I don't even like mustard."

He reached over and pulled her on top of him and suggested, "We could pretend. I love to pretend, especially if it ends up with us kissing."

She leaned over and kissed him soundly and said, "Back in a minute, and we can explore that after I tell you something."

She flashed him a smile as she dashed out of bed. Jacob frowned as he wondered what she wanted to talk about. He thought they were okay, but he had thought that before. He decided to straighten up the bedding and prop up the pillows when he heard her gasp behind him.

"Oh, my goodness, Jacob. When, er, what, um, how, I mean wow!" She sat behind him and traced the outline of the dragon with gentle fingers like she was afraid to hurt him. "It is beautiful. Does it hurt? Does it have a name? Fierce and graceful with lines that cover your whole back. I like the look in its eye of protective malevolence as it stares back at me."

Jacob swallowed as he realized he'd been holding his breath since she had gasped. "It doesn't hurt anymore, though it did for a while. I hadn't thought about a name. I am glad you said fierce and gentle. It will remind me of you. I, um, missed you and felt my life was upside down. I did it for a lot of reasons I don't even recall now. I thought I did it to help forget about you, but that didn't work. Perhaps, um, I don't know. I am glad you like it. Do you want to name her?"

Petra chuckled and wrapped her arms around his back, pressing into him as she admitted, "I might want to name her, but I don't know her yet. Let me get to know her, then we can name her, perhaps.

"I wanted to talk to you about something, and I think being behind you is the best place to open the conversation, for now."

"Okay." Jacob felt a mild fear run up his spine that she couldn't face him and talk.

She leaned her head against his back and quietly stated, "Last night in the pool, I said I wanted to apologize, and I do, but I also wanted to let you know some things. I am very self-conscious of this scar on my face, which you have not mentioned even once.

"My speech is mostly back to normal, though the jaw is still a bit sore. That is a time thing. The scar, though, is not pretty and brave like your dragon but red, jagged, and covers most of one side. I was very happy when the wires were removed from my jaw and grateful that my balance and agility have returned with hours of exercise. The scar will continue to be ugly to me. It made me ugly inside until Julie and, frankly, everyone here helped me to regain my confidence. I pushed you away when you were trying to do the same thing. I realize now you have never seen it, not really. I made a mistake thinking I was a burden."

Jacob murmured, "Well, I am glad you see that. I wish I had just told you. Perhaps that would have been easier. Some things men are just not so good at saying. You are beautiful because you make my heart whole."

"Thank you, Jacob, you make my heart whole, too. That is important to me, but sadly I also want a balanced face, like I had before. To do that, I have two choices. The first is three or four surgeries to repair the damage and reduce the scarring to fine lines, easily concealed with makeup. The drawback is that as I get older the side that has surgery will remain mostly unchanged and averse to natural aging."

Jacob interjected, "I can appreciate you wanting to look like you did, but again, you are beautiful to me. Three or four surgeries could take a very long time and sound painful. I would not like you to be in pain again."

Petra sighed and continued, "I am not certain I want any more pain. You are correct in that the doctors said it would be painful for several weeks after each surgery and that I would have to heal well before the next surgery.

"The second choice is one I had not even considered. I am not certain if you will support me, but I think I have decided it is the path I need to take." Petra paused as she worked up the courage to complete her explanation. "Su Lin and I spoke, and she suggested I could be tested and possibly be a candidate for some DNA modification if the markers aligned."

Jacob tensed just a bit and replied, "Like what she did long ago that seems to have worked on Franklin and her from a tissue regeneration perspective? Don't forget I read all her experiments and data sheets. It could work, as she said, if you have the right markers. Not trying to live forever, are you?"

Petra laughed, "No! In fact, Su Lin said it would focus on certain types of cells and would take time. Not an overnight miracle but gradual, like her skin changing from the first time you and I met her. The lines are gone, the skin heals very quickly, and she showed me some before and after pictures of where Franklin had scars from being tied up. Do you know how old Franklin really is?"

Jacob laughed, "Yes, but don't say it aloud, please. I won't be able to un-hear it. Is this what you would prefer?"

Petra raised her head and released him. She scooted around to the side and settled upright into one of the pillows. Jacob took up an adjoining pillow and covered them both with the sheet. Petra reached over and took his hand in hers. They were quiet for a few minutes, contemplating their own thoughts.

Petra finally replied, "Jacob, it is what I want if you will give me support and strength for the testing and the waiting that will follow."

Jacob confirmed, "You should know that for all things, I am your dragon."

CHAPTER SIXTY-SEVEN

A New View of an Old Tale

Tuck and Quip howled again at the curious adaptation of the 1880's folklore story, now carefully brought forward to the digital age. As with any successful outside barbeque that gets mixed with fermented grapes or hops, men tend to regale one another with amusing anecdotes. The tendency is, of course, as the quantity of adult beverages consumed goes up, the more outrageous the story. The unfortunate part of this universality among men is that it is the women who have to endure the escalation.

Quip was finally able to regain some semblance of normality, and the same was true of Tuck. Their laughter had died down. A little bit of tranquility had descended upon the small group. It was the final evening that Quip and Jacob would be in Melbourne. The rest of the group had returned to their respective destinations that morning. The only requirement remaining was securing the multi-year contract with Tuck.

The barbie had been a wild success and would be talked about for years by all who attended. Between the steaks, chook, shrimp, snag, and all the trimmings, there wasn't a person for miles around who would be hungry tonight or for the next week. The three-day event had the eskys ever full, sheilas serving, bartending, and cleaning up, and each one prettier than the next. Old Tuck had been crowned the Barbie Prince early on and had accepted the role with wit and charm. Quip had tried several times to get the commitment to the contract in writing from Tuck, but he'd either pulled a beer from the esky or insisted on more snag off the barbie.

Quip asked, "Tuck, wasn't this barbie the best ever?"

Tuck grinned with a lopsided look that spoke of a few beers and replied, "Good onya, Quip. It was indeed a grouse barbie. The crowning at the beginning will be remembered forever in these parts.

"Gina suggested I go ahead and sign your document but added some caveats for extra charges for short notice, calling outside of business hours here, and advanced funds from you I can draw up. If those changes are agreeable, bloke, we can sign it now in front of these fine gentlemen."

Quip laughed and then they each signed a copy, one of which Jacob secured into his jacket pocket. He wondered if either of them would remember the conversation tomorrow. They had been matching drinks for hours. Not that Jacob hadn't, he just never had the appetite to compete with others in drinking. These two had attended university together and had saved a small country. They deserved to cut loose. Tuck went to replenish his beverage of choice as well as Quip's while Quip and Jacob relaxed and enjoyed the evening sounds. Jacob was still grinning from the telling of his story, now having completed its telling for the third time.

After Tuck returned to his seat and settled in, he toasted Quip.

Quip struggled to suppress a smile as he asked, "Jacob, one more time, please?"

Tuck and Quip both stared eagerly at Jacob, who chuckled a little, and offered, "You got it! This is the tale of old Br'er Rabbit

Coder and his struggle with old Br'er Fox Doctor. Old Br'er Fox Doctor had set up a trap to capture Br'er Rabbit Coder, seeing how Br'er Rabbit Coder had the Fountain of Youth programs on his trusty Br'er laptop. Now, old Br'er Fox Doctor was mighty cagey, and he decided to hold old Br'er Master Po hostage, figuring Br'er Rabbit Coder might be willing to bring him what he wanted there in old Br'er Finland.

"But old Br'er Rabbit Coder figured that there was a trap a-waitin' for him, but he couldn't leave poor old Br'er Master Po to the diabolical Br'er Fox Doctor. So old Br'er Rabbit Coder boldly marched in to retrieve poor old Br'er Master Po, but the Br'er Fox Doctor said, 'Ah-ha! You were right foolish, Br'er Rabbit Coder, to walk into my trap! Now I have you, the laptop, and Br'er Master Po! I've won! I've won!'

"Now Br'er Rabbit Coder, who is a rabbit that thinks fast on his feet as well as cranks out fast code, said, 'Well, you got me dead to rights, old Br'er Fox Doctor. Just one thing I beseech of you, please! Please don't fling Br'er Master Po's programs into that awful briar patch you call a supercomputer! That old briar patch supercomputer will tear the coded routines clean off the programming logic poor old Br'er Master Po spent months building! You can do anything you wants with me, but please don't fling Br'er Master Po programs into that awful briar patch of a supercomputer!'

"Now old Br'er Fox Doctor's face turns into a big ol' grin as he said, 'So that will hurt you most, huh? Then that's exactly what I'm going to do to your programs, Br'er Rabbit Coder!' With that Br'er Fox Doctor uploaded all of Br'er Master Po's programs to the briar patch supercomputer and then turned to Br'er Rabbit Coder and added, 'There, what was once yours is now mine, Br'er Rabbit Coder! Now that I have the programs in the briar patch, I won't be needing either of you! So this is where...'

"Old Br'er Rabbit Coder just laughed and laughed and then finally admitted, 'I'm sure glad you done uploaded all the programs of Br'er Master Po, because now you not only have what you wanted, I now have what I wanted. A way to go home with my dear old Br'er Master Po.

"'You see, being the smart Br'er Rabbit Coder that I am, I added several other Br'er virus routines that will be munching on your data, unless I feed in the cancel codes. My only problem with building the Br'er virus codes was how to get them onto your system, but then you were mighty obliging to upload them Br'er virus routines. Now, Br'er Fox Doctor, it is actually you who has been caught!'

"Now Br'er Fox Doctor was furious at having been tricked, yet again, by Br'er Rabbit Coder, but he holds his temper as he asks, 'When can I have my briar patch back from your Br'er viruses?'

"Br'er Rabbit Coder smirks as he helps Br'er Master Po to the transport as they were leaving, then turned and offered, 'Well now, a deal is a deal, so I want you to go to the computer terminal on Br'er patch supercomputer and type in It's me! By and by you will have everything you deserve.'

"With that, old Br'er Rabbit Coder and Br'er Master Po closed the door to their transport to take them home.

"Poor old Br'er Fox Doctor ran back to his terminal and entered *It's me!*, which promptly launched all the Br'er viruses that had been uploaded to briar patch supercomputer.

"Once in the air, Br'er Rabbit Coder said to Br'er Master Po, 'It'll be a long time before that briar patch hurts anyone again.'"

Tuck and Quip howled with laughter again at the re-telling, just one more time, of how Br'er Rabbit outsmarted Br'er Fox in the 21st century. Unwilling to recount the tale again, Jacob got up to leave, smiled, and said, "Gentlemen, good night."

CHAPTER SIXTY-EIGHT

Changes Coming to Accommodate the Internet of Stuffs

...The Enigma Chronicles

ICABOD stated, "Dr. Quip, I have completed the analysis you requested. All the parameters were fed into the program that we discussed. Would you like the output or just a summary?"

Quip swallowed hard and hesitantly questioned, "You appear to have done that rather quickly. Did you get all the information installed into the program to give it all the relative impact points? I don't want to present this to the team and then notice some of the parameters were overlooked."

ICABOD responded, "Then let me recount the inputs, and you can verify none were overlooked. I do not believe any were missed.

"First and foremost, there is the arithmetic growth of food production as extrapolated from the food production enhancements over the last fifty years. Some of that food production enhancement was offset by the backlash against genetically enhanced food stuffs. Therefore, the gains in food production were somewhat retarded.

"The loss in arable land to shopping malls was somewhat countered by more urban-based food production and an accelerated demand for locally produced food. That, coupled with the demographic shift for more people to live inter-city rather than in the suburbs, reduced some of the strain on the cannibalization of arable farm land for single family dwellings.

"I have accounted for shifts in weather patterns and calculated the evolving effect of rainfall changes, heat, cold, evolving crop diseases, possible harvesting improvement techniques, and violent storm patterns as they adversely affect or benefit the different food production regions around the planet. I incorporated a standard deviation model that factors in plus or minus ten percent to make the mathematics a little more interesting.

"After the food production model was sufficiently polished and a suitable chart built, I then began to look at the life and death cycle of humans and their domesticated livestock, coupled with food used in energy production, such as ethanol. No X-factor modeling in food production is anticipated in the calculation of either scenario, Dr. Quip. In other words, no disruption in global food production is accounted for, such as aliens landing on earth and all food production being confiscated for their off-world consumption."

Quip, momentarily caught off guard, questioned, "ICABOD, have you been watching Saturday afternoon science fiction movies from the 1950s again?"

ICABOD ignored the question and continued, "It is easily demonstrated that humans are living longer and that the population is growing. The impact factors to people living longer and thus consuming more food are *Diseases, Religions, and Governments,* or DRAG. The loss of human life to the DRAG effect has had a negative effect on human culture since humans began living together. The DRAG value has held the human population growth in check for a value of twelve percent. At any one time this figure may balloon horrifically or dive precipitously, but over millennial the aggregation of these three factors is consistent in limiting population growth.

"However, when I introduce zero deaths from disease and unchecked birth defects, and as longevity goes up to a thousand-year life span, I received some unusual results. I had to differentiate the death from disease from all other forms of death like driving drunk and other ill-advised activities, including the use of dynamite for fishing which yields life-shortening results. Upon further investigation, it appears that there are several activities that men in particular attempt, and they almost always begin with, Hold my beer and watch this, for which the forever code was not designed to protect."

Quip grinned and clarified, "Natural selection at its best. So, what happens when you feed the forever solution into the population mix? Does the removal of genetic flaws in our DNA programming cause the population to overwhelm the food supply as we expected?"

ICABOD responded, "The answer is yes, the population growth did overwhelm the food supply, but the equation became unbalanced because it overlooked the impact of political tempering. Once the political factors were included in the model, two result outcomes emerged. There are two branching alternatives here, Dr. Quip, which appear to yield the same unique population growth results.

"The first is, with an altruistic release of the forever solution to all, people quickly realized that food stuffs come under population pressures. Governments quickly begin to eye other territories for *Lebensraum* and additional food production. Sovereign conflicts flare up, and the land rush to support longer life spans quickly soaks up the net gains from the forever code. The governments discover that the longer life spans of those who survive will easily cover their lost tax base since people will then pay taxes longer. Additionally, pension plan funding for retirees will be deferred farther out so retirement benefits will be pushed out in the timeline continuum, with the tendency to spend, rather than prudent money management."

Quip stared blankly at the audio/video screen of ICABOD, letting the first analysis sink in before he asked, "Was that the good news scenario or the bad news scenario?"

ICABOD replied, "No attempt was made to categorize these two scenarios as good or bad, Dr. Quip. Continuing with this line of reasoning, water and energy consumption would become vital considerations for food production as well, so conflicts would increase to secure the needed resources to maintain the sovereign population. It would result in a determination that the forever solution will need to be retracted from general offering and strictly licensed. However, the model suggests that several pockets of forever solution recipients will coalesce into small communities. These communities would become self-sustaining and lost to the government control. I categorize this as the *Shangri-La* syndrome that has no use for outsiders and no one would feel compelled to leave. After a while these small communities would vanish from the collective human conscience of the outside world and would evolve along a separate path. Birth control for these pockets of survivors of the forever solution would be a matter of legislative permission rather than biological capability. Otherwise, unsanctioned births would put undue strain on the local food production."

Quip's imagination poured over this last statement from ICABOD. He absentmindedly noted, "The legend of Shangri-La, or maybe Atlantis, where highly evolved technology vanished from mainstream human consciousness. Hmmm...interesting.

Hey, wait a minute! You mean that I would have to have permission from the government to increase the number of animals in the herd? I am not going to ask permission to play with my significant other! I can see birth control as the price of admission in this scenario. What could happen to the ones who stay with the sovereign program with the forever solution?"

ICABOD answered, "These people would become the new ruling class. With almost forever lifespans, they could amass great wealth by simply using compound interest and, over time, accumulate great volumes of knowledge. You would expect this new ruling class to be either benevolent or cruel based on their appreciation of human life or the lack thereof. It is unlikely they would have a middle ground, though not impossible."

Quip, becoming quite uncomfortable, commented, "Maybe we should look at this topic through the future coding solution we confiscated last year from the Werewolf Clan. Perhaps it is time to dust that off and use it in the manner intended."

ICABOD stated, "I was not given permission to use that program so that lens was not applied in this forward-looking analysis, Dr. Quip. That program requires more data sets and much more processing power than the time frame I was given to render an analysis for the team's consideration. However, I am prepared to begin that process if instructed to do so. This analysis is not nearly as exhaustive as the future solution, but it has yielded some important tendencies and points of consideration."

Quip qualified, "No, this analysis will be enough for our preliminary discussions. If the team believes more effort should be expended, then we can make that decision as a team. I do not want to authorize the use of the future solution without everyone's consent." After a few moments of thinking, Quip asked, "What else does the first scenario model suggest?"

"Dr. Quip, great effort will be given to restrict new births as well in an effort to optimize food consumption for the new millennials while trying to accommodate the food producers. We could easily expect religious customs and lower class resentment of such policies, thus leading to open warfare between classes, not just between governments. Also, a significant class war could result between those who understand the need for restricted births and those in the opposing camp, driven by the fundamental need humans have to reproduce. This is as far as the modeling takes us for the first scenario."

ICABOD added, "The case for bio-genetic warfare to control the population growth could be introduced here as a means to limit the impact on food consumption, but this was not included in the model. A good argument can be made that if humans can be engineered to live longer then a virus could also be designed as a biological weapon for targeted population control. I would need more time to incorporate that into the current modeling, however. Simply removing food consumers with an effective biological virus is infinitely more efficient than a standard ground-based warfare operation with all of its collateral damage to civilized buildings and infrastructure."

Lost in thought, Quip didn't respond right away. After a few moments of reflective thought, he asked, "And what of scenario number two? What does that look like? Or at least the tendency of scenario number two?"

"In scenario number two, the new knowledge is immediately recognized for its disruptive power, and the forever solution never goes mainstream. People of power, influence, and wealth isolate the forever solution to build themselves a secret order but leave the rest of the planet to continue their normal lives so that the more difficult issues of who gets to live forever can be deferred. Basically, the new millennials use the forever solution to maintain their control over the population of the planet, and the standard humans do not know they have been excluded. The top one percent jealously guard their secret elixir of life, and the ageless aristocracy run the planet behind the scenes. In this scenario, the forever solution becomes an enslaver rather than a liberator for the human race. The death penalty would be invoked against anyone looking for the forever solution, since it would have to be classified out of necessity for the common good of the people."

Quip blinked several times, sighed, and then offered, "So the net-net of the forever code is that increased life spans won't solve any problems, fighting over resources will continue under the new model, and most probably those in power will get to rule longer. In reality nothing changes. The fountain of youth that everyone has been after for millennia is truly a myth. Living longer only hardens our bad attributes, and it will take longer to overthrow tyranny after it gets ensconced."

ICABOD confirmed, "The fundamental flaw with the forever solution is that IF it cannot be for everyone, then no one should have it. If any group of people get the forever solution, then they are automatically isolated from the regular public, because how could anyone who will live forever socialize or even mate with someone not of the thousand-year life span? Who would want to watch a friend or loved one die before you had lived only a tenth of your life span? The forever solution is poisonous, Dr. Quip.

"Unless everyone can have it, then no one should have it."

Quip sheepishly asked, "But we could sneak the solution for ourselves, right? I mean, no one would have to know, yes?"

ICABOD replied, "Your perpetual youthful look would not go unnoticed, Dr. Quip. After a decade of no aging, your friends, family, and colleagues would spot the issue. Then either you would take to using make-up to disguise your youth, or you would simply become a recluse and be terrified of anyone with a camera. Once the suspicion was made public, you would be hounded for the secret, or you would be forced to kill the desperate youth seekers. The forever solution is a one-way trip with no happy ending for the traveler."

Quip, still trying to justify keeping the forever solution, said, "I was talking about bringing my whole sphere of family and friends along, so no one gets left behind. Not just me!"

"Dr. Quip, those friends and family also have friends with their families. No one would want to leave all their friends behind, so some very hard choices come to the forefront rather quickly. Also, because the forever solution will make you an outcast with anyone not taken along, you would have the choice of being persecuted or being in charge. The forever solution will tend to make you be in charge as a defense mechanism, which will make it easier to cloak your ageless life span. Out of necessity you will be the new dictators, ruling the planet because of your uniqueness.

"The other problem here is that with a reduced gene pool for the new millennials, new genetic flaws begin to surface, and inbreeding becomes a high-risk issue for the participants. Reduced genetic diversity of these new rulers will be an unexpected threat long term. This could be mitigated by fresh DNA being introduced into the ruling class or perhaps a continued tweaking effort on the forever code. In any case, this was not accounted for in the model."

Quip absentmindedly stared off into space as he extrapolated, "So scenario two is my destiny even if I had no intention of ruling the planet, huh? ICABOD, I just want to cheat in my favor without any consequences! And I don't want my progeny to suffer due to a reduced gene pool! Can you understand that?"

"Dr. Quip, in order to have everything work in your favor as you desire, you will have to modify all human behavior, a product often thousand years of evolution, to achieve the desired outcome. The collective human psyche is very elastic and almost always returns to its original charted course, even after the last game changer has tried to alter the direction of the human race. I believe the phrase commonly used gets stated, *It is what it is.* No more and no less, Dr. Quip."

Quip sulked a moment, then decided, "Well, poop! I knew that the end game would not really better mankind. Get a summary of the analysis out to the core team so we can discuss it at the team meeting."

Otto thought things had recovered to some degree. Jacob and Petra were back together and seemed to be working things out, albeit much slower than anyone expected. At least they had both returned to Zürich and resumed living at Wolfgang's. Things seemed more settled from his perspective, and following the meeting later today with the team, he and Haddy would spend a week back in their home taking care of the twins while Julie and Juan took a long holiday in Mexico. A win/win scenario from Otto's perspective.

Wolfgang arrived and seemed to have an extra bounce in his step as he entered Otto's office. "Morning, Otto," he greeted. "I am ready for our meeting at the top of the hour. Have the others arrived yet? I have all the documentation ready, and I reviewed every last detail last evening with Jacob and Quip. The data in the *Fountain of Youth project* has essentially been lost forever in unrecoverable data bits and bytes. Jacob reiterated that Eric's eyes and ears, that is Jim, will corroborate that in his report which was to be filed a few days ago."

Otto smiled and explained, "As long as Eric believes that and we can add some additional funds, courtesy of Master Po, I think that case will be closed."

Wolfgang elaborated, "Master Po, umm, Su Lin, I mean Ling Po, has requested to be left alone to spend her time in Atlanta living with Andy, who is happily recovering. After everything she has been through, she said that just living would be a lovely change of pace. It shouldn't surprise anyone if she decides to permanently accept her Su Lin identity, based on the comfort level it has with Andy, and forever abandons Ling Po, aka Master Po. When I spoke with her a few days ago, we reviewed her funds and investments, and she willingly provided access to the Pekoni funds. Originally, she had planned to donate it to help some endangered species, but felt it was best in the hands of the American people, though she insisted not the open hands of the greedy politicians. I told her we would do our best to stress that request.

"Leroy Bacon has vanished, though we have alerted authorities with Homeland Security in the United States and Interpol. How he slipped out of Finland is still a mystery. I suspect that the funds he withdrew from Pekoni's accounts before he left will keep him in style for a while, but manipulators like that usually only go away permanently if it is in a casket."

"How true!" chuckled Otto. "Let's go and set up projects for the next month so I can get out of town. Haddy warned me that no late excuses would be tolerated. I know she has a buffer though."

"Doesn't Haddy always!" Wolfgang muttered.

When Otto and Wolfgang entered the conference room, Quip, Petra, and Jacob were all quietly situated with their laptops up and running. Quip had an outline of their various open projects on the big screen.

"Nice to see you all present and accounted for," Otto commented as he took his seat.

Wolfgang smiled and added, "It is indeed."

Otto asked, "Are we ready to place a final update call to Eric?"

Quip nodded and suggested, "We might want to review the status of the project and then let him know about the funds transfer. I want him comfortable that we have closed on that job.

"I think everyone has had time to read the analysis that ICABOD extrapolated from the data and the possible outcomes. I have also checked that all the data sources applied with the extracted files from Master Po matched to the files originally held on STINKIE. Su Lin agreed that no one is ready for most of the findings, and she has no intention of pursuing it outside of the application of genetics already widely used. We can vote for further analysis or simply bury the correlated programs. Jacob's program successfully wiped the information from STINKIE as well as the laptop of Master Po. All backups of the information were also hunted down and wiped from existence as well."

Jacob explained, "I have also planted some very deep-rooted programs that would be triggered by certain combinations commands and data handling processes. These sleeper/sentinel programs have been quietly parked in all major ISP peering junctions around the planet like Los Angles, New York, and Amsterdam and will passively watch for certain query combinations and alert us if they begin to surface. Basically, if the search engines begin returning answers for this line of questioning from the growing family of supercomputers, ICABOD will be alerted, and we can be engaged. It is a self-governing routine to add a layer of protection."

Otto fingered his chin, looked at Wolfgang, and then asked, "Does it dictate human behavior, Jacob?"

Jacob looked around the room and replied, "It merely processes alerts to very complex routines that can be reviewed for possible intent. Nothing that takes away human creativity or their ideas for solving problems."

"Then with Jacob's programming, combined with the analysis provided in Quip's summary, are we in agreement that the Fountain of Youth project be relegated to the archives?" asked Otto. He looked around the table for the agreement and added, "That does not, of course, have any impact on the ongoing scientific efforts on DNA for finding cures to various diseases or altering cellular behaviors which could have a positive impact on the quality of life."

With nods from everyone, the forever code passed into urban legend.

"The next item on the agenda is a review of our current projects. Quip, if you can walk us through the list of items and the order we have committed to our customers."

Quip presented a slide on the screen which listed their current projects and the initials of those responsible. Most of the projects were their standard customer deliverables that covered security and audits, and in some, system updates were due. Quip gave everyone a few minutes to review the list and then commented, "None of our current financial or investment customers have any new requests, so these are very standard projects that require our completion and documentation, things we already do. Jacob, I was hoping that you could do a review of all of our system testing processes to make certain we are taking advantage of all the gains you have made in breaking into systems to prevent those activities for our customers, in addition to the projects already tagged with your initials."

Jacob replied, "I was going to make that suggestion myself, so thanks for reading my mind. I also wanted to work with Petra on the process changes to help with any encryption modifications."

Petra smiled and nodded in agreement. Quip was ready to continue when the screen flashed, and an ICABOD interrupt comment appeared as a bubble above a picture of a phone screen.

Eric calling to speak to either Otto or Quip. Do you wish to accept in your meeting?

Without even thinking, Otto pressed the counsel of the conference phone, "Eric, how good to hear from you. Quip is with me, sir. We had just finished our review of your invoice, planning to send it to you today."

"Otto, thank you for taking my call. You too, Quip. Yes, send along the invoice. My operative's report is also completed and aligns with our prior discussion.

"I am sorry to catch you so late in your day, but I wanted closure on this so we can begin to assess a new peculiarity that has just surfaced. It looked modest at first but we have some reports of random interruptions in standard routines that track equipment shipments and validate inventories. My team is checking it out, but has not yet discovered anything concrete. One item in particular involves the International Space Station. The ISS is a multinational cooperative effort that is funded and supported by many countries. One of the joint efforts involves sending replacement parts and routine maintenance items to the crew that is based on the ISS. A recent standard transport was received but only ninety-five percent of the materials received were actually to the required specifications. The other five percent were boxes of doggie treats in place of some food supplies."

The team looked at one another, and Quip in particular grinned at the thought of the poor crew sitting and begging for their doggie treats.

Otto cleared his throat and asked, "Eric, this is really not funny as it could potentially endanger the crew. Is there any danger to them?"

Eric chuckled a bit, then continued, "Quip, I can almost see your grin! I smiled myself and thought of my wife's dog, Hope, begging for her snacks.

"No, there is no present danger other than the crew is requesting a dog be brought up, but that is a different issue that thankfully the directors of those programs are dealing with. We are trying to find out why at random times information that is static and known is now shifting. The alarming part is that the error rate of mismatched parts, wrong sized couplers, empty battery cases, and flat wrong part numbers is accelerating. Another example which seems unrelated is in an auto plant in Europe where the color for the day was slotted for blue, yet the cars off the line were yellow, and I mean *yellow*. This factory is essentially all automated with a human quality assurance as the last process. They are running a root cause analysis routine, but so far nothing looks like it was even incorrect. What is most disturbing is that the internal diagnostic system doesn't see the problem as incorrect even with the facts. It is like there isn't a problem with the equipment's function but that the fundamental assumptions that it was built with have been or are being tampered with.

"Have you had any reports of this sort of oddity or inconsistency with any of your other customers or projects?"

Otto looked around and noted the negative responses of the team. "Eric, we have not been alerted to anything. I assume you have ruled out your standard computer viruses as a possible culprit, but this does sound a little bit dodgy. Do you want us to officially start looking around?"

Eric laughed. "Not yet. This was merely a social call. I start asking for your help, and the dollar signs appear in my dreams. I haven't received your current invoice. How about, as friends, you alert me if anything unusual starts appearing on your radar, eh Otto?"

Otto added, "Eric, we also located some additional funds that we are transferring to your standard account which were asked to be returned to the people of America for a good use, not to line your politicians' pockets. The amount will be summarized with the invoice and was a portion of the grants that were bestowed upon Dr. Pekoni for his failed project. We hope it meets with your approval. We did not subtract our invoice from this as we wanted no impropriety of commingling funds."

Eric was speechless for a moment and then replied, "Otto, my thanks to you and your team. Your team is good – pricey, but honorable."

Otto grinned, then replied, "Always good doing business together. We will let you know if we hear anything, Eric. Good evening."

The team finished reviewing their meeting and Otto bid his farewells, saying he could be reached by phone if needed.

Wolfgang, Petra, and Jacob headed out but not before inviting Quip to join them for dinner and to bring Eilla-Zan, which he declined with a glint in his eye. He smiled as he noted the incoming number of the call and waved the others off as he answered while walking toward his office to finish up. The conversation with his dream lady didn't quite go as planned, however.

"Hi, honey, I was just…"

She lit into him before he could finish his greeting as she groused, "Quip, can you get this stupid smart refrigerator repaired? It keeps ordering more groceries over the Internet even though it's full! This is the third time this week I have had to turn the delivery away!"

Quip puzzled a moment and suggested, "Okay, let me access it over the 'net to see what the problem is.

"Oh, okay, I think I see the problem. For some reason the refrigerator has been recalibrated for cubic meters, rather than cubic centimeters. That's weird. Honey, did you make any modifications to the refrigerator programming?"

EZ, really annoyed at the inference, retorted, "No, I didn't futz with the programming on your refrigerator! Geez! It's like some giant conspiracy out to get me! First the Internet-enabled refrigerator and then my missed doctor's appointment because the damn cell phone calendar has the wrong time!"

Quip agreed, "Yeah, I know what you mean about the wrong time on a phone. That's why I wear my trusty Swiss made, self-winding watch that I set to the atomic clock in Zürich. One can't be too careful about your time source."

EZ was livid at the situation and barked, "I don't want to hear about your superior wristwatch! Technology that I get over the Internet or that my appliances get from other technical sources should be correct! Last week, when I was working with Carlos to triangulate with cell towers, things kept coming up wrong! The dumb smart tower kept giving us wrong geo-location coordinates and screwing up our tracking of Jacob's plane! If Carlos hadn't known how to fix the coordinate information, I would have placed him in the Arctic Ocean!"

Quip, now more puzzled than consoling to EZ, said, "Hmmm, that's interesting. This doesn't sound like virus-based issues but possibly disinformation. Have you noticed anything else, honey?"

Bordering on exasperation, EZ loudly questioned, "What are you doing, taking a survey here? But, yes, now that you mention it, my favorite recipe website has started giving out dishes where the ingredients are all out of whack! Tablespoons of salt instead of teaspoons, stuff like that. Pepper instead of sugar, which would have cracked me up if I wasn't in such a hurry to fix your dinner!"

Quip, realizing EZ was overwrought, tried to defuse her mood and offered, "Honey, I am on my way home, and we will work through everything when I get there. Okay?"

EZ, trying not to let Quip placate her, responded, "Oh, alright, fine!"

After disconnecting from EZ's rant, Quip recommended, "ICABOD, please put this topic on the top of the list. Perhaps a survey is a good way to start.

"I think we need to look a little closer at this topic in conjunction with what Eric told us. The Internet is the greatest tool ever invented, and it would be a shame if no one could trust its output. I, for one, do not want to return to the days of the slide rule and abacus for engineering and accounting for world business operations."

"Yes, Dr. Quip. Enjoy your evening with Miss EZ."

"Thank you, ICABOD."

Specialized Terms
and Informational References

http://en.wikipedia.org/wiki/Wikipedia

Wikipedia (wɪki' pi: diə / *WIK-i-PEE-dee-ə*) is a collaboratively edited, multilingual, free Internet encyclopedia supported by the non-profit Wikimedia Foundation. Wikipedia's 30 million articles in 287 languages, including over 4.3 million in the English Wikipedia, are written collaboratively by volunteers around the world. This is a great quick reference source to better understand terms.

Amyloid plaques insoluble fibrous protein aggravates sharing specific structural traits. They are insoluble and arise from at least 18 inappropriately folded versions of proteins and polypeptides present naturally in the body. These misfolded structures alter their proper configuration such that they erroneously interact with one another or other cell components forming insoluble fibrils. They have been associated with the pathology of more than 20 serious human diseases in that abnormal accumulation of amyloid fibrils in organs may lead to amyloidosis, and may play a role in various neurodegenerative disorders

Anonymize An anonymizer or an anonymous proxy is a tool that attempts to make activity on the Internet untraceable. It is a proxy server computer that acts as an intermediary and privacy shield between a client computer and the rest of the Internet. It accesses the Internet on the user's behalf, protecting personal information by hiding the client computer's identifying information.

Australian Terms/Slang Used:

Barbie Barbecue, as in "I'll throw some shrimp and chook on the barbie."

Bugger off A more polite way of telling someone to 'f**k' off

Chook Chicken. Often served barbecued at fancy turns. If your hostess is befuddled and/or overcome by trying to do too many things at once, one might say she was "running around like a chook with its head cut-off!"

Esky Portable icebox or cooler - it's always a good idea to have one in the boot stocked with some cold ones just in case the party's bar runs dry.

G'arn Go on, you're kidding.

Grouse Rhymes with "house" - means outstanding, as in Grouse barbie.

Sheila A woman.

Snag A sausage.

Strewth Pronounced "sta-ruth" ... general exclamation of disbelief or shock.

Cloaking is a search engine optimization (SEO) technique in which the content presented to the search engine spider is different from that presented to the user's browser. This is done by delivering content based on the IP addresses or the User-Agent HTTP header of the user requesting the page. When a user is identified as a search engine spider, a server-side script delivers a different version of the web page, one that contains content not present on the visible page, or that is present but not searchable. The purpose of cloaking is sometimes to deceive search engines so they display the page when it would not otherwise be displayed (black hat SEO). However, it can also be a functional (though antiquated) technique for informing search engines of content they would not otherwise be able to locate because it is embedded in non-textual containers such as video or certain Adobe Flash components. For *cloaked* devices as used in extended DOS device drivers.

DDoS Distributed Denial of Service Attacks - A distributed denial-of-service (DDoS) attack occurs when multiple systems flood the bandwidth or resources of a targeted system, usually one or more web servers. Such an attack is often the result of multiple compromised systems (for example a botnet) flooding the targeted system with traffic.

Encryption In cryptography, encryption is the process of encoding messages (or information) in such a way that eavesdroppers or hackers cannot read it, but that authorized parties can. In an *encryption scheme,* the message or information (referred to as plaintext) is encrypted using an encryption algorithm, turning it into an unreadable cipher text (ibid.). This is usually done with the use of an encryption key, which specifies how the message is to be encoded. Any adversary that can see the cipher text should not be able to determine anything about the original message. An authorized party, however, is able to decode the cipher text using a *decryption* algorithm that usually requires a secret decryption key that adversaries do not have access to. For technical reasons, an encryption scheme usually needs a key-generation algorithm to randomly produce keys.

Enigma Machine An Enigma machine was any of a family of related electromechanical rotor cipher machines used in the twentieth century for enciphering and deciphering secret messages. Enigma was invented by the German engineer Arthur Scherbius at the end of World War I. Early models were used commercially from the early 1920s, and adopted by military and government services of several countries — most notably by Nazi Germany before and during World War II. Several different Enigma models were produced, but the German military models are the most commonly discussed.

German military texts enciphered on the Enigma machine were first broken by the Polish Cipher Bureau, beginning in December 1932. This success was a result of efforts by three Polish cryptologists, working for Polish military intelligence. Rejewski "reverse-engineered" the device, using theoretical mathematics and material supplied by French military intelligence. Subsequently the three mathematicians designed mechanical devices for breaking Enigma ciphers, including the cryptologic bomb. This work was an essential foundation to further work on decrypting ciphers from repeatedly modernized Enigma machines, first in Poland and after the outbreak of war in France and the UK.

Though Enigma had some cryptographic weaknesses, in practice it was German procedural flaws, operator mistakes, laziness, failure to systematically introduce changes in encipherment procedures, and Allied capture of key tables and hardware that, during the war, enabled Allied cryptologists to succeed.

Genetic sequencing a part of DNA sequencing and human genome sequencing.

Hackers and Crackers *Hacker* is a term that has been used to mean a variety of different things in computing. Depending on the context although, the term could refer to a person in any one of several distinct (but not completely disjointed) communities and subcultures Cracker, or Hacker (computer security), a person who exploits weaknesses in a computer or network. People committed to circumvention of computer security. This primarily concerns unauthorized remote computer break-ins via a communication networks such as the Internet (Black hats), but also includes those who debug or fix security problems (White hats), and the morally ambiguous Grey hats.

Human genome the complete set of nucleic acid sequence for humans (*Homo sapiens*). Encoded as DNA within the 23 chromosome pairs in cell nuclei and in a small DNA molecule found within individual mitochondria. Human genomes include both protein-coding DNA genes and noncoding DNA.

INTERPOL or International Criminal Police Organization Is an intergovernmental organization facilitating international police cooperation. It was established as the International Criminal Police Commission (ICPC) in 1923 and adopted its telegraphic address as its common name in 1956.

MPLS Multiprotocol Label Switching is a mechanism in high-performance telecommunications networks that directs data from one network node to the next based on short path labels rather than long network addresses, avoiding complex lookups in a routing table. The labels identify virtual links (*paths*) between distant nodes rather than endpoints. MPLS can encapsulate packets of various network protocols. MPLS supports a range of access technologies, including T1/E1.ATM, Frame Relay, and DSL.

Nanotechnology the manipulation of matter on an atomic, molecular, and supramolecular scale. The earliest, widespread description of nanotechnology referred to the particular technological goal of precisely manipulating atoms and molecules for fabrication of macroscale products, also now referred to as molecular nanotechnology.

Supercomputer a computer with a high-level computational capacity. Performance of a supercomputer is measured in floating point operations per second (FLOPS). As of 2015, there are supercomputers which can perform up to quadrillions of FLOPS.

Unified Communications (UC) Is the integration of real-time communication services such as instant messaging, presence information, telephony (including IP telephony), video, video conferencing, data sharing (including web connected electronic whiteboards, interactive whiteboards, call control, speech recognition, with non-real-time communication services such as unified messaging. UC is not necessarily a single product, but a set of products that provides a consistent unified user-interface and user-experience across multiple devices.

Yaqui Indians Native Americans who inhabit the valley of the Rio Yaqui in the Mexican state of Sonora, Mexico and the Southwestern United States. The Pascua Yaqui Tribe is based in Tucson, Arizona.

Read a snippet from the seventh book in the series…

the
Enigma
Gamers
BOOK 7: Award Winning Techno Thriller Series
Breakfield and Burkey

So far and yet so very near

The drone of the commercial aircraft was unmistakable, though First Class was undeniably quieter than the Coach seats behind the engines. Conversations were muted, or passengers dozed. The distinctive aromatic smell of heated nuts wafted from the forward galley. The aircraft had almost reached the cruising altitude that would allow comfort services to begin. They were on the last leg of the long flight from Zürich to Macau. Juan had grumbled about taking a trip so far away, but Julie had sold him with her vivid description of the small peninsula across the Pearl River Delta from Hong Kong. As a Portuguese overseas territory until 1999, it reflected an extraordinary mix of Portuguese and Chinese influences. What seemed to put the glint in Juan's eye was its nickname, "The Las Vegas of Asia".

Macau was one of Julie's favorite places, but she had never gone for pleasure, only for work purposes. Julie, also known as JAC or Cyber Assassin Julie at work, had originally visited the city to meet with a customer. Julie was hooked the first time she walked over the beautiful black sand on Hac Sa Beach, her thick light brown hair ruffled by the breeze. Her legs, which made up most of her 1.6 meters, gobbled up the sand as she'd traveled to her destination.

That seemed a lifetime ago. Since then, Julie had maintained her peak physical condition with martial arts training sessions with Juan and by chasing after their twins. Even now, she carried almost no fat on her supple body, just the way Juan liked it. She was delighted with their current lifestyles even though they still had some elements of risk in their professional endeavors.

So much had happened since the last trip she'd made to Macau. It felt as if she were looking through an entirely different lens. She and Juan had started their own business, known as the Cyber Assassin Technology Services or CATS team, shortly after they were married. Their business was supported by her family's business yet thrived nicely on its own merit. She leaned back into her seat to relax as the fragments of their history went through her mind.

Julie, adopted as a baby, had grown up in a family which was part of an ongoing business formed during World War II that now stretched around the world. The business, which was referred to by the family and close associates as the R-Group, had interests in real estate, finance, technology, security, and information resources. Their clientele included private elite families, initially serviced post-World War II, and public entities including Interpol and the intelligence agencies of various countries. The primary pillars of the R-Group were to uphold the rights of the individuals or governments that stood for freedom and justice.

Originally, the family founders, three daring young men, had taken a copy of the Enigma Machine as they fled Poland. These intelligent and resourceful men had joined their skills to slightly modify the device and then had used it to undermine the German Nazis through encryption of information shared in just the right places. Though many of the core family members had changed over the years, the foundational beliefs of the operations had not. Their span of power and influence had increased, though much of the operation was only known within the family business.

Juan and Julie had met during an R-Group assignment where Julie had worked to locate an heiress, Lara Bernardes. Lara, the head of a now successful fashion house of Brazil, was also the love of Juan's brother, Carlos. Julie had provided both Juan and Carlos with new identities at the end of that assignment, though he had mightily protested erasure of his past.

Juan, the crazy flyboy, had captured Julie's heart with his quick wit and ability to love her unconditionally. She knew she was in love with Juan when she had beat him in a martial arts challenge at a gym. He told great stories, kept his cool under pressure, loved their twin children, and was deliciously passionate.

Julie glanced over to her resting partner. His thick ebony hair was a nice topping to his nearly 1.83 meters of rippling muscles and clean-shaven face. When he smiled, she had no doubts that he adored her. Julie was known for her never-ending smile and leveraged it often with her delightful husband, as well as in her undercover roles. As if aware of her stare, Juan's hand reached over and gently cradled her hand in his with a slight smile appearing on his generous lips. If they weren't on a commercial flight with people all around, she might have started something, hoping Juan would finish it.

Juan rested comfortably against the window and almost dozed, though he was aware of his surroundings. It was odd to be flying somewhere and not piloting the aircraft. The feeling of Julie's hand in his, warm and soft, was not exactly the scenario he had been thinking about, but it would do until they reached the resort. Julie had told him that the resort offered more private and scenic rooms than the large, over-crowded casino hotels. But a promise to go and check out the gambling at some point was fine with him. Juan liked to gamble a bit and had even brought some of his reserves from his pre-Julie Mexico investments to play, thus presenting no risk to their business. The business was doing well, and Juan knew that Julie's family had money, but it was something they were building together for their family dynasty.

Juan missed the twins, Gracie and Juan Jr., with their constant babbling and laughter. Regardless, he was going to make the most of four days alone with his beautiful wife, partner, and love of his heart, right next to him where she belonged. He opened his eyes at the sounds of services beginning, and Julie rewarded him with one of her megawatt smiles. He toasted them when their wine was served and knew he was very lucky to have her.

Julie and Juan were laughing while they deplaned, finally at their destination. Their driver was there with the correct placard on display as they walked outside. Julie's father, Otto, who was enjoying the time with his grandchildren almost as much as her mother, Haddy, had insisted they have a driver on call so they could go anywhere, anytime without needing to worry about the vehicle itself. It had been his gift for them to enjoy.

Otto, as one of the primary heads of the R-Group, rarely took time off, but the twins seemed to somehow make it easier to set aside those responsibilities. Maude was the children's full time governess, but Haddy and Otto insisted on staying to enjoy Gracie and Juan Jr. in peace. Their time with the twins was also being referred to as the Grand Spoiling Time. Julie chuckled as her phone indicated another text message with likely a candid photo arrival. Her giggles erupted anew as she showed the picture to Juan, and he laughed too.

Their driver, Chen Lee, smiled as he greeted them and proceeded to tell them, in his perfect English, that his name meant morning. His non-stop oration included the points-of-interest they drove past, things he liked, his family, and how much he approved of their choice of the beach front villa that afforded privacy. Privacy and seclusion was expensive and limited in

Macau. Chen was lean and a bit shorter than Julie but had a welcoming smile and a twinkle in his dark eyes that reminded Julie of espresso. Chen boasted about his twelve children, and Juan privately remarked that working must be the only time Chen was able to speak, so Chen obviously made the most of it. After delivering them to their villa and making certain the arrangements were in place, Chen indicated he would pick them up that evening for dinner. At their request he promised to provide several options for after-dinner activities.

Their room was magnificent! The floor to ceiling windows dominated the two sides reaching into a corner with a breath-taking view of the water on one side and the city on the other. Quiet music was in the air but gentle, like a breeze. The furniture was sparse with the oversized bed, covered in white and ivory silk covers and overflowing with huge pillows, as the dominating feature. Bold-colored silk flowers offset the whites and ivories of the interior and bedding. The bathroom contained a shower as well as a four-person, sunken Jacuzzi with a private window view toward the sea. Everything was elegant and yet seemed practical to a fault.

Juan called for room service while Julie made quick work of unpacking and settling into the luxurious suite. Room service had already arrived when Julie emerged from the bathroom. She was comfortably garbed in a barely-there bikini that perfectly matched the blue in her sapphire and diamond wedding ring. Ahead of where she walked, she spread fairies of light across the room as the sun caught the surfaces of her ring.

Juan leered at her, grinned and then groaned, "My darling, if you keep dressing like that we will never see more of Macau than this room."

Julie wagged a finger toward Juan as she firmly explained, "Juan, we need to establish some rules. I want to go curl my toes in the black sand and perhaps bring back just a little for our kids. I want to swim with you in the South China Sea and enjoy all the historical sites with you." Then she insisted, "Juan, you need to behave."

He handed her a glass of champagne and raised his to toast to them both. Juan grinned, then replied, "Sweetheart, it is far too late to start trying to establish rules. I will, of course, behave as your servant and lover. All your wants will be fulfilled as will mine. Then, I promise, we will see about the sights on your list."

He pulled her close as they sipped the champagne.

The glasses were magically resting on the table empty as Julie found herself horizontal on the giant bed with Juan leaning over her with a familiar look of passion burning in his eyes.

"We have not been alone in far too long, my beautiful wife." Running his hands over her skin that somehow had lost the minor inconveniences of the bikini, he continued, "Your skin is so soft, so smooth, and well, so kissable."

Juan kissed her lips and every available inch of her body while she returned the kisses and the touches, lost in the wonder of the magic they shared. She had never felt as much heat or ardent pleasure as she did when he had her in his arms. Juan knew all the right places to touch and lick until she begged for him to get closer and deeper.

"Sweet mercy," he groused as her inner thigh muscles clamped down on him as she pushed her hips up against his to continue the pleasure, "why did I wait so long to finish."

Another woman might have been insulted at the comments had she not known, heart and soul, that to this point he had only considered her fulfillment and her pleasure. He had repeatedly given her everything she wanted and needed. He cared about her satisfaction in a way that was absolute until the precise moment when it shifted to being about him. He allowed her to be on top and drive him to the end of the precipice as he pulled her bottom into him, growing bigger and harder with each thrust until they both felt as if they were launched into space and flying. Afterward they tumbled as an entwined pair and drifted into a soft slumber after their exhausting lovemaking.

Minutes or hours later, Julie murmured, "We really need to see the sights while we are here."

Juan shifted them slightly and gripped her a bit closer as he whispered, "From my perspective, the sights are perfect from here."

CHAPTER TWO

Rambling Gambler

Frieda questioned, "So what do you want to do? The communications infrastructure is crumbling, plus we need more personnel and sizeable upgrades just to keep things running!"

Jamie looked at her rather dispassionately and remarked, "Just tell them this is what we need. What's the big deal?"

Frieda and Jamie were certainly an unlikely pair. He was blond-haired and blue-eyed, but she was a dark-haired beauty with her stoic, logical German temperament that often clashed with his romanticized Irish temper. When her temper flared, her cheeks got rosy and her curls seemed as if they were on springs. When he was annoyed or angry, he held his temper in check until the last possible moment and then he bellowed. She had seen that once and it wasn't pretty.

They lived together in a poor excuse for an apartment with the only saving grace being that it was furnished. Their knowledge of technology complemented one another with her specialty in hardware, networks, and high-end databases and his in programming, especially cowboy style. He had the inbred flair for the blarney with a side of manipulation.

This job had been advertised as high-paying and filled with bonuses for making or beating deadlines. To date, the pay was less than advertised. They were tired of the frustrating situations that occurred daily. Lousy work and no extra money did not a happy couple make.

Becoming annoyed with his illogical approach, she angrily countered, "They'll argue the cost. Then argue over the estimates. I'll be sent away with no funding and told to deal with it. We have a major technology implementation sunk into this wretched continent. These idiots won't listen to the logic of expanding which requires spending. You found us a once-and-done bunch when it comes to WAN communications infrastructure. I'm so mad, I could just spit!"

He sighed and replied, "Frieda, why do we always have to have this same discussion? Come on, get dressed. Let's go fix this."

She stared at him incredulously and exclaimed, "Jamie! What are you talking about? Didn't you hear what I just said? They don't listen. They won't spend! THEN they complain about the poor service! They'll dock our pay because they'll never pay our bonus."

Oblivious to her remarks, he asked, "How much do you need again to up gun the project the right way?"

Not completely comprehending the situation, she answered, "Uh, 14.5 million euros. But I have already…"

Jamie clucked his tongue and suggested, "Okay. Let's go see the finance group of Ebenezer and Scrooge so we can get the necessaries for your problem, shall we?"

Jamie was a high-stakes gambler with an unjustified self-confidence that always seemed to court disaster. One time he'd rounded up several investors to buy up a toilet paper manufacturer that had seen better days. He figured that the price was right, and that with his marketing prowess, they could turn the company into a dominant player in the toilet paper manufacturing business. Unfortunately, his marketing instincts were wrong, and the company imploded before it could get off the ground.

The truth was no one from the wholesaler down to the retail buyer could accept a product based on a design intent called Break on Through to the Other Side, regardless of the old rock song of the same name being used in the commercial messaging. Toilet paper labeled Break on Through to the Other Side was simply a marketing nightmare on steroids. The customers avoided the product in droves.

Jamie had what was known as the Reverse Midas Touch in his endeavors, but it never seemed to bother him when he launched into his next con game. Frieda had been a part of his world for a couple of years now. He always seemed to make strides and get out of situations. Then he'd turn around and step into a bigger puddle of muck.

She numbly followed him into the manager's office where Jamie launched his verbal assault. "Which one of you race car drivers has this Formula 1 car stuck in second gear?"

The finance manager looked up from his computer, somewhat puzzled, then asked, "Whadda you two want? If it costs anything, the answer is no. Unless you are here to deposit money, you can leave now."

As usual, the finance manager retrieved the parked #2 pencil from behind his ear as if he was going to write down something, even though everything he did was on his computer keyboard. The office was cluttered, dusty, and screamed for a good cleaning. Rather than being dressed for success, the finance manager was a perfect match for the office décor of messy and shaggy right down to the hair that he combed over from the back to minimize the reflection from his shiny scalp.

Jamie, as close to disinterested in the manager as possible, replied in a very tired voice, "We are here to advise you that you need to pony up 38.5 million euro to stay in business here. I am ordering this gear and consulting services to be shipped in for installation the week after next. Are you interested in having it installed or not?"

Jamie tossed a handwritten list of gear on a piece of paper at him that Frieda had hastily assembled during the walk over to this office. In Jamie's mind, the desk reflected the disorganization of the user, which made this plan easier. A wobbly desk, a dusty ten-key adding machine with mountains of paper flowing out in ribbons behind it, and a tired looking computer with a smaller screen than the old man's eyes needed.

After his chuckling subsided, the finance manager focused a puzzled expression at Jamie and asked, "Has the jungle fried your brain? I can't begin to authorize that kind of expenditure! If you have really ordered that gear, you'd better find a way to cancel it, or you're fired! Then after I fire you, I'll cancel the order and extract the order cancelation fees from your last check.

"What kind of clown are you anyway? No one approved any expenditure of that size. You're lucky I let you order your own printer cartridges and paper!"

Jamie looked at him hard, shook his head, and with a sour look on his face informed Frieda, "You're right, sweetie, he's sharp as a soccer ball."

Then, after a moment of silence, Jamie turned toward the finance manager. Using slow, carefully enunciated speech, he explained, "No, genius, you don't get it! If you don't buy it, I will take it to the competition, and we'll set it up for their entrance into the market. Haven't you noticed all the free goods that have been circulating around in the area? While you have been squeezing pennies, the competition has been dropping serious folding money to soften the market up for a switch to the greener pastures of your competition. You seriously didn't think you guys would be the only game in town indefinitely, did you?"

Now starting to panic slightly, the finance manager responded, "We simply cannot spend that kind of money! We must fight for market share another way! We intend to stay in Africa, and no one is going to push us out by giving some bars of soap to the natives."

Jamie looked at Frieda straight-faced and snorted. "See, I told you he was dumber than he looked."

He turned his head back to the finance manager and flatly stated, "Oh wow, slow down, lightning! We are not talking about spending our own money! And we are not talking about spending only for this state in Africa. Your competitors are coming in to offer them the expertise if THEY pony up the money. And by THEY, I mean all the surrounding African states as well. You think so small! That's why you'll fail."

The finance manager stared blankly, unable to comprehend, until Jamie sighed again and clarified, "WE don't write the checks, they write the checks! We get all the surrounding states to come into the game because we can't operate in a vacuum. We invite them in on the game, and we get them to pony up as well. No one will refuse because no one wants their country left behind. Are you beginning to see or do we also need to get your glasses checked?"

After a long pause the finance manager replied, "Yes, Mr. Rafferty. I now begin to see. We invest, but we use their monies. You said the gear is coming in two weeks?"

Jamie smiled and asked, "Yes, how do you want it invoiced? My alternate client is standing by, in the event you don't want it. In fact, I'm not quite sure I know what I'm going to tell them if you actually use your never used #2 pencil to approve the purchase."

The finance manager nodded and agreed, "We'll take it. Make sure your team gets it deployed as soon as possible."

Jamie grinned and remarked, "Actually, it will go quite slowly since we will be training the local IT students on its installation and operation. No local politician would dare to cross us, because we would have to lay the students off if we're ejected from this market. Then they would lose voters. Remember, invest locally and your competitors will struggle to displace you. Am I right?"

The finance manager almost smiled as he responded, "About the time I think you two have outlived your usefulness, you pop up with something to help extend your contract."

Outside the finance manager's office, Jamie smiled at the bewildered Frieda as they walked toward their work area. "See how easy it is to steer the weak-minded? Of course, they do have to be greedy like this guy." He tossed a thumb back over his shoulder. "I am going to approach the competition about upgrading their systems to see if we can move on to a better deal.

"However, before we do that, I'd like to get some more wine, get you back out of your clothes, and see what kind of erotic calisthenics can be executed in your hammock. But, this time, no falling out as we rotate positions!"

Frieda smirked. "So you're going to let me participate in the pole vault game this time instead of doing all the work yourself? That's mighty big of you! …Well, not really."

Jamie clucked his tongue in mock annoyance with the disparaging comment. "Just wait until I get you naked, sweetie!"

They had returned to their humble accommodations. Frieda had remarked she was going to change into something more comfortable as she walked into the adjoining bedroom. About that time, Jamie saw the incoming email he had been waiting for pop into his PC screen. He grinned broadly as he read the awaited response. Straining to contain his exuberance, he loudly stated, "Hah! The competition took the bait! I mean, my career destination is now on target! Pack our bags, babe! We are heading to China and our newest gig!"

Frieda's mouth hung open slightly in disbelief as she watched Jamie doing his happy dance around their grimy living quarters. Finally, shrugging off her dumbfounded state, she reminded, "We're under contract here, my soon-to-be-in-jail-for-fraud humping-buddy. We haven't saved anything to just pick up and leave this cesspool that has been downgraded from its earlier status in the travel brochures as the Armpit of Africa. You just conned the finance dweeb of this disgusting manufacturer of personal hygiene products for animals and larger primates with a fabricated story that rivals the Wall Street financial derivatives debacle of 2008. None of that now matters because you think we are leaving for China instead of jail! By the way, where in China? I don't speak Chinese and neither do you as far as I know."

Jamie, still elated that his dream-scheme was unfolding the way he needed it to, waltzed over to Frieda. While smiling tenderly, he pushed her dark hair behind her ear. He then moved his head over to whisper in her ear but instead began teasing her ear with his tongue while his right hand moved to begin caressing her breast. He would have undone her blouse if her indignation hadn't kicked in, prompting her to pull away.

After a few retreating steps were made, she rebuked, "So it's going to be like the last time, right? Me desperately trying to keep us out of jail, and you ready to drop and run to the next scam. Jamie, I can't ask my folks for more money to underwrite this lifestyle! Don't we ever get to do what I want? Will there ever be a time when we can just have a normal life? Is this just one big con game for you? Is that all I am as well?"

Jamie, always the gambler, offered, "If you don't want to go, you don't have to. After all, apparently all I am is your humping-buddy anyway. Surely someone as pretty as you can get that anywhere.

"Look, Frieda, I don't have anything but my wits to leverage. I've taken all these backwater IT jobs that no one would take to learn just one thing. I wanted to know how computers communicate, how information flows, and most importantly how to profit from that knowledge. Not to do it for the rest of my life, but how to win at their game.

"This job in China is exactly where the payoff comes in. I will be the lead IT engineer in a fully automated gambling casino, in what is probably the newest version of the old Wild West. Since this part of China is similar to Hong Kong, English is spoken as well as Chinese and Portuguese. I need to do this. If you want to go with me, I promise you will be wearing diamonds as big as horse turds before I'm through. Are you with me?"

Frieda could feel the old con game being staged again with her emotions simultaneously pulling for and pushing her away from the blue-skies offer. How many times had he taken her along for his roll-of-the-dice only to lose everything except the clothes they wore? She fought the tears and the tidal wave of anger, but it boiled down to only one of two choices. Each time he promised something better, and every time they were the losers.

She really wanted to go home to start over in a normal life. Trouble was, she wanted him to go too! He simply wasn't the reliable, home by five for dinner, kind of man. She knew this would be like the last time, and the next gig he signed on for would be like the one previous. She told herself that he was the one with the gambling problem, but if that were true, then why couldn't she just leave? The tears streamed down her face as she made up her mind on what her future was going to be.

In that short moment of thought, Frieda stared at Jamie for a few minutes and then slapped him hard across the face.

CHAPTER THREE

I thought I saw ...

With their last full day in Macau, Julie and Juan were planning to spend it in the historical district and then on to dinner and gambling in the casino. Juan had heard that this casino had some of the best payouts, which Chen had also confirmed. Julie was comfortable in a flowing dress with small flowers scattered across the pale blue background and strappy sandals that were like walking barefoot. Juan was casual yet elegant in his khakis with a linen shirt that accentuated his dark skin and barely concealed his powerful build. He wrapped a protective arm gently around her waist while his eyes scanned everything nearby.

The historical district was a dichotomy of the merging of Western and Eastern culture that spanned decades. Each of the more than twenty ancient monuments and urban squares contained various stories of history, with religious foundations right in the forefront. The chapels, temples and churches were erected from the early 1500s well into the twentieth century. Even the Protestant cemetery they walked through highlighted the diverse community profile of Macau, as it was nestled next to a fabulous and expansive garden with sweet flower scents filling the air.

Juan called for Chen to retrieve them and take them to the casino. Both of them smiled when Chen arrived within moments with a bright smile. At their request he took a picture of them with the garden in the background and then held open the door of the car. All the way to the casino, Chen chatted about what to do or not to do.

"This casino is very different than others you might have encountered. You can speak for anything you want, and it will magically appear at your elbow. No one speaks very loud as there are ears everywhere. Just know that what you say will be heard, interpreted, and analyzed for the best way to fulfill the speaker's wants or needs. It is said the information gathering is second to none.

"The food is excellent, and the wines are brought in from all over. Madam, I suspect that you might find favor with the wines from France, while you, sir, might enjoy the richness of the Jamaican rum."

Juan laughed and asked, "Chen, how is it you have us pegged so well?"

Chen smiled and replied, "I listen too! And I have very good ears, a necessary requirement with so many children. However, you, sir, actually asked me where to find the best of each the first day I picked you up."

Julie flashed him a smile and suggested, "Chen, you have an excellent memory. You let me know if you ever tire of this job. I have good use for those that pay attention to details."

Chen stopped the car in front of the casino and then walked around to open the door. He offered his hand while Julie emerged and said, "Pretty lady, you have a nice evening with your husband. I think he will take care of you." Then Chen winked and quietly added, "I will keep your job offer in mind, perhaps part time."

Julie laughed as she took Juan's arm, and they walked in through what looked like a door, but which magically disappeared as they approached. Other guests that preceded them also looked impressed with the unique surroundings of Chinese art and artifacts. The ambiance was very different and bespoke the locals' name for the casino, Chinese Dragon. Juan escorted Julie into the dining hall where they were seated at a secluded table near a meandering brook that seemed to encircle the restaurant area like a mote, but with water that bubbled and danced over the rocks like a natural stream.

"Juan, this is exquisite. I never imagined that a casino could house this quiet, elegant restaurant. I can see others at the nearby tables, but I cannot hear a word they are saying."

Juan cocked his head as he surveyed the area, then commented, "It must be a series of white noise columns that somehow isolate each of the guest tables. I, for one, will enjoy this quiet time with you while I sit back and sip some of that Jamaican rum that Chen mentioned. And you, my love, would you like a glass of the French chardonnay we shared earlier at the resort?"

Julie flashed one of her coveted smiles and said, "I would like a glass and perhaps some fresh vegetable bits to snack on."

Soundlessly, within seconds of her response, a robotic waiter placed their glasses on the table followed by a tablet for each of them that flashed pictures of the available cuisine for the main courses and desserts.

"Juan, this is amazing. All the food is pictured, so there is no confusion on what will be served."

"You're right, honey. This is fun, but let's skip the octopus. The tentacles, cooked or not, still give me the creeps."

"I agree." Julie laughed and then added, "I think that a nice scallop salad with the main entree of rice with shrimp would be more than enough for me."

"That sounds pretty good, except I think I would prefer the filet mignon, medium, with the steamed vegetables on rice for the side, more to my liking."

Their snack of cold vegetables with a wasabi ranch dipping sauce arrived while silent mechanical hands removed the tablets. Juan offered a toast to their love, good fortune, and their last night in Macau. It promised to be totally memorable.

After a delicious dinner culminated with a fresh lemon mousse, Juan declared he was ready to try his hand at the tables. Julie was happy to walk along or sit next to him as he moved from one table to another. Julie looked around when they stopped at the Baccarat table as Juan declared there was no skill required to play this game of chance.

There were people dressed up with flashy jewelry that advertised their wealth. Couples and groups laughed and chatted at all the tables within sight. Some laughed and clapped with their success while others asked the mechanical waiters for additional drinks. In many ways, Julie thought it very efficient, yet still inviting. Juan had found some level of success at each table they had encountered, including this one. He promised that he would spend only a short while at each type of game.

The casino floor was enormous with muted lighting and soft rugs of gold and red with dragon characters of various colors seemingly creating a path to walk from one area to the next. There were only a handful of casino personnel that could be identified by their name tags and non-descript apparel. These people smiled at the guests and looked around to make certain all were having fun and all robots were functioning. Julie noticed the sensors on most of the items and recognized that what Chen had said regarding their spoken words was very real.

A young man caught her attention as he appeared to be fixing a machine. His well-groomed blond hair along with his tailored black uniform and polished boots were enough to get him noticed. Yet, what Julie was drawn to was his rapid hand movements and flipping of switches. She studied him closely, trying to put words to what she was seeing. She scanned the ceiling for the monitoring cameras and easily detected four or five that should have him in their sights. Then she wondered why anyone would attempt such a clumsy skimming play on coin slots with that many cameras present.

Juan leaned over very close to her ear and whispered, "That young rogue has quite the moves. Do you find him that attractive, my love, or are you trying to see exactly at which point he is lining his pockets with the euros he is extracting from the machine while resetting the counters? Makes me wonder if the management is even aware."

Julie shot Juan a smile and laughed, "That was exactly it. How did you spot it so easily? I thought you were playing your game."

"I told you, sweetheart, this game takes no skill. I can play and still enjoy watching you and seeing what fascinates you, or what captures your attention."

Julie leaned in and kissed Juan soundly, then commented, "You, honey, fascinate me. I like seeing you play and win. Show me some more of your winning streak.

"I hope he doesn't get caught. I suspect they would frown upon that sort of action. Glad it's not our problem."

CHAPTER FOUR

Something or not

D mitry asked, "Are you sure you can deal with the gaming interface to the program? Some people in the older generation are uncomfortable with the new graphics and high-definition interfaces. I know your system can support the heavy rendering demands being made on it. However, if that is fully offset by having a fully animated Avatar playing a role for you in the game space, it's not going to be much fun."

Dmitry glanced over to make certain the outer office door was closed and then looked through the window across the room to the data center. The office had huge furniture suited to older European tastes and the darker colors favored by ostentatious males. The floor was marble with large area rugs in darker shades that complemented the furniture. The heavy drapes on the single large window overlooking the garden were open, letting in natural light. The large room also boasted several large digital screens and a couple of soft leather chairs of varying styles with remote control devices on adjacent tables. The man himself was dressed for comfort in dark fine wool slacks and a grey cashmere sweater that was near the color of his groomed hair.

As the Russian Minister of Information Propagation, Dmitry had access to some of the most sophisticated computers and software in the world. As a former Russian war hero, now bored with minimal daily efforts of state, he thought the adrenaline rush from this digital competition was nearly as good as being in battle, without the limited rations and wet socks. He'd paid his dues and now he played his games with his supercomputer and his brains versus his once fierce enemy, Chairman Chang.

Chang was the head of the Chinese Cyber Warfare College, as well as politically connected and virtually untouchable. Dmitry had been battling the old goat for many years with differing battle strategies, both winning and losing at times. Now they were more like global associates that knew how to work their respective countries' politics and resources for their own gain, using one another as needed to reach their dutiful goals. Dmitry shrugged off thoughts of their history and focused on the game, feeling quite certain the programming experts of his Dteam had outdone themselves with this competition. It was a virtual game, with virtual machines and players, connected by an open conference bridge which either side could mute on demand or add video, depending upon their ego for the day. This was a no holds barred game with each player committed to the win, period.

Chairman Chang, frowning at the conference phone, responded, "Ever since I gave up my slide rule and abacus, I've been able to keep up with the digital world just fine. What's the matter, you old goat, afraid that I will win in this child's digital contest? I've loaded up the program on my supercomputer here, and I believe I understand the rules of engagement. I'm ready to do the gaming combat, as we discussed.

"It has to be better than that non-event we had where you said let's launch a digital onslaught against the Finnish super-computer. I mean how funny was that? We teed up to pound the Finns with both our supercomputers, and you sent us both to a website that was recruiting suicide truck drivers for some Islamic

Jihad movement. But I digress and am now ready to bring up my Avatar."

Dmitry sulked at the unpleasant reminder of that event but quickly retorted, "That's just typical of you, Chang! I offer up the best Russian gaming environment to help improve your disposition, and all you can do is grouse about a missed target! You didn't have to apologize to the Muslim fanatics or promise to increase their monthly stipend to get them to calm down!"

Chairman Chang soothed, "Oh, come now! After a few more atrocities they will have forgotten about the incident. Anyway, I was just teasing you. Let's get down to the game because, truth be told, this does look like an interesting diversion from my normal mundane workday. A person does need some good wholesome activity to break the work monotony. Wouldn't you agree?"

Dmitry brightened a little and replied, "Well, alright, since you put it that way, let's go over the ground rules for this event.

"Now, as in all games, it's the amount of points and money you accumulate over the life of the gaming challenge. These programs are designed to credit our attacks, the number of end points rendered inoperative, and, most of all, how much booty each side is able to acquire in the allotted time frame. Understood?"

Chairman Chang, growing excited by the prospects of the digital contest, offered, "I'm ready! Let's wind 'em up, Dmitry!"

Grinning enthusiastically, Dmitry roared, "The game is now live!"

Breakfield – Works for a high-tech manufacturer as a solution architect, functioning in hybrid data/telecom environments. He considers himself a long-time technology geek, who also enjoys writing, studying World War II history, travel, and cultural exchanges. Charles' love of wine tastings, cooking, and Harley riding has found ways into the stories. As a child, he moved often because of his father's military career, which even helps him with the various character perspectives he helps bring to life in the series. He continues to try to teach Burkey humor.

Burkey – Works as a business architect who builds solutions for customers on a good technology foundation. She has written many technology papers, white papers, but finds the freedom of writing fiction a lot more fun. As a child, she helped to lead the kids with exciting new adventures built on make believe characters, was a Girl Scout until high school, and contributed to the community as a young member of a Head Start program. Rox enjoys family, learning, listening to people, travel, outdoor activities, sewing, cooking, and thinking about how to diversify the series.

Breakfield and Burkey – started writing non-fictional papers and books, but it wasn't nearly as fun as writing fictional stories. They found it interesting to use the aspects of technology that people are incorporating into their daily lives more and more as a perfect way to create a good guy/bad guy story with elements of travel to the various places they have visited either professionally and personally, humor, romance, intrigue, suspense, and a spirited way to remember people who have crossed paths with them. They love to talk about their stories with private and public book readings. Burkey also conducts regular interviews for Texas authors, which she finds very interesting. Her first interview was, wait for it, Breakfield. You can often find them at local book fairs or other family-oriented events.

The primary series is based on a family organization called R-Group. Recently they have spawned a subgroup that contains some of the original characters as the Cyber Assassins Technology Services (CATS) team. The authors have ideas for continuing the series in both of these tracks. They track the more than 150 characters on a spreadsheet, with a hidden avenue for the future coined The Enigma Chronicles tagged in some portions of the stories. Fan reviews seem to frequently suggest that these would make good television or movie stories, so the possibilities appear endless, just like their ideas for new stories.

They have book video trailers for each of the stories, which can be viewed on YouTube, Amazon's Authors page, or on their website, *www.EnigmaBookSeries.com*. Their website is routinely updated with new interviews, answers to readers' questions, book trailers, and contests. You may also find it fascinating to check out the fun acronyms they create for the stories summarized on their website. Reach out to them at *Authors@EnigmaSeries.com, Twitter@EnigmaSeries,* or *Facebook@TheEnigmaSeries.*

Please provide a fair and honest review on amazon
and any other places you post reviews. We appreciate the feedback.

www.ingramcontent.com/pod-product-compliance
Lightning Source LLC
Chambersburg PA
CBHW060940190726
48286CB00005B/1361